A Reluctant Side Character

A. L. Brooke

Also available

Sharp's story
An Unwanted Escort Mission
An Inconvenient Tournament

Other stories
Time Tripper
Destined To Fail
Animal Control

A Reluctant Side Character

A. L. Brooke

Copyright © 2019 A. L. Brooke

All rights reserved. This book or parts thereof may not be reproduced in any form without prior written consent of the publisher.

ISBN: 9798871367155

Any references to historical events, real people or real places are used fictitiously. Names, characters and places are products of the authors imagination.

Front cover image by A. L. Brooke
Book design by A. L. Brooke

For Phill, for helping when others did not.

And my parents, for arguing about the rain.

Chapter 1

Jasper Sharp was on a mission. Or at least he WOULD be on a mission when they gave it to him. He absent-mindedly tossed a bag onto the bed and automatically packed all the things an adventurer would need, something he had done so many times before that he didn't need to concentrate on the task. The King was looking for a hunter. The reason for why was unclear but the word had come from his mouth rather than the many retainers he employed who would usually deal with small time problems such as rampaging goblins and the like (it should be pointed out that rampaging goblins was only small time in Sharp's mind). What WAS clear however was that Sharp would, in fact, be chosen. Everyone knew his name as he'd taken down ogres, giants, lichs and on one occasion a chipmunk that had been enchanted to grow in size until it was the size of a large mansion and was rampaging in search of a meal that would satisfy its hunger, a hunger which had grown with the chipmunk itself. That one was one of his proudest but it was hard to get to the impressive part of the story once one's audience had devolved into laughter upon the word chipmunk.

A number of other 'hunters' had also booked into the same tavern as Sharp with the same goal in mind as him - the invitation wasn't a personal one after all. One couldn't just assume that the hunter one wanted was willing the take the job (some kings maybe but King Torrell The Just was a rather understanding ruler. Some might say a pushover but those people had quickly learned that this was incorrect from behind the bars of their cell) and so the decree had gone out to a small number of the top hunters, meaning of course that the word had instantly gone out to absolutely everyone and even small timers had rushed to the cause. Sharp was fortunate he could afford better accommodation than your average person or he might have had trouble finding any in this now bursting town but it did mean he was sharing the building with some of the most big headed of the hunter world. He had managed to avoid most of them so far but he was going to have to leave the room at some point and his grumbling stomach informed him that time was now.

Sharp poked his head out of the door and, seeing the way was clear, slipped out into the corridor and straight into the beaming smile that was Lydia Sterling. Presumably there was a woman attached to the smile but it was like looking into the sun, blinding to the point you saw nothing else for the next few hours.

"Sharp! Fancy meeting you here!" said the grin.

Sharp replied a non-committal grunt.

"Did you see who else is here? Herbert and Slick! Been wanting to chat to them ever since they took down that troll over in Tellwood! And guess who else?"

Sharp allowed his brain to take a short break. He had no interest in other hunters at all. The only reason he was willing to let Sterling at least have SOME of his time was that she was considered to be the number two hunter (also he could tell a conversation he couldn't back out of when it was staring him in the face). Sharp could at least see the fame thing, her exploits were well known and she even LOOKED the part. Blonde, shoulder length hair, green eyes, not an overly attractive face but friendly (a small scar here and there) and that grin that tended to drag people into believing that she could easily take down anything. To be fair this was mostly correct. In comparison, Sharp had short, brown, uncontrollable curly hair, dull brown eyes, a tendency to loom over prospective clients and a scowl that, while convincing those he spoke to that he was tough enough to get the job done, did little to convince them he wouldn't be taking first born children as payment. He was twenty-eight. He would guess Sterling to be maybe younger but over twenty certainly, old enough to trust with the jobs she had taken anyway.

"Yeah, that's er, great but I really should be getting down to breakfast." Sharp said while backing towards the door in an attempt to escape the black hole that was this conversation.

"Oh great! I haven't eaten either!" Sterling replied and continued where she had left off.

Sharp went back to his happy place. His happy place varied but right now it was anywhere but here so he settled on the image of accepting the King's fine offer of that mission and Sterling's disappointed face in the crowd, that grin finally slipping away. Everyone else in his dream was disappointed also but understanding, of course, that he was the most deserving of them and they all knew it. He could see the eyes of the people, full of their usual respect, as he set off into the sunset.

Sterling continued to follow him for the rest of that morning. Sharp wished he hadn't already packed so he would at least have an excuse to return to his room and maybe break off that grip she seemed to have decided to keep on him that day. He considered just flat out telling her to get lost but she was well liked and he could find his own popularity slipping if he said as much in public or, worst case scenario, having a sword swung at his face - not that Sterling was the type to do so.

The town they were in was the capital city, Golden, the largest city in the land of Mistmore by a large margin. What had started off as a small town (although the name seems to suggest the founder had big plans for it) originally had been built out and then up and now sported buildings several stories high in some places. People vied for a place in the 'big city' but as the edges of Golden now reached Dreary Bog on one side and the Riff Sea on the other, expanding out was no longer an option. The streets branched off at different points like the spokes on a wheel, only stopping when they reached the spokes of another 'wheel'. Each section was a different size depending on where it had begun being built and how close to another 'wheel' it was. As a result, the city could feel oppressive down the smaller streets, dark even in the daylight and a cut-throat's ideal hunting ground at night. The buildings themselves looked eclectic at times as the latest building materials were used each time a new level was added. This made the higher stories look far more modern than the lower ones and at some points people had built walkways between the towering houses, more as a means to stop them from toppling into each other rather than a way to cross to another person's home. They were stable to walk on but Sharp didn't like the look of them, not that he had a reason to use them at all. The whole effect made him think that from a bird's eye view the city would look like a mass of spider webs connecting to each other (not that he would give it a try, his one brief flirtation with flight hadn't been a pleasant one). Golden wasn't all like that though as wide open spaces were dotted here and there to accommodate the various markets and there had to be a certain width to main streets in order to let carts travel around. At some point there must have also been a fountain enthusiast in the King's employ as many different varieties of the things appeared in random places but with no real theme between them. Someone had obviously just liked fountains but at least they made the place look cleaner than it actually was.

Of course, there were other places to live, with small villages scattered over the landscape. Monsters were not uncommon however and one couldn't always rely on a nearby and affordable hunter to come to the rescue, especially the villages outstretching towards the gloomy outer lands far in the distance approaching Moremist. Moremist contained no villages itself which was due to the thick fog that covered the area going no one knows how far. Certainly, anyone who returned hadn't managed to get far in due to various reasons. Some said a canyon blocked their way, some said a jungle, others said they simply returned due to the feeling of being watched. Some juggled with the idea of sailing around the planet and seeing it from the other side but never got further than it being a simple thought when they hit on the question of why they were doing it to begin with as the mist wasn't expanding and there didn't seem anything of interest inside. Sharp wasn't overly sure whether anyone trying it wouldn't simply drop off the edge of the planet anyway. The round planet society was fairly new and people were still hazy on whether to make fun of the group and risk being wrong or join in and risk being considered one of the weirdos that believed things such as the gods not pulling all the strings.

Sharp always felt rather at ease in the city. Outside of it he always had to work so even though it was crowded here with Sharp's least favourite of all monsters, people, they were all clumped together and tended to drown each other out and pay no attention to Sharp even though he was rather widely known. People have no time for celebrities when they're too busy organising the mundane details of their own dreary lives. The whole place just felt so impersonal that he could let his mind drift and relax, no need to watch out for rampaging monsters here. Or at least said monster would have to bash its way through the general populace first, allowing Sharp ample thinking time.

Of course, Sharp didn't usually have to deal with his own personal chaperone like today. Most of the time he was able to avoid talking to people with the odd nod or non-committal noises but Sterling had a habit of asking him very specific questions about places he'd been, or monsters he'd taken down, or the same topics but involving other hunters. She didn't seem to mention her own adventures unless Sharp asked (he presumed she would anyway as he didn't ask) which he assumed was her being modest but just came off to him as being a massive pain in the arse. All he had to do was put up with it until he was named and then he could immediately leave her in his dust.

The King had decided to hold the meeting with his chosen hunter in the courtyard of his castle and at midday, the two hunters made their way to the gleaming landmark in the distance. It was the only building kept spotless (cleaning the rest of the town to that extent would have been pointless. The city seemed to have a constant air of grubbiness to it) and had a habit of blocking out the sun when one got close. The guards were currently fending off a wave of potential hunters. The ones actually invited were being let through but a number of lesser fighters were trying their luck as if breaking into the castle might be a good way to show their cunning or something. Sharp was positive it was a good way to show their ability to get themselves hanged but what did he know? He WAS invited.

The guards indeed waved them in without much of a glance as they waded through the crowds, making sure not to accidentally impale themselves on various stabbing implements being waved around. On top of the wave through, Sterling got a smile from the guards who she made eye contact with. She was popular, not just well known. Sharp felt a twinge of annoyance as it wasn't as if being liked was part of the job. Respect was more what you should aim for.

Sharp had never actually been in the castle itself. He'd had jobs from the castle before but they were given by intermediaries and though bigger than the usual job, nothing he couldn't handle. The fact the King himself would be here suggested that this job was tough, one to really cement a person in history. Perhaps a statue... Sharp was torn between wanting endless respect and wanting people to leave him alone. Being respected at a distance, that was the way to go. He wasn't sure how he would manage this but whatever he was going to get paid for this job would probably go a long way towards making it happen. Wave enough gold in someone's face and you'll get them to admit you're whatever you choose to be.

The unfamiliar corridors were easy to manoeuvre due to the guards set at positions clearly to guide them and frustratingly in front of the most important and interesting looking doors. A craning of the head would result in a glare from the heavily armoured soldiers and clenching of a hand on a sword hilt. Sharp noticed Sterling attempt a glance with a grin to ease the attempt but got the same reaction as everyone else. It was fairly satisfying to see her treated the same way as a regular person as he was starting to really get ground down by the fact she appeared to be charming her way through life. Sharp gave up spying and kept his head straight until they arrived in the throne room.

It was magnificent. The ceiling seemed to stretch away high into the distance, eight pillars spread along the sides of the room (Sharp doubted they were for support, probably more for the aesthetics of the room). There was a mural on the ceiling of the city (Sharp could just make it out while squinting) although with less of the grime and the general populace milling around, just a shine of gold and silver over spotless streets and unfamiliar looking perfect beings Sharp could only assume were people of various species. He had never seen such good-looking people in his life. There were windows in the room but high up and the only one at eye height looked out on a beautiful courtyard with the most colourful flowers Sharp had ever seen arranged in such a way that they blended perfectly with each other. He suspected the King preferred to gaze upon his perfect garden and perfect image of the city than the real thing. Sharp couldn't say he would be any different. King Torrell might not have even been ignorant of the outside world but his advisers tended to do most of the actual work after getting their orders from the King (advised by those same advisers, it would have probably saved a lot of time not even asking. In fact perhaps that was indeed what happened, how would he know?). A glorious perfect red carpet with not much wear stretched towards a small set of stairs that led to two thrones on a slightly higher level than the floor. The King had to be higher than his guests of course. The thrones were gold with purple coverings and Sharp couldn't see the backs of the thrones themselves due to their being occupied. The King wore a smile that would have put Sterling to shame, his glorious silk outfit and a blindingly shiny crown. The other throne was taken by Queen Vera, a stern looking woman with a probing stare that Sharp found boring into him before she moved to Sterling and then down the line of the other hunters. She had a green dress with a silver lining and a smaller but no less impressive crown.

There were three hunters already there. Herbert and Slick were two of these. They worked as a duo so Sharp tended to lump them together in his mind. Having someone to watch your back could be good (he had done so in the past. After finding a hunter already on the quest you had just been given, it would often be better to team up rather than having a race to the target or risk a sword in your back) but splitting the reward from jobs wasn't a prospect Sharp liked. He supposed felling that troll had brought them into a sharper light since before they hadn't been much of note. The fact that Slick was a ralli was also worth mentioning. Rallis were small and quick when they wanted but without much intelligence to go with it. They relied more on slow and steady mostly to get a job done and usually with their rather extensive families to share the load. A short layer of brown scruffy hair (although an attempt to brush it could be seen) covered Slick's small frame (about 4 foot tall) and he had short pointy ears like a cat's and short spines ran down his back. He had an animal like snout with a black dog nose and small pointy teeth. Rallis bred fast, had short lives and tended to live away from humans unless hired for an extensive job but you still saw them often, weaving in between the larger folk living in the cities or villages. Sharp wondered how many were hiding in their own villages but he supposed he would have to deal with a surprise ralli army if it came or when it came. Herbert himself wasn't worth much of note. A tall, heavy-set human with a quiet demeanour and an arm strong enough to hack off limbs. What more did you need in the job he was in?

   The other hunter Sharp saw was a woman by the name of Karla. Women tended to be a rarity in the profession and this one Sharp didn't know too much about. She was about medium height, with a short, sensible haircut and a thoughtful expression as she took in the room and its occupants. If she recognised Sharp and Sterling (and why wouldn't she?), she didn't show it. Sharp wondered how she got an invite. She didn't look tough but she must have done SOMETHING of worth to be here. He decided to keep an eye on her but not be too worried. After all, the King would make his decision and that would be that. All other contestants could return from whence they came and the hunter chosen could be on his merry and very profitable way.

The King beamed down on them and the Queen glowered. Queen Vera didn't tend to approve of hunters but then again she didn't seem to approve of anything as far as Sharp could see so he supposed this wasn't that important.

"Welcome hunters! So glad you could all make it!" declared the King with gusto. He looked like he meant it. A lot of fans of hunters were children and would look upon them with a sort of awe and wonder. The King had this same expression on his face.

"So sorry I can't give this mission to everyone! It's for only one of you but there are, however, other jobs the others can do for me. For, of course, great rewards!" The King gestured to one side and a servant hurried forwards with a velvet cushion. On the cushion was a circle of metal, small enough to slip into a pocket, large enough to look impressive when you shoved it in someone's face. The Seal Of The King. Sharp had never seen it before as it was rarely given out. It was essentially a skeleton key to people rather than locks and gave the wielder the right to demand anything they wanted under the order of the crown. Any order given as such should be treated as if the King had given it himself and Sharp could almost feel himself drooling over the sight. He instinctively found himself creeping closer and could see the other hunters also craning forward at the sight. Sharp was going to use it a LOT. Maybe even for things he didn't really need for the mission just to prove he could. He would have to return it at the end of the quest, after all, can't have multiple people with the power of the King walking around but for a short period of time he could say "For the mission!" and anything could be granted.

The King reached out and took the seal in his hand, flipping it over between his fingers and watching his audience's heads follow it like a kitten watching a piece of string. He stood and walked towards... Sterling. He abruptly stopped twirling the disk and held it out to her. All eyes were still on the seal but Sharp could see every one narrow as she took it carefully as if it would break.

A small explosion happened in Sharp's mind. It started at the base of his skull and crept slowly up, setting off smaller blasts as it covered the rest of his brain. A wild impulse to grab the seal and run flashed for a split second before his common sense, which was distracted by the earlier mentioned explosion, stepped in and pointed out the very large guards surrounding the place.

Sharp was aware the King was speaking to them but all he heard was a slight buzzing and was easily led out of the room by a guard's not ungentle, hand on his shoulder. He saw the others (minus Sterling) similarly led back towards the sunlight outside. A sun that once looked cheerful now seemed to mock him and his companions as they took a furtive look at each other then walked in opposite directions. The King had said they could collect other jobs but he knew that none would take them. He had been so sure he would be chosen and the look on the faces of the others suggested they too had

had these notions and no one here was willing to accept second place.

The next time Sharp was aware of his surroundings was at sunset. He was leaning against a fountain (The Goddess Surilla with her magic bag, producing a stream of water into the base below). The coins at the bottom of the fountain shone in the light of the declining sun and Sharp wondered how and why he had got there. After the minor meltdown his brain had suffered he had let it reload and had obviously wandered aimlessly around for a while. He hoped he hadn't hit anything (hitting things tended to be his default action) but there was no sign of a fight on his knuckles. He sighed. That mission had been his plan for the foreseeable future and now he found himself at kind of a dead end, annoyance at his stupid certainty scratching in his mind.

The area was quiet at this time of day and so the sound of someone clothed in metal walking and then stopping stood out like thunder to his shattered mind. He looked up at Sterling who had an expression of what Sharp assumed was meant to be sympathy. He hated that. She walked over and sat next to him.

"You really thought you would be chosen right? I'm sorry." She was sorry? Damn that expression really WAS sympathy. Sharp was taken momentarily aback which Sterling took as a cue to keep talking. For the first time all day he found himself actually paying attention out of a sort of curiosity.

"You want to know the truth?" Sharp did. "I thought it would be you as well." Okay, that one HAD to be a lie. He looked for any sign of it but there was none. Either this woman was a master of deception or she really WAS that naïve.

"So give the mission to me if you think I'm so

much better to handle it." Sharp retorted, finding his tongue. He sounded like a child who had had a toy taken away and he could hear it but he couldn't help himself.

"I can't. Mission was given to me by the King himself. I feel sorry for those not chosen but I AM still a hunter and I was just given the biggest mission of my career." Sterling replied.

A grunt from Sharp.

Sterling took a deep breath.

"You er, want to join me on it? Split the reward."

Sharp's brain rewound that comment.

"Wait. You want me to JOIN you?" he asked.

"Sure. I actually don't know what my chances of success are if I go it alone. The King said I could invite whoever I deemed useful to my quest. Technically I could just order you to come along or offer to pay a small amount but I wouldn't want to join up with someone with that sort of feeling in the air."

"Worried about a sword in your back?" Sharp inquired.

Sterling actually looked shocked at the notion. Sharp was fairly certain at this point that she had not, in fact, ever teamed up with another hunter before. The fact she was still alive and spouting this optimistic rubbish was proof of that.

"Just want to make sure we both put in our all and the reward itself is massive, even split between two." Sterling's reluctance to name the actual price was suspicious but Sharp was in no doubt it would be worthwhile so didn't dwell on it. He debated with himself as she watched his face for any clue as to what was going on in there. He could refuse out of pride. He certainly had that foremost in his mind but there was the money and perhaps somewhere along the line an... accident might occur. He would have to carry on the quest in her stead if that happened. It would be the right thing to do of course.

Sterling was twirling the seal in her fingers as he wrestled with himself internally.

"Why DON'T you just order me to go. I'd have already used that thing a hundred times if I had it." Sharp said irritably. The seal had gone from being a thing of desire to one of annoyance, now it was out of his metaphorical reach.

"I plan on using it as little as possible. People shouldn't be forced into doing things. If we take away free will from people how does that make us better than the monsters that prey on them?" Sterling said thoughtfully as if she was talking to the seal rather than Sharp. Sharp felt a pang of annoyance run up his spine to add to the constant irritation he already felt around Sterling at her superficial statement.

"Because people are stupid and don't KNOW what's good for them."

"That's horrible! You think we should dictate how people run their lives? I thought you were someone who SAVED lives!" Sterling replied, shocked.

Sharp was already bored with this conversation. Debating ethics with someone who had just offered him a lot of money was probably not the right thing to do anyway. Especially when that person was probably the furthest away from him, opinion wise.

"Look, I promise never to go into politics, okay? I'll just keep killing the things killing the people, which I happen to be very good at. I'll leave the life improvement to you."

Sterling surveyed his face again. What was she trying to do? Read his mind? He doubted she'd actually want to see what he was currently thinking. He doubted some of the ruder words were even in her vocabulary.

"Fine. We split the money and the work." Sterling finally said.

"I'm guessing you're in charge though."

"We're equals." She paused. "Well, MOSTLY equals. Come on, I'll explain the mission when we're out of earshot." She turned on her heel before he could respond and took a route towards the tavern where they were both staying. Sharp was silent on the way back. He knew he had made the correct decision but he was finding it hard to push down that knot in his stomach that told him never to work with someone else. Especially if that someone else made him want to choke the life out of them every time they opened their self-righteous mouth or grinned at him with it. Why was she so HAPPY all the time?

They entered the tavern and she led him to her room. It was better than his. And they said he had been given the nicest room! Nicest price definitely for the innkeeper. He was glad he had stashed all those tiny soaps they kept refreshing every day in his bag and left boot marks all over the bed. Sterling's room was immaculate, however, (and she had brought her own soap. It smelled of strawberry. As if they made soap with a scent!). If the maids had come by he doubted they had much to do here since the bed had clearly been made by Sterling herself (it didn't match the way his had been done) and she hadn't even raided the tiny crisps they left in the cupboard! Sharp shook his head incredulously.

"Apparently, there's been problems with Moremist." Sterling started. She had obviously decided to get straight to the point, maybe the niceties had been getting to her as well. "The villages in a five-day radius have been destroyed by something. Golden so rarely gets messages from out that far so this could have been going on for a while. It was only recently a messenger got to the castle to report it. The villages seem to have been... smashed. There were bodies. Not all villagers have been accounted for but blood trails into the mist suggest the offenders live in there."

"Reason for deaths?" Sharp cut in.

"Smashed is the only word I got in that meeting. I guess no one knows what's been going on." Sterling was flipping the seal agitatedly. She continued. "We have to go and see what the problem is and, if at all possible, stop any further incidents. The villages further out have reported strange shuffling sounds and growls as well as flashes of lightning when no lightning is in the sky itself. The King decided to send a hunter as he thought this sounded the sort of thing we do but to be honest it sounds like something from a ghost story that ends with the protagonist finding out the cause, only to succumb to it herself. I know I could back off and return if I find this to be something I can't handle but people are dying and whoever it is isn't picky about who to destroy. The bodies of all species, genders and ages have been found, so it really does seem like a wild beast or several. I know hunters are better equipped to take monsters down than villagers but those that live in the outer villages are tougher than the rest due to having less help. They shouldn't ALL be succumbing so easily." Sterling took a deep breath after saying this last part at breakneck speed.

"So walk to Moremist, which, by the way, is going to take us months, stop some super beast (or several) going on a rampage, walk BACK, celebrate with a feast and vast mounds of gold. Got it." Sharp summed up

"Er, I guess?" Sterling had expected more of a reaction it appeared, but to Sharp, this just seemed like more of the same as his day to day only on a bigger scale and with more walking. Really, two hunters were probably far more than the job needed but hey, he wouldn't have benefited at all had Sterling not decided to overreact at a story told by someone who had probably exaggerated on a story told to him by someone else who could have done the same.

"Right then I'm off, meal then bed. Early start I suppose?" Sharp stopped leaning against the wall (deliberately leaving a muddy mark) and made a move towards the door.

"Guess I'll join you for the meal, we can discuss buying supplies for tomorrow!" The grin was back in full force and Sharp found himself pulled along in its dazzling wake. This meal was not going to be fun but then again the next few months were going to be exactly the same. He wondered idly if covering a partner with griffin bait would be traceable back to him.

Sterling wiped the mud from the wall before following him down to the bar.

Chapter 2

It was an early start. Sharp didn't mind mornings. He enjoyed the slowness other people seemed to feel until the day hit its peak and he was particularly enjoying this one as Sterling, it appeared, was not a morning person. It was the quietest he'd ever seen her and although she was not unpleasant (that would probably blow a fuse in her brain) she was definitely irritable. They bought the supplies they needed fairly quickly (Sterling wasn't in the mood for haggling) and headed towards one of the exits to the town without saying much. As soon as the sun crept higher so did Sterling's spirits and she was soon in her usual optimistically annoying mode.

Their first destination was a village not so far from Golden. The plan was to go through towns as much as possible without deviating too far from the journey. They both knew that things could happen and having somewhere nearby where you could stock up and sew appendages back on was usually the sensible option. Hunters were often portrayed as being a wild bunch of people but the truth of the matter was that a crazy hunter was usually a dead one and their exciting life was about ten percent heroics and ninety percent preparation.

After walking for a few hours, Sharp was beginning to realise the magnitude of the quest he had undertaken. Not for the difficulty of the mission itself but he was fully convinced this quest would be the death of either himself or Sterling. The question was really whether he would throttle her or if he would jump off a cliff first. He supposed the cliff idea might be quicker but the throttling would cut off the talking and she would probably still be audible on his trip down the cliff if he picked that option. Sterling didn't seem to be aware of his irritability either but prattled on about whatever happened to be going through her mind at the time and Sharp was realising that teaming up was a bit of a novelty for her. At least this mission was going to make him rich. Okay, so the respect would be lowered by teaming up with someone else but half the glory was better than none. He found his new happy place on the heap of gold floating around his head and found the clinking of coins drowned out most of Sterling's drivel.

The first few days were uneventful (fictional murder plots in Sharp's head notwithstanding) and they reached each village with ease before the sunset each day. They were both seasoned hunters and knew how to pace themselves well. Ironically the two knew this area less well than further out as their talents were utilised closer to places involving danger but, because of the relative safety aspect, the towns were closer together and maps were more clearly marked. People were eager to mark their homes as 'Near Golden' without having to actually put up with living in the place. Some of the shine but without the noise and smog. Sharp noticed the fountain designer had made his way out here also as on occasion he noticed his handiwork scattered about. He guessed it must be a sign of dignity to have a fountain near one's house.

The villages themselves had little to comment on. The closer they were to the city, the neater they were. Older, but well taken care of with plentiful fields filled with plentiful crops and people wearing plentiful smiles. It was all very peaceful and Sterling was happy to return the smiles people shot her. Sharp was unsure if they knew her or if she was just being polite. That smile seemed to be infectious so more and more people were sucked into its wake. Sharp got some of the run-off of the smiles himself but his usual gloomy expression stopped them fairly quickly.

"Smiling takes up fewer facial muscles than frowning you know!" Sterling said once.

"This is a NEUTRAL expression." Sharp retorted. "Uses even LESS." To which she didn't seem to have a response and, with an expression he was unsure of, turned away leaving him with a feeling that he had somehow lost a battle. What that battle was or how he had lost it he hadn't a clue. At least she seemed to have gotten over the initial delight at having someone to talk at. Either that or she had realised he wasn't exactly replying or even acknowledging her at all.

They eventually reached Turnhill Village. This was a regularly visited one for Sharp as it stood next to a forest. Apparently, the builders had decided the resources found in it were more valuable than the safety of not building their homes right next to a monsters' natural hunting ground. Sharp headed straight for the tavern (the bartender owed him a free drink or three) and Sterling followed behind.

"Sharp!" yelled Dorn the bartender.

"Dorn!" yelled Sharp in kind.

Dorn slid a beer across to him from the other side of the bar and Sharp could smell that trademark scent of alcohol mixed with whatever Dorn happened to have in his cellar at any one time (Sharp chose not to ask).

"Hello, Dorn." said Sterling and Sharp found himself slightly irritated at the thought Sterling and he might actually have a mutual acquaintance.

"Hello, Sterling." Dorn replied and slid a drink over to her also. Sharp got a whiff of an actual drinkable substance as it zipped past his nose.

"Sooooo, you guys actually here... together?" Dorn had a faint look of bemusement on his face.

"There is a LOT of money involved." said Sharp.

"Ah, fair enough." Dorn understood money. Gold was gold. You didn't have to come to an agreement with it and it might get you different amounts in different places but it was always respected.

"So you wouldn't be after a bit more then?"

"Kind of on a mission Dorn. Just staying the night then cutting through the forest while we have daylight." Sharp said into his beer.

"What about you?" Dorn turned his attention to Sterling. "Wouldn't take long. Two days max. We got some kind of crazy beast in the forest scaring the women and children. The howls get louder each night and it's going to reach the village eventually."

"We're working together. So if I don't have time for your mission then she won't either." Sharp cut in. Women and children indeed. Glad Dorn didn't try that schtick with him.

"Hhhmm, how close are we talking?" Sterling ignored Sharp's response.

"Whaaaaat? Come on, you know we have a schedule! No one has even been killed here! And we have women and children in trouble at the END of our journey."

"So what's the difference then?" Sterling replied. "People in trouble here are worth the same as people there."

"I highly doubt Dorn is willing to pay the same rate as a KING, so probably not." Sharp snapped back with what he thought was a good response but was met with a genuinely shocked look on Sterling's face. He thought she should be used to his attitude at this point but maybe not.

"We're taking the job. Forget the reward." said Sterling

"WHAT?! Not even taking the gold?! No way am

I on board with that."

"Well I'm not leaving until it's done and since we're working together I guess you'll just have to like it or lump it." Sterling was flipping that stupid seal again.

"Going to use that thing on me?" Sharp said eyeing the disc.

"No. You can wait here and the job will take longer if you wish." Sterling seemed to know enough about his feelings towards the reward to know he wouldn't bail to say this with confidence. She downed her drink in one. "You say the noises are at night, correct?" This was aimed at Dorn who was watching the back and forth with a straight face. Sharp could only assume he had had to deal with this kind of clientele before. Dorn nodded.

"Then I'm taking a room to rest up." She practically snatched the key from his hand and strode upstairs. Dorn turned to Sharp.

"Knew you were cold but always thought you considered the lives before the money. Surely there are more lucrative jobs with less likelihood of getting your head torn off out there if that's all your interest is in." Dorn didn't sound like he was judging. Just saying a thought out loud.

Sharp was silent. What he had said had felt natural but it HAD been harsher than he had planned on. He nursed the beer while feeling himself in a bit of a dilemma. He supposed it would be faster to help and it was going to be a long journey with Sterling pissed off at him. An annoyed Sterling could be worse than an endlessly chatty one for all he knew.

He was still there two hours later when Sterling returned at sundown. She ordered a small meal (stew) and at a half glance towards Sharp, he raised two fingers to indicate to double the order (although he was tempted to raise a specific single one). The food was more edible than he remembered but it still tasted bitter as he followed Sterling out into the darkening village. He felt like a child as he scuffed his feet along the dirt path but couldn't help himself. If Sterling noticed it, she didn't comment and they walked in silence as they entered the gloomy interior of Turnhill Forest.

Sharp started paying attention as they entered the dark woods, claustrophobic in the night time. He craned his ears for whatever was lurking but all he could pick up was the ambient sound of a soft breeze rushing through the grass and trees, crickets chirping and the odd owl hooting. After they had been walking for roughly an hour, Sharp was about to suggest they turn around. Certainly, nothing this far in could be heard in the village. He felt no disappointment. It may have been a wasted trip in a mouldy smelling forest in the middle of the night but at least he had the satisfaction of being right, which was always a good feeling to have in his opinion. Suddenly he became aware of, not a sound, but a lack of one. Sterling had detected it also and stopped to take in the silence. They craned their ears and in the distance they could suddenly hear... music? Their eyes met and as one they softly started walking in the direction of the strange beat. As they drew closer, Sharp could definitely make out a tune now although he couldn't pick out the song or even the instruments playing and a dim light grew brighter as the torches lighting a clearing became visible. They both stopped at what they saw there.

There was a circle of yeti dancing in a state of what seemed like mania. In the centre of the circle was a statue of a yeti with crossed legs and a serene expression, completely at odds with the motions of the dancers. Surrounding the dancers were a further circle of onlookers, although these seemed merely as viewers and not part of whatever ritual (indeed the dance seemed too stilted and wooden to be for fun) was happening. Many of their number were children, the smallest being held in their parents' arms. The music was coming from various yeti gathered close to the circle of dancers, watching their movements with a sort of intensity. Sharp couldn't tell if they were waiting for something to happen or were simply concentrating on keeping to the beat of the dancers. He had seen many a musician without much grasp of the song they were playing with the same expression, as they concentrated on the unfamiliar score. The instruments themselves were also strange. Sharp could see they had basic features of say, drums or the lute, but with strange shapes that created different sounds than the ones he was used to.

  Perhaps more surprising than the strange ceremony was simply the species of the group. Yeti were an extremely rare species, thought to have fled to the outer lands nearing Moremist after they had been hunted around two hundred years back. They had mixed poorly with the other species, being large and aggressive. Eventually, they had been declared as monsters and the hunters turned on them to keep the peace and their pockets lined. An intelligent foe would always fetch a good price to match the challenge. The few beasts that survived disappeared from society and many people believed them to have died out, if they even knew of their previous existence at all these days. Sharp had never seen one except in books (research being a crucial part of any hunters repertoire) but those books hadn't done the creatures justice in the slightest. The tallest stood around 8 feet by Sharp's guess and had human looking features but on a slightly flatter looking face, with the ears rounder and higher on the sides of their heads. They had a thin, wiry type of fur covering most of their bodies, with the faces, hands and feet being the exception. The dancers were clothed in what seemed to be ritualistic attire but their audience was dressed in regular, if sparse, looking garb. Certainly their appearance seemed to be different from the books, as their literary counterparts had wild features, long fangs and claws, all with wild expressions and drawn in poses indicating an aggressive nature.

The creatures danced in perfect unison, their voices chanting along with the music, their feet stomping and hands clapping. The two hunters put their hands on the hilt of their swords with their backs to the way they came. They would be no challenge for the whole group of yeti in front of them but curiosity stopped their feet from leaving.

The music hit a crescendo, the dancers dancing faster and faster and then suddenly...

"STOP!" A voice boomed out loud and broke the hunters from their stunned staring and the dancers from their reverie.

"NOW what? I definitely didn't miss the A sharp THIS time!" said one of the yeti who was holding one of the stringed instruments.

"Ah, it was probably She Who Weaves With Style. She was TOTALLY off key in verse three."

"Oh sure and you totally weren't clapping off the beat or anything." retorted one of the dancers who, Sharp assumed, was the accused.

The bickering went on in this vein for a few minutes, Sharp and Sterling standing there in confusion, at a loss as to what they should be doing. A number of the yeti had taken out long parchments, seemingly instructions (Sharp had to squint to see them). The dancers had footprints on theirs in various step sequences, the chanters had indistinguishable words (with their pronunciations written phonetically underneath) and the musicians had long notes written neatly on scored paper. All were studying their various aids carefully for any trace of a mistake they had made.

"Look are you SURE this needs to be exact? I'm certain they didn't have it pitch perfect in the past!"

"They had PRACTICE. This was part of their culture!"

"Why are we even thinking this is going to work? This was meant to be our last ditch attempt at fixing the problem!"

All the voices of the yeti mixed together as they started to bicker among themselves.

Sterling coughed loudly to get their attention, all tension from the maddening scene gone. As one group they all turned to face the two hunters. Sharp's hand was still on his hilt but he could see Sterling's was not. Seeing the beasts as one might see everyone else certainly was a reassuring feeling but Sterling clearly had a more trusting opinion of the whole situation. Sharp preferred to know he had a stabbing implement in his hand when dealing with pretty much anyone at any time anyway so technically he was also treating them the same way as he treated anyone else.

A yeti stepped forwards.

"Oh I'm sorry, were we too loud? I knew the village would be able to hear us! We'll try to keep it down!"

"Er, actually we were investigating reports of a beast in the woods..." Sterling trailed off.

The yeti all looked at each other a bit furtively. They turned and looked at one of the larger of their number who was considering the new arrivals with a calm and steady look. His fur was grey, giving him the impression of an older individual and he had a decorative, important looking necklace, giving him an air of authority. Indeed, the yeti were looking at him with reverence.

"I believe our attempt at the ritual is over for this evening. I'm aware that everyone has jobs or learning to attend to tomorrow so we should all retire for now. Please look over your parts for our next meeting. Thank you." He shooed the curious looking crowds away before turning to the hunters. "Please come with me. I can answer any questions you may have."

He turned and walked further into the woods. The yeti stood out of the way to allow him and the two humans to follow him and Sharp could see them either craning their necks to get a glimpse of the strangers or nonchalantly pretending NOT to be trying to do so.

"Are you sure we should...." started Sharp, turning to Sterling but he could see she was already striding after the chief without a hint of concern about the towering creatures either side of her. Without much of a choice Sharp scuttled after and had to walk fast to keep up with the yetis' long strides. As they left the clearing he saw that there was a village a short distance away. The houses were made of wood and cloth, painted and dyed in various colours, giving the whole place a cheerful appearance even in the dim light. They looked sturdy and clean, unlike the grubby brickwork that made up most of the buildings in other towns and though they were mostly single storey (some smaller structures were nestled in the trees), they were tall in order to accommodate their larger occupants. Various pots and cloths had been hung outside as well as an assortment of other items. In other villages most of these things would have been taken inside because of a fear of thieves. Some people would take anything just to take or vandalise just to vandalise but that situation didn't seem to be in effect here. Sharp stumbled and found he had tripped over a wooden model of a fox with uneven wheels, a bright paint job and surprising attention to detail. He carefully placed it off the path and continued to follow the two people in front of him. They were leading him to the largest of the buildings with a symbol painted on the large front door matching the symbol engraved on the chief's necklace. The beast in question led them to the front door and held it open for them, Sharp followed Sterling's continued confident stride into the hut even if he didn't agree with her attitude as the unfamiliar location made his hunter senses flare up (as if anyone's common sense wouldn't tell them that this was not a safe situation to be in). Sharp glanced over at Sterling who didn't seem to share his discomfort and instead she seemed to be absolutely fascinated by what she was seeing. She wasn't touching anything but Sharp could tell she was itching to, instead probing everything she could see with her eyes. Sharp's own eyes were on the door. And the window. And the stairs. In fact, he was pretty sure he could fit up the fireplace in a pinch. The chief motioned to two oversized chairs although Sharp was sure they were regular chairs for the yeti. Perhaps it was specie-ist to think thought like that but these days what WASN'T?

"My apologies for the way you have been introduced to my people. We don't usually partake in..." The chief paused "...uncivilised behaviour. My name is He Who Rules With Wisdom. You say you are looking for a beast in the forest, yes? I would suggest speaking about this in the morning but as you are clearly here at this time of night for a purpose, perhaps now is more convenient for you and I wouldn't want to appear unhelpful to a very rare guest."

"First of all, it is an HONOUR to meet you! My name is Lydia Sterling and this is Jasper Sharp. We go by our surnames mostly if you don't mind!" Wisdom shrugged but Sharp could see half an eyebrow raised and the yeti leaned back slightly away from the ball of enthusiasm that was Sterling. Unperturbed (or not noticing this), she continued, "Well, the sounds we were looking for do seem to occur during the night but as you live much closer to the source and we have had no sign of our creature this evening, perhaps we would gain from gathering information among your people which we would, of course, do during the day and only at their convenience. If we could stay nearby for the night, perhaps get a meal from somewhere we would, of course, pay for anything we require." Sterling's need to breathe was probably the only reason she stopped talking and appeared to find this entire situation to be the most exciting thing she had ever encountered in her life.

Wisdom held up a hand and Sterling managed to hold her tongue long enough for him to speak.

"You may stay and speak with my people but," he paused as if mulling over his next words. "we ourselves require aid and perhaps you may be of assistance. Or at least, more assistance than an ancient ritual dug up by a superstitious librarian." Sharp decided he didn't care about this particular backstory and waited for the man to continue. Sterling's face seemed to indicate the same as it had gone into the expression Sharp had come to know as her listening for the details of how she could solve the speaker's current problem and possibly any other issues that would make their lives better in any way, shape or form. He was starting to wonder if they would ever reach their destination with all the sidetracking Sterling seemed eager to do.

"In fact..." Another pause, "Our problems may

actually be one and the same. You see we have also been plagued by a beast. It seems to move between our village and the one you came from. It has yet to claim a victim but it has injured many and it will only be a matter of time before it kills. We would be grateful if you could rid us of the menace. In exchange, we offer you shelter and food. I imagine you have a further reward waiting back at your previous village."

"I'm not sure spending a night here would be..." Sharp started.

"We accept!" blurted out Sterling. Sharp was beginning to think that he would get more respect if he was completely helpless like most of the people they had encountered on this journey thus far. Sterling certainly seemed to listen to them more.

"Excellent!" said Wisdom. "I know you plan on speaking with my people but I can give you all the details you may require. The others have taken on more and more... desperate acts in order to scare the beast away. This ritual is merely one of many foolhardy attempts and, in fact, our people have not believed in the occult for quite some time. Solitude has given us time away from our old habits and time to think has made it quite plain that simply thinking in itself has dramatically improved our state of living." He turned and faced Sharp. " You will find our people to be peaceful. Please ignore your introduction to them earlier." Sharp narrowed his eyes but gave a curt nod. Probably better to agree with the man who towered over him.

"Now then," Wisdom stood and strode towards the door. "One of my people will show you where you may spend the night and then tomorrow we shall discuss the details." He opened the door, or at least he would have done had someone not been leaning against it. He sighed and, instead of trying to see who it was first, put his back into it, throwing the door open with a SLAM and sending the leaner several metres away. Sharp could instantly see the figure wasn't a yeti. Indeed, she was smaller than he was and had a thin frame. As she felt around for a pair of fallen glasses and then wobbled to her feet he instantly recognised her species as a fletchin. It seemed he was bumping into all the rare species this evening.

Fletchins weren't all as small as this one was but none were tall, making up for their size with their overwhelming ability to wield magic, something that was exceedingly rare in every other species and never as strong as even a very young fletchin could manage (not that there wasn't the odd one that was weak in this respect or even completely without it). Fletchins were basically human shaped, all slightly, if not greatly, overweight due to their over-reliance on magic. When you can bring anything you want to yourself without leaving your seat you tend to not bother getting up very often. Their faces tended to be more angular even in the more portly of members, and their ears were larger in relation to their head than a humans with a ridged edge to them. Generally their skin wasn't the same as a human's, their hues could be almost any you can imagine along with hair or eye colour. Indeed, their appearances were far more varied than any other species. The only thing they shared was a piercing glare they affixed onto whoever they were speaking to (Sharp wasn't sure if they could even blink but he hadn't met many in his life to check) and a sneer they always wore while dealing with anyone who wasn't one of their own. They kept themselves away from all other species, only mixing with them when it came to trading. Friendships between them and another who didn't share their own magical ability were non-existent and they hoarded magic as though it was the rarest of treasures (as perhaps it was) as it was granted to them almost exclusively. Sharp had no idea of how they lived as no one outside of their species was allowed into their cities. One could see such cities towering high if one desired. They didn't keep them hidden, probably out of pride as they were the cleanest and grandest of metropolises in the known world (larger than Golden but Sharp didn't count them as they weren't open to everyone). They covered them with domes of magic, unseen to the human (or inhuman) eye, but walking into one could sometimes prove fatal. Such power had granted the fletchins a feeling of importance and dominance and their overinflated egos had made them consider the other species to be unworthy of conquering. Sharp wasn't sure on how a war like that would go, perhaps their magic would make up for their lack of numbers but they probably bled just the same as any other people.

    This fletchin was thin, which was odd, and had an expression Sharp had never seen on a member of her species (even in illustrations). It was embarrassment. He recognised the expression of one who felt guilty and at a guess he would say she had been listening in on their conversation with Wisdom. Her skin was a pale blue, her hair was a darker blue and her eyes were piercing orange. Her clothes were unlike the usual fashion of her species, looking well worn and sturdy, missing all the jewels and expensive but useless looking material.

    "Tolah. What are you doing?" inquired Wisdom who knew exactly what she was doing.

    "Erm... not invading your privacy?" Tolah's reply sounded more like a question as she returned her glasses to her face. Wisdom sighed.

    "Do me a favour Tolah. Take Sterling and Sharp to the guest houses and answer any questions they may have." (from the way Sterling was fidgeting, Sharp could see she had plenty). Wisdom turned to the humans. "Tolah is... visiting for a spell. She seems... fascinated with my people. Perhaps she could... tell you all about it." Sharp nodded in agreement. Any more pauses and this could go on for a long time. At this point Tolah had the same expression of practically exploding with questions that Sterling had. Wisdom nodded in a direction and Sharp put a hand on the backs of each of the women and pushed them gently in the direction the yeti had indicated. They got the idea and started walking, both obviously not wanting to start talking, possibly out of politeness, not that that had stopped Sterling before.

After a few minutes, they reached a section of the village that was set slightly apart from the rest. It consisted of about four small huts and, although it was built to what seemed like the same standard as the rest of the village, looked as though it had been less well maintained and less lived in. One of the huts had piles of books in front of it. Sharp could see reams of script in careful, neat writing alongside rather skilful looking sketches . He recognised some of the faces from the village.

"This area is where you can stay. This is my place." Tolah indicated the book infested hut.

"How long have you been here? It's so rare to see a fletchin outside of their cities and I've never seen a yeti in the flesh at all and yet here you both are!" Sterling managed to fit all her current thoughts into a single question.

"I KNOW, RIGHT?!" Tolah clearly couldn't hold herself back any more. "NO ONE has seen a yeti in YEARS and here they all are! A WHOLE village! And the books were all WRONG! They aren't violent at ALL! I've spoken to so many of them and they all have more knowledge than ANYONE I've spoken to!" Sharp had never heard a person talk in so many capital letters before. Surprisingly, Sterling was still holding her tongue. Sharp thought maybe she had finally met her match but she wasn't even trying to interrupt. She seemed genuinely happy to see someone so passionate in what they were talking about. All Sharp could see was the manic look in an obsessive fan's eyes. Being so absorbed in a single thing never ended up well in his opinion. He had seen people destroy themselves or others just to get to what they wanted. At least in this case Tolah seemed not to be hurting anyone unless you counted Wisdom and his sanity. Or his own. Or possibly anyone's she had ever spoken to ever. Sterling appeared to be the exception but to be fair she didn't seem to be affected by anything except impoliteness.

Tolah continued to talk about the workings of the yeti. Sterling didn't seem to be in the mood to interrupt so Sharp knew he would have to.

"TOLAH." he said in her ear. She jumped, her train of thought derailed for a second. "This is all very... fascinating but we need information about the beast currently rampaging around the place. We have a LONG journey to make and unless we can get past this road bump of a mission we seem to have encountered" he shot a sideways look at Sterling who seemed unmoved, "we may end up here for a LONG time. I can see that that is something YOU wish to do but it's not really my idea of a good time."

Sharp watched Tolah's thoughts rearrange themselves after being knocked off their current track.

"Oh yes! He hasn't actually been in the village but he seems to be causing a bit of a stir! The locals don't really know what to do about it as the village is meant to remain secret. They can't really go out and hire a hunter as history has taught us that their own species is also to be hunted. Of course, history doesn't know what it's talking about here as the people are..." Tolah was at risk of wandering back into fan girl territory.

"Has anyone actually SEEN it?" Sharp prodded her back on subject

"Er, maybe?"

"Maybe?" Sharp asked dryly.

"Well, we have a fair number of reports but they don't seem to... match up. I guess living in a peaceful forest with people who don't cause any trouble is safe but not exactly... exciting. Everyone has a habit of embellishing whatever they've seen. Some reports say a giant with blood dripping from its teeth, others say a jet black demon with claws the size of your head, others say a creature of mist that can move in between shadows."

"And your opinion?"

"The logistics of any of those things existing is very unlikely." Sharp could have told her some stories but let her continue. "However, it seems to be a large, hairy creature with two arms and two legs. It has teeth, claws and a bad temper."

"Like a yeti then." said Sharp. He heard a sharp intake of breath from Sterling.

"WHAT?! No! I THINK the yeti would know what another YETI looks like! And they are NOT beasts and do NOT have bad tempers! I've been here for MONTHS and never seen one get angry!" Tolah exploded.

"What, never? That seems unlikely for anyone." Sharp replied. Tolah paused, seemingly caught off guard. She regained her composure fairly quickly.

"Don't judge everyone by your own standards! As a hunter, you must only see the worst of everything! These people are better than that. They have evolved past the point that they fly off the handle and then go on a rampage!" Sharp was fairly sure that wasn't how evolution worked but he knew better than to say. Tolah had started on a rant again but Sharp's mind had already started working out what the next course of action would be. Clearly, they needed to take the beast down, no matter what. He had no qualms about taking down a yeti if it meant they could continue on and it wouldn't be the first time he had to take down a foe that could think for itself. People did as much damage as monsters did, just in a different way. In the end, if he got paid for it or if someone stood in his way badly enough, he would kill. Obviously Tolah idolised these people but she also seemed to have the most knowledge about them. Access to her notes would be useful as they probably held information about how to kill yeti as well as whatever else she had been looking at.

"Well?" Tolah's voice brought Sharp back to the one-sided conversation. He had absolutely NO idea what she had been saying but he could hazard a guess.

"I apologise." said Sharp "I will admit I have a lack of knowledge on the yeti but you don't seem to have the same problem. May I perhaps study your notes?" Tolah's eyes lit up. He may not have said the right thing but it was generic and following up with an interest in her obsession was a good idea. He realised his mistake as soon as he'd made it.

"It would be FAR better if I just TOLD you!" Tolah looked as if her birthday had just come early.

Sharp was fairly sure some of what she said was probably useful but he was also fairly sure listening to the entire thing would dissolve his mind. A glance at Sterling saw her trying to not to laugh. Sharp knew he didn't have the patience to sort through the haystack to find the needle so he let his mind wander. Time passed.

Perhaps it was minutes, perhaps it was weeks, but in the end, the talking stopped and with a half-hearted mention about needing food he grabbed a dozing Sterling by the arm and dragged her towards a random hut.

"Oh, er, okay then, I'll get someone to bring you something! Talk to you later!" Sharp heard the voice disappear into the distance, silenced as he slammed the door and braced himself against it as if Tolah might break in to tell him about the finer points of yeti dental hygiene. Sterling had a bemused expression on her face.

"Learn anything?"

"Oh yes." replied Sharp "Nothing about how to take down the beast but a lot about Tolah. Not sure why a fletchin even CARES about any of this stuff let alone bothered to leave her comfy house with all the amenities a magic word away at all times."

"You could ask, you know. And people aren't always going to be the same. She just found something she was interested in and went for it. Isn't that what you did when you decided to be a hunter? It's hardly safe work and I'm fairly sure you had people tell you that you shouldn't."

"I became a hunter for... other reasons. It was just something to do and it paid. It was a good way of elevating my status as well. Although I didn't realise I also had to be NICE about slaughtering bloodthirsty beasts to gain that. I was fairly sure that simply saving lives would be good enough."

"You can save people in other ways. Sometimes killing something trying to kill them will do that. Sometimes you can do the same with just a smile." Sterling seemed to be talking like a normal person today (albeit a bit preachingly). The eager non-stop tone had slipped from her speech, although Sharp still couldn't take her that seriously while she was spouting her new age opinion. If people were placing a smile at the same level of life-saving as stopping an ogre from tearing off their face then they clearly needed to re-evaluate their priorities. He decided just to change the subject and use her current lucid state to get some actual advice.

"Perhaps we could talk about our reasons for doing what we do when there isn't a creature rampaging about?"

"You really think it's a yeti?" she asked.

"Sounds like it by Tolah's description. Her notes could be useful if it is and if it isn't then we just change our tactics when we get there. Between both of us, we've probably fought whatever it is before but if it IS a yeti then I'm guessing neither of us has any idea of where to stab the thing."

"They just seem... too peaceful." Sterling sounded almost sad that there could be something off in a place so serene but she was clearly up for talking about it. Sharp guessed it was her hunter's instinct taking over. When it was your own life versus your ideals it was nice to know she had the sense to pick the right side. She must have to to stay alive.

Sharp decided to throw her a bone.

"Look we're just going to be prepared. If I'm wrong then nothing has been lost and you can keep your happy picture of these people. Just remember what they used to be. A dog will still act like a wolf when it's cornered and we have no idea what happened in this village before we arrived. To be honest I don't even care. We have a bigger picture to get back to."

Sterling mulled it over.

"Fine. But we can't tell Tolah that's what we're doing. There's no way she would go along with it. Hopefully her notes alone will tell us what we need to know."

Sharp was immediately behind any plan that didn't involve being chained into another conversation with Tolah. A loud knock jerked him out of his thoughts. It had come from the door so he turned to open it, revealing an overlarge platter of food with a fletchin's legs sticking out underneath. Tolah's limbs were clearly shaking from the sheer weight of what she was carrying but Sharp decided to see how long she could keep it up. Sterling ruined it, however, by grabbing the other side of the platter and placing it on the table. She shot Sharp a look which he pretended not to see as he took in his surroundings for the first time. Not that there was anything of note in here. A couple of beds, the aforementioned table and a few chairs, all with that same unused look to them. Clearly, the yetis didn't get a great deal of company but were too polite not to prepare for it.

The platter was full of vegetables and fruit and no sign of meat. Everything Sharp had read on the yeti said they were omnivores but trying to imagine the people he had seen earlier actually out hunting was an extremely jarring image. If Sterling or Tolah regretted the lack of meat they said nothing as all three ate without pause and Sharp tried to keep his attention as the other two chatted. Tolah was talking abut the yeti non stop but Sharp found her mile a minute way of talking to be extremely hard to keep up with. Sterling may have been doing so, he wasn't sure, but if she wasn't then she was doing a good impression of a person who WAS. The strange change in her personality had him confused as she wasn't trying to butt in or anything and although he welcomed said change, Tolah was filling the gap. He switched his brain off and the rest of the evening went a lot smoother.

After a suitable amount of time he managed to shuffle Tolah out of the door and he and Sterling sat in silence for a few minutes.

"You're going to steal her notes aren't you." said Sterling with a raised eyebrow

"Stealing implies I won't be giving them back. I don't suppose you managed to get any information out of that conversation? I drifted off after that part about yeti mating habits. Actually I kind of wish I'd drifted off BEFORE that part."

"Oh, er, partly?"

"Partly."

"Okay I get that she's found something to be passionate about but it was extremely hard to keep up with her." Sterling actually seemed embarrassed that she hadn't been able to keep up with the crazed ramblings of a mad woman.

They sat in silence until Sharp saw the light go off in the window opposite their hut and Sterling said nothing as he left the hut and re-emerged with an armful of notes that had looked the most useful and that Tolah had conveniently left on her porch. He dumped the pile on the table and Sterling grabbed some and started sifting through it. Most of the work involved finding the genuinely useful information in the ravings Tolah had committed to page. If anything else, he had to respect Sterling's professionalism as, without speaking, they were both able to work together, building a pile of useful material and writing information down and occasionally passing pages across the table to the other person.

It was almost dawn when they had completed their work, less information gathering and more separating the wheat from the chaff. He gathered up the materials and quietly returned them to where he had taken them. Tolah didn't need to know anything. The late night had taken its toll on the both of them and on returning to the hut, Sterling was already asleep on one of the beds. He decided not to take the other bed. Experience from their camping out had shown Sterling to be a grouchy riser and he didn't want to deal with it. He left the hut and found the one next to it unlocked. The interior was identical to Sterling's. Gratefully he collapsed onto one of the beds and fell asleep as soon as his head hit the pillow.

Chapter 3

It was late when he awoke but still morning. A loud banging on the door jerked him out of sleep and he managed to roll onto the floor before remembering where he was. Shaking the blankets he was now tangled in off of himself he opened the door to a subdued looking Tolah.

"You slept late." she said. He shrugged.

"Was up late. Going out late tonight as well so it made sense." Tolah nodded and beckoned him towards Sterling's hut.

"We have breakfast if you're interested." Sharp's stomach told him he was so he followed her in silence. Her own silence was unnerving him slightly, both the motor mouths he had met so far had reversed their trait. They entered Sterling's hut and ate. Sterling looked rested enough, he and she were hunters after all, missing sleep was fairly commonplace if you wanted to keep an eye out for your target. They ate the way they spent the next day: quietly. A few side glances at Sterling showed the same confusion about their new friend's sudden quietness and Tolah answered questions in a far more tolerable way although he didn't gain anything useful. Seeing the yeti in the daylight and not doing crazy rituals made him see them behave the same way any villagers would. He could see bakers, builders, housekeepers and the usual activity. The fact that the people in question towered over him didn't make much of a difference as their body language wasn't aggressive in the slightest. How could these people have changed so much from the brutes he had read about?

He was ready to leave as the sun sank, as was Sterling so they left Tolah behind and made tracks. As soon as the village was out of view, her chatter started up again. He had no idea what had caused her to shut up in the first place but he knew that asking about it would just extend the tirade. This went on until they reached one of the ambush points that they had been told of the previous day. She flicked over to professional mode as they split up to look for anything that might lead them in the right direction. Scuffs on the trees and disturbed grass were everywhere, along with a rather distinct footprint that matched those of the yeti. They didn't wear shoes so it was easy to identify.

Suddenly there was a rustling behind him and he had unsheathed his sword before his brain caught up and he heard the same sound from Sterling's direction. He looked sideways at her and she indicated he should stay where he was. She crept quietly towards the sound and in one quick motion lunged forward and pulled the invader out of the bushes. It was Tolah. Sharp hoped that Sterling could tell that before she plunged her hand into the brush as he was fairly sure she wouldn't have been able to haul out a yeti the way she now held the fletchin aloft. Tolah had the decency to look embarrassed at least.

"You aren't very good at this spying thing are you?" asked Sharp bluntly.

"You didn't hear me last night."

"Ah, you knew I took your notes. I suppose that was why you were attempting the silent act earlier. Feel free to keep that up by the way." Sharp re-sheathed his sword.

Tolah looked annoyed even as she still dangled from Sterling's grip. Sterling lowered her gently to the ground and Tolah tried to look as dignified as she could while rearranging her crumpled collar.

"Why did you follow us out here? We wouldn't want you to get hurt while we're hunting." Sterling said, genuinely concerned.

"Because you think you're fighting a yeti! I want to see your faces when you find out how wrong you are! The yeti are kind!" She slammed her foot down and Sharp saw a few pebbles jump. "The yeti are peaceful!" This time Sharp could feel the ground judder under his feet as hers hit the ground. "THE YETI WOULD NEVER DO THIS." She yelled this last statement and Sharp felt the ground shake noticeably.

Sterling was the one who parried the first blow as the giant creature bounded out of the trees, roaring as it did so, its shaggy, matted fur hung low over mean, flaring eyes. Sharp grabbed his sword back out of its sheath, cursing himself for focusing on the fletchin as she drew the monster towards them with her pathetic temper tantrum. Close up it was clearly a yeti, slightly larger than most, he thought, but it was bent over slightly so it was hard to tell. Its hands were callused and its eyes wild which changed it completely from the people that were occupying the village. A fist clipped Sterling and she was pushed back. Sharp took the opportunity to leap out and take a free swing which took a chunk out of the beast's shoulder. It felt like trying to hack at a rock. The yeti roared in pain and tried to punch him but Sharp darted out of the way in time as Sterling dashed in and took a free shot herself without much more success than him. The hunters made eye contact and she nodded. He rushed forwards and launched himself up, aiming at its face. As it reached up to swat him like a fly, Sterling swiped at its less protected chest and succeeded in opening a wide gash. It backed off, a hand trying to stem the blood while it growled savagely at them. Sharp could hear Tolah whimpering slightly behind them. The yeti's eyes darted between the two hunters then found Tolah at the back. With a roar, it lowered its head and charged right at her. This was going to be a hard one to stop and already it seemed unbothered by the wound on its chest. A yeti at full charge was like a boulder rolling down a hill, just get out of its way and let it reach its destination. Tolah was stock still so Sharp ran at her, managing to reach her in time, pushing her small body out of the way. Sharp had been hit by many things in the face (not all in battle) but the yeti was solid muscle and he felt his nose shatter and one of his eyes go dark as he was shoulder bashed into the tree directly behind him. As it stood out in front of a bright full moon, he saw the shape of the yeti as it rose up to deal the finishing blow on him but out of the corner of his good eye, he saw a flash of lighting as it snaked across the ground and struck the creature in its side. It shrieked with pain and crashed to the ground slowly like a giant oak tree after being felled. The ground shook like a small earthquake as Sharp stumbled to his feet, blood pouring down his face from his broken nose. He looked in the direction of the lightning bolt and saw Tolah, a shocked expression on her face, shaking slightly, her hand still outstretched with small sparks dancing around her fingertips. He moved behind her, gripping her shoulders and held her in front of him like a weapon, aiming her at the yeti who was still on the ground but moving and growling again.

"Hib ib again!" He mumbled through a blocked nasal passage and a mouthful of his own blood.

"I'll kill him!" Tolah said indignantly.

"Kinb ob the ibea!!" Sharp rolled out of the way of the now up and charging yeti, its fur still sparking from Tolah's spell. Sharp dragged the protesting fletchin with him, the floor crackling where her feet touched the ground. The yeti threw a fist and Tolah raised her hands again, a wall of fire leaping between the creature and the other two. Sharp could feel the air in front of his face shimmer and burn the stubble on his chin. He fell backward and scrambled away from the blaze. In the light, he could see the silhouette of a figure fly at the yeti who swung a fist in her direction and he saw it connect. The silhouette grew bigger as it came towards Sharp before breaking the wall of fire. He ducked as Sterling's body flew over his head and crashed to the ground, clothes and hair ablaze. She yelled and rolled in an attempt to put out the fire but it was Tolah that succeeded at this as she hit the other woman full in the face with a stream of water. Sterling choked and wiped the water from her face with one hand while supporting herself with the other.

"Are you alright?" asked Tolah. Sterling gave her a thumbs up with her head pressed against the floor, steam still coming off her back, armour showing through charred spots in her clothing. She seemed to have been extinguished before any damage had been done. Suddenly Sharp was aware that the shadow still behind the fire was getting bigger and he scurried backward on all fours to get away from what he knew was coming through the flames. The yeti showed no fear as it strode forward, its fur and its eyes on fire (the fur literally, the eyes figuratively) as it came to a stop and fixed its eyes on Tolah, the only one who seemed to be posing any kind of a threat as the blood from the previous sword slices had stemmed, leaving lines that looked as if they wouldn't even leave a scar. Sterling stumbled to her feet and went to stand in front of Tolah, though the hunter was struggling to stay upright, steam still pouring off her. Coupled with her determined glare, Sterling would have looked intimidating had her opponent not been... well, a behemoth currently on fire and not showing any signs of being bothered by it.

"We need to finish it." said Sharp, finding his feet and proper speech somehow. Sterling nodded. Tolah looked back and forth between the two of them as they stood there bleeding and charred.

"Erm, how?" she asked.

"You could always throw something magicky in its direction if you wanted to lend a hand but I'm thinking you wouldn't want to give it a splinter or mildly inconvenience it, so maybe instead we repeatedly stab it until it stops TRYING TO TAKE OUR HEADS OFF." Sharp replied, his voice rising with annoyance.

"You can't kill him! He's a thinking person!" Tolah genuinely seemed outraged that anyone would ever consider killing a sentient being any time in history.

"Fine. You want it alive, YOU knock it out but after that it's still going to be rampaging through the forest, threatening people's lives!"

Tolah looked as if she was going to cry for a brief moment but quickly recovered.

"Fine!" she said, striding forwards and pushing Sterling aside. Ice formed on her fingers and a cone of ice blasted outwards. The yeti looked at its hands, but the ice hadn't hit its body at all. As a group, they all looked down at the sheet of ice below the beast's feet. Tolah shot another ice blast out, this time hitting it IN its feet. The creature skidded on the ice and smashed to the ground, stunning it momentarily. Sharp strode forward and pushed the yeti with his foot, exposing its neck and swung back, readying a final blow.

"STOP!"

Sharp stopped. This protest came from Sterling rather than Tolah.

"Why do YOU want me to stop?" he enquired.

"Well... I guess... what if he IS a person?" She looked at Tolah. "Tolah obviously knows things we don't. We learned what a yeti is from a book like we learn about everything we fight, but she learned from watching them. What if we snuff out a life that can be saved?"

"Wait, you HAVE killed people before right?" Sharp asked, the beast was moving under his boot but not much.

"Only when I had no other option. The people I killed were beyond hope, beyond help. This one hasn't racked up any kills to our knowledge. We should tie it... HIM up. We can always finish him later if need be." Sterling reasoned.

"If you won't kill it now you certainly won't be able to do it when it's helpless. Come on! This is just a needless waste of time! Needless AND dangerous! I have no idea how you're still alive with thinking like that!" Sharp looked down at the creature and could see it looking back at him with anticipation in its grey eyes, all fight seemed to have faded from them.

"JASPER SHARP PUT DOWN THE SWORD."

"I don't think you know what partner means." Sharp said, still making eye contact. Why was it just... watching him? He managed to tear his gaze away (it was started to creep him out) but the view he changed to wasn't any better. The two women were glaring at him. Sterling had her sword gripped tightly in her hand, hair looking wild from the crazy atmosphere changes it had undergone and Tolah had shimmers of magic running through her skin.

"Dammit FINE!" Sharp conceded, reaching back and taking a rope from his pack. "But you're dealing with the aftermath." The yeti didn't struggle as he tied it up and he wasn't gentle about it. The way it stared at him was really starting to freak him out now. When he was done he found the least uncomfortable stone he could to take a seat and gestured to the women to talk about whatever it was they wanted to ask this thing about.

"Hello!" Tolah chirped brightly. The yeti's head turned so it was staring at her now. "Can you tell me your name?" For a moment it looked confused at the question.

"He Who Angers Quickly." rumbled the yeti.

"Appropriate." Sharp mumbled under his breath.

"So you can talk. Why were you rampaging through the forest? Seems you've been doing that for a while now." Sterling asked him

"I get... angry sometimes. Father told me to leave when I feel as if I'm going to lose my head. Crashing around in the forest calms me down and no one in the village knows about my... affliction." explained Quickly.

"Do the other yeti not feel anger?" Sterling asked both Tolah and the yeti.

"Well, I know they feel annoyed. I may have... overstayed my welcome on occasion, but I've never seen one actually shout or anything." Tolah admitted.

"Our people have a bad history with anger. We used to let it rule us so we changed, but what is the point when we don't go anywhere near other people? Even the fletchins trade with the other species but we don't even talk to anyone! They say that we have plans to meet with other species but they've been saying that my whole life! When Tolah showed up they took her in but they still tiptoe around her and show no signs of wanting to see more of the outside."

"If you know about me then how have we never met?" asked Tolah.

"Father made me leave the house when you came by. He's important in the village and having me as a son is shameful. He hides my... problem from the other villagers and they don't know I'm the beast that's rampaging in the forest." Quickly continued.

"What?! Who's your father?!" Sterling's mouth

was open but the words came from Tolah. Sharp was looking forward to losing Sterling's doppelgänger, this was a real pain in the arse.

"He Who Rules With Wisdom." answered Quickly. Even Sharp was suddenly interested, but mainly because someone was probably going to get maimed and it was nice to have that person not be him.

"But... he asked us to find you and..." The unfinished sentence sounded confused but her voice was sad. His own father had ordered him killed and Sharp could see Tolah wrestling with whether to tell him or not.

"We going back to the village now? Because standing around in stunned silence isn't going to solve anything." Sharp asked. He was clearly not going to be getting any sleep tonight, at least not in a comfortable bed so he may as well move things on. Quickly turned to look at him.

"Did something happen?" he asked. Sharp opened his mouth to answer but found he couldn't. He didn't like people and right now he was with two he REALLY didn't like and one who until very recently had been trying to cave his skull in. He was tired and his nose hurt but telling someone (and he now classed Quickly as a someone) that their father had paid a couple of strangers to kill him was causing him some discomfort. Sharp got to his feet.

"We should go back to the village. We're going to have to have a discussion with your father." Sharp said. Quickly nodded and Sterling stepped forward to cut him free of the rope (could have just untied him and saved the rope since it WAS Sharp's but he supposed cutting it was more dramatic or something). Quickly moved in what seemed like a random direction after the party had been turned around somewhat during the fight but he clearly knew the area well. The other two stayed silent on the journey back to the village but for the first time, Sharp kind of wished for some kind of noise as the stillness in the forest was making him feel uneasy. After what felt like a week, a torch could be seen in the distance. Sharp could see the women slow slightly but Quickly picked up his pace and they were forced to scurry along in his wake. There were no yeti outside when they reached the village, that single torch left out, perhaps for the hunters' return. Sterling took it from its holder and held it aloft so they could see without walking into a building. Quickly had ignored the torch, seems he didn't need it. They stopped in front of Wisdom's house and Quickly pushed his way in with the others following behind. There was no sign of life inside, it was very late after all.

"Perhaps we should wait until tomorrow." said Sharp. As one, the two women turned and glared at him. No such luck on the sleep it seemed. They were only a few days into this mission and he had never wanted to walk out so badly. The money, the fame, his pride, did they really weigh more than his current level of annoyance? He sat on a nearby stool and decided just to watch this play out.

"Father?" called out Quickly. "I'm home. Sorry to wake you." Wisdom drew back a curtain that had separated the room into two and stepped towards the group.

"I didn't think your kind usually stopped to talk to your targets." This was directed at Sterling.

"Tolah convinced us to. It was only after we halted that we realised who it was we were about to kill." Sterling's voice was tinged with anger. She continued. "How could you? I don't understand why you would send us to kill your own son!" Quickly was taken aback and turned to face his father.

"That can't be true... right?"

"Son... it has been getting harder and harder to hide your anger from the rest of the town. I'm supposed to be the head but I can't control my own son when he decides to flip out for whatever reason he has at any particular moment. Our people have tried too hard to overcome the image the rest of the world has of us but how can I possibly reveal the yeti when there's an example of everything they hate about us standing right in front of me! Dismissing you every time Tolah came by seemed to work wonders, she seems to love how peaceful we are." Wisdom turned to face the fletchin who had been watching but started when she was suddenly involved. "You seem adamant about how we have overcome our previous reputation, yes? Surely you can understand how I would want to keep this the way it is? When we finally reveal ourselves to the outside world we need to all be safe in their eyes."

"How... how can you assume I'll agree with you? You sent us to kill your son for your own reputation! You're a MONSTER!!" Tolah stopped at her own words and looked between Quickly and Wisdom. "I... I think I should leave now." She looked down at her feet, voice quavering. "I don't know where I'll go but I don't think I can stay here any more."

"You can come with us." said Sterling.

"Whoa, hang on a minute!" Sharp was suddenly interested. "I was in this for half the reward! I am not sharing with anyone else!"

"Relax Sharp, she can share my half. I keep my promises." Sterling looked tersely in his direction. Sharp was also feeling antsy about having more people around that he couldn't stand but Sterling looked as if she considered him to be her most expendable party member right now and he had not put up with what he had so far to lose the reward at the end.

"I'll also be happy to take your 'problem' with us." Sterling directed this at Wisdom with a side glance at Quickly. "I think you'll find he does fine being himself for once." She turned towards Quickly "If he wants to of course. It's your choice."

Quickly looked at his father who had a steely gaze to his usually calm stare and then back to Sterling.

"I think I would like to come with you." He glanced towards Sharp as if to see if he had a similar outburst to his recruitment but Sharp just shrugged. Sterling was going to do what Sterling was going to do and he just wanted to sleep now. "I'll collect my things."

The yeti disappeared and the other four were left in awkward silence. Tolah opened her mouth as if to speak but when the other three turned to look at her she shut it again and looked at her feet. After a short time Quickly returned, a bag slung over his shoulder. It was fairly small but it was packed tight, Sharp could see a few flower stems poking out under the flap.

"Well, Father... goodbye for now. I will try to become calmer and then I can return, I'm sure of it." Quickly sounded hopeful but Wisdom just looked back with a look of sadness in his eyes.

"We shall see. You will be the first of our species the world will see. Their opinion of your actions may well impact our own arrival so make sure you behave." He turned and walked away, drawing the curtain behind him.

"No pressure." mumbled Sharp, turning and walking out of the hut. Outside were a few of the other yeti. They looked at him expectantly but Sharp didn't know what they were looking for. He was joined by the other three and at Quickly's appearance, they broke into smiles and came towards the group.

"We haven't seen you in a while, we were worried!" said one.

"I'm sorry you know how I am, out gathering what I can." Quickly patted the bag. "Seems there are many different plants where these people come from." He gestured to the other three "So I'm going to go visit. An adventure, sounds as if it should be fun!" His voice was confident but Sharp could see his hands shake as they gripped his bag. The group of yeti crowded forwards to give hugs, thanks and tearful goodbyes as Sharp and the others squeezed out of the furry clump before they could get crushed. Tolah had a sad smile on her face.

"They aren't all monsters." she said quietly to herself.

"Like everyone else I suppose." replied Sharp, looking at the group of yeti.

"I guess." Almost a whisper. Sharp looked down at her but she had already turned away. When Quickly had untangled himself from his friends they walked back to town in yet more silence. Everyone seemed to be dragging their feet so it was Sharp who entered the tavern first, the sun starting to creep above the horizon as he did so.

"Two rooms, four people." said Sharp to Dorn without looking at him. "No questions before tomorrow morn- er whenever we get up." Dorn had seen a lot in his time and a lot of those things had been following Sharp back through town, although perhaps not as non-threateningly as the two newcomers currently were. He squinted inquisitively at Quickly but nothing else. Sharp was sure he had never seen the man raise his brow once in the years he had known him, even when Sharp had contracted that weird face rash (long story). He tossed two keys on the bar and in response, Sharp threw a few coins. He tossed one of the keys to Sterling without looking to see if she had caught it and headed straight for the stairs, practically dragging his aching bones up them, fumbling the key into the keyhole and through the door to collapse on the first bed he encountered. He heard Quickly shut the door behind him (Sharp would certainly have more to say on the roommate situation when he was more conscious). He heard the yeti shuffling in his bag through the muffling of the blankets, then a shock as he was hoisted up and placed carefully in a sitting position. Before he could say a word, Quickly reached forwards and grabbed him by the nose, jerking it into position. Sharp gave out a pained yelp and Quickly took the opportunity to shove a plant of some kind into his mouth. He was forced to swallow and the plant was bitter to the taste. Quickly kept hold of his nose as he felt a warm glow descend down his throat and up his nasal passage and swollen eye socket as it dulled the aching pain that was his face. He was able to reopen his blackened eye fully and as he did, Quickly slowly removed his hand from Sharp's nose. It still ached but as he wiped the remainder of the blood away he found he could breathe easily again and his nose had healed back into the position it should be in. He opened his mouth to raise an objection but failed at the smiling face in front of him. Without a word, Quickly returned to his own bed, feet hanging over the end of the human sized cot. He was certainly the quietest of Sharp's current companions. Sharp decided to take this as a good thing for now and rolling back into the blankets he sank into a deep, dreamless sleep.

Chapter 4

It was late afternoon when he finally awoke. The curtains were still drawn but he could see a bright light leaking into the room. Quickly was nowhere to be seen so he took his time getting himself ready before ambling down the stairs.

The other three were already eating whatever you would call a late afternoon meal, the few other patrons staring at the hulking yeti carefully trying to work his way around human sized cutlery and the fletchin reheating her tea with her own hands. Sharp sighed and drew up a chair, part of the circus attraction. He was greeted by a smile from Quickly, a nervous side glance from Tolah and a glare from Sterling.

"I was just bringing the other two up to speed on our mission." she updated Sharp. "They seem willing to join us. Of course, I will be splitting my half of the reward with them." If she was expecting her guilt trip to have any effect on him then she didn't know him very well. He simply shrugged and helped himself to their leftovers, pausing when he heard that stupid flipping sound. Sterling was twirling the seal again. Sharp was sure she did it to piss him off.

"Can we at least go in a straight line from here?" Sharp raised his voice in an attempt to drown out the sound.

"Unless we see anyone else in need on the way." Sterling replied.

"Fantastic. Say that louder why don't you? We could do with a queue lining up for more free work while the outer reaches of Mistmore get devastated waiting for us. I'm sure they'll understand their loved ones dying or disappearing while we clear bugs out of people's gardens and do general repairs on leaky roofs, probably while picking up any waifs and strays we meet along the way for our small army." Sharp said irritably.

"I'm not suggesting we do menial jobs but I won't refuse to help someone who needs it! Also, you'll be grateful for the extra help when we DO find that whatever our target is is too powerful for just the two of us!" Sterling was raising her voice. Sharp was finally starting to grate on her nerves, it had taken her longer than most. Tolah had been watching their conversation, her head moving back and forth. Quickly was staying out of it and quietly ate his meal.

"You guys argue a lot, huh?" asked Tolah. She seemed a lot more passive this morning. Sharp suspected her shock at the yeti village had done something to her brain.

"Lives and the contents of my wallet are in danger of disappearing. What would you want to do?" Sharp asked.

"Are you actually asking my opinion?" Tolah sounded surprised. Such a small amount of time and already she knew what he was like. Hopefully, this would reduce the amount of interactions they would have but he doubted it.

"Sure, why not." Sharp replied.

Tolah thought for a moment then said slowly "Well, perhaps we should just start walking and if an opportunity to help someone comes up, we decide then? We should judge based on the situation, not just lump all side missions into a must do or must avoid decision right off the bat."

Sterling looked at her frowning. It hadn't even occurred to her that there might possibly be a person not worth helping. Sharp guessed Tolah had learned some kind of lesson about her own personal brand of positive stereotyping. Well good for her: she had grown as a person, but he was more interested in the fact she might be a voice of reason for Sterling's save the whole world crap.

"Fine by me." said Sharp, leaning back on his chair. Sterling's flipping abruptly stopped as she came to a decision.

"Agreed." Sterling rose and looked at her company of... adventurers? Hunters? Random idiots? Yeah, that one seemed right. She had a stupid expression that Sharp could only describe as pride. Tolah beamed back at her, Quickly sat up straight and Sharp lounged back in his chair to ruin the effect. He was met with that look she kept reserved just for him. It wasn't anger, more as though she felt sorry for him maybe? He shook off the feeling and stood.

"We going then?" He strode off without looking back, a half-hearted wave at Dorn who returned it without looking up. Sharp would be back sometime in the future.

It was Sharp who led them that day as Sterling stayed back to chat to those she knew wanted to actually hear from her. From what Sharp could make out she was trying to give Quickly a pep talk whenever she could about the importance of being who you are. A berserker has his place in battle to be sure, but Sharp had never liked them. Someone who couldn't control their anger was useless when faced with a foe who was using their brain but Sterling was going on about it as if he had a superpower of some kind.

The next village was in easy reach and nothing of note happened while there. However, the following day they made sure to buy camping gear as from this point on the towns were further apart and they would not always be able to get to them before nightfall. Sharp preferred to sleep out on his own anyway but he supposed that wasn't really an option with tag-a-longs.

The villagers stared at the group of course. This was going to be a problem, Sharp could tell, but Sterling had a way of acting as if he was meant to be there wherever she went and by just ignoring the whole giant creature and snobbish recluse following her around thing, it didn't exactly go away but there wasn't really anything anyone could do. Neither Quickly nor Tolah were actually doing anything wrong so people were more keeping an eye on them to make sure it stayed that way more than anything else (as if they COULD do anything if Quickly raged out or Tolah decided to set fire to things). There were plenty of other races that WERE common of course and being racist just tended to lose you business if you were a merchant and lose your vital signs if you were weaker or more unlucky than the one you were insulting. Many people had never even heard of the yeti but by Sterling acting normal they probably just assumed this was one of those new-fangled species they hadn't heard of in their backwater town which only had humans, dwarfs, rallis and whatever Ray who lived under the bridge was. Well, at least they got no trouble from the owner of the inn who only judged what colour the coin in front of him was as opposed to the colour of the hand holding it.

His sleep schedule disturbed from the previous day, he woke in the night and wandered downstairs to the empty bar and took a seat with a view over the deserted street outside. A noise alerted him to Tolah taking a seat next to him and he sighed.

"Plenty of seats." He waved an arm to indicate the multitude of tables and chairs.

"Maybe I want to talk to you."

"I have no idea why."

"Seems we got off on the wrong foot." Tolah seemed geared up for a conversation.

"Unfortunately this is the only foot I have. If you don't like getting kicked in the face, feel free not to talk to me." Sharp went back to looking out the window.

"Sterling was right." Tolah said, pushing her glasses further up her nose. Sharp turned to look at her. She was looking at him with a curious expression.

"Now I'm concerned. Sterling was right about what?"

"Something's weird with you. She says you're here for the money and the glory but I'm not sure why anyone would have stuck with a situation for so long for such a superficial reason. To be honest I'm not sure why you even want the glory since you seem to hate attention so much."

"You and Sterling have the same idea about me, huh?"

"She... pities you."

So that was the expression she always had. She pitied HIM? Sure people looked up to her but they did that for him as well. He certainly wouldn't want the sort of attention she received.

"I don't see what's so hard to understand. A lot of people want to be in the position I am. I just have the skill and persistence to attain it. That's all." He replied sharply, moving forward into her personal space.

Tolah backed off out of his face. "Just so you know, I don't like you. But I like Sterling and she likes you so I'm willing to try to at least not try to set you on fire."

Sharp grunted.

"I wouldn't take it as a compliment though. Sterling likes everyone. Don't mess it up." Tolah stood up and started to walk back out of the room.

"If you give everyone the same thing then how can it be worth anything?" said Sharp to her retreating back. Tolah paused as if to reply but instead continued to walk out of the room, leaving Sharp to his empty room.

The next few days were uneventful. Tolah wasn't speaking to Sharp and Sharp wasn't speaking to anyone. Sterling, on the other hand, was talking to everyone as per usual although her main target still seemed to be Quickly.

"You shouldn't pay any attention to what your father told you. If you feel angry you have the right to be angry! You'll find out that everyone else expresses their emotions all the time! It's your father who will suffer when he meets everyone else. How is he going to cope with other people getting mad or being upset or anything else when no one in his village is allowed to feel anything at all?" She was lecturing as if she was a guidance counsellor and Sharp wondered how many more multiple personalities she was hiding away in there. Every time she spoke to the other two she would revert back to Sharp's chatty Sterling or Tolah's listening intently Sterling. He was starting to feel a bit dizzy when she spoke to more than one of them at a time.

Of course, they had a few scuffles on the way with enemies but not from other people. A couple looked as if they were interested in the contents of their wallets for a moment but shortly returned to looking straight ahead at a glance from Quickly. Most of their trouble was from the odd beast that had decided to wander up the road, the most interesting being an encounter with a bear that Quickly ended up scaring off with some kind of stink bomb.

Quickly had turned out to be a herbalist of a kind. Around their campfires Tolah took the time to lecture them all about various creatures, people and whatever she had decided to become obsessed with in the past (the latest being the yeti) but Sharp tended to tune her out and watch Quickly work. He had many different plants Sharp had never seen before. Not that he paid a lot of attention to plants as a whole. If it wasn't trying to eat him he wasn't overly bothered with something (there was that weird plant with a face and all those teeth he killed that one time. That one he paid attention to). But Quickly had such a wide variety and could combine them to make pretty much whatever he wanted. He always made sure to have a good supply of the healing plant he had used previously on Sharp. It didn't heal severe damage but light cuts, bruises and sprains could be fixed and, according to Quickly, it would speed up recovery of worse injuries although broken bones and such would have to be held in the position they needed to end up in. Sharp had also seen him use the previously mentioned stink bomb (self-explanatory), a bomb that made the target's eyes water and what looked like a slightly oozing concoction he made while wearing gloves, carefully wrapped individually and then placed in a bag. Sharp could guess what it was for although he hadn't seen Quickly use it at all. For the last few nights he had been working on some sort of oil. Sharp hadn't asked what it was for and Quickly hadn't been forthcoming about it but he tossed it into the campfire every so often. He always watched what it did when it hit the flames but Sharp couldn't be sure that he wasn't just disposing of a failure. For someone with anger issues, he sure was able to concentrate on long, boring tasks for extended periods of time. In fact, Sharp hadn't really seen much of the temper since they met. He had seen a few hints of it in the fights they had had and once when Tolah had gotten a little into a haggling argument which had turned a tad colourful. He had to hope it was Sterling's pep talks or just the fact that he felt more relaxed in his new company rather than bottling it all up.

It was at the town of Silver that they next made a major stop. Silver only wished it was Golden. It was certainly more of a city and less of a town but didn't have that claustrophobic, stepping on people all the time thing going on, at least for the most part. Also, it had considerably fewer fountains (but some).

"Meet at the Kings Head at nightfall!" said Sharp and without waiting for an answer, he separated from the group and melded into the crowd and towards blissful solitude. He turned to the side streets which were doing their best to emulate the spoke-like streets of Golden but without the more talented builders the effect was more wobbly than anything and the paths curved in places. The buildings weren't as high either but that meant more light reached the pedestrians down below and Sharp had no trouble finding his way, stepping around various people, striding as fast as he could past those that gave him looks as they recognised him. His target was a garden he knew about. It was far enough away from the centre of the town that he knew he wouldn't be disturbed and peace and quiet was what he was craving after weeks of having to deal with people. He found a suitable tree pointed away from the crowds and took a seat in its shade. He was dozing when he heard the whispering. Sharp didn't know what it was about but whispering always made him want to listen harder.

"Yeah, they got here a few hours ago. Lost track of Sharp but the other three seem to be sticking together and it's Sterling who has the seal. We might have a problem with the hairy bodyguard she seems to have picked up and I've been hit by magic before so maybe watch out for the fletchin as well." said a scratchy voice.

"Want to try to separate them while in town?" said a booming voice in reply. It was still whispering so the effect was that it sounded like a regular person talking normally.

"If we do then they won't leave town before meeting up and we can't do anything while surrounded by the locals. We wouldn't want to harm anyone else." said Scratchy.

"Look, we really weren't prepared for multiple targets, seems Sterling is really making use of that seal. I say we go with plan B and just try to pickpocket it." suggested Booming. "Think you can do it?"

"I can pickpocket anything, you know that." Scratchy sounded insulted. "I guess I'll wait until they bed down for the night. They're staying at the Kings Head, should be easy to get into that place."

"Then that's the plan. Let's go get something to eat!" Booming stomped off before Sharp could get a good look but one was small, not human, and the other probably was human but was on the bulky side.

Sharp sighed. He got to his feet and took off in the direction of the inn. It wasn't time to meet the others so he took a sidetrack through the market. It was about time he bought a new sword. The last had been a gift but was starting to look the worse for wear (using it as part of makeshift mountain climbing gear had probably been a bad idea). He managed to find one he liked but refused the offer to sell the one he currently had (he was rather attached) and through the stalls he saw Sterling carrying a pile of books, probably for Tolah though goodness knows how she was going to carry them when they left Silver. Tilting his head he saw Quickly towering over everyone else, he probably should have looked for him first come to think of it. Sharp made Quickly his focus and weaved his way towards the group.

"Need to talk to you." he said to Sterling.

"Perfect!" Sterling dumped half the books in his arms.

"In private and now." He grunted under the weight. Sterling's face turned serious and she led the party back towards the inn.

The others had already booked the rooms without him so they were able to find privacy there.

"We have a couple of stalkers after your seal." Sharp said.

"What? Who?" Sterling was astonished. The seal came with the power of the King after all, stealing it was tantamount to stealing from him directly.

"Didn't see them well but it's a couple of men. One human, one shorter, dwarf or ralli probably. Perhaps someone should keep her voice down when proudly declaring she's on an epic mission for the King when she stops in every single village." Sharp glared at Tolah.

"Well, I wasn't aware that people were going to be nasty enough to want to steal from us!"

"Tolah, we've been over this. People are jerks." Sharp replied.

Sterling waved them both to be silent. "It doesn't matter how they know, we just need to avoid the problem. We could inform the guards or simply change our sleeping arrangements for tonight. I was hoping we could stay here for a couple of nights to recharge but if we leave tomorrow we could put some decent distance between us and them before they realise and hopefully lose them in the Silver Dales. The creatures down there would scare anyone away from us."

"Or we could wait until they try something and set up an ambush. Why run when we can take the problem completely out of the picture? Better yet, wave that seal around and get a few swords to help us out.

Guards would probably be best, mercenaries will still want paying even if the King himself asks." Sharp reasoned.

"We're avoiding blood when we can." Sterling said stubbornly

"They want the seal, that's treason! There WILL be blood. I'm just concerned that it will be ours! For once we have the upper hand! Let's use that!" Sharp was starting to lose his patience.

"I've made my decision. We inform the guards of what is going on, NOT USING THE SEAL, and then we change sleeping arrangements. You two," she indicated Sharp and Quickly "will be staying at The Hunters Mark and Tolah and I will stay at The Silver Coin. I'm leaving the seal with you in case they follow me. You will SHARE A ROOM." Sharp had been taking a single room whenever he had been able. Sharp groaned. He hated The Hunters Mark. It was owned by dwarf brothers who had been hunters in their heyday. As a result, they had mounted so many stuffed trophies all over the walls you could barely sit in the bar without being poked with an antler or two and if they saw someone they knew was a hunter they wouldn't leave that person alone, comparing stories until a victor was announced. While Sharp was sure he could win such a contest, that chipmunk story always came up and Sharp would rather not have to talk to anyone full stop. At least his only companion would know how to shut up.

Sharp didn't reply to Sterling but pushed Tolah's pile of books he had been carrying back towards her.

"Good." said Sterling. "I will inform the Captain of the Guard on what is happening, you go check into the inn." She reached into an inner pocket and brought out the seal. She paused, turning it over in her hand a couple of times before handing it over to Quickly. The yeti gave a look at Sharp, who was practically drooling as it passed by his nose, before carefully placing it in the middle of his bag of herbs. Sharp had no idea how he would find it again but Quickly seemed to have some sort of order in the chaos that only he knew about. Without another word, Sharp left, Quickly lumbering along behind him. He toyed with the idea of asking Quickly to hand him the seal. Quickly tended to just go along with whatever the others asked him to do but so far he hadn't had to choose between two of them. Quickly caught Sharp staring at him and gave him a smile. He rummaged round in his bag and came out with what looked like a small tightly tied ball of herbs but what Sharp recognised as one of his home-brewed sweets. He handed it to Sharp who took it (those things were delicious) and put out of his mind all ideas of asking for the seal. He couldn't do that to Quickly, no matter how annoyed he was with the company and what would he do after he got it? He had no plans to abandon the mission. Despite Sharp not liking anyone, Quickly was extremely close to breaking that, there was something you couldn't really hate about him.

  The Hunters Mark was exactly as Sharp had remembered it to be. A huge troll head loomed over the bar and a variety of other heads stuck out of the rest of the walls (most of them griffins, Sharp didn't know what their issue was with the beasts and he was surprised they weren't extinct) but the centre of attention was, as usual, the two dwarfs currently arm wrestling each other on a table in the middle of the room. They had a crowd of people around cheering and sloshing their drinks everywhere. Cries of "Trent! Trent! Trent!" and "Tag! Tag! Tag!" blurred together as the two men wandered in. Sharp wondered whether the spectators even knew which of the dwarfs was Trent and which was Tag seeing as they were identical in both looks and attitude and the current condition of the crowd could only be described as 'completely plastered'.

Dwarfs were probably the second most common species after humans. The tallest usually didn't break four foot but tended to be stout and people were fools for thinking they could defeat one simply because of their size. Other than that, they shared a lot of the same looks and traits as humans. These two had short, scratchy beards, bald heads (shaving was less embarrassing than a receding hairline) and cunning eyes under bushy eyebrows.

This match could go on for a while. He worked his way through the crowd.

"HEY! WE NEED A ROOM!" he yelled into the ear of the nearest dwarf with no reaction. "YOUR KITCHEN IS ON FIRE!" He tried.

"Finally get something that isn't raw then!" said a jokester in the crowd to a roar of laughter.

"I BET YOU TEN GOLD YOU CAN'T BEAT MY FRIEND IN ARM WRESTLING!"

The two simultaneously stopped so that their hands hadn't moved from the dead centre before they parted.

"Well, well, well if it isn't Mr Number One himself! Haven't seen you since you were just starting out! How's that crying into your drink problem getting along?" said Trent/Tag.

Sharp rolled his eyes and put a bag of gold on the table. All eyes in the room went to it.

"Arm wrestling. You win, the gold is yours. My friend wins, you give us free board and food and you leave us alone the whole time we're here." As one, the crowd turned and craned their necks at Quickly who gave a nervous smile and waved then turned back to look at the dwarfs who had their mouths wide open.

"You er, want us to arm wrestle that or hunt it?" asked Trent/Tag.

Quickly looked nervous.

"Just the arm wrestling please. I hunted him earlier. Ster- er another hunter with me convinced me to let him live. He's been rather helpful so far." Sharp said.

"Wait. You have people who will work with you?!" asked Trent/Tag.

"Yes, that was the weirdest thing about what I said." replied Sharp. "You in?"

"Heck if YOU beat him we'll have no trouble!" The dwarfs grinned. "Get the er, man? a chair!"

Someone managed to find a barrel that would support Quickly's weight and Sharp showed him the position to put his arm in on the table. The two dwarfs nodded to each other with a grin and set up chairs opposite then proceeded to both put their elbows on the table to a resounding "OOOOOOO!" from the crowd. Sharp crossed his arms and shrugged nonchalantly which earned him an "OOOOOOO!" of his own. The two dwarfs grasped Quickly's hand then at a nod to each other pushed as hard as they could. The crowd resumed their cheering for the two dwarfs but as the yeti's hand remained where it was they faltered. Sharp looked around and started chanting "QUICKLY!, QUICKLY!" over and over which the crowd soon realised was Quickly's name and took up the chant themselves, allowing Sharp to stop and try to regain some of the dignity he thought he had or that anyone cared about. The match went on for about three minutes before the chanters started to trail off slightly and look a bit bored. Sharp shuffled forwards and whispered into Quickly's ear.

"You're supposed to force their hands to touch

the table." Quickly's eyes widened with understanding and with no effort he pushed the dwarfs' hands carefully backward so as not to hurt them. There was a pause, then a cheer started up then rippled round until everyone was raising their voices and stomping their feet.

"Let's see how he handles his beer!!" said a voice from somewhere.

"Coming right up!" said Trent/Tag, nonplussed from his defeat as he slid over the bar and started filling the biggest tankard Sharp had ever seen.

"Hey, don't forget the leaving us alone thing!" but he was drowned out by the crowd chanting "CHUG! CHUG! CHUG!" as the tankard was pushed into Quickly's hand. He gave a look towards Sharp who shrugged so he lifted the drink to his lips and downed it in an impossibly small amount of time. Sharp gaped and suddenly he found himself as simply part of the crowd, craning to see what his companion could handle next. Tests of strength, tests of endurance, tests of speed - Quickly smashed all records. At some point in the evening a drink was pushed into Sharp's own hand and after that, the evening kind of blended together into one long blur.

Chapter 5

When Sharp woke up he was looking at a wall. He shook his head, pain flared up and he felt himself swaying. Swaying? He turned his head and he realised he wasn't looking at a wall but the floor. A rope wrapped around his entire body and he was hanging from the pole that until yesterday had held the sign for The Hunters Mark. He craned his head and saw Quickly tied in a similar fashion to the gate leading to the inn. Someone had painted a moustache on his face in some sort of black paint and the yeti was snoring like an earthquake. Someone cleared their throat and looking around he saw Sterling and Tolah with unimpressed looking expressions.

"Oh, er, hey." Sharp said. Quickly continued to snore on. Sterling drew her sword. "Whoa, hey watch it!" said Sharp as she readied a swing. Sharp closed his eyes and heard her cut through the rope. He crashed head-first into the pavement. As he shook himself free from the ropes, Tolah was cutting Quickly free and trying to work out how to wake him up. Sterling was rummaging around in Quickly's bag which had found its way outside but was still full (there was only a certain kind of herb that interested the people in The Hunters Mark).

"Wha, where's the seal?! I leave you for one night and you lose the most valuable thing in the country!!" Sterling was livid.

"Just calm down woman." Sterling's voice was cutting through his aching skull. He stumbled back into the Mark and up to the bar.

"Need some hair of the dog that bit ya?" asked Trent/Tag.

"Just give me back my coaster Trent." groaned Sharp.

"I'm Tag." said the dwarf pushing a tankard off the seal and handing it back. "You are one depressing drunk by the way." Sharp snatched the seal back.

"And you still owe me a free room and a meal. I spent the night outside somehow."

"You can claim it on the way back through, assuming you survive whatever quest needs a furry giant to help you out. He's fantastic by the way, you should actually attempt to hold onto a friend for once. I can imagine him to be an asset in battle as well." continued Tag, leaning on the bar.

"Don't need the help but I'll keep that in mind." said Sharp as he left. Sterling was looking pissed, arms crossed, tapping one foot. Sharp didn't think people actually did that outside of comics but there you have it. He flipped the seal, caught it and then threw it to Sterling who caught it deftly without breaking eye contact. She inspected it, wiped it on Sharp's jacket and returned it to her inside pocket again. Quickly had been roused into consciousness somehow and with a groan, lumbered to his feet.

Their punishment was to carry the books. Quickly had the majority but Sharp found his load to be more than enough. They walked behind the other two (who apparently had a safe, if boring, night at The Silver Coin) and although neither of the men said a word, there was something to be said about a shared hangover and punishment.

They had no trouble for the next three days. Sharp was feeling less stressed lately. He still blocked out Tolah's lectures over the campfire but Sterling seemed to have loosened up slightly or at least was leaving him alone more and there was something almost hypnotic about watching Quickly make whatever he was making during the evenings. He threw his oil substance into the fire and, from a cheer from the other three, it flared up then made the blaze larger. Sharp had no idea if that was what he was aiming for but having oil that would sustain a fire was exceedingly helpful, especially as the nights had started getting colder. They had entered the Silver Dales a couple of days before, a series of valleys that led away from the city and heralded the start of the sparser inhabited areas of Mistmore. Forests dotted the landscape as well as more open sections with long grass, waving in the breeze. The party met a cliff edge and followed it for a time, the edge dropping off into darkness. Sharp could see treetops if he squinted. They adjusted their direction which caused them to walk into a small forest with trees spaced rather far apart. This was where they met the two hunters.

They were Herbert and Slick. The company stopped and for a moment no one spoke.

"We wanted to do this in town, no fighting, but it seems we'll have to go with plan B." said Slick. Sharp recognised Scratchy from back in Silver. So they knew about the seal from the King himself rather than Tolah's big mouth.

"Not sure what you think is going to happen here." said Sharp, dropping the books he was currently carrying and saw Quickly do the same (though more carefully than Sharp had done). "There are four of us and only two of you. Feel free to try your luck though. If we kill you, that's two fewer hunters to compete with out in the field."

Their two opponents shared a look. Herbert drew a large, two-handed battle axe and Slick nocked an arrow. Sharp and Sterling each drew their own swords. The first move was by Slick. Sharp felt the arrow zip past his head as he barely moved out of the way in time, leaving a small red line across his cheek. He and Sterling charged forward and swung at Herbert who blocked Sterling's swing and a mighty kick hit Sharp in the stomach and knocked the wind out of him at the same time without Herbert showing much effort. Slick jumped onto the tall man's shoulder and used it as a springboard to gain more height. He loosed another arrow and it whizzed through the air and hit Quickly in the shoulder who had been pacing the outside of the fight waiting for an opportunity to help. He roared with pain and slammed his fists into the ground, shaking it. He charged and Sharp recognised Quickly's berserk mode, diving out of the way of the stampeding yeti. Herbert grabbed Slick and dodged the charge, turning to block another strike by Sterling as Slick shot another arrow towards Tolah who was trying to aim a lightning bolt at one of the two enemy hunters. She reacted by shooting the arrow with lightning which redirected it, everyone making sure to keep their distance. While everyone's attention was on the arrow, Slick dashed forwards and through Sharp's legs. He turned quickly to track the ralli and slammed face first into Sterling who was trying to take a bash at the annoying little beast. While they were stunned, Slick dropped his bow, climbed up Sharp's side and pulled out a knife from who knows where and tried to find a gap in Sharp's armour under his outer clothes. Sharp preferred leather for the ease of movement so Slick found no such gap but he couldn't dislodge the ralli who was crawling all over him. Sterling was trying to find an opening, afraid to use her sword so close to Sharp and instead, swung a fist just as Slick jerked Sharp's head back, earning Sharp a knuckle sandwich. In the background, Sharp could hear Herbert laughing as he dodged reckless attacks by Quickly, using the yeti's giant frame to block

Tolah's view and, subsequently, any magic.

"Any comrade you can't seamlessly fight alongside is your enemy!" Herbert taunted. He swung his giant axe and the hilt caught Quickly's ankles, causing him to go flying and disappearing into the foliage. Tolah combined a water spell and a fire spell, shooting boiling water towards Herbert who blocked it with his axe. He yelped as some of it hit him in the face and at the noise, Slick left his targets and ran at Tolah who hadn't been expecting the sudden rush and reacted by shooting fire straight in front of her. Slick kept coming, coat and fur ablaze. He hit Tolah full on and proceeded to take short stabs at her. Blood rose from her arm where she tried to block him and fire crept from his fur onto her sleeve. He jumped off her as she desperately tried to put out the fire, gasping with pain. Herbert rushed forwards and threw his coat over Slick, extinguishing him before the blaze could do any damage.

"This is ridiculous!" cried Sharp. He untangled himself from Sterling and rushed Herbert who raised his battle axe to repel the sudden attack. Sharp used his superior speed to duck under the swing and took a slash at Herbert's face. His sword caught Herbert's cheek and bounced off his shoulder armour. He backed off to find Slick in his way, swinging at him with both the original and a second blade he suddenly had. Blood spurted from slashes on Sharp's face and arms and the ralli was doing a number on his leather chest-piece but so far it had held. Sharp got some distance from the duo as the ground shook and Quickly suddenly reappeared, arms swinging. Their two enemies separated and, in the yeti's crazy state, didn't know which to target, allowing Herbert to take a free swing at Quickly, gouging a chunk out of his side and taking him down as the yeti roared and held the wound. Tolah had managed to put out the fire on her clothes and obviously decided a less self-damaging spell was in order. She raised her hands and roots crept out of the ground wrapping themselves around Slick who had been distracted by dodging Sterling who was taking swipes at his face. Slick managed to twist his upper body around slightly and grabbing a rope he had wrapped around his waist, threw it at Sterling's legs, wrapping around and sending her flat into the dirt. Herbert ran at Tolah who was concentrating on maintaining the spell and Sterling, who was struggling with the rope, yelled out.

"SHARP! GET TOLAH!"

Sharp could see this fight was going poorly for them, the other two clearly had the upper hand in working in sync. Anger rose in his chest until all he wanted was to end this embarrassing farce. He chose Slick as his target and charged full speed towards the still trapped ralli. A well-aimed swing hit him full in the chest, carving a line all the way up and over his neck, ending with a slice through his muzzle and sending him crashing to the ground with an agonised scream, cut off as he lost consciousness. A yell from Sterling made Sharp turn to see the giant axe slicing through Tolah's side. She gave a horrific screech before crashing to the ground herself. Herbert didn't stop to finish her off but instead bull rushed Sharp out of the way and scooped up his fallen friend, covering him in his jacket, trying to stem the flow of blood. Herbert looked up at Sharp and he was surprised to see tears in the man's eyes.

"I guess I can see where your priorities lie." Herbert said bitterly and turning his back, ran off as fast as he could. Sharp turned to see Sterling bent over an unmoving Tolah. Sterling's jacket and hands were covered in blood as she cradled the fletchin in her arms. Her eyes met Sharp's.

"I told you to get Tolah." Her voice quavered, it sounded almost like a question.

"But I... I just... thought..." He trailed off, his chest tight, heart pounding. Suddenly he heard a growl and turned to see Quickly rise to his feet, blood dripping down his front and pounding the ground, he charged towards the two women. Sterling clutched Tolah to her in an attempt to shield her. Sharp dashed forward and, disrupting the charge, was rewarded with a fist in his side, flinging him away and cracking some ribs. The team quickly became tiny as he flew horizontally away, hitting multiple branches but somehow missing any tree trunks. He protected his head with his arms and saw the edge of the cliff pass by underneath him. Gravity finally took hold and he fell down, hitting further branches and tearing his clothes. The ground rushed up to meet him and he had nothing to slow him down as he slammed his head on a protruding boulder, his vision immediately going black.

Chapter 6

When Sharp woke up it was raining. He had no idea how much time had passed but it was now dark, luckily with a bright enough moon that he could see well enough, even with the trees blocking out much of the sky. His whole body ached, and there was a shooting pain in his head where he had hit the boulder. He struggled to his feet, his ribs complaining, and took a look at his surroundings. He was in a wood somewhere. Glad that cleared it up. He sat backwards on the boulder to collect his thoughts but all he could think of was Tolah. He had killed her as surely as if he had struck her himself. She had been annoying sure, but she was still his companion. How could he have chosen to do what he had? All he could remember was his blood boiling, anger at being mocked alongside the knowledge that they were losing the fight. He was so unused to working in a team and Tolah was experienced in exploring but certainly not in any kind of full-on fight. It was easy to forget she wasn't as capable as he or Sterling when she was lobbing giant fireballs around.

He had no idea what he should do next. He was certain they hadn't gone to look for him after what he had done, perhaps Sterling and Quickly had simply carried on over the Dales. He wasn't sure that Sterling wouldn't put a sword through his face if he managed to catch up with them. He wasn't sure that he wouldn't let her. For the first time in ages, he wasn't sure. He wasn't sure.

"I'M LOST!" Sharp cried out but all he got in reply was the howling wind and the battering of the rain on his tattered clothes and damaged armour. He looked up and could see where he had fallen, almost completely vertically down. He pointed himself in the direction of where he had come off the cliff and with no other idea, or inclination to think of one, he started to trudge forwards, each step sending pain through his crushed ribs and through his head. At least the pain was something he could concentrate on besides the crushing guilt, the feeling of loss. It had been a while since he'd had to deal with either emotion.

He managed to reach the cliff edge. The rock surface was dark and foreboding but Sharp could see handholds in the surface so he put his aching hands forward and started the long, slow climb to the top. It must have taken him around two hours, the odd outcropping gave him opportunities to rest his weary arms and he made sure to take his time. He was in no rush. When he reached the top of the cliff he rolled over onto his back and let the rain wash over him. He was exhausted but he knew this was no place to rest. Monsters made forests their home and Sharp was in no shape to fight them. He hauled himself to his feet and found the way he had come through the forest. A clear path lay in front of him, he must have hit every branch he possibly could on the way through, it looked as if a small tornado had been there. He felt his heart sink the further he walked and instinctively started moving slower the closer he got to the clearing where the fight had taken place.

The moonlight was shining through a gap in the clouds when he got to his destination but the rain was still coming down. Sharp walked towards where Tolah had fallen. The rain had mostly washed the blood away but had left a red trail with a streak of black in it which was still flowing freely. He followed the black to its source and found it came from Tolah's pile of books, still left where they had been dumped. They were now completely ruined by the rain, the ink seeping out of the soggy pile of paper and leather. Sharp bent over the pile and dug around, seeing if something, anything, could be salvaged from Tolah's collection. Salvaged from that fight. Deep under the pile, he found a single tome which had been protected from the rain by its kin, a few hours more and it too would have been turned to mush. The title read 'Exotic Rocks And How To Distinguish Them From Other Similar Rocks Found In Non Exotic Places And Their Properties' by John Smith. Even the guy's name was thrilling. Clearly the most valuable of the whole collection. Sharp was brought back to the present and he gently placed the book inside his jacket so it wouldn't get wet.

Now he had to decide what to do. He got to his feet and took a look around. The rain had eliminated most of the evidence of the fight but Slick's abandoned bow was still lying where he had dropped it. It was small to match its user but it had some intricate designs on it and was clearly well made. After slight hesitation, Sharp took this too.

"My priorities huh? YOU attacked US for a bit of metal." he mumbled to himself, turning the weapon over in his hand. They were to blame, so why did he feel like it was his fault? That's when he noticed the tree.

It had the word 'SILVER' carved in deep, hastily made gashes. Sterling had left him a note of where they had gone. He didn't dare to hope she actually wanted him to join them, but she must want him for something and at least it was something he could set his mind to doing. He could, of course, just walk in the opposite direction and just keep walking. For one crazy second, he imagined getting to the goal before Sterling could. Perhaps saving every life would make up for failing to save one. He turned back towards Silver and started the long walk back to the city.

The walk took four days. The rain hadn't let up for more than a few hours at most and the terrain was slippery and had not much of a path to begin with. Sharp was mentally and physically exhausted but every time he tried to get some sleep he would wake up after only a couple of hours, his brain buzzing and rather than lie where he was he decided to trudge on. He didn't bother trying to set up a camp but curled up where he could find any shelter, wrapping his arms around the reassuring shape of the book beneath his jacket. He had little appetite, which was convenient as he had little food on him and so, although he was on the road more than he had been on the way out of Silver, he still took longer returning. He found the first guard he could at the entrance, who had been idly watching Sharp as he approached with a bored sort of interest. Sharp enquired about Sterling and Quickly. The guard looked him up and down, he must have looked like a crazy person. Sharp had been out in the rain for days, bags under his eyes, torn clothing and with a slightly manic look in his eyes.

"Yeah, they came through here about three days ago, maybe a bit less. I remember the giant one. They were both covered in blood and he was holding a fletchin, desperate for the best healer I knew about they said. The little one looked too far gone to me but they insisted so I sent them to Doc Rothkar since he's the best in Silver." The guard gave Sharp the address so that was where he headed. So Tolah made it to the gates somehow. The others must have run the entire way back, goodness knows how they managed it. He tried to stop the hope that was welling up but it was hard. No one should survive losing that amount of blood and she had been in that state all day. Quickly's healing herb was good but it wasn't THAT good and how did they get her to eat it?

Rothkar's clinic was a rather healthy size for a single doctor. Sharp assumed he had others working with him but the only name on the shiny, oversized plaque on the door belonged to the man himself. Sharp pushed his way through the door and was met with a small waiting room. There was a dwarf behind the reception desk who scowled at him over tiny glasses, and two patients, an elderly looking elf tapping her foot impatiently and a human who was staring blankly ahead and shaking.

"Well?" said the receptionist in a voice that clearly didn't say 'I got this job for my bedside manner'.

"Er, I'm looking for my friends." Sharp replied "Came in three days ago. Human, yeti and fletchin. Covered in blood."

"Well the covered in blood thing is common," the woman said casually. "but the yeti and fletchin not so much."

"Did..." Sharp trailed off before trying again. "Did the fletchin survive?" Before the receptionist could reply, the doors to the clinic proper opened and Sterling was there. She looked tired but well apart from that. Sharp was surprised to feel genuinely pleased to see her.

"Ask her." said the receptionist and turned back to whatever she had been doing when he had walked in. Looked like a crossword. Sharp strode up to Sterling and gripped her by the arms. She stiffened at the sudden touch.

"Tolah... tell me she's alright."

"She's alive. She hasn't woken up yet but for now, she's still with us." Sterling looked torn between anger and bewilderment at Sharp's current attitude. Sharp let go of her in relief.

"Can I..." Sharp found he couldn't complete the

sentence and Sterling's expression softened into a sympathetic look as she pulled him by the wrist and through the doors.

Tolah's room was at the back and was sparsely decorated. A bed, a couple of chairs and a table with some medical looking bits of equipment Sharp could only guess the use of and Tolah's glasses. One of the chairs contained Quickly who looked outright miserable. He looked up at their entrance and shot straight up, the chair falling backward as he did so. He ran forward and Sharp found himself in a bear hug. He could hear Quickly sobbing slightly.

"I thought I killed you... I thought you were gone." It hadn't struck Sharp that Quickly might have been going through the same thing he had. A new wave of guilt washed over him. Messed up again. His ribs were agony but he managed to return the hug briefly before pushing Quickly away, gasping for breath slightly.

"I wasn't sure you would come." said Sterling. "We couldn't look for you. Tolah still had a pulse so we decided to take a chance on her recovering. We didn't even know if you survived the fall."

"But how did you even make it? There was... so much blood." Sharp asked.

"Quickly's healing herb did a lot but we had to burn the wound closed to stop her losing any more blood. Thank goodness she was unconscious for that." Sterling said.

"Where did you get the fire?" Sharp asked.

"Quickly has acid bombs. We broke one apart to use it but it still needed diluting. Those things are nasty." Sterling said and Sharp recalled the concoctions Quickly carefully wrapped. Quickly himself looked as if he was going to cry.

"They aren't meant for people! They melt through things in your way! They really hurt her, even mixed with water!" Quickly was indignant.

"They saved her life Quickly." said Sterling, placing a hand on his arm to soothe him. "She would have bled to death and the doctor says they didn't do too much damage."

"Not that I condone it in the slightest." Doctor Rothkar had managed to sneak into the room somehow but now he made his presence known as loudly as he could, his eyes seeming to judge everyone present.

Doctor Rothkar was an elf. Apart from the pointed ears, elves looked fairly like humans although they were probably the species that interbred the most and, as a result, many had features from the other parent, shorter ears, a shorter body, perhaps a slight fur covering parts of their bodies (Sharp didn't want to know how one could breed with a ralli). The Doctor seemed as pure-bred as they came however, ears that could take your eye out if he spun too fast, a chin that matched the pointedness of the ears and a lean body he probably didn't have to diet for (though being a doctor, one would assume he ate well) and his tall frame meant he loomed over most of the party.

Rothkar looked down his extensive nose at the newcomer.

"And what have you been doing to yourself, eh?" He grabbed Sharp by the ear and turned his head to look at the wound on his head. "You realise I'm the only doctor working in this clinic, yes? I can't take care of everyone who comes rolling in off the streets WITHOUT AN APPOINTMENT." he glared at Sterling. "You're lucky I happen to have some free time." Without waiting for a response he dragged Sharp out by the ear into a room opposite, containing a tired looking woman.

"Nurse. Head wound, exhaustion." he poked Sharp in the ribs who winced. "Broken ribs, malnutrition, dehydration and probably some bruises and scrapes. Fix him up, he'll be paying PREMIUM." The doctor left the room and Sharp could hear him barking orders at another nurse who was trying to steer the human from the waiting room into one of the side rooms. "AND WHERE'S MY TEA?!" He yelled at someone else. Sharp saw him walk past the open door shaking his head, a newspaper tucked under one arm.

"Runs this place on his own does he?" Sharp asked. The nurse wearily shook her head and worked on cleaning Sharp up. When she was done she pushed him out of the room with an order to get a meal and some sleep. In Sharp's opinion, she looked worse than him and he'd been walking the rain for four days. Sterling was waiting outside, turning the seal absent-mindedly in her hand.

"Everything okay?" She enquired. Sharp wasn't sure if she cared, her expression was carefully neutral.

"I guess." He touched the tender part of his head but at least it was no longer oozing blood (he hadn't dared to touch it or think about it on the walk back). Sterling looked him up and down.

"You look like a mess. Just go sort yourself out then and, I don't know, do what you want I guess. You're good at that." She turned and walked back into Tolah's room. At a loss of what to do, Sharp decided to take her advice. He paid his (extensive) medical bill and wandered over to The Hunters Mark. He decided free board was worth the annoyance of trying to dodge Trent and Tag. The place was exactly the same as when he had left it. If Trent/Tag was surprised to see him again he didn't show it.

"Cashing in that free board." said Sharp "Also

give me something that will make me forget my own name."

"Sure about that? You have to drink it down here." said Trent/Tag, placing a tankard of something that smelt like paint thinner and a key on the bar. Sharp looked around him. Many of the other patrons he remembered (albeit through a beer induced haze) and they had grins slapped on their faces. He had been here not long ago and if he wanted to be left alone, this wasn't the place to be. He said nothing but left the drink, swiped the key and trudged up to his room. The way he was feeling right now alcohol might actually finish him off anyway. A meal tomorrow would be good but for now, he collapsed on the bed and immediately fell asleep.

He slept all day. It was already dark again by the time he rose. He definitely felt better but not great, a grooming session and a meal in the bar improved this further. He decided to check on Tolah and although it was late, wasn't stopped by the disgruntled looking receptionist or the fatigued looking nurses he passed on the way. Tolah's room was empty of visitors. He supposed the other two had returned to wherever it was they had holed up. Well, Tolah looked the same as she had done yesterday. He really had no idea what one was supposed to do when confronted with a person in a coma. At least she was finally quiet. He mentally kicked himself for even thinking it, it was his fault that she was in this state in the first place. What was it Tolah had wanted from him? To listen to her he supposed but that was off the table, so talking would be the next thing to do. He drew up a chair. What to talk about? He didn't like talking to people even when they were awake and so found himself at a loss.

"I guess I should start with... I'm sorry." Sharp stuttered and fell silent. He felt embarrassed talking to a sleeping person. "Oh, I brought you one of your books. The others were kind of ruined. I'll replace them." Sharp was hoping she couldn't hear him. His bank balance was fine but spending a lot in quick succession made him nervous. He liked to earn but not to spend. Sharp pulled out the book and flicked through the first few pages. Smith definitely had a different definition of exotic to Sharp.

"You like this stuff?" asked Sharp. He had no idea what the other books had been about but if this one was anything to go by she had some weird reading habits. "This rock changes colour depending on the weather. That's kind of interesting I suppose. Pointless but interesting." He was grasping at straws but with nothing else to talk about he lapsed into reading the book out loud. He managed to plough his way through a couple of chapters before his brain threatened to become rock itself.

The following few days went the same. Sterling would avoid him but Quickly stuck to him like a bad habit whenever he could. He only eased off worrying when Sharp acted as friendly as he could but in his current mood he found that to be a challenge and after managing to sneak away, Sharp would often stalk the streets of Silver until they were almost empty before returning to Tolah for another enthralling episode of 'what's that rock?' A routine made him feel as though he was on somewhat solid ground.

On the fifth day, he woke up to the rain once again. It had been on and off for the whole time he had been there. Today he felt the thing that had been bending in him snap and he realised he really, REALLY wanted to hit something with a sword. He snuck quietly out of the room so as not to wake Quickly (he had decided to share a room with Sharp as soon as he found out where he was staying. Trent/Tag were happy to allow their new favourite sideshow to stay) and he grabbed his fighting gear and made his way down to the training yard on the outskirts of town. It was mainly used for the training of new guards but no one wanted to use it in this weather and who cared if some random idiot wanted to hit their training dummies in the rain? He was surprised to find he wasn't the only one with this idea and he could see Sterling furiously hacking away at a rather devastated looking target which he assumed used to be human shaped at one time. He walked up to her.

"Wondered where you went during the day." said Sharp. Sterling jumped at the sudden voice. She didn't reply but had at least stopped her violent attack on the undeserving, well at this point, firewood would be the best description. "Want to hit something?" Silence. "You can be pissed off at me you know. I know you want to be nice to everyone all the time but I... really messed up this time. If you want to hit me I'm totally up for it. It would probably make both of us feel better." Sharp turned around to face her and was met with a fist flying at his face. He was knocked on his arse and could already feel the bruise forming on his cheek.

"You are an IDIOT!" shouted Sterling. "NEVER do that again or I will KILL you!"

"I get it! You honestly think I would repeat what I did?" Sharp asked.

"I don't know! I honestly don't understand how your mind works. I thought you were just rough on the outside but then I thought maybe you were rough on the inside and when you abandoned Tolah I thought you were rotten but now you genuinely seem sorry about it. You're giving me whiplash!" She clutched her head as if to hold it together. Well, he didn't know how he did it but he had finally broken Sterling. Good job Sharp.

"I'm not good with people Sterling. It's been... quite a while. Honestly, I prefer the monsters, at least I know where I am with them. But yes, I feel guilty about Tolah and I can't say I particularly like her but I would never want what happened to her to actually happen to her." Sharp hoped she would say something soon. Sitting in the mud in the rain was starting to become uncomfortable. Sterling sighed and held out a hand to help him to his feet.

"Okay I believe you, but you have to be in this for more than the money you know. If we don't work together the same thing is just going to happen again. I honestly don't see how we could have won that fight the way we work as a team. Two should not be winning against four so easily but they worked as an extension of each other." Sterling looked depressed. Looks as if she had more than Tolah on her mind. Sharp had found little room in his head to think of anything else but she was right, that fight had been embarrassing.

"So you aren't kicking me out?" Sharp asked. Sterling sighed.

"Well, I think we definitely need more than just myself and Quickly if we have any hope of completing the mission and this is before I really even know what the goal is! Tolah will be laid up for a while. As soon as she wakes up we can be sure of her living but it's going to be a while before she can walk properly. When I know she's going to survive I'll feel as if we can leave. The weather has been foul lately and if it turns to winter we'll have to fight the snow on top of everything else." Sterling had thought this out. Sharp had been sure she hadn't thought any further than Tolah's current situation.

"I agree on the weather front, though it will hopefully slow down whatever is attacking those villages." Sharp agreed. "On the terrible teamwork front,

I think we have a solution in front of us." Sharp drew his sword. Sharp hadn't seen Sterling smile in a while but he saw a small suggestion of one here. She drew her sword in response and charged him. He dived out of the way then went to strike only to get blocked by her blade. She pushed him back and he went for her again, trying to use his speed against her. They both used one-handed swords but he could see she favoured strong, slow strikes while he preferred faster, more reckless attacks. They were fairly evenly matched. Sterling increased her attacks and Sharp found himself being forced backward. His feet tripped on something and he fell back onto the mud only to see it was his own pack that had caused him to become undone. He saw a hilt sticking out. His old sword was still there! He blocked an attack by Sterling with his current weapon and grabbed the sword from his pack with his other hand, swinging it towards her legs (flat edge of course) and she ended up on the ground. He leapt to his feet and carried on the assault, Sterling finding it now impossible to block both the swords. With her blade defending her face she grasped for anything she could use and her hand found a discarded wheel that had somehow found its way onto the training grounds. She bashed it into Sharp's stomach and he was forced back, winded. She gave him a moment to regain his breath and he decided to keep both the blades as she had obviously decided the same with her makeshift shield. This was fun! It had been so long since he had had a sparring partner! He felt some of the tension melting away and with a grin, Sharp charged forwards as she did the same but they never connected. Sharp found a giant palm in his face and from the muffled grunt from Sterling, she had encountered the same problem. Sharp pushed Quickly's hand out of his face. He smelt like a wet dog.

"Stop fighting!" Quickly sounded distressed. Sharp was fairly sure he was giving the yeti a nervous breakdown.

"We aren't fighting, Quickly. We're training. It's okay." said Sterling gently putting a hand on his arm. Quickly looked at Sharp who nodded.

"You want to join in? We probably should be practising at fighting together anyway. Herbert and Slick had a perfect team." Sharp suggested. Quickly looked at Sterling.

"You have a shield." he stated.

"Yeah. I kind of like it." she said. Quickly turned to Sharp.

"You have two swords." Quickly said.

"You have two fists." Sharp said. He brandished the swords. "Wanna see how they stand against each other?"

They trained for the rest of the day, teaming up in twos against the other. Sharp found he rather liked the feel of dual-wielding and Sterling was finding the shield to be effective. It probably suited her constant need to protect everyone and could give a rather severe shield bash when he wasn't paying attention.

The evening meal was a lot more animated than before but Sharp found he didn't mind for once. Quickly was looking a lot happier than he had the last week and the topic of the conversation was battle tactics, something Sharp could add to. The following evening was spent with Tolah, Sterling filling her in on the day's events in case anything they voiced would somehow sink in. Sharp carefully kept to himself the way he had been trying to keep her entertained and to be honest, he couldn't be sure his reading material choice hadn't been further sustaining the coma.

Two weeks later, Sharp's new found enthusiasm

for teamwork was starting to wane. Actually, it had started to wane as soon as it kicked in, but now he found himself craving his own space again badly enough for him to want to do something about it. He managed to slip away after the latest training session and walked until he found a tavern he had never heard of. A tiny dive on the outskirts of Silver called The Rusty Dagger. The city was large but also had a disturbingly large number of places to drink your troubles away. This one had the sort of clientele you didn't want to bump into in a dark alley but, more importantly, contained no one he knew or who knew him. Except for one person. He had lost the cocky expression and was leaning over the bar with a half-drunk beer in his hand but it was unmistakeably Herbert. Sharp hesitated for a moment but ended up taking up a seat next to him. Herbert didn't look up. Sharp took the small bow out of his jacket, he had been carrying it with him as it was small enough to fit under his coat and served as a constant reminder of what he had done (that thing poked in really uncomfortable places). He placed it on the table and slid it across the bar to Herbert. A shaking hand let go of the beer and took hold of the bow. It looked tiny in his large hand.

"He won't be using it again." Herbert said.

"Did he live?" Sharp felt no sympathy for the man. They had been the attackers and Sharp attributed part of what happened to Tolah on the duo. No one involved would have been hurt had they not attacked at all but Sharp's conscience still blamed Sharp himself more than anyone else.

"Yeah." The fact that Herbert was drinking alone and with that expression meant Slick couldn't be in any shape to have another go at them any time soon. "The fletchin?"

"She'll be fine." Sharp replied with a more upbeat

tone than he felt. Actually, he had never said anything with an upbeat tone so that might have been a bit much but it seemed any acting was going to be lost on Herbert anyway. He didn't seem to be registering even the words, let alone the inflection. Sharp took the beer that was offered by the barman and they spent the next few hours drowning their sorrows. Neither of them spoke but there was something uplifting about the other man's misery, Sharp felt no guilt in admitting this to himself.

When he returned to The Mark, Quickly and Sterling had already retired for the night. Quickly was still up when he got to the room but at Sharp's return he said nothing and rolled over on his bed and fell asleep. Sharp allowed himself a small smile. He was still looking forward to going back to being a solo act but the people he was stuck with at the moment were at least half decent. He supposed he could learn at least one thing from Herbert.

Chapter 7

Tolah woke up the next day. The trio had been training as usual but Sterling had snuck away when they broke for lunch. Sharp had had no idea the clinic was where she went every day but the silence was welcoming so he never complained. She came back a few minutes later, completely breathless. She attempted to talk but it came out as an incomprehensible splutter. Quickly stood up with alarm. Sharp took a slow bite of his sandwich.

"GUYS COME QUICK TOLAH IS AWAKE!" Sterling exploded. Quickly had the widest grin Sharp had ever seen on him but Sharp himself had a weird mixture of feelings inside his stomach. Relief was in there, sure, but guilt and concern over what Tolah would say were stabbing him repeatedly. He trailed behind all the way to the clinic and made sure to be the last to enter her room. Sterling was hugging Tolah who looked as if she was choking but seemed okay with it. Quickly was just standing there but still had that stupid grin, Sharp was starting to think he was stuck that way. At Sharp's entrance, her smile turned to a scowl.

"You're still here I see." she said. Sharp said nothing.

"He's REALLY SORRY." said Sterling pushing him forward.

"Guessing you won't believe that though." Sharp added. He wasn't sure of the expression he should wear, this wasn't really his area of expertise.

"You could try to convince me." Tolah didn't seem immediately ready to set him on fire which was more than he could hope for.

"There isn't going to be anything I CAN say. I almost got you killed for a chance to grab a victory. It's not something I'll ever do again but most people shouldn't need the lesson in the first place. You and I both know I'm not going to be falling on my knees and asking for forgiveness but anything you need I will try my utmost to do. Changing the past is impossible." He paused. "But I'll do what I can for you in the present." Speech done, he pulled the book out of his jacket and placed it on the bed. Tolah reached forward (wincing slightly) and took a look at the title. Her eyes lit up.

"This is one of the best ones!" she exclaimed. Sharp literally could not think of anything worse than that collection of words masquerading as a book. "Thank you." she said quietly, turning the book slowly in her hands. "I suppose I bought too many anyway."

"You could have read them in here though. I have no idea when we'll be returning through." Sharp shrugged.

"You can't go without me!!" Tolah said outraged. This was the reaction Sharp was expecting from simply seeing that he still existed, not the rather obvious statement that implied a crippled person would not be able to join a world-saving expedition.

"Tolah, we have to. We can't wait until you can walk again, the winter will be here shortly and we won't make it to Moremist if we tarry here any longer. No animal would make the journey carrying you either." Sterling had obviously been thinking about this.

"So I can come if I don't slow you down right?" Tolah's eyes lit up worryingly.

"Yeeeeeees I suppose?" Sterling said slowly.

Sharp should never have returned to Silver. He should have walked in the opposite direction and kept walking. But he didn't and now it was too late.

"Come on Sharp, they're pulling ahead again!" Tolah dug her heels into his ribs. Sharp sighed. He HAD said he would do anything she asked but she could at least have let him take turns with Quickly carrying her. It was a week before they reached the end of the Silver Dales, avoiding the clearing with the fight had cost them a few hours but other than that it was simply the fact that a person had to be carried that was slowing them down. At least no one stopped him when he crawled into his tent each night after their meal without staying to chat. The whole idea was absolutely ridiculous but he had no right to argue. If Sterling had thought the same then either her desire to see Sharp suffer or her desperation to allow Tolah to continue with them had prevented her stopping Tolah.

"Look I'm going as fast as I can! You weigh almost nothing but you're still a whole person! I just thank whichever god who feels like paying attention that you aren't the more... usual size of your species. I have no idea how you manage to keep the weight off more than them." Sharp grumbled. Tolah was silent for a time.

"My people aren't exactly active. When magic comes to you easily then you tend to use it for everything. Why farm when you can magically make the vegetables grow, levitate them into the kitchen, cook them with your own fire then levitate them onto your plate all without leaving your chair? Why search for a water source and set up an irrigation system when you can just make pure water out of thin air? I could go on but so few of the fletchin even have jobs and anything that can't be made with magic we import from the outside. Gold comes so easily to us, it can be made by magic also, but since we rarely need anything out of the city we make little of it, not that many of us care about disrupting the economy outside our protective bubble. The world outside is like an ant farm for most of my species." Tolah sounded bitter.

"So why are you so different?" This sounded like a history lesson waiting to happen but he needed a distraction from his aching shoulders (and ribs) and he was genuinely trying to make an effort to at least pay attention enough to be able to answer the question "What was the last thing I said?!" in case it was randomly asked.

"Present situation excluded, I'm usually quite active. Sitting around in an easy chair and rearranging the elements to clean your bathroom isn't my thing. The outside world was always so exciting! There are other species! Other plants! Monsters!"

"Rocks." muttered Sharp

"Exactly!" said Tolah. "I practised my elemental magic, ignored all the magic that gave me an easy life and as soon as I knew I could hold my own I just started walking! My family thought I was crazy but I was losing my mind just drifting around there. In hindsight, I probably should have learnt some healing magic but I wasn't expecting to have half my stomach ripped out by an axe." Sharp stayed silent. "I learnt so much but there's always more to learn. When I'm done exploring I'm going to write down all I've learned in books and teach the younger fletchins that their whole life doesn't have to be in one room." Tolah had long-term goals. Sharp tried not to think further than his next payment (this trip was involving more thought than he usually needed) and thinking of other people wasn't something he tended to bother with. What had they done for him lately? Improving an entire species was insanely over-reaching but he had to play nice.

"When do you think you'll be done exploring?" Sharp asked.

"I have no idea." Tolah said leaning heavily on his shoulders. "I guess I'll just decide when it's time."

"There you go Sharp, you almost stopped an entire species learning about how life can be better." Sterling cut in, she and Quickly had slowed down to allow the other two to catch up.

"Fairly sure sitting around on your arse all day without having to work for anything is always going to be the dream." Sharp replied.

"Perhaps Sharp would like to hear the fascinating mating habits of the birch squirrel." Sterling said casually.

"Oh yes! That's an AMAZING topic!" Tolah squealed. Sharp gave a weary look towards Sterling who averted her eyes but couldn't hide that irritating smile. Sharp had to listen to this topic for the next few miles, it was hard to ignore when the person talking was right next to your ear, not that he didn't try.

A further two days and the next village was in sight. Sharp was ready to drop after his solid march with Tolah. Sterling had been determined to make good time both despite and because of the weather remaining foul, as if they could outrun it but Sharp was hoping for at least a couple of days here. If all else failed he could always guilt trip Sterling into staying, using Tolah as the reason.

Their entry to the town was pretty much the same as everywhere else. A few stares at the famous hunters, more stares at the fletchin and many, MANY stares at the yeti. This appeared to be a town mainly of ralli. The further away from the main cities you got, the less varied the species tended to be in each town. Sharp was a little concerned the tavern would be too small for Quickly, taking the height of the general populace into account but he didn't have to worry. The ralli behind the bar looked Quickly up and down before clearly taking a count of his current beer barrel supply then turning back towards the newcomers with a massive grin slapped on his face.

"Two rooms, four people." said Sterling as usual. The keys hit the table.

"How about a drink?" asked the bartender, his hand twitching near the pump.

"Maybe later." replied Sterling at the same time as Sharp said "YES." The fastest poured beer Sharp had ever seen appeared in front of his nose and he downed the drink as quickly as he could. The bartender looked unimpressed at the feat but happy at the cash. One of the other patrons, however, was staring, stunned. He was a ralli, rather nondescript as rallis went, short brown fur, dull brown eyes and no notable features.

"You wanna meet the yeti?" Sharp asked him pointing a thumb towards Quickly.

"You're Jasper Sharp!" exclaimed the ralli.

"Say what?" said Sharp. It had been a while since he had been picked out of the bunch.

"And you're Lydia Sterling!" The ralli sounded as if all his birthdays had come at once. They had a hunter fan apparently.

"That's right." said Sterling with a smile. Oh great, they were going to humour him.

"What are you doing here? Are you on a mission? TOGETHER?!" the ralli asked.

"We are temporarily WORKING together." said Sharp, emphasising the word working in case the guy was going to rush home and start writing erotic fan fiction. "The mission itself is on a need to know basis. You don't need to know." He put down the tankard, picked up the key and started subtly edging backward. Sterling, however, had the ralli in full conversation mode.

"What's your name?" she asked. Great, first name

basis with a random fan. His favourite. The ralli drew himself up to his full height (about 3" 8).

"Macgillivray Jarzembowski 27th." he announced proudly.

"That is the weirdest name I have ever heard and I once spent a week in Mthwndl, and they don't have any vowels there!" said Sharp.

"Don't be rude Sharp!" snapped Sterling.

"Screw that, I already forgot what it was. I'm calling you MJ" Sharp directed this at the ralli. Macgillivray blinked a couple of times before the corners of his mouth stretched further and further apart in a strange sort of slow motion.

"I love it! I've never had a nickname!" MJ somehow managed to look more pleased than he had before, at least if his head exploded from excitement Sharp wouldn't have to be in this conversation any more. "How long are you staying? Maybe I can hear some stories? Please?"

"Ah, probably leaving in the morning." Sharp replied. He decided aching bones were better than an aching brain.

"You know what? I think we can stay a few days." said Sterling. "Tolah could do with the break."

"Oh yeah, I'm exhausted." Tolah said nonchalantly with a side look at Sharp.

"Then let me buy you all dinner!" MJ proclaimed.

"Very kind of you." said Sterling. Sharp was hoping the rest of the trip wasn't going to be like this now they had something on him. At least the towns would be sparser after this and as they approached their goal, even more so.

MJ did indeed buy them dinner but Sharp and Sterling paid for it in the sheer amount of questions the ralli had. By contrast, he had no questions for Tolah or Quickly but they seemed to be enjoying the break and Tolah was especially enjoying Sharp's discomfort at having to deal with a fan. Sterling also had a few questions for him which she managed to crowbar in when MJ had to stop to take a breath.

"So MJ, you must have a large family, what with you being the 27th." MJ fell silent, then slowly said,

"I... used to. There was an accident that claimed many, and as time went on I lost the others through various reasons." MJ fiddled with his beer. "I live on my own now. No family, no reason to stay really. I don't remain in one place very long. Roaming far from town tends to take my mind off things."

"Oh, that's terrible! I couldn't imagine what it would be like to lose my family!" Sympathy dripped off Sterling's words. Oh great, another one of Sterling's personality shifts. Sharp had no idea how she seemed to have one for everyone she met but he was really not in the mood.

"Ever been close to Moremist?" Sharp cut in before Sterling could really get into it.

"Oh, all the time!" exclaimed MJ. "I enjoy the quiet and the mystery of that fog. Sometimes," he paused for dramatic effect, "I even go inside the fog and listen to the creatures moving around."

"That's really dangerous!" gasped Sterling.

"I can defend myself." MJ puffed himself up. "I don't go too far in of course, but I'm rather an accomplished fighter if I do say so myself. Of course, nothing compared to you two!" He seemed to remember who he was talking to and dialled himself back a bit.

"Been there lately?" Sharp cut him off before he could go further.

"A few weeks ago."

"Notice anything dangerous? Well, more dangerous than usual for those parts. There's been some trouble." Sterling carried on Sharp's line of thought.

"Is that why you're here?! Wow, there must be a LOT of trouble to have two hunters, a magic user and your trained erm..." MJ faltered at the looks he was getting from everyone in front of him. "Trained battle companion?" he tried. Death glares were dialled back.

"We aren't telling you why we're here." said Sharp. "And as I'm not really one for after dinner conversation I think I'll be taking my leave. Good to meet you Mister 27th. Good luck with the slow drowning in your own ego thing." Sterling liked entertaining the masses so much she could do it solo. To his surprise, Sterling grabbed him by the belt and yanked him back into his seat. Sharp spluttered a protest which she ignored.

"Would you be able to guide us to Stillhaven?" Sterling asked MJ.

"Wait, you aren't thinking of taking this guy with us are you?" Sharp asked.

"Why not? He knows the area and we were going to have trouble locating any of the outer villages, let alone the specific one we're aiming for." Sterling reasoned.

"I totally accept!" said MJ, leaping onto his seat for added height. He put his hands on his hips and declared, "I will make sure to get you to your destination safely!"

"Tone it down Peppy." said Sharp. "This seems like a vote situation. Who votes for the sketchy looking guy we just met in a pub to guide us on a life or death mission with a load of innocent lives on the line?"

Sterling and Tolah both raised their arms. They all turned to look at Quickly who looked worried. MJ slowly started raising his hand but without turning his head Sharp pushed the hand back to the ralli's side.

"You don't get a vote. You aren't in the team."

"I won't be any trouble! And I can guide you to the one behind the whole problem. I take it you're investigating the deaths in Stillhaven?"

"Wait, so you already know about what's going on? The one behind the disappearances and the ravaged villages?!" Sterling gasped.

MJ crossed his arms smugly. "You let me lead you there and I'll tell you."

"Tell us who we're after first." Sharp wasn't buying it.

"If I tell you then you won't take me with you." MJ's smug look wasn't improving Sharp's mood any.

Quickly raised his hand.

"What are you doing man?" asked Sharp.

"He wants to help. When I wanted to help, you took me with you and now I feel better. We should let him show us the way."

"Three against one. The ralli comes with us." said Sterling.

"Nice!" MJ sat back down.

Sharp dropped his head on the table. "Why don't we just stop this mission and open up the circus Sterling clearly always wanted to run. I'll be a clown."

"You don't have the ability to make people laugh. Maybe a lion tamer?" Tolah was having a whale of a time.

"NOW can I go to bed?" Sharp asked.

"Sure, we're staying up." said Sterling. Sharp got to his feet and started to walk off.

"WAIT!" said Tolah.

"What?"

"Is there really a country which doesn't use

vowels?"

"Sure is. Don't bring up Y though." Sharp turned on his heel and went to bed. A couple of hours later he heard Quickly enter the room.

"Sorry." the yeti said quietly. Sharp didn't bother to reply.

Chapter 8

It was early when Sharp went down to breakfast. He decided to ignore the inn (bar food was always a bit ropey for breakfast. Actually, it was a bit ropey for all meals, but the most important meal of the day probably shouldn't be whatever the bartender could scrape off the plates from the previous night) so he decided to find somewhere else. However, someone was definitely following him. He didn't turn but whoever it was wasn't exactly subtle. He could hear them tripping over things, annoyed exclamations from people as he presumably got in their way and at one point he could swear the stalker was humming their own theme tune. Sharp sighed.

"Morning MJ."

"Wooooow, how did you know it was me?!" MJ sounded impressed.

"Just a hunch. I usually eat alone for breakfast."

"Well, today you don't have to!"

"Fantastic."

Even if Sharp had wanted to talk he wouldn't have found a space in the conversation. MJ had a habit of asking a question then answering it himself. He had certainly done his homework on his favourite hunters and if he was going to be like this the whole way it was going to be insufferable. Sharp had to hope he would calm down as they went along, surely he would have to run out of stories at some point.

Three hours later and he still hadn't stopped. He had trailed after Sharp the whole time and the hunter was at least impressed at his ability to keep up as he took paths only a tall person could manage or tried to sneak away when the ralli's back was turned. He would always turn up again a couple of minutes later with no recognition of the fact that Sharp had tried to ditch him.

It was a relief to see Tolah when they did, which was probably the first time he could ever admit to that (to himself. He would never admit it, full stop to anyone else). She was sitting on a bench so Sharp made his way over to her.

"Hey."

"Oh, hey Sharp, I see you found our new friend." Tolah didn't seem as enthusiastic as the previous evening. MJ gave a nod to her but otherwise kept his attention on Sharp.

"MJ, Sterling was looking for you back at the tavern." said Tolah. MJ's eyes lit up.

"Oh, I'd better go right away! See you later Sharp!" He ran off to a relieved sigh from Sharp.

"Did Sterling ACTUALLY want to see him?"

"Well, she was wondering when he would turn up today but wasn't actively looking for him." A pause. "Thanks."

"No problem. He was getting rather grating last night and he wasn't even paying any attention to me."

"Maybe that was WHY you were irritated."

"I'm not an attention hog you know." Tolah sounded irritated.

"I suppose not. You aren't interested in his species or back story or anything? I thought you were interested in everything."

"Nah. My people know enough about rallis already since they're everywhere. And before you say anything, I don't care about humans either. You know, as a species. There are some individuals I like." She looked at Sharp. "SOME individuals."

"Ouch. And his back-story?"

"I know his back-story from last night. Dead family. That's pretty much all. He's going to milk it for all it's worth though." Tolah said wearily.

"Think he was the one who killed them?" A snigger from Tolah.

"You're the one who's going to have to share a room with him when we get to each town. Better watch your back!" Tolah got a brief laugh from Sharp in return.

"What are you doing just sitting here anyway?"

"Not a lot else I CAN do." Tolah moved awkwardly, wincing. Sharp felt a pang of guilt.

"Need a lift somewhere?"

"No, but thanks for the offer. I have to get used to walking on my own if I ever want to join in with the fighting again."

"You don't have to join in with that part if you don't want. I'm sure Sterling wouldn't mind." Sharp didn't say out loud he was going be paranoid if Tolah got back into the fight again.

"What, so I can be a drag on you guys? No, I'm going to be earning my keep. Don't you think magic is really great in a fight? Not many people can use it and most opponents aren't going to have any defence against it." Tolah sounded almost desperate. "And you three seem to have a really good rapport going in a fight now. I guess you were training while I was sleeping."

"Well, we can train when you're feeling up to it then. I'm not going to refuse an ally who can set things on fire. That root thing was good as well. I like that you can hold people down for me."

"Maybe make sure I'm covered by someone next time." Sharp looked over at her with concern but she was smiling. He relaxed.

"I guess I don't really know everything you can do. You want to go over some battle strategies while you can't train?" Tolah's eyes lit up.

"DEFINATELY."

The other three found them in the tavern a few hours later. Tolah had insisted on writing things down so they were now also half buried in paper. Sharp was fairly sure magic didn't require research into various angles or material of various armour, just shoot it at the squishiest looking parts. Fire on clothes and fur, lighting on metal things, roots on stuff that wouldn't stop moving, that sort of thing, but Tolah did like careful plans. Sharp had knowledge of a lot of the things he hunted and definitely understood the value of research but after about thirty seconds into a fight the opponent would do something you hadn't planned on and that would derail your whole strategy. Instinct was far more important but he could drill that into her head when they started doing actual training, he supposed. Right now he was still trying to stave off shame so he decided to stick to her way of doing things. At least it took him away from MJ who he had known for less than a day but he already knew was going to be the most annoying thing he had encountered in a while. Ugh, fans.

"Enjoying yourselves?" asked Sterling with the now all too familiar smugness Sharp had come to expect.

"Sure am." replied Sharp without a hint of irony. Sterling's smug look changed to one of suspicion. MJ picked up one of the reels of paper that had reached down to his level.

"Wow, Sharp did you draw this? It's amazing!" he said holding up a rather gruesomely detailed picture of a human impaled on ice shards. The other two winced.

"Nah, that one was Tolah's. This one is mine." Sharp held up a picture of a stick figure (maybe also a human?) on fire.

"Oh erm. That's er..."

"Yeeeees?" asked Sharp leaning on the table. He

could hear Tolah sniggering quietly. At last some common ground. Shame it had to be irritation at the same person but, let's face it, it was hardly going to be LIKING the same thing.

"Well, you don't need a complicated drawing to show what you mean." To be fair, the stick figure did get across what he was trying to show. "Why do you need all these notes? I thought you acted without a plan?" MJ asked curiously.

"Oh, I always have a carefully detailed plan to follow. Can't move away from it even slightly or I could fail miserably."

"Didn't you once defeat a minotaur after it impaled itself on a broken fence?" asked Sterling.

"Totally planned."

"After it tripped on a stray root?"

"Saw that root when I checked out the place before the fight."

"Did you also see the thunder that shocked it into losing its balance?"

"The weather forecast was extremely accurate that day."

"After you started the fight on top of a cliff before falling off?"

"Of course."

"After you started the fight INSIDE a cave on the top of said cliff before breaking out the back of it?"

"Definitely."

"After you started the fight with no sword, completely blind drunk, wearing only a pair of boxers?"

"You've been talking to Stuart."

"Maybe."

"Okay so I don't always have a plan but now we have team up combos and everything which involves," Sharp held up the picture, "planning ahead."

"Maybe we can train together!" said MJ.

"I don't know... I wouldn't want you getting hurt." said Sterling. MJ looked downcast.

"You don't think rallis can fight do you?"

"Oh that is definitely not what we think." said Sharp, running a finger over his cheek where Slick's arrow had grazed him (no mark remained now). "What's your choice of weapon then?" MJ rummaged around in his bag and placed two gloves on the table. Sharp picked them up and, on further inspection, they had five long, metal claws attached. The gloves looked unworn, the metal shiny and clean. "You know what, let's see what you can do. Why don't you lead us to where you train?"

"Yes, sir!" MJ jumped up and out of the room. After a shared look with the rest of the team, they followed him, Quickly scooping up Tolah and Sharp's homework and Sterling supporting a limping Tolah who was refusing to be carried. They followed him quite a way. There was a small wood at the side of the village and in that there was a clearing. This is where MJ led them. There was a target on one of the trees which had uneven circles drawn on it and many arrows stuck into the surrounding trees and the ground. None were in the target itself which seemed a statistical impossibility. There were two of the ugliest dummies Sharp had ever seen in the centre, they were clearly home-made. Misshapen bodies made of sacks stuffed with hay, bits sticking out the side, oddly sized branches added as arms, what looked like broom handles for supports shoved into the ground and crudely drawn on expressions to round off the whole effect. One was cross-eyed and had its tongue sticking out, the other had spiky teeth and an angry look. Neither looked that damaged, small sword and scratch marks covered them. Sharp drew his swords but Sterling pushed him back.

"I'm going to be the one to fight him." she said. Sharp was disappointed as Sterling drew her sword and shield. Sharp doubted she would need either weapon to beat him but she was probably going for a not disrespecting her new friend thing. MJ probably wouldn't have noticed. He put on his claws and decided to take the first shot. He ran forward and took a swipe at Sterling's chest. She blocked it easily with the shield and he stumbled back, swiping around the shield for a chance at her face. Sterling used the flat of her blade under the shield to take his legs out from under him and he fell back, scrabbling to get back to his feet. Sharp was reminded of a beetle tipped on its back.

"This is ridiculous. The kid can't fight, Sterling. We all knew it." He looked around, Tolah and Quickly nodded their quiet assent.

"He deserved a chance."

"Why? Because he says he knows what we're looking for? Or because you felt sorry for him? That's why we ended up with the other two but at least they can defend themselves! I know you want to help everyone you meet but it's neither possible nor advisable! You can't keep focusing on the individuals or the masses will suffer! They feel just the same as the ones you meet personally. Just because you haven't spoken to them all doesn't mean they deserve to be helped any the less and there are so many more of them!" Sharp was tensing up again.

"We're still just baggage to you, huh?" Tolah said. Sharp was jerked out of his line of thought for a moment. That wasn't what he wanted to imply but it had just come out.

"Well... not any more. You definitely carry your own weight and having you guys around is... fine, sometimes it's nice to have someone to talk to... dammit,

I'm bad at this!"

"No kidding." Sterling said dryly.

"MJ though is just going to get himself killed and maybe even take one of us down with him if we're unlucky."

"He's coming with us." Sterling was adamant. MJ had been listening to this, cowering slightly from Sharp's outburst but at Sterling's response, he stood up straight.

"Of course." Sharp turned on his heel and stormed off.

"Why do you think I invited YOU along?" He heard as he left but didn't stop.

This was starting to get a bit repetitive. Just as he thought he was getting used to the group, Sterling did something that pissed him off and he ended up leaving. Again. Part of him thought that this was Sterling's fault. He knew he was being sensible and her attitude was way too soft. But another part of him knew he was acting like a child. Storming off solved nothing. With that in mind, he didn't return to his room but instead took a walk in the chilled air to cool himself down while mentally preparing several speeches to say to the others but kept stumbling when he got to Sterling. She still pitied him and this pissed him off more than anything else. Her holier than thou attitude was a pain in the ass. Well... he always thought he knew better as well, he supposed. Guess they had that in common but it didn't make getting along with her any easier. He felt he had gotten to a good place with Quickly and had started working towards getting along with Tolah, but Sterling was more difficult. Her bipolar attitude confused him, how can you get used to a person who always changed how they acted and the only constant she DID have was her obsession with being nice, something that Sharp was finding really hard to get behind. It wasn't as if he didn't get it. Being happy was something he remembered fondly but it didn't get anything done. He sighed to himself, time to do what he did best first. Looking after himself. His current issue was MJ, but the ralli wasn't going to be going away so he would just have to get the guy to a place he was happy with. With a plan in mind, he went back to the tavern. A peek inside showed the party members he didn't want to strangle sitting around quietly. Sterling was there as well, looking as though she wanted to erupt so he slowly closed the door and returned to the street. Next place to look was the clearing where MJ 'trained'. No sign of the ralli here either. Sharp sighed. Information gathering was the dullest part of the hunter job but it had to be done. The bar was usually a good place to start but the trio was in there so he decided to head to the market. The first few stands yielded no result but the third (selling the sweetest looking confectionery Sharp had ever seen) had a woman who knew him. Her spiky teeth stretched into a smile (grins on a ralli always looked creepy to Sharp).

"Oh yes, he comes here all the time! Such a sweetheart!"

"Know where I might find him?" The stall tender looked at him a bit suspiciously.

"What for?"

"He wants to be a fighter. I'm planning on making him one."

"Oh, he won't get hurt will he?!"

"Not when I'm done with him. I already have one person to look after in a fight, I'm not having another." The stall owner looked a little confused but seemed to accept his answer.

"Well, he does like hanging out with his friends." She gave him the name of a park and the directions.

After a thought, he also asked for MJ's favourite sweets and was handed a bag of pink squares. He had no idea how you could make a sweet square or WHY you would, but there you have it. They tasted way too sweet for him, so he left the rest of the bag untouched. When he got to the park there were a number of groups of people who looked around MJ's age. There was a group of rallis playing a fast-paced game involving a ball, a mixed group of different species with no rallis (probably the entirety of the non-rallis in the village) and a final group of rallis in the corner of the park, away from the others and collected around a makeshift table. One had a helmet made of cardboard and another had a wooden sword. Dice were involved. Sharp sighed and made his way over to this group.

"Excuse me can I-" A hand lifted up to silence him without any of the participants looking up.

"I use shield bash on the ogre to push him into the fire!"

"Roll for it!" The ralli with the helmet declared.

"You aren't the storylord Clyde." said a disgruntled ralli with glasses.

"Sorry." said Clyde.

"Roll for it!" said Glasses. The ralli who had declared shield bash rolled a die with a ridiculous number of sides.

"CRIT!" yelled the players in unison.

"You hit the ogre in the stomach, knocking the wind out of him and thrusting him into the blazing inferno! The ogre is dead!" said Glasses, pushing his specs up his snout.

"Actually shield bashing an ogre is more likely to result in your wrist breaking or possibly forcing your shoulder bone out of its socket. Also, an ogre's skin is naturally resistant to the elements as they live in harsh weather and as such would be more protected against fire." Sharp cut in. The group turned slowly to look at him. As one their mouths dropped open.

"Romas' hide! You're SHARP!" gasped Clyde.

"That's what my mirror tells me. Listen I'm looking for someone."

"Then you have come to the right place! We know EVERYONE."

"Yeah, you look like a really popular guy." Clyde puffed up proudly. Sarcasm was apparently not something he knew. "Listen, I'm looking for a guy called Mac... something or other."

"Mac?"

"Oh I don't know, his name is unpronounceable. I've been calling him MJ. He has the number 27 in there somewhere."

"Oh, you mean Macgillivray! Wow, what do you need with him? Because I totally know this town better than him!" Glasses was suddenly interested.

"Just tell me where he hangs out."

"Ooooo, maybe he's in trouble! Can we watch you beat him up?" said Clyde.

"Are you people actually his friends?"

"Sure are! I mean REAL friends pick clerics to heal their team-mates rather than dps all the time but whatever, we totally have his back!" said Glasses.

"So tell me where he is." Clyde and Glasses looked at each other as if trying to decide how to persuade Sharp to pick them instead for whatever he had planned.

"He likes to go to the lake." said the guy with the sword quietly.

"THANK you." Sharp said. "Er, which direction?" Sword pointed in a direction. Sharp headed towards it as quickly as he could. These people were insane.

"Aw, come on, we could have hung out with a HERO!" he heard as he walked off.

"Come on guys, give Macgillivray a break. He needs one."

MJ was at the lake. He was sitting on a rock just staring at the water and looking miserable.

"Contemplating something?" Sharp asked. The ralli almost jumped out of his skin.

"Oh, hello Sharp!" MJ did his best to look upbeat.

"What's on your mind?"

"Look, I'm sorry if I'm in your way. It's just the idea of travelling with my heroes is my dream! And I really CAN help you!" MJ pulled a roll of paper out of his bag and handed it to Sharp. It was a map. A very detailed map showing the area around their current location. Sharp couldn't be sure if the direction they were heading was accurate on the scroll but he recognised the one they had come from.

"Where did you get this?"

"I made it." Sharp looked at him suspiciously but he didn't seem to be lying. Who could tell with MJ though? "I'm sorry I made Sterling yell at you."

"Fairly sure that was my fault. She does that a lot anyway." Sharp said casually, his attention still on the map. MJ looked cheered up enough. That would do. "Listen, when Sterling decides something, it's going to happen, but I wasn't kidding before. I can't be watching you to make sure you don't die horribly all the time. So I'm going to train you." He handed MJ the sweets to add weight to his offer.

"That's AWESOME! LET'S GO!" The sweets might have been unnecessary and sugar was probably a bad idea in hindsight.

They went back to the clearing. The dummies may have been shoddily put together but you could hit them just fine.

"You er... didn't get on with a bow then?" Sharp eyed up the target. It would be nice to have another long range fighter and it would keep him out of the way.

"Oh, I was just getting the hang of it when I hit my friend Clyde in the, erm, backside. He broke the bow so I decided to use the claws until it was fixed."

"You know what, let's stick with the claws." Clyde probably deserved it though.

It really was as if he had never picked them up before and he wasn't going to be a fast learner. By the time they broke for lunch MJ had learnt how not to stab yourself in the eye with your own claws. Good job too, Sharp was running low on the stash of healing herbs he got from Quickly. MJ was never going to be a powerhouse of damage so he tried to teach him speed, which had the added benefit of making sure he could keep out of the way when he needed to. Sharp didn't foresee him being as big a threat as Slick had been but having a small, quick ally on his side would be handy. This, however, was a long way off. At least MJ seemed to be having a whale of a time. his stamina was something impressive at least, Sharp was more tired than he was by the time they were ready to leave for the day.

The other three were back in the tavern when they returned. They all had angry expressions prepared but these changed to shocked when they saw him enter with MJ.

"Booze. Now." demanded Sharp.

"What kind?" asked the bartender.

"I don't know. Let's just go down the list alphabetically and see what happens." A selection of drinks was laid out in front of Sharp which he happily started on.

"So what have you been doing?" Sterling asked.

"We've been TRAINING! Sharp is teaching me so we can fight together!" As one they turned to look at Sharp.

"I'm teaching him not to die, which he WILL do if he fights the way he currently does." Sharp kept his attention off them and on the alcohol. MJ was happy to supply Sterling with more details than Sharp had given though he was pretty sure MJ would take longer to explain than the training session itself.

"You planning on doing something painful to me?" Sharp asked Tolah under his breath while MJ had Sterling distracted.

"Can't think of anything more painful to happen to you than hanging out with MJ. Look, we know you're a jackass already, we've kind of accepted that. Sterling seems to be the only one holding onto the idea that you're salvageable."

"I kinda thought you liked us." Quickly said. Sharp was torn.

"It's been a while since I had actual friends you know."

"So we ARE your friends."

"Yeah, I suppose."

"You have to stop pissing us off then making it up to us later."

"Agreed." Sharp looked over at MJ. Sterling was starting to look a little worn out. "Sterling always gets her way anyway. I may as well just put up with her decisions and skip the drama afterwards."

"So an old dog CAN learn new tricks." said Tolah.

"Just let it go." Sharp continued drinking, the

bartender happy to feed his habit. He was fairly sure he hadn't drunk as much in the last year combined as he had on this journey.

"You annoyed with me as well?" Sharp asked Quickly. The yeti shook his head.

"Unless you keep peace with others, how can you make peace with yourself?"

"You hear that from a fortune cookie?"

"No. My Dad."

"Well, I got some advice for you. Unless you say what angers you, people are going to keep doing it and nothing gets better. Shutting up and putting up doesn't solve a damn thing." Quickly thought this over but said nothing. Sharp didn't push it, he was starting to feel nicely buzzed and wanted to ride the feeling. Sterling bustled over, taking the drink out of his hand.

"Hey!"

"You have training tomorrow, remember?"

"You can have custody. I'm fine with it." grunted Sharp. Sterling laughed.

"We can share custody. Also, he's a guy, so he's rooming with you. We start first thing after breakfast so don't get a hangover."

"He can sleep at home until we leave town."

"He has no one to go home to! Let him stay with you tonight. Can we get an extra bed in their room?" This second part was directed at the bartender.

"It'll cost you more, but sure." The bartender knew the value of money.

"Excellent!" said Sterling taking the second tankard out of Sharp's hand as he tried to take a swig from the next drink down the line.

"Eventually you are going to have to let me get my way, even if it's just once."

"We'll see." Sterling replied. Sharp always

thought Tolah would be the hardest person to get along with, but Sterling still held that position. MJ might give her a run for her money though.

Sharp didn't get much sleep that night. He had no idea how it was possible for someone so small to snore that loud but MJ kept him awake until the early hours. Quickly slept right the way through, nothing bothered him, really. Sterling seemed to take over training MJ for the next few days which was a relief. Tolah was clearly feeling a bit left out, however. Until MJ had joined, Sterling had been primarily focused on her, not only for the injury but they seemed to be developing a best friends sort of relationship. Sterling's equal treatment wasn't as fair as she thought. Sharp and Quickly took to helping Tolah back on her feet. She still wasn't able to walk for long but it was a start. It was a long way to the next village (according to MJ's map anyway) and although Tolah accepted Quickly's offer of sharing the piggyback duties with Sharp, she would have to do some of the walking herself if they were to get there before the snow set in. Sharp could see the others were also getting rather tired of the constant stops, although the latest one had been for MJ's benefit more than Tolah's. Every day was spent training and every night was spent trying to block out MJ's snoring. Sharp was starting to get tired. On the fifth night, he finally shuffled out of bed, took a roll of tape he had bought the day before for this very moment and wrapped it around the ralli's snout. MJ woke up with a start. Sharp returned to bed and fell asleep before he could hear MJ's response.

Chapter 9

"We should head to the next village." MJ said at breakfast the next day. Sharp noticed he still had a patchy strip of glue round his snout. "I can train on the way, right?" He laid the map Sharp had previously seen on the table. Sterling was as impressed as Sharp had been.

"How are you Tolah? Can you walk?" asked Sterling.

"Well enough. The guys have offered to help as well." Sterling gave them a look of appreciation. It was still early so they stocked up on supplies, MJ disappeared somewhere and reappeared with a backpack the same size as him. Sharp could see a small wooden leg sticking out.

"Ah, MJ you might want to leave some things behind." Sterling said.

"Oh, I'm sure he knows what he's doing. He's done this a LOT, right?" Sharp recognised the boot on the foot of the wooden leg. He had the real version in his safety deposit box in Golden.

"Definitely." MJ took the lead, leaving Sterling to follow. She shrugged and went along with it.

The scenery didn't stay the same for very long. After only a day the forests faded. Sharp was getting tired of MJ kicking the fallen leaves around so it wasn't all bad. Stretching in front of them was a vast wasteland. Sharp had never been this particular way before but he had been out this far on occasion and knew that the wasteland stretched miles in each direction. It housed fewer monsters than the forests for obvious reasons but the ones that it DID have were the sort to survive in pretty much any situation and seeing them charge at you from so far away was not a fun prospect. They camped where they felt like it as the landscape didn't change until they saw a single tree in the distance.

"Oh thank goodness, I was getting sick and tired of the same landscape constantly." said Tolah. As they approached it, it was casting shade over a boulder with a small pool of water. In the summer it may have appeared as an oasis but in the autumn it just looked miserable. Still, a break from nothing was welcome so they set their tents up there.

Sharp woke in the night to a scream. It sounded feminine but was highly unlikely to be Sterling so Sharp rushed outside his tent to save Tolah. Tree branches were wrapped around MJ's legs who was hanging upside down screaming and swiping in front of him, nowhere near the monstrous face in the trunk of the tree that was attempting to eat him. The boulder had sprouted legs and arms and Sterling was sizing it up and strafing around it. With no head on her opponent she was trying to see how it was tracking her movement so she might have a place to strike. Quickly was currently inside the water that had now become a sphere and the yeti was occupied with simply trying to grab air instead of fight. Tolah had appeared from her own tent shortly after Sharp had. Seemed the scream had been MJ's.

"Whaaaa?! What's going on?" Tolah asked.//
"Elementals. I HATE elementals."//
"What do we do?!"//
"You did all that homework. Use that to work it out! I'm going to stick to my intuition." Sharp went for Quickly first. He was in the most danger, water elementals were always a pain. He took out his rope (newly bought after his old one was HACKED APART by someone) and tied a loop in the end. Sharp whipped it around his head like a lasso and attempted to hook it

around Quickly's foot. It was going pretty well until it hit the water but then sank pathetically.

"Okay, this is going to suck." Sharp looped the rope around the tree (MJ screaming at him to help, which he ignored) which attempted to bite through it but failed as the bark inside its mouth wasn't sharp enough to do any damage. Holding both ends of the rope, Sharp took a deep breath and launched himself into the elemental. It had been sitting out in the wastes for a while and bits of gravel, leaves and small rocks hit Sharp in the face as he swam towards Quickly. He looped the hoop over the yeti's foot and pulled the other end of the rope. What was SUPPOSED to happen was Quickly was meant to be pulled out and then he, in turn, could pull Sharp out. What ACTUALLY happened was Sharp gave a massive yank on the rope and found himself instead launching out of the elemental to face plant on the rocky floor. Physics and Sharp were not on good terms. Spitting out a mouthful of dirt, he carried on pulling on the rope resulting in Quickly having the same experience that Sharp had, the yeti gasping for air. The elemental gave a gloop of annoyance but before it could attack the two men again, a bolt of lightning shot from Tolah's direction and shocked it. The elemental's surface spiked and shuddered and finally fell as a waterfall. As it hit the two on the ground a residual amount of electric in the water travelled up their bodies. They fell backward with a splash, their hair standing on end.

"I did it!" Tolah said.

"Good job." wheezed Sharp. Quickly blurped. They wobbled to their feet. Two to go. The three turned their backs on MJ (still screaming, he had impressive lungs) without consulting each other. Sterling was still dodging rock smashes, taking swipes when she could but not denting it.

"Can you make ice under its feet?" Sharp asked Tolah.

"SURE CAN!" Ice shot out under the rock elemental. It slipped but managed to keep its balance, legs wheeling. Sterling stood back to see what they had in mind.

"Quickly?" The yeti nodded and charged it, knocking it on its back.

"Sterling! Take off its legs!" She nodded and they both swung at the creature's cartwheeling legs. The limbs went flying.

"Bet I can get mine further than yours!" Sterling said, winding back for a go at an arm. Sharp grinned and did the same. They both hit the arms at the base and the limbs disappeared over the horizon, spinning as they went. All four squinted after them.

"I honestly don't know who won that one." said Tolah. Quickly kicked the rock elemental and it rolled away slightly, now just looking like a normal boulder again. They turned to look at MJ. He had finally run out of breath and was gasping while weakly swiping at the air still. The tree elemental was unable to bend its branches and so MJ wasn't, in fact, in any danger. Actually Sharp wasn't sure how the tree had managed to pick him up in the first place.

"MJ, cut the branches man." said Sharp. MJ stopped swiping and looked at his claws. At least he had the foresight to grab them before going into battle. He bent up and swiped at the spindly branches wrapped around his legs. They split easily and he plummeted to the ground. Sterling ran forward and caught him easily. The others hadn't bothered moving. He was still for a second.

"That was AWESOME! Did you see that! I totally defeated that tree monster!" The tree roared and swiped harmlessly in his and Sterling's direction with its remaining branches. The others looked at each other.

"Yeah, good job there man." Sharp said absent-mindedly and returned to his tent. The tree's growling was at least quieter than MJ's snoring.

"You know what? I'm fine with monotonous wasteland." He heard from Tolah outside the tent.

The end of the wastelands wasn't far after that. The treeline they saw made them all grateful to see something other than grey featureless ground. As they got nearer, Sharp could make out a building. On closer inspection, it was a mansion and although it was grand it was also clearly long abandoned, cracks appeared in the walls and plants had grown up the sides. MJ had taken out his map and was peering at it carefully. At a look from Sharp, he shook his head and shrugged. Spots of rain had been threatening to increase for the last hour and it was getting dark so the five of them made their way towards it. Plenty of time to explore it before bed though. The entranceway had obviously been grand once but now a thin layer of dust covered almost everything. Looking down, Sharp could see footprints of varying freshness. The most recent were small and were probably made by a number of rallis.

"Whoa, people live in places this big?" Quickly's neck was bent almost completely back in an attempt to take it all in.

"I wonder who owned this one and what happened?" Tolah mused. "Let's take a look around! I bet we could find out!"

"Sure, why not?" Sterling said. "We should try to find a bedroom or somewhere to sleep anyway."

They split up to look around. A lot of rooms had holes in the walls and on the top floor one wall had been caved in by an enormous tree that had obviously toppled a long time ago. Any documents that had been in there had been destroyed. Sharp found nothing of interest in any of the other rooms he looked at (all expensively decorated once upon a time). The only bedroom he could see at a glance held only a single bed, half eaten by woodworm, unsuitable for the party. He deliberately avoided any that looked as though they might contain something interesting (to Tolah anyway) so that the others could have the pleasure of discovering it themselves. He didn't personally hold much interest in this place. The kitchen, unfortunately, had nothing of note in it, although it had been long since abandoned so any food left there had probably grown a pair of legs and walked off itself a while ago. By now the rain had really picked up and it battered against the large bay windows. Sharp always found the rain outside to be satisfying. It made one feel warmer and happier simply by being inside, especially if he could see other people outside getting drenched. He wandered back to the lobby and saw a large pair of doors in the shadow of the stairs. They were hard to see in the encroaching darkness so he grabbed a nearby candle, lit it and shouldered his way into the room. It was the largest room Sharp had seen in the mansion by far. Had he not been in the King's throne room previously he would have said it was the largest room he had ever seen. The ceiling stretched above him, painted with murals of angels and rare creatures the world had a habit of romanticising. Fairies danced together in shining swirls of silver. The hunter in Sharp told him most fairies were actually gruesome in looks and nature. The artist, however, seemed to have different ideas from the way they were portrayed. The walls originally had expensive looking wallpaper, now old and peeling and there were pillars, finely carved, matching the decoration on the various tables around the outside of the room and the chairs that littered the middle. The main feature in here though was the most glorious grand piano Sharp had ever seen in his life, slightly elevated on a stage. He walked slowly up to it. The chairs in the room had been pushed backward to leave a large clear circle but had once been set up in neat lines. This must have been an amazing venue for performances at one time and to see it so dilapidated was a sobering sight. Sharp ran his hand over the back of the piano. It was made of what looked like fine mahogany and as Sharp's hand wiped away a line of dust, the surface underneath seemed undamaged. Sharp could see his face in it. The candle left creeping shadows dancing up the walls as he placed it carefully on the piano. As he looked around he could see the dust on the seat was almost gone, the same could be said of the dust directly around the piano itself. Sharp looked at the circle the chairs were surrounding, he could see the centre had almost no dirt in it at all. At a guess, he would say a passer-by had hosted a dance recently.

"Wow. This room is amazing!" A glow of candlelight revealed that Sterling had seen the door Sharp had left open and had come to check it out. The other three appeared behind her and spread out, muttering admiration for the contents of the room also. Sharp was still focused on the piano. He raised the lid of the keyboard and the keys themselves were perfect. Protected by the lid, they were unmarked and as shiny as the main body of the instrument. He ran his fingers over the cool ivory.

"Why don't you play us something?" asked Mary.

"What?" Sharp was jerked out of his reverie.

"I said, why don't you play us something?" repeated Sterling. Of course it hadn't been her voice.

Sharp paused for a moment then tentatively played a scale. It was in tune. The scale turned into a simple melody so easily. It came back to him as if he had played it yesterday. Before he knew it, he had sat down, the tune evolved and suddenly he found himself playing a memory. Light danced on the piano, the smell of cut grass floated through the open window. The tune was light-hearted, simple and sweet. He closed his eyes and found the song working its way up his throat and out of his mouth and suddenly he was singing. He could sense her just out of eyesight, she was listening as she always did. He could almost feel her hand on his shoulder, smell the spring air mixing with the scent of the blueberry pie that was floating through the air. There was a nagging thought at the corner of his mind trying to warn him about something approaching but he pushed it down and focused on the song. He knew it by heart and he let himself get lost in it, a feeling of bliss rising in him. He smiled for what seemed like the first time in forever. Why had he ever stopped playing?

The average song isn't long and this one wasn't an exception. A few minutes to forget who he was, where he was. As he played the last note, reality came crashing back down and the nagging thought became a roar in his mind. The light faded and the oppressive darkness wrapped itself back round him like it had before he placed his fingers on the keys and the smell became the mustiness of an old, damp room covered in dust. The ache in his chest was back but intensified from the sudden return to a memory he had been gradually moving away from over the years. The smile faded.

"That was incredible! You can play AND sing! Who taught you?" Sterling's voice yanked him back into the room.

"My wife."

"You're married?!"

"No."

Sterling fell silent, the only sound being the rain beating itself against the window, the sound now made him feel cold and lost.

"What can I... What do you...?" Sterling tried and faltered.

"What do I ALWAYS want?" he said to the piano keys. Quickly started to walk forward but Sterling took him gently by the wrist.

"To be left alone." Sterling said quietly. She pulled a hesitant but unresisting Quickly out of the room, the yeti trying and failing to find words. The other two were at a loss and simply followed the others out of the room. Finally Sharp had found a way to shut them up. Shame it required an assault on his heart to achieve. He carefully replaced the lid and lent on it, letting his mind wander to whatever empty void it could find.

It was only when the candle snuffed out that he realised how much time had gone past and suddenly was filled with the urge to leave this room and never return. He felt his way using the piano and the chairs that littered the floor before groping forwards to find the door out of the piano room. The giant window in the lobby afforded him no light as the clouds blocked out any moon there might have been. A sudden bolt of lightning lit up the room and he was able to memorise the way to an old candle on the wall which he lit. He used the small light to return to the bedroom he had previously seen and with no concern over the half-eaten wood, rolled onto the old sheets and with a cloud of dust, fell into an unsettled night of scattered dreams that he was unable to recall the following morning.

Chapter 10

"FOUND HIM!" Quickly's suddenly roaring voice woke him. Sharp's eyes sprang open at the sudden noise, sounding as if it was right next to his ear. He sneezed at the dust he had probably inhaled some time during the night, the bed dishevelled as he had tossed and turned.

"Good nose man!" shouted Sterling's voice in reply. Sharp groaned. It was going to be a fun day, he could tell. Quickly looked at him with concern before gripping him by the back of the shirt and gently lifted him into a sitting position.

"You can tell where I am by smell? Perhaps I need a shower." Sharp sniffed tentatively at an armpit and winced. "Sorry about that."

"You smell like sword oil."

"I suppose Sterling smells like unbridled optimism." Sharp yawned and got to his feet.

"Sterling smells like strawberries."

"Oh right, that stupid soap." They had reached the top of the stairs and looked down at a distraught looking Sterling, a wary looking Tolah and a curious looking MJ (he had probably already written the revelation of last night down in his journal).

"Quit looking as if you found out I'm dying. Let's just get something to eat and leave this place in the dust." Sterling nodded, looking more upbeat (but tired. She had better not have lost sleep over HIS problems). Despite what Sharp said, the breakfast was still silent and awkward and it didn't help that the food itself was on the pathetic side. They had been in the wastes for long enough that all they had left was the dried stuff they only ate when nothing else was available.

They left as soon as they were able. The rain had stopped and everything had a fresh feel to it. They spent the first day getting as much distance from the mansion as they could by unspoken agreement (Tolah allowed Quickly to carry her for the time being) but after that, they spent time replenishing their dwindling stocks by hunting and foraging. According to MJ's map (he had carefully drawn the mansion on it. It seamlessly matched the rest of the map, revealing that he had at least drawn the thing. This, at least, was not a lie Sharp supposed) it was another week before the next town and they all decided another day on basic supplies was a day too many. The forest spanned almost the whole journey to the next village and as they were in wilder lands now, the monsters became wilder to match and also more numerous, allowing the group ample time to practice their teamwork. Tolah was able to take part finally (they still had to take rests more often than they would have liked but she seemed determined not to slow down the party) and so managed to win back some of the attention from Sterling she clearly craved. Sharp managed to swallow some of his annoyance to take the lead in MJ's training some days to give her a chance for some 'girl time'. He may have had to cope with MJ practically drooling over his feet but he got Sterling out of his way for a while as well as helping out Tolah (she was always going to be able to feel that injury even if it didn't hold her back too badly).

MJ was still getting on Sharp's nerves. He was the only one to attempt to talk to him about his wife, a mistake he did not repeat (to his credit Sharp didn't leave a permanent mark). He was learning slowly and seemed unhappy to work with either Tolah or Quickly in battle, making their fights disjointed. He always needed to be watched due to his inexperience and the fact that his fighting style meant that he always had to be close to his opponent. He at least had enough fear to get out of the way when he was going to get hit by something and seemed to have the innate speed rallis tended to lean towards which Sharp tried to encourage when he could. None of the other party members had particularly high agility except Sharp himself but he tended to try to attack fast before the enemy could respond whereas MJ seemed more adept at a hit and run approach. At least his backpack had become smaller as they had gone along, the weight had clearly been doing a number on him. Sharp imagined a line of knick-knacks, action figures and dice leaving a trail behind them.

Settling down for the night wasn't as relaxing as Sharp would have liked either as Tolah still wanted to talk about whatever had her interested at the time, but now she had to compete with MJ. He had been mostly quiet during the walk over the wastes, the empty feel of the place tended to do a number on the hardiest of travellers and MJ certainly didn't seem that (although he confessed to having made the walk several times before). MJ's topic of conversation tended to lean towards his depressing life. Apparently, he had at one point had a commonly large family. He had had two sets of grandparents, a set of parents and twenty-eight siblings, not to even mention the whole slew of aunts and uncles, nieces and nephews who presumably weren't all deceased (he didn't dwell too long on these). Rallis were born in litters of around two to six children (although more was certainly possible) and more than one litter could be born in a year. The main topic of the mansion forest chapter of their journey was his parents.

"Did you know there is a type of rock that has pure white speckles that glow only during a new moon? It attracts the green-maned griffin of the Thundercrash

Hills who will often bump into another of its kind there and either fight to the death or mate depending on the gender!"

"Please don't mention griffins... My parents were killed by a griffin." MJ muttered. Sterling gave a slightly accusatory look as if Tolah was supposed to have already known this.

"Oh, I'm sorry. I had no idea."

"They were on their way to attend a friend's wedding the next town over." Apparently, it wasn't too painful a subject that MJ wasn't willing to talk about it in great detail. "They never made it. The griffin was attracted by the food they had brought as a gift (my father was a fantastic chef) and attacked them mercilessly." MJ stood up and made his fingers like claws to add emphasis to his words. "They found them the next day. My father had been trying to protect my mother but she had obviously refused to leave him and they both fell to its relentless attacks." He sank back onto the log he was using as a seat, head in his hands. Sharp was impressed 'they' had been able to tell exactly what had happened when 'they' investigated the scene (he had no idea who 'they' were. He both sensed it wasn't the right time to ask and also he didn't really care) although there were people who were really good at working these things out. He knew a man who could walk into a crime scene and in an hour could tell you the perpetrator after simply examining where things had fallen, things that had been touched, things that had been taken and the relationships the victim had. It was all a bit modern for Sharp who liked the criminal to be covered in the victim's blood or holding the thing that had been stolen in their hand at the time. That was how monsters acted and how he tracked them down. People were too complicated for him. Plus he didn't have much faith in any kind of official law enforcement.

"That sounds terrible!" said Sterling. Sharp was impressed with her capacity for sympathy since the group was really pushing that to its limit. He wondered how so many people with issues had managed to drift together like this. Personally, he found it hard to accommodate any problems other than his own. MJ said nothing further but simply stared miserably at his feet. The group fell into silence and Sterling looked desperate to break it. The seal was back, turning in her hands.

"Actually the phos rock glows all the time, not just in the new moon, it's just easier to see in the dark. The phosphor in the rock is what makes it glow and that reacts to the air." Sharp said casually. As one they all turned to look at him. "What? It was in Tolah's exotic rock book."

"Whaa really? I haven't read that part!" Tolah whipped the book out from wherever she had managed to hide it away and started flicking through the pages. Sterling gave him an amused look. MJ looked as if he didn't know what to say, his back-story stopped for now. Even rocks had their uses Sharp supposed.

The town of Bullshorn was their next stop and was a gloomier place than they were used to. The area around the place itself was surrounded by farmland but this late in the year it was mostly empty. A few late year crops still maintained a desperate grip on life and the few farm animals brave enough to venture outside grazed on patchy grass. The odd farmhand gave them suspicious looks as they passed, Quickly was a bit too beast-like for this area and even regular villagers were tough enough to take on monsters, so he would have to watch himself. It was purely a necessity to be tough around here as if you weren't, you were dead, due to the increase of monsters, especially this close to the forest. Sharp rarely bothered coming out this far for that one reason. The creatures may have been tougher but the bounties were exceedingly rare due to the townspeople taking care of business themselves. Any job they COULDN'T handle was generally too dangerous for how much they were willing and able to pay. The current mission they were on was starting to grate on his mind slightly. Before now he could ignore it but now they were past the halfway point he found his mind wandering back to the conclusion more and more. He still would have taken it on solo had he been given it but there was something reassuring about having four other people to rely on. Well, three people. Hopefully, MJ wouldn't need babysitting when they got to their goal, although he could always be conveniently pushed in front of something injury inducing before the end. Not enough to finish him off (wouldn't want Sterling out of sorts in the main event) but enough to take him out of commission.

    There was only one tavern in town and it was small. The majority of it was made up of the bar area and also a separate eating section. Apparently, this was the main source of income for the owner rather than the inn. Bullshorn didn't see many visitors it seemed. As the team walked in the front door all heads turned to watch them with suspicion.

    "Er two rooms, five people?" Sterling asked.

    "We only got one room. Twenty gold." said the bartender.

    "What? That's extortionate!"

    "Feel free to sleep outside. That guy looks as if he's already used to it." He pointed at Quickly to the laughs of the various patrons. Sterling looked taken aback. It seemed hunters weren't respected in this town.

Sharp doubted they even knew (or cared) who he and Sterling were.

"We'll take it." Sharp said laying the money down. As soon as Sterling stopped being stunned she would probably tell the bartender off and he had the only room in town. Sharp didn't want to sleep outside unless he had to. He took the key so they could check out the room. Well, there were three beds at least. No doubles but he was damned if he was sharing with anyone anyway. Better to take the floor. They made no conversation over their meal and they felt as if every eye was on them and every ear as well. The towns were probably all going to be like this going forward, perhaps just a restock and move on from now on. Sterling certainly didn't like the oppressive atmosphere and it was surprising how much her bad mood brought the rest of the group down. She always seemed to have such a high opinion of everyone that to see people who didn't smile when they saw her was a bit of a blow. At least she had the rest of the group. Had she come all this way on her own it might have been a bit depressing for her. Well, whatever, it wouldn't have been Sharp's problem in that case.

He did end up on the floor. Quickly wouldn't have fitted in a bed anyway so he was the other floor user. They were the last two to fall asleep, they could still feel the hard floor through the clothes they had laid on top of it. They didn't speak but just knowing someone else was as uncomfortable made Sharp feel better (although Quickly did have a layer of fur as well). He might like his companions more than he used to, but he was still Sharp.

He dreamt he was sleeping face first in a cloud and woke up to find Quickly's arm on his face. He pushed it away and spat out a mouthful of yeti hair. The others woke up shortly after, looking more well-rested than Sharp and Quickly but still uneasy. There was something about Bullshorn that made you think you were being watched all the time. Breakfast was the same as dinner had been and Sharp was looking forward to escaping the oppressive atmosphere. However, the tenseness was disrupted by one of the other patrons. He wandered up to the table, his target Tolah.

"What're you meant to be then? One've those magic people, right?" He took a swig from his tankard.

"Er, yes." replied Tolah.

"Well we got one o' you people come through a couple months ago. Throwin' 'is weight around 'e was and ended up burnin' down 'alf the town an' killin' a bunch o' people in the process." So it was Tolah they were looking at.

"Maybe you should tone the drinking down at eight in the morning. Also, why are you the only one in this town who has an accent?" said Sharp.

"Oh, Bruce always talks like that when he's been drinking and he drinks at eight am because a crazy, arrogant, green-skinned, fire flinging jackass killed his brother." said the bartender, not taking his eyes off Tolah, who was sinking in her chair.

"You can't talk to us like that! Do you know who these people are?!" MJ jumped on his seat.

"Never seen 'em 'fore in m' life." MJ looked a bit taken aback.

"No need of hunters really, this far out, MJ." Sharp said.

"Well, we just have to BEAT the knowledge into them!"

"We aren't beating up anyone." Sterling cut in. Sharp realised it had been a while since he'd heard her speak. She stood up and looked at Bruce. After a thought, she changed her mind and addressed the bartender. "Is there anything we can do to help?" Sharp sighed. Why had he expected any different?

An hour later, Sharp was attempting to thatch a roof. No wonder the whole place went up in flames. The whole row of houses currently had one of their team members on their respective roofs except Tolah, who had been banned from being anywhere near anything flammable. Sharp had a supervisor with him, someone who actually knew what he was doing. Sharp was doing most of the grunt work.

"Mind if I ask you some questions?"

"As long as you can work at the same time."

"Of course. This magic user who did all this." Sharp gestured to the surrounding area, a corner of the village of several houses with various stages of fire damage. "Why did he do it?"

"Who can tell? Crazy people those fletchins, big-headed all of them. He came through saying some crap about working for a chosen one. Must be some fletchin with a crazy amount of power to impress another into being his lackey. Maybe someone here insulted his messiah and he flipped."

"Doesn't mean the fletchin with us will do the same."

"Only ever seen two fletchins and the first one destroyed the livelihoods of many people I happen to care about. Ain't going to make the same mistake twice."

"Do you remember the name?" Perhaps someone on the rest of the journey had seen the man. Sharp didn't care about this man's agenda, but sounded like someone to avoid. Magic was too unpredictable for him to want to mess with.

"No. Just get on with your work." And Sharp

couldn't get anything else out of him.

Next job was stocking up on firewood. Apparently a couple of the people who had been killed would have done the job and they needed someone to fill in. Sounded a bit far reaching but Sterling seemed up for just about anything they were willing to throw at them. Sharp was going to have to talk to her about this later. Tolah wasn't with them on this one either. He saw her earlier so he knew they hadn't done anything to her but she had looked completely miserable. He would have to address that one later also. When had his life become about sorting out his friends' personal issues? He probably would have had to have had friends first but still, this was getting a bit out of hand. Sharp could handle this job a lot better than the last due to brute strength being involved and it felt cathartic to have a weapon in his hands. They still had a supervisor on this job though. Supervising was all he was doing as well and Sharp wasn't even sure why he was there. Couldn't have been to keep an eye on them seeing as they volunteered to do all this (or at least Sterling had). During a break, Sharp sidled over to him and asked him the same questions he asked the thatcher. He seemed to have the same level of knowledge except Sharp did get a name out of him. Arborious Augury. Sharp didn't think he'd heard a more pretentious name but perhaps all the fletchins had similar ones, how would he know? More tasks followed the lumberjacking, Sharp was seeing less and less relevance to the whole repairing the damage thing in each job, the various supervisors seemed to be enjoying themselves more and more. The worst was the mayor who was the one assigning the various tasks to them. He did have a pretty nice hat though. Fedora, but ruined with a kind of stupid poofy feather in it. He finally let them break for the day when it was clear they were ready to drop and they were faced with an overpriced meal and another night in the overpriced room without any space. At least this time he was so tired he dropped straight off to sleep although it did mean he had no chance to talk to either of the people he wanted to talk to. He didn't even argue about the bed assignments and no one else seemed to have the energy to either.

The next day he felt as if he'd been run over by a cart. All of his limbs told him to stay in bed er, floor. The mayor, however, had other ideas. A repeated banging on the door roused them all and they struggled downstairs, struggled their way through breakfast and struggled out of the door to the mayor and his stupid hat's new list of jobs. None of the tasks had any semblance of being anything remotely related to the fire damage today, and none of the villagers were trying to hide their amusement. Sharp made it until lunchtime. The next job he was given was repainting a house. A completely fine house that was nowhere near the fire damaged part of the town. The brush was in his hand, the grinning supervisor in front of him. Honestly, what was he meant to do with that set up? He probably could have stopped at dumping the paint tin on the man's head but he decided to just go with the flow. To be fair the wall DID end up painted, he just didn't use the brush.

Sterling found him back in the room. He was enjoying the feel of a mattress for the first time in what felt like a lifetime and was in that moment between dozing and sleeping.

"SHARP!!"

"Mph."

"Get back to work Sharp. You also have some apologies to make!"

"Doing manual labour for no reason isn't my idea

of a good time."

"Of course there's a reason! We're helping a town get itself back together after a horrible attack!"

"We shouldn't even be helping in the first place. This isn't our concern. It was somebody else who did the damage. I'm not even sure how much we're sorting the problem anymore either. They're clearly making fun of us."

"They are not making fun of us! They needed help and that's what we're doing for them in whatever capacity they need!"

"It is not our PROBLEM Sterling! I know you want to help everyone but sometimes you just can't! And people past the wastes are going to screw you over because they have to do that sort of stuff just to survive out here! People don't know who you are and they won't treat you special. You are going to have to make a CHOICE!"

"And I choose to help them! You can do whatever you want but I am staying here!" Sharp pondered over his options. Sterling was breathing deeply and fuming, it had been a while since she had gotten like this with him. He stood up and carefully took her by the wrist. She didn't seem happy but his calmness seemed to have her put off balance. He pulled her out of the inn (stares but no one stopped them) and went in the direction he had seen Tolah go that morning. As usual she was given a different task to the others. He was hoping he would guess where she had gone if he walked far enough and luckily he didn't have to walk long. A farmhouse lay right on the edge of the village and attached to it, a large barn. He took his chances and went inside, climbing the stairs along the outside leading to the platform overlooking the ground floor (the upper floor was for storage apparently). Sterling was still saying nothing and not resisting. Clearly, she was curious as to where this was all going. They reached the top and Sharp looked down. Bingo. Tolah was there, knee deep in whatever filth the animals in there had left (and there was a lot with the animals staying inside in this weather) with a shovel clutched in both shaking hands and sobbing. She too had a supervisor who was leaning against the wall with a stupid grin on his stupid fat face, obviously not lifting a finger. Sterling seemed momentarily paralysed, her own hands shaking slightly as she gripped the wooden guardrail.

"Remember to look after your own before looking after everyone else."

Sterling didn't turn to look at him but her face changed to show resolve. She looked angrier than he had ever seen her (even at him) and her hands stopped shaking. As she made her way down the stairs to the people below, Sharp rummaged round in his pocket and found an apple. Leaning on the rail Sterling had vacated he took a bite and settled in for the show. It was glorious. He had never heard her swear before but here he learnt words he hadn't even heard before. The whole encounter ending in the supervisor being covered in, well, it wasn't paint. As the man spluttered and pushed his way out of the barn in an attempt for some fresh air, Tolah had been watching the whole thing with her mouth wide open. Sterling turned to face her, tears in her eyes spluttering apologies. Tolah smiled and as she went to hug her, Sharp left. Fun part was over.

He took in the view of the town from the elevated height at the top of the stairs. It was a miserable sort of place and Sharp had no idea why anyone would want to live this far out. It can't have been an attempt at being unsociable since the hard life they had out here insisted on working together. Those that didn't, didn't live long.

The fire damaged part of the town could just be seen from his viewpoint, Augury had really let rip. Sterling may have gone about it in the wrong way but she really had been trying to help people in need. He shook his head. This wasn't like him. He waited until Sterling and Tolah emerged from the barn and went to join them as they returned to the town centre.

"Thank you." said Tolah almost inaudibly to him then strode ahead to walk beside Sterling without looking to see if he had heard.

Quickly and MJ were waiting for them with the mayor who seemed to be angrily quizzing them as to where their companions were. Quickly looked unconcerned but MJ was looking a bit nervous, hiding behind the larger man. They all looked relieved at the arrival of the other three.

"So there you are! What is your excuse for the mistreatment of these men?" The mayor gestured to Sharp's supervisor who was literally red-faced still and Tolah's, who everyone was attempting to stand downwind from.

"And what is yours for the mistreatment of mine?" Sterling retorted.

"You offered to help!"

"And you abused that offer. You worked us almost to unconsciousness, charged us a fortune for subpar bed and board and you humiliated one of my friends! How DARE you!"

"Your 'friend' is an unstable ball of destruction who belongs to a group of people who hate everything that doesn't look like them."

"You can't paint everyone with the same brush!" Sterling bristled at the racism.

"Stereotypes are there for a reason." The mayor looked suspiciously at Quickly and Tolah. The both of them were silent for a moment, staring each other down.

"Ask for payment for our work and a refund on the room." whispered Sharp.

"We're leaving. Now." Sterling said, ignoring him.

"What?! But we did all that work! And the room was terrible! And the food was awful! I prefer MJ's cooking and I swear he moults in the damn pot!" MJ looked shifty.

"I just want to be gone." Sterling said.

"FINE." Even when Sharp got his own way apparently Sterling ended up getting it partly her way as well. Sharp narrowed his eyes then whipped the mayor's hat off his head. "But I'm taking your hat." The mayor opened his mouth to say something but then changed his mind at Sharp's expression.

They didn't walk far as they were all tired but they made sure the town was out of view and found a hill to shelter them from the wind. They silently set up their tents then all fell asleep, Sharp's mind briefly brushing his own single-minded views on the fletchins aside.

Chapter 11

When Sharp woke up it was dark, his early night and his empty stomach compelling him to consciousness. No one else was up so he found one of Quickly's oils that burnt and lit a fire, throwing what he fancied foodwise into a pot. As the food was almost done he heard Sterling get up and join him. He split the meal without a word from either of them.

"Thanks." Sterling said finally. Sharp knew she wasn't talking about the stew.

"It's fine. I still think we should have got some cash out of it though." He picked up the hat he had left outside the afternoon before. A few more moments of silence.

"Do you think I should stop helping so many people?" Sterling suddenly asked. "You know, stop being so soft on everyone?"

"I think you should dial it back a bit. Wouldn't say stop completely."

"Why not? I really screwed up in Bullshorn and you wouldn't have stayed for even a day more than we needed had you been in charge."

"I just do what I want. That's no different from you doing what you do. If it makes you happy then go ahead, just make sure you aren't screwing your team over."

"Thought you'd take the opportunity to make me change my charitable ways."

"And turn you into a bastard like me? No thanks, we don't need two of me. Besides, I hate people telling me what to do, I'm not going to do it to you."

"Thank you. I know you were annoyed when I invited the others to join."

"Still am." said Sharp, examining the feather in the hat, it was glued in pretty well.

"Well, be honest, one of us would probably have killed the other had we not had them along."

"I suppose you're right. Way too many witnesses now." Sharp took a grip of the feather and ripped it out of the hat. He examined it and, happy with the result, placed it at a jaunty angle on his head. Sterling gave him a suspicious look before shaking her head and smiling to herself. A noise behind them indicated the other three had decided to join them so Sharp added more to the stew and they were all happy to eat whatever he had improvised, his food was always at least half decent, a hunter had to learn how to survive on what he or she could get his or her hands on.

"So erm, that didn't seem very heroic." MJ said looking into his stew after they had settled.

"What? Helping people?" asked Sterling.

"Well, I thought we'd be all like defeating evil and stuff."

"That's the majority of it and I suppose that's also all you're going to hear about." Sterling said.

"It's all *I* do." said Sharp. MJ turned to stare wide-eyed at him. Great, now the focus was back on him. Time for some damage control. "Look. Sometimes helping people is killing the thing that's trying to kill THEM but for most people, that's never going to be a problem. Sometimes just giving a meal to help someone live through the winter is what they need, or helping to bring in the crops." Sterling gave a surprised but grateful look. Sharp was hoping he wasn't going to have to start pretending to be a decent person as well as the current trying to get along with his friends challenge.

"I'm not sorry I decided to try to help but I am sorry I couldn't see what was going on and what it was doing to you all."

"You don't have to be perfect all the time. Especially not in this part of the world." Tolah said.

"Okay, here's a question for you Sterling. Everyone says both of us are at the top of the hunter list but my screw-ups are still pretty well known. Never heard one of yours though. Tell us a story of how you failed." Sharp enquired. The rest of the group leaned in to hear her answer.

"Oh, er, are you sure?"

"Sure. You know how terrible WE are. Give us a chance to judge you for once."

"Well, I have bad things about me as well. Doesn't mean I want you guys to know about them."

"We aren't going to think less of you if you have a fault." Quickly said.

"Yeah, if we ditched people for their horrible, horrible faults we'd have left Sharp long ago." said Tolah. Sharp gave no reaction.

"Well... I guess just one." Sterling said. The four leaned back in again. "I've only gone past the wastes twice before now. Got a job back in Silver. An old couple wanted me to track down their granddaughter. Apparently, her parents had vanished over the wastes when she was young and she had gone to track them down now she was older, still only a teenager though. The pay wasn't much but, well you know what I'm like so I took the job. The wastes were pretty uneventful. I weaved around in the hope of picking up some kind of trail but I was grasping at straws. A gust of air and a footprint is gone. Other than dust the only thing I found was a pack of overlarge wolves, easily defeated. The forest was easier to deal with, it didn't take me more than two hours to find broken branches, a tear from her jacket, you know the sort of thing." Sharp nodded.

"When I found her she was with a manticore. She had managed to crawl into a cave small enough for her but not for the creature that was trying to bite her through the entrance. It was tougher than the usual manticore, they seem to be hardier this side of the wastes, but I was able to dispatch it without too much trouble."

"Oooo how did you do it?" MJ cut in, breaking Sterling's flow.

"Oh, I broke a wing over a rock then stabbed it in the heart."

"Awesome."

"Anyway. She was miraculously unharmed. Not a scratch actually, which was impressive for the journey she had taken. She was frightened and agreed to return with me to Silver, the chances of her finding her parents alive was practically nil and it took almost dying herself to see that. More of those damn wolves on the way back but we got to Silver without too much trouble. Her grandparents were overjoyed to see her of course. Paid me more than they had promised actually. I don't think they were expecting me to bring her back alive. Of course, I tried to refuse the extra."

"Of course." muttered Sharp.

"But they insisted. That night I was woken by a terrible screeching. It was coming from the direction of the old couple's house. There was screaming and a mixture of scared villagers running from the scene and guards running towards it. There were a number of bodies and in the middle of it was a changeling, dripping in blood and snarling. It still showed features of the girl I had 'saved' only now they were twisted into a grotesque visage. The guards and I managed to take it down together, for a creature so small it sure could fight. Of course, the people who had given me the quest were dead. No one else knew why the changeling had come into town but when I went to the captain of the guard and explained, he decided to hush the whole thing up. I was... insistent on being punished but he was right. Having someone to blame wouldn't have made anything better. Changelings did wander into towns, however rarely, so owning up to what I had done wouldn't have set any minds at rest, plus the current captain had by this point made me kind of a champion of the town. My fall would have only created more panic. He did, however, give me a great deal of community service under the guise of me just helping the local populace under my own steam. Before that though I took my only other trip across the wastes. Starting my search from where I had encountered the fairy made short work of the investigation. I found the girl's body just a few metres away, incompetently hidden in a ditch, badly mutilated from the changeling's attacks. I took her body back with me and buried her next to her grandparents. After that, I had no inclination to pass the wastes again, not that there are many calls to do so. This mission is a different case seeing as so many lives are on the line and... I'm not alone this time." Her story finished she looked around nervously at her friends.

"That's why you invited me along." said Sharp.

"Well, that was part of it. I could have invited any of the other hunters rather than you, but you seemed so crestfallen that the mission had gone to me and I wasn't lying when I said what I did. I really did think you should have been the one to be picked."

"It wasn't your fault." said Tolah.

"A lot of people died because I didn't notice I had a monster with me. It took a week to cross the wastes and I didn't notice that whole time! They aren't self-aware, they just imitate looks and actions they've seen the victim perform. She didn't say much but that should have tipped me off."

"How were you supposed to know she wasn't just a quiet person? Or that she wasn't in shock? Quickly is quiet too but it doesn't mean he's a monster!" Tolah said. Quickly said nothing but carried on eating.

"Changelings are tricky though. They have to get their act to perfection or they die." Sharp interjected.

"You ever meet one?" asked Sterling.

"Once that I know of, I suppose I could have been fooled and never found out but they usually kill their dupe by the time they reach their goal, usually a large group of people. They often break character to murder everyone in their sleep. Your fairy, I think, overestimated its chances. The one I met waited until we reached a small group of traders. Of course, I was more than happy to ditch this random tag-along I'd acquired so I convinced them to take him. I stayed with them that night as they offered me a meal but woke to claws trying to take my eyes out." Sharp indicated a number of small scars you could barely make out on one side of his face. "I reacted by stabbing it in the stomach. No one else had died seeing as it went for me first, I was the biggest threat, I suppose. I was only with him for a day but I didn't suspect anything. Why would I? Changelings are rare."

"My brother was killed by a changeling." MJ chipped in.

"Are you sure you don't black out and bodies just happen to appear next to you?" Sharp asked. Sterling hit him on the back of the head, making his hat fall off.

"Don't be insensitive!" Sterling said. Sharp put his hat back on in a defiant way as if that was some sort of reply.

"It happened on a summer morning when my

brother and I were-"

"SO MJ CAN I LOOK AT THE MAP FOR TOMORROW?" Sharp said loudly, cutting MJ off. Sterling looked a tad annoyed but let it pass. MJ had been giving a lot of relative demise tales lately and it was probably grinding on her nerves as well. He was momentarily jarred but it was a request from Sharp so he immediately rummaged round in his bag and drew out the map, presenting it proudly in a flourish.

"Thanks." Sharp took it. "Wait, is this the same map as before?"

"No. That one only went up to Bullshorn remember?"

"Oh yeah. So how many of these do you have?" He couldn't help but notice the area they had walked through already was more detailed than the area they were going to.

"Oh, I have loads!" MJ opened his bag. Inside were about ten maps. Sharp pulled them all out and examined them, each one showed the area they were heading through except one which seemed like no land he had ever seen before. It seemed to be one large island named 'Awesomeland', with towns marked with names such as Clydesville and Blastzone. It looked real other than the names. "Ah! Give me that!" MJ snatched it back. "Oh I mean, sorry, I erm, this one isn't real. I just made it... for fun."

"That was for your game right? Your friends were playing it in the park."

"What?! They were playing without me?! They can't beat any encounters without the warrior! The rest of the party is way too squishy!"

"They had a shield user."

"WHAT?! Did someone re-roll a warrior?! They had better not be using my character! They're going to use all my stuff!"

"Er, maybe?" Sharp spoke six different languages but he had no idea what MJ was saying. He went back to the real maps. They covered all the way up to Stillhaven if he laid them side by side. "This is really nice work." he said.

"YOU REALLY THINK SO?!" MJ had stopped mid outrage to respond to the only compliment Sharp had ever given him.

"Well yeah. I guess I thought you were lying about the whole leaving town thing but you couldn't have made this if you hadn't. You may fight like a drunk jackrabbit with three legs but you really know your stuff as a cartographer." The others crowded around the maps and murmured their impressed agreement. MJ was so puffed up he couldn't speak. At least that had shut him up for the time being. Could be he caused more trouble down the line but future Sharp could take care of it himself. Present Sharp was just glad of the silence.

Past Sharp was an idiot. The next few days passed with no towns at all and MJ didn't shut up for a moment. Even in random scraps they had he kept proclaiming how awesome each move he did was. Sharp realised that they had seen no other people on the (for want of a better word) roads in a long time, monsters roaming where they liked. MJ was good at guiding them no matter the terrain and at one point saved them a few days' travel by avoiding a large chasm that had split the earth from some natural disaster or another. He did, however, lead them through a field marked on the map with crosses.

"What are these?" asked Tolah.

"Oh, er... I forget. It's been a long time since I walked through here."

"Let's go around." said Sharp.

"We save a couple of days going straight through. If MJ can't remember what it was then it probably isn't so bad." Sterling said.

"Your funeral. Ours as well assuming one of us is left alive to bury us." Sterling didn't reply but instead just led the way. The first hour was uneventful but then...

"I hear something." said Quickly. The others all stopped, craning their ears to try to match his better hearing. Sharp heard it faintly after a time. It was a soft but consistent moaning, coming from somewhere below their feet.

"Amazing." said Sharp. The first hand to emerge appeared next to MJ who screamed. Sharp was starting to get used to that noise by now but it was still annoying. MJ darted out of the way and Quickly carefully picked him up by his jacket and out of reach of the grasping hand that flailed around without its target. "I hate zombies."

"What do we do?!" asked Tolah, jumping out of the way of another two hands near her. Quickly also looked nervous, only the two hunters were unconcerned.

"Just keep walking." Sharp said and strolled off at a leisurely pace. Sterling matched him, Tolah scuttled after them and Quickly followed with long strides, still carrying MJ.

"Erm, are we not concerned?" squeaked MJ, looking at the sea of hands shooting up below him.

"You know how old these things probably are? Most break apart before they reach the surface." Sharp kicked a hand which snapped easily at the wrist and went flying.

"What about those ones?" Tolah pointed a shaking finger at a few that had managed to keep their arms mostly intact and were in various stages of unearthing themselves. Sharp crossed his arms and waited. The first made it to the waist before the heavier upper half (still had skin and presumably some rotted organs) snapped at the bare brittle spine. The upper half flailed around before attempting to crawl its way towards them using only its hands, one of which snapped at the elbow and the other broke off at the fingers. The second got all the way out but had no feet so it toppled over and shattered as it hit the ground, bones and skin scattering. The next two suffered similar fates. Quickly lowered MJ to the ground and, chuckling, the ralli stomped on a few fingers poking out of the ground.

"What about that one?" Tolah pointed to one that had managed to get itself out of the ground with only the loss of one arm. It ambled slowly towards them. Quickly put a hand on what was left of its forehead and it continued to attempt to walk towards them while swinging its arm.

"Alright, I guess we've wasted enough time here. Let's go." said Sterling.

"What about him?" asked Tolah, pointing at the zombie.

"Ah just leave him, he's not doing anything." said Sharp. They turned and carried on the way they went, stepping over hands, heads and one time a foot, leaving the one intact zombie shuffling far behind them.

"How did you not remember that was a zombie field?" Sharp asked MJ.

"Oh, erm, I don't know..."

"Just leave it Sharp." said Sterling.

"I just don't want to wander into a griffin nest or something because he can't remember what a mark on his own map is." Sterling didn't reply and he could get no more out of her until they were far past the field of decaying bodies.

They next stopped when they reached another forest. As they were serving up dinner, Sharp peered over at MJ working on his map. He was carefully drawing tiny zombies where the crosses had once been.

"Hmph, give me a minute. Nature calls." Sharp gestured in a random direction. Sterling waved him away. He got some distance from the camp to do his business. Along the way, he noticed the remains of what looked like another campsite but set up in an ill-advised area, too open for here especially. They had clearly used green (or orange this time of year) foliage which would have made more smoke than fire. Nothing like seeing someone else make a bad job of things to make your own efforts seem more satisfying. The fire had obviously gotten a bit out of control as well with scorch marks around the outside of the fire pit. On the trees too, weirdly enough. He carried on walking away. As he was finishing his business he heard a sudden noise. Next thing he knew something slammed into the back of his head and he blacked out.

He opened his eyes but his vision remained black. He felt the ground under him shift slightly as he moved so he immediately stiffened up. At least whoever attacked him had taken the time to pull his trousers back up. He slowly turned his head and saw a line of light above him. He had been thrown in a hole somewhere but luckily he seemed to have landed on a ledge on the way down. He reached his hand out in front of him but couldn't feel the opposite wall at all. He was really hoping the line of light had indicated the hole was narrow and not that he was just reeeeeally far down. It was hard to tell with his neck at that angle, the pounding in his brain from the blow and the feel of blood collecting on the back of his head. Okay, options... He reached up to the wall he was lying against (almost dislocating his shoulder) but the surface was mostly smooth. No way he could climb that side unless there were handholds further up but he had no way of knowing with no light. The other side might be better but he would have to hope the wall was close and had handholds as well. The ledge started to shift under him PLEASE BE CLOSE, PLEASE BE CLOSE. He jumped. The opposite wall hit his searching hands. He felt his fingers scrape against it with the impact and desperately tried to scrabble for something to hang on to but found this wall to be as smooth as the other. He pushed off the wall and managed to wedge himself between that one and the other, using both his arms and legs. Below, he heard the remnants of the ledge disappear into the darkness. He craned his ears but couldn't hear them hit the ground. Legs shaking, he raised his arms and after putting all his weight in them he managed to shift his legs up slightly. Okay, that was a start. He repeated the process and found himself a couple of centimetres higher than when he began. This could take a while.

  He lost all track of time but managed to keep going until he felt as if his arms were going to fall off. He left the weight in his legs to give his arms a break. Great now his legs felt as if they were going to fall off. He tried to think of anything except his screaming limbs but finally, finally the line of light was within his reach and he hauled himself over the edge with the last of his strength.

  The light was almost gone now and the sunset gave a layer of red over everything. He lay there for as long as he could allow himself to, then rolled himself into a sitting position to take in his surroundings and checking the back of his head. The blow didn't seem to have done that much damage and he could see scrape marks where he had presumably been dragged. Either his assailant hadn't been strong enough to completely carry him or just felt like causing him a bit more pain. Sharp stumbled to his feet and followed the marks back to where he had walked and was subsequently knocked out, then the path back to camp. As he approached, he could hear the others talking, no, they were arguing. He took a look and saw Sterling with himself in a headlock. Wait... himself?

"Okay changeling, what did you do with Sharp?" Tolah was saying. Quickly drew himself up and roared in Other Sharp's face.

"GUYS LET IT GO!" Sharp yelled running forward. The other four stopped in their tracks but Other Sharp twisted his form and suddenly lashed out at Sterling who reeled back, small lines of blood forming on her cheek. Quickly zipped forward and pulled Sterling out of harm's way as Other Sharp became a grotesque banshee, her razor claws shining in the firelight.

"Crap, I hate banshees!" Sharp said.

"It's fine, changelings don't actually become the thing they look like. They're just imitating how they look, remember!" Sterling replied. The banshee opened her mouth and SHRIEKED. The entire party covered their ears in pain until the noise was over. Sharp pulled his two swords out of his pack he had previously left by the fire and ran towards the creature, stumbling slightly as his damaged ears ruined his balance. The creature was slow and he succeeded in slicing her shoulder and kicking her away from the others. The banshee's form twisted again and suddenly became a minotaur, looming over them all.

"-----t's going on?" someone yelled. Sharp's hearing was coming back to him.

"It's not a changeling!" Sharp yelled over the ringing in his ears. "It's a shifter!"

"How did you find that out?!" Sterling shouted back.

"It knocked me out then dumped me down a hole. It showed intelligence rather than," he dived out of the way of the minotaur's charge, "animalistic behaviour. It would have torn me apart instead of what it ACTUALLY did!"

"So what's the difference?" Tolah asked, shooting a lightning bolt towards the creature which only seemed to mildly annoy it.

"Shifters can BECOME the thing it imitates as long as it knows how it works. They're also self aware as opposed to changelings that only LOOK like what they're copying and," Sterling stopped to rush forward with her shield to block an attack on MJ and was pushed back but was able to slow the minotaur long enough for Quickly to ram into it and send the beast rolling, "will act like like an animal."

"What did it want from you?" asked Sharp.

"It wanted the seal! When I refused it was" Sterling moved her shield to block another minotaur charge and sliced under the metal at the beast's legs, "...polite."

"Wait, that's how you knew it wasn't me?" Sharp asked, charging the minotaur as it fell to its knees. Sharp's swords met air as the bull turned into a cloud and Sharp fell flat on his face. MJ rushed forward and swiped uselessly at the cloud. It surrounded the ralli and suddenly became a giant python, choking the life out of him. Quickly roared and rushed the python recklessly, Sharp recognising the start of his berserker mode.

"Keep it together Quickly!" Sharp yelled. Quickly didn't stop his charge but wound up a punch to accompany it and knocked the python full in the face which freed MJ who fell to the floor gasping. Sterling dragged him out of the way. Quickly backed off, still in control for now.

"This thing knows a lot about the creatures it's turning into!" Tolah said.

"Books will only get you so far, really. Shifters need to see how a thing works to really become it." Sterling mused. The python slithered its way towards Tolah who shot a cone of ice towards it. It slowed down and in a panic, shifted into a warm-blooded creature, probably the one it was most familiar with. It was human. A human Sharp recognised. It was

"Karla!" Sterling completed Sharp's thought.

"Er who?" Tolah asked.

"GAAAASP!! KARLA TRIED TO KILL ME!" MJ squealed. Sharp was fairly sure you weren't supposed to SAY the word gasp.

"Oh, a famous hunter." Tolah answered herself.

"This is both very bad and very good." said Sharp.

"Explain please." said Sterling not taking her eyes off Karla who also seemed to be waiting for what Sharp had to say. All hunters were big on research and if you walked into a fight you didn't have the knowledge for, you collected it on the job. Karla was searching for an edge, same as Sharp's group.

"She's a hunter. The very bad is she probably has in-depth knowledge of a lot of very scary things. The good is that we know how to beat those very scary things." Karla looked amused. Sharp had no idea what that meant. Sterling took the brief moment to try to talk to the enemy of course.

"Karla, why did you attack us?"

"Why are we talking? She tried to kill me! Fairly

sure that's a reason to pay her the same courtesy!" Sharp was getting nervous about the lack of light. He had fought battles in the dark before of course, but not because he had planned to. Fighting someone who could become something with perfect night vision while all they had was a failing campfire wasn't something Sharp relished.

"Ah, you're always alright."

"You sounded pretty concerned earlier."

"ENOUGH!" Karla cried and her body suddenly became vines that shot out and under the ground.

"Everyone move! She's remembering where we are to strike!" The five scrabbled out of their original spots and stood waiting with bated breath.

"Think she got lost down there? She doesn't have any eyes." Tolah asked. A vine shot out of the ground suddenly near Quickly who grabbed it and with a grunt of pain realised it now had thorns before it turned to water, splashing down to the ground. Tolah readied a lightning bolt.

"Stop!" Sterling shouted. Tolah did and noticed the pool of water had collected around Quickly's feet. She killed the sparks immediately.

"She's trying to get us to take each other out. I've used that one a few times!" said Sharp. "Make sure you don't throw an attack that has a chance of hitting an ally. There's five of us, we can take her and she knows it!" The water rushed towards him. She seemed to be having issues with deciding the biggest threat of the group or perhaps she was just picking a random direction, water had no more eyes or ears than vines did so he was unsure of how much she could sense. Karla became a harpy as she reached Sharp, lunging at his face and before he could react she had wrapped her arms around him, pinning his own arms to his sides. Beating her wings, she took to the air. Unwilling to drop his swords, he gripped them tightly. The ground started to get smaller, the faces of his friends as they craned their necks to keep Sharp and Karla in sight getting unfocused in the dim light. Sharp started throwing his weight as much as he could in first one direction then the other, unbalancing the harpy's flight pattern. As she spun, he kicked at her shins. He felt her grip loosen slightly and managed to push one of her arms away, freeing one of his own which he then thrust up, his sword slicing into one of her wings, making sure to avoid anything that would seriously damage it. He did want to reach the ground in one piece after all. Karla cried out in pain and tried to drop him but he let go of his other sword (praying it didn't hit anyone below), grabbed hold of her wing and yanked it down in an attempt to get her closer to the ground. They spiralled and Sharp lost track of what was up and down and when finally Karla was able to dislodge him, he had no clue of how far he had to fall. He closed his eyes, the spinning making him nauseous and finally hit something soft. He opened his eyes to find Quickly had caught him. He breathed a sigh of relief.

"Thanks man." Quickly grinned and set him down carefully. Staggering slightly he looked around for the harpy but saw nothing. "Where did she go?"

"She turned into something small and scuttled away." Sterling said, craning her eyes for any kind of movement.

"Got any more of that oil?" Sharp asked Quickly. The yeti nodded and handed some to Sharp who threw it on the fire which flared up and revealed a vampire, the shadows from the fire spiked outwards, adding a level of horror to the scene. Sharp jumped at its silent appearance. It hissed, its teeth bared. It shot forward and turned into a bat, dodging the two hunters who had charged forward, Sharp grabbing his second sword that was sticking out of the ground where it had landed.

"This is getting really old!!" Sharp said, swiping at dead air as the shifter dodged yet again. Karla reached Quickly, became the vampire again and dug her claws into his shoulder. He roared in pain and tried to pull her off but she had a solid grip. She sank her teeth into his exposed neck and MJ ran up and launched onto the vampire's back, swiping rapidly at anything he could reach.

"Go for the neck MJ!" Sterling yelled but before the ralli could actually target something that would kill it, the vampire twisted its head around and bared its teeth in the ralli's face. He stiffened up with fear and was shaken off as Quickly finally lost his temper and, ignoring all the pain, grabbed Karla by the arm and wrenched her off his neck, sending her and a good deal of his own blood flying.

"Now we have to look out for two of them!" Sharp shouted. Quickly charged Karla who spat out a couple of teeth and easily dodged the attack. His moves were easily telegraphed so she was able to avoid him and take shots in return without much trouble.

"We have to help him!" said Tolah.

"How?" asked Sharp. That whole area was full of fangs and claws and any attack they made was more likely to hit Quickly.

"What kills a vampire?" Tolah asked.

"Beheading, stake in the heart, daylight, fire." Sharp and Sterling said in unison.

"Okay daylight is out, I don't think any of us has a stake?" Sharp and Sterling waved their swords also in unison.

"Oh right. You think you can hit her heart?" They all looked at the mass of yeti and vampire. "Okay, so beheading? Probably hit Quickly..." They all turned and looked at the fire.

"So how do we get her and not Quickly in the fire?" At that moment, Karla slashed out at the yeti who stumbled backward and fell on the flames. It was immediately snuffed out and Quickly gave a pained noise before leaping out of the way. Luckily his fur and clothes hadn't set on fire but they were all now draped in pitch black. They heard a hiss and the vampire's eyes shone through the darkness, one disappearing as they finally heard a blow from Quickly make contact with the side of her face. Karla was sticking to her vampire form. The darkness and her speed were working well for her and the others couldn't even approach the fight while Quickly was in the way, even if they COULD see it. Tolah lit a flame in the palm of her hand.

"We can't fight anything like this!" Sterling said.
"Bail?" asked Sharp.
"We aren't leaving Quickly!"
"I wasn't suggesting we do that."
"Then how do we get HIM to bail when he's currently like THAT?" Tolah asked. Quickly seemed even more beast like in the darkness, eyes flashing, fur darkened, teeth shining. If Sharp didn't know him he would definitely be hunting him.

"We'd have nowhere to go anyway." said Sharp. "He's not a beast." he added quietly.

"We know, Sharp." Sterling put a hand on his shoulder. He averted his eyes and his sight fell on... Quickly's pack. He rushed over and rummaged around in it. He still had no idea where anything was but he managed to find two of Quickly's oils. He tossed one to Sterling who looked confused but caught it, grimacing as the goop covered her hands. Sharp covered his swords with the stuff and Sterling realised what he was doing and started to do the same with her own sword and shield.

"Light 'em up!" Sharp said holding his weapons towards Tolah. Sterling did the same. Tolah caught on and she lit her other hand up with a blue flame. Sterling took the blue and Sharp the red. Sterling had drawn a simple little skull on her shield which blazed.

"Cute." said Sharp dryly. Behind them, Quickly finally fell, shaking the ground. Karla stood gloating but as she preened from the victory she was hit simultaneously by two flame sword attacks by the hunters, taking her by surprise. They swung their swords at her neck. She ducked but didn't stop her hair from setting on fire. She shifted into an ogre in response.

"Ooooo shield bash it!" shouted MJ from the darkness somewhere.

"Shut up MJ." replied Sharp, swinging a sword as close to its face as he could reach. Ogres were resistant to fire but they didn't have very good vision. They tended to swing large objects at people and he didn't intend to allow Karla to grab anything. Sharp's sword swing didn't connect but the fire's light blinded the ogre momentarily. Sterling and Sharp darted around her, waving their swords close to her face to repeat the result and after a few laps, they took a few slashes at her legs. she grunted in pain but remained standing.

"Sterling, give me a boost." Sharp saw the disk of fire go horizontal so he took a run up and with their combined effort was launched into the air. He swung back and took a mighty swing at her face, slicing deep and spraying the area with blood. As the ogre hit the ground, Sharp thrust his other sword deep into her throat.

"Yeah, don't help or anything." he said.
"Ah, you guys had it." said Tolah from

somewhere in the black.

"That was the best thing I ever saw." said MJ. Sharp was fairly sure all he had been able to see was fire moving around but he didn't push it.

"Is Quickly okay?" asked Sterling. Sharp used a sword to ignite the fire again. Quickly was unconscious but breathing. He was bleeding badly from several claw marks, however, so Sharp rummaged around for a healing herb while Tolah attempted to stop as much blood as she could. Sharp was just hoping he could feed him the herb while he was still asleep, he would be in a lot of pain if he had to wake up first.

"We never did find out what she wanted." said Sterling looking at Karla's dead body. It was still an ogre. No one really knew what a shifter's real form looked like, perhaps they didn't actually have one, who knew? He found a herb and tossed it to MJ who proceeded to shred it as small as he could.

"Wanted me to leave her alive?"

"Would you have done it had I asked?"

"Probably not. You saw her, she was way too dangerous to keep around. Besides I'm fairly sure she was just after power, hence the seal. Shifters have always seemed power hungry to me." Sharp looked at his swords, the fires now dying and saw that Sterling's weapons were doing the same. He sniffed and found MJ some water to mix with what remained of the herb.

"No need to get snippy."

"I think he wanted the blue flame." said Tolah.

"Did not." Why would he care about something so trivial? The LOGICAL thing to do would have been to give the blue to the guy but what did he know? The others laughed. He went to help MJ get Quickly into a sitting position and managed to pour the solution down his throat without him choking. To his relief, Quickly's wounds started to heal. At least he wasn't going to bleed to death. He sat down at the campfire and only then did he remember how tired he was. Adrenaline had made him forget his cliff climb momentarily but now his legs gave up and he lay back on the cold, slightly damp ground. He saw Sterling appear above him.

"You okay?"

"Oh yeah. I was almost murdered several times today and no one cares, but par for the course right?"

"I WAS worried, you know. We just... had other things to concern ourselves about at the time." They heard a snort and Quickly woke up, immediately falling back like Sharp had done as his pain took its toll.

"We're going to have to do something about Quickly. I know you want him to be himself but himself happens to be an uncontrollable monster." Sharp said. Sterling took a deep breath and Sharp could see a speech coming on. "I don't think he's a monster because of what he is, I think he's a monster because he loses his mind in a fight." he followed up quickly.

"Sorry." said Quickly quietly.

"It's fine. It's just something we need to stop ignoring and work on. I know plenty of people who I'd describe as monsters."

"And you'd compare him to them would you? People like that maniac who burnt down half a town?" Sterling said.

"Look, all I'm saying is he's like that a very SMALL amount of the time! Most of the time he's great. Stop putting words in my mouth that you know I don't agree with. That Augury guy obviously has a few screws loose all the freaking time." Every eye turned to look at him.

"Who's Augury?" asked MJ.

"That was the name of the fletchin with the arson

problem. Did NO ONE ask questions in Bullshorn but me?" Sterling turned to look at Tolah who had gone pale. "What?" asked Sharp.

"You ask questions of strangers but not of your own friends apparently." Sterling said bitterly. "That's Tolah's surname."

"What was his first name?" Tolah asked.

"Arborious."

"My brother."

"He burn stuff a lot at home?" Sharp asked.

"No, but he LIVES there. I have no idea why he left though, he's always been happy having everything done for him." The party pulled some seats up. Ironically Tolah now had a captive audience but it was for something she didn't want to discuss.

"How long have you been away from home?" asked Sharp.

"About five years."

"Did he ever find religion?" Sharp asked. Tolah looked at him confused. "He was talking about following some kind of messiah in Bullshorn apparently."

"Arborious didn't believe there was anything more powerful than himself. It would have to have been a person of massive power to have won him over."

"Maybe it WAS an actual god?" Sterling said.

"They ever speak to YOU?" asked Sharp. "Because they sure never spoke to me at all."

"I have no idea." Tolah replied to Sterling. "I write home every so often to let them know I'm okay but I never stay in one place long enough to be able to have them reply to me. I guess I'll have to go home to find out after this." Tolah didn't look happy at the prospect. Sharp could understand the appeal of being in a conversation where the other party was silent.

"I guess everyone has family issues." said Sharp.

"How about you Sterling? Got any skeletons in the cupboard?"

"Not really."

"None at all?"

"No. Actually I had a rather bog-standard upbringing and everything I did I was supported by my parents and siblings. I still visit and apparently, everyone is doing fine. I may have a stressful job but nothing has made me ever want to stop. I'm not sure I could say the same if I'd gone through what you all have."

"Well, it's not as if we're alone." said Tolah "I still have my parents (not that they like what I do), MJ still has some relatives around somewhere, albeit distant ones. Quickly has his father but I'm not sure who else. Sharp I don't know about but we all have friends right? Better than family a lot of the time since you can pick those. Most of the time." Sharp knew who the exception was.

"Well you're stuck with me now." he said.

"I guess I am." Tolah didn't sound sorry about it to his surprise.

"Want us to look for your brother?" asked Sterling. "I'm sure we can spare some time." she glared at Sharp before he could open his mouth.

"No. We have a time limit and it's been getting colder. It's going to be really tricky to do any kind of fighting if we get there after the snow sets in." replied Tolah.

"Actually." Sharp had been thinking. They all turned to look at him. "I don't suppose he'd know anything about camping would he?"

"Highly unlikely. To be honest I'm not sure how he'd stay alive out here."

"Then I think I found his camp. Thought it might be Karla's but she was a hunter so she'd have put hers together far more competently. Looks as if he lost his temper a bit with the local trees as well." Sharp said. "I'd also like to know about his messiah. I don't like thinking there's something more powerful than a mage out there. Might even have something to do with our mission. Smashed was the word you were given to describe our target right? Seems vague enough that magic could have been involved, it would certainly lend credence to the idea of villages being taken out that close to Moremist. The toughest people live there."

"We should at least check it out tomorrow then. For now, let's just turn in for the evening." Sterling said. They all turned to look at the dead ogre. "Maybe somewhere else."

Chapter 12

The campsite looked as poorly put together in the daylight as it had in the oncoming darkness.

"Definitely his camp." Tolah said running her fingers over the burn marks on the trees. "He always did like fire magic. Not that Dad let him use it in his sight. Other than cooking, the fletchins aren't keen on it. It causes too much destruction if it gets out of control."

"Nothing like forcing someone to get out of their chair as a reason to stop flinging fireballs around." said Sharp.

"Campfire doesn't look too old. Less than a week I'd say. I suppose he's been walking round in circles or going back and forth if he really does have something to do with the villages being destroyed. We still have a bit of a distance to cover." Sterling mused, ignoring Sharp's comment.

"Don't suppose you know anything about this?" Sharp asked MJ.

"Huh, what?" MJ had been daydreaming, he was a bit useless here. And everywhere else.

"You know who's behind the whole problem, right? So is this messiah our big bad and is Arborious a right-hand man or what?"

"Erm, I don't really want to say who it is. And I don't know who his allies are."

"Fine, forget it. You should know we aren't going to dump you in the middle of nowhere for lying to us though. Would give me bragging rights over Sterling at least and your map skills are worth keeping around even if I WAS inclined to drop you into a certain hole I know of."

"I do know stuff!" said MJ. Sharp sighed and turned to his USEFUL companions.

"Anything?" he asked Sterling.

"I have a trail. I don't know how far he'll be but we can follow it if we wish."

"He won't have been walking far. He gets out of breath if he has to go faster than an amble." said Tolah a little sadly. "Our people... aren't the healthiest. They think healing magic is all we need health-wise, but healthy living could probably extend our lives by a lot."

"Let's do it." said Sharp.

"Sure? Not worried about a time limit?" Sterling asked.

"Hunting is about risks. I think risking the weather is better than risking losing this guy who might have some answers."

"Okay with you Tolah?" asked Sterling.

"Yes. He may be an egotistical idiot but he's still my brother. I'm sure what he's got mixed up in he shouldn't have done so let's see if we can talk him out of it." Tolah looked determined.

It took them four days. The man wasn't subtle in his movements and left a clear trail of destroyed foliage, random scorch marks and occasionally a dead creature, both dangerous and not. As they got closer, they saw more smouldering bits of scenery and at one point the stench of burning flesh led them to a dead griffin, wings and fur still burning, the creature's mouth open in a grimace of pain.

"He's not going to be confrontational is he?" asked MJ, hiding behind Quickly as if Arborious would suddenly leap from behind the smoking corpse.

"Oh, he was definitely that." said Tolah. "Thing is, before he would just say stuff and not actually DO anything. Now he seems more... active I guess."

"So are you LESS likely to get attacked by this

guy or more? Because I kind of like not being on fire. I've been trying it out for a few years now and I'm rather addicted."

"I guess we didn't part on good terms but I'm his sister! He won't hurt me!"

"Convincing. You're going first." Sharp pulled Tolah to the front of the group. She took a deep breath and strolled forward with the others shuffling after her. He wasn't far away. He didn't look very active to Sharp. He was sat in the most luxurious chair Sharp had ever seen outside of a noble's house although a better description would probably be that he was wearing the chair. Sharp wasn't sure how he got up without taking the thing with him. He had a ralli with him, a black-furred female with blue eyes. She was currently giving him a foot massage.

"Arbo?" Tolah said tentatively. He looked up at the group of people who had invaded on his privacy.

"Tolah? What are you doing here? Stop! Read the mood you stupid thing." The second part was directed at the ralli. She scuttled out of the way and sat quietly, waiting for further instructions. MJ stared, mouth open.

"We were looking for you! You caused a lot of trouble in Bullshorn and now you're walking around setting things on fire! Why did you leave Eternal Heights?" Oh great, they were from Eternal Heights. The biggest eyesore built by magic and Sharp considered all things made by magic an eyesore.

"It was a command."

"From Dad?"

"From a man who came to the city. He wasn't a fletchin but he was able to just... walk in!"

"Wait, only those with magic can enter the city! What species was he?" Tolah actually sounded excited.

"He was an ORC!"

"What?! No way! Orcs don't have magic! Not even a bit! And they keep to themselves in groups! Was he massive? Did he walk through the streets?"

"Oh no, he was the smallest orc I have EVER seen! Smaller than you even! About the size of a ralli I would say. He was a sort of muddy brown colour with blue eyes and he just strolled in! He knew exactly where to go, he went straight to the King's palace and demanded to see him! He said he had been granted great power by the Gods themselves and as his people weren't worthy to stand with him he had come to seek out superior company. Of course, the only option was the fletchin!"

"Did any other orcs follow him to the city?" asked Sterling. The man's expression turned to one of annoyance.

"No. I just SAID he came looking for people to stand with him didn't I?"

"Calm down Arbo. These are my friends. We just all want some answers."

"Thought you would know better than to mix with people of lower status than yourself. Though, of course, you would always hang out with those kids from the street over from ours. Their family made pots as I recall. Workers indeed." Arborious seemed amused at the idea.

"They were good people and they worked hard. You used their pots all the time!"

"And you used the toilets but didn't hang out with the people who emptied them did you?"

"Well, the waste left the city via sewer so that would have been impossible..."

"Exactly. Anyway. He said his name was Duke and as promised showed he had excellent control of all types of magic, besting all challengers presented. He even beat the King's vizier!"

"Wait. He beat Father?! He's the most powerful mage in the city! Except the King of course."

"You didn't know about the whole second to royalty thing did you?" Sharp whispered to Sterling. Sterling shook her head slightly. This whole conversation seemed to have scrambled her brain, she was just letting it take its course.

"He most certainly did! He quoted from the Godscroll, he said he was the prophet mentioned by the Lord of Lords!"

"And you believed him?"

"Well, it said one of power would rise to lead us to enlightenment and domination. It never said it would be a fletchin that would be the one! Duke already had armies who he commanded but he needed those of higher importance to help him rule, his lackeys are all so far beneath him it must have been unpleasant to have only them as company. Although I have found those of lower classes to be useful as servants." He gave a glance towards the ralli who was sitting to attention.

"Who does he have serving him?" asked Sharp.

"You let them talk out of turn all the time?" Arborious flipped back to bipolar mode number two.

"They're my friends, not my underlings! We're on an important quest and what you have to say may collide with what we are trying to do!" Tolah repeated. Sharp was expecting him to flip out again but instead, he laughed.

"You had better pray you aren't going to get in Duke's way! And for your information," he turned to Sharp. "He has tremendous beasts, twice the size of YOURS," he nodded at Quickly. "A great army of them! They obey him without question although they're wild by nature! He has devoted followers," here he nodded at his ralli. "who will work tirelessly without rest or food if asked! He has people from many races who simply want to join in with his glory, people of great strength! And finally, he has US! The fletchin's magic will help to elevate him above all others! He lives in a dangerous and unforgiving land but nothing in there touches him, and his followers may walk through unheeded! He truly has the support of the Gods!" He had risen to his feet as his speech had gone on, the effect slightly ruined by having to shake the chair loose, which then fell over. The ralli scuttled forward and set it upright again before returning to her vigil. MJ was wringing his hands.

"I don't know man, it all sounds a bit culty to me." Sharp was unmoved by the dramatic speech. "Were ALL the fletchin behind this?"

"Well, of course, there were naysayers. The King, however, is behind it and when Duke gets results they will be won over in time. They won't gain as many rewards as the original believers though."

"Arbo, it really does sound a bit dodgy. What did Father have to say about it?"

"He was the one that volunteered me to join! To become Duke's right-hand man, like he is to the King! Why don't you join me! You won't have to follow these 'people' round any more. You can have a position of power (not as high as mine but still pretty high) and you won't have to almost starve to death." He poked Tolah in the ribs (Sharp wondered if he had ever felt his own ribs in his life). "And you get servants who DON'T TALK BACK." Arborious glared at Sharp.

"I'm sorry Arbo. I don't consider people to be worth less than myself just because they can't shoot ice out of their hands at will. I made good friends, better than I ever found in the people that Father picked out for me. I could never help you make them feel like you made me feel every time you spoke to me as a child. As though I was somehow worth less because I didn't think the 'correct' way." Tolah had walked up to Arborious, she was far smaller than him both vertically and horizontally. Sharp wasn't sure if she was going for an intimidating stance but if so she failed. "I really hope you aren't mixed up in whatever we're on our way to stop, because we WILL succeed and I'd rather not have to hurt my own brother."

"I'll do it." said Sharp. Sterling elbowed him in the ribs but Tolah simply turned to him.

"Okay, you can do it."

"Nice."

Arborious growled, his hands shimmered with the heat from his flames.

"Nothing is stopping Duke's rise. I'll stop you here so you don't get in his way."

"You're going to kill your own sister?" Tolah stood in front of Sharp. He wasn't sure how much she expected to block any attacks but he supposed the thought was there at least.

"If you get in my way then definitely." Arborious looked serious. Tolah's shoulders dropped.

"We aren't even sure if you're the threat we're supposed to be neutralising." Sterling had said nothing before but now she spoke up. "So perhaps it would be prudent to go our separate ways for now. I'm sure neither of you wants to kill your sibling." Sharp wasn't sure about that part. The Augurys stared each other down for a moment. Arborious snuffed his flames.

"Yeah, I guess Father would be annoyed if I killed you. I'll just have to show you. Come to Stillhaven. You'll change your mind once you see what's there." He stood back, his piece said. Tolah didn't have anything to reply so they just stood there for a few seconds. "Er, I kinda have a whole set up thing here so you guys are the ones who are going to have to leave."

"Oh right, sorry." As the group turned to depart MJ went over to the ralli. She looked at him expectantly.

"You should come with us." Sterling turned to Sharp but he said nothing. He had a feeling about how this was going to go.

"Why would I leave? I'm serving a higher power than myself and as part of a larger machine where each piece works hard so we can accomplish whatever we set out to do!"

"But you can be so much more than that. Don't you want to do anything as yourself?"

"Why would I do that when I can do more as a group?"

"You can't see yourself as a part! You're a whole just on your own!"

"You should leave. And I know I'm speaking out of turn but you shouldn't come to Stillhaven. You'll gain nothing but your own deaths." She returned to her original position and wouldn't say more.

"Come on MJ." said Sterling softly. He gave one last look towards Arborious who was looking smug before following his friends away from the area.

They walked for a couple of hours without talking. MJ didn't seem up to map reading and they didn't feel like asking him for one to follow themselves so they just chose a random direction for now. They turned in early as they had no idea where they were going and it had been a rather trying day. Sharp usually liked silence but by this point it had been going on for a while so he decided to break it.

"So Tolah." she turned to look at him. "How much does your brother over-exaggerate?"

"A LOT."

"But how much exactly? Because I don't know about everyone here but I'm fairly sure we can't take on an army of beasts, magic flingers and whoever this random cult has picked up along the way and you know what people are like with new religions. They tend to be extremely zealous."

"I'm fairly sure he wouldn't have left home if he didn't really believe in this guy. Quite honestly I wasn't sure I'd ever see him leave his house. Man, he really lost weight." Goodness knows how much he must have weighed before.

"So... we still doing this?" Sharp asked.

"Of course! Why not?" Sterling inquired.

"Well I have faith in my skills but I can't say I've ever gone up against an army. Oh except that gnome army but I don't think it counts when the members only come halfway up your shin and you can kick them a mile away."

"We'll work it out! We can't just let them mow down the rest of the world like they've been doing to the villages on the outskirts of Mistmore!" said Sterling.

"The good guys don't always win you know."

"So we just ignore this and go home?"

"Well you know... we should certainly tell someone. When we die there won't even be anyone to do that."

"So you go back and tell someone. We'll go on and save the day."

"Uuuuuugh we're all going to die." Sharp wasn't going to back out now. He still thought they were going to lose horribly but Sterling did have a point. They already had no time left and to go back might be the last nail in Mistmore's coffin. Also Sharp didn't really want his friends to die. It was an annoying new feeling to be sure. "I suppose you all side with Sterling?"

"I don't know." Everyone turned to look at Tolah with surprise. "Well, Sharp has a point! How are we meant to beat a whole army? It's not as if I'm going to abandon the group but we need to think it through at least."

"I agree. I can't even keep my head in a battle. If I'm against an army there's no way you can look after me." Quickly said. They all turned to look at MJ.

"Well, you know I think you two can win ANY fight and you guys," he gestured to Quickly and Tolah, "Are also amazing. I'm sorry I never said so before, you should really be famous as well! But, well, I can barely fight... maybe I should go back to warn everyone, I'd just be in the way here."

"Wow you get brushed off by a woman and you get all depressed, huh?" said Sharp.

"Wha... that's not... I mean I wasn't..." MJ stuttered.

"I'm not worried about your skills man, after all, you haven't been fighting for long. If you want we can up your training. You work hard when you train and we probably shouldn't have slacked off but it's been so long since I've needed to train myself so it kind of slips my mind." MJ looked starry-eyed.

"Okay, that sounds great!"

"Still doesn't solve our current dilemma." said Tolah. Sterling seemed a little stunned at the direction the conversation had gone in and was quiet. Not everyone thought that being optimistic was an army destroying power. A splatter of rain hit Sharp in the face.

"Weather is probably going to be bad for a while. Why don't we walk to the next town at least? We can talk about it then and get out of the rain for a while. MJ's map said there was one a couple of days away." Sharp said. "Sound good to everyone?" There was a murmur of consent except from Sterling.

"You okay Sterling?" Tolah asked.

"Huh? Oh yeah of course. Talk about it on the way. Good idea. Well, I guess an early night then." She stood and went into her tent.

"Did we... say something wrong?" Tolah asked

"I think she's used to being nice being the solution to everything. Plus everyone kind of agreed with me which must have been a bit jarring." If he was being honest, it was a bit jarring to him as well. "Nothing stopping us from actually going with the suicidal five against many plan later but at least we can talk about what we want in our wills."

"Let's just turn in." Tolah turned and headed to her own tent. Without a word, the rest of them followed suit.

MJ's screaming woke Sharp up. He REALLY hated that noise. He struggled out of his blankets and out of his tent to see the zombie with one arm had bitten down on MJ's own as he slept. He had managed to kick the tent down in his struggles and Sterling had pulled the tangled mess off him.

"Wow, that thing has been following us all this way?!" Sharp said.

"I guess so. A bit embarrassing that it actually caught us though." replied Sterling.

"Erm should we be helping him?" asked Tolah

"IT'S EATING ME!!!!" MJ squirmed around. Sharp bent down and peered between the zombie's ribs.

"That'd be a trick. It has no stomach."

"Calm down MJ. Zombies don't eat people. The undead don't have working organs but they don't really know it so they act like this one is doing. They only retain some of their minds after undeath so they still feel the need to eat." Sterling was trying to be reassuring but Sharp supposed it wasn't very comforting when one had a zombie attached to one's arm. MJ wound his feet up and with a pretty impressive kick, forced the zombie away. He looked at the bite mark oozing blood.

"I'M GOING TO BECOME A ZOMBIE!!"

"You aren't going to become a zombie." said Sharp. "That's a myth. How on earth does one pass on the ailment of death through a bite? That's insane."

"I suppose it could get infected." said Sterling, staring at the bite mark with interest. "That might kill you. Someone would have to cast a spell on you to actually turn you into a zombie after that though. People rarely do it now because what's the point in a slave that can barely even hold itself together?" MJ looked terrified and was on the verge of tears. Sharp was having an amazing time. Quickly took out one of his healing herbs and gave it to MJ who took it and chewed it slowly.

"Will this stop it getting it infected?" Quickly smiled at him and nodded slowly. "Okay." MJ said quietly.

"What do we do about Boney?" asked Tolah.

"You named it?" asked Sharp. Boney was still trying to get back to its feet after being knocked on its back from MJ's kick.

"Sure why not? He made all this effort to catch up with us!"

"Tolah, it's a monster." Sterling said.

"I don't know. He seems mostly 'armless' to me." said Sharp. "OW! Quit it!" he said as Tolah repeatedly punched him in the arm. Quickly burst out laughing, a very rare event.

"Well, it can't come with us." MJ said. He seemed insulted at the lack of attention now he actually had a reason for people to feel sorry for him.

"Why not? We could take all the zombies we can and form our own army!" said Tolah. Everyone turned to look at the zombie's slow attempt to get back to its feet. It finally managed it and then its other arm fell off. It shambled towards them so Quickly turned it around. They watched it take a couple of steps before turning slowly around again and came back towards them.

"There's a reason people don't make zombies anymore." Sharp said. He swung his sword and beheaded the zombie.

"BONEY!"

"You want it following us through town and causing a ruckus?" Sharp asked.

"I guess not. But I'm still leaving the zombie idea on the table. If we got enough of them they could do... something, right?"

"Zombies? No. An army of USEFUL people? Maybe. Not sure where we would get the people from though." Sharp wasn't happy about having more people join but an army versus another army?

"We don't need an army. We can do anything with just us! We got this far didn't we?" Sterling actually seemed... kind of desperate.

"Okay, I guess we think of something else then." said Tolah loyally.

"Oh sure if STERLING feels bad we try something else." Sharp said.

"Well yeah, I care what SHE thinks." Tolah said. Sharp sighed.

"Let's just go to the next town already."

The town was closer than they thought, it only took a day. It was one of the nicest villages Sharp had seen in a while, a rose in a bush of thorns. MJ was peering at the map (probably to work out why he drew it wrong) so Sharp leaned over to read the town's name.

"Starglade. Fancy." Sharp looked around. The buildings were well tended but, unlike the other towns they had passed by after the wastes, the residents had also clearly made an effort to make them look good. Paint was clearly visible and plants grew up the sides of houses into trellises. Benches were well varnished, flowers bloomed and grass was GREEN. The further out they got, the greyer it had become. "Let's find the inn. I bet they have REAL alcohol rather than the watered down vinegar we've been drinking since we left civilisation."

The inn was indeed nice. It was small like in the rest of the towns in this neck of the woods but it had two rooms with two beds each and after a request, a cheerful effort was made to find an extra bed. All in all, it was like a breath of fresh air after being in the back end of nowhere for so long. They ordered a meal and it was the best one Sharp had had in a long time.

"So I have a question." Sharp asked the bartender. "How come this place is so nice? Most people out this far don't bother making an effort."

"Ah, that would be the mayor. He turned up about four years ago now, half dead both in body and mind. We took him in and restored him to health and in return, he helped anyone who asked. After that, he started working on improving our quality of life. He was well versed in farming, food preparation, beer making, building, you name it he was skilled in it! He was so well liked we made him mayor after he'd only been here a year and he used his position to improve things even more. We may not get a lot of trade, being this far out but anyone who DOES come out this way makes sure they stop by Starglade. You'll probably meet him soon. He tries to greet everyone who passes through and he'll be the nicest person you ever met." Sharp wondered if this mayor had a religion about him. He certainly had a devotee right here, probably had a photo of him on the mantelpiece.

"Well, he did a marvellous job! The place looks amazing! I look forward to meeting him!" Sterling was gushing again. It had been a while. At least she seemed to have gotten past whatever was bugging her before and Sharp was hoping she would be more open to the whole army idea than before when it got brought up again and he couldn't see any other way around the problem of being horribly murdered. The rest of the people they met were also paid up members of the Church of the Mayor. They were, however, extremely friendly and helpful about other subjects too so Sharp figured it wasn't a bad thing. As long as this guy was all about peace and not about killing everyone it wasn't hurting anyone and made this town a splash of colour in an otherwise sweep of grey. He stretched out his legs and allowed himself to enjoy his meal.

"We should talk about our options." Tolah said. Sharp hadn't wanted to start the conversation but it did need to be started. As nice as this place was, they couldn't hang around long. Be nice to stay for a while on the way back though, presuming he was still alive of course.

"I was given this mission by the King. I only picked people to come with me whom I trusted. An army is so... impersonal. I like knowing the people I'm working with." Sterling said.

"You asked most of us to join after a day. Fairly sure we can spare that to let you chat up an army." Sharp was probably being unfair but this was serious. They couldn't indulge her in her fantasy that best friends forever would get over any hurdle put in front of them.

"A small group working together can accomplish

more than an army that doesn't know each other."

"Then we find an army that DOES know how to work together."

"From where?" This was the question he had been avoiding of course. There were tough people out here but other than individual groups of guards for each town, there were no large bodies of people working together to keep any kind of peace, and guarding a town is nothing like fighting a war. They all fell silent and sat back in their chairs.

"Sterling, we aren't going to stop." Tolah put her hand on Sterling's arm.

"It sounds like we're giving up. I believe we can do this with just us. It's a good team and I don't think we should take on an army but there has to be a way we can win with just us."

"Well, you're the boss." Sharp said. "As much as you tell me this is an equals situation, we all know it's not. I'll follow. I've come this far and I assume the others feel the same." He looked around and they all nodded. "Your word means more than ours but if you lead us poorly we WILL die. Can you live with that?"

"It's a good job I AM in charge if you have so little faith in us." Sterling stood angrily and stormed off to her room. The friendly sounding buzz of conversation around them ceased as she left, slowly starting up again after she was gone. The remaining four sat in silence until they were sure no one was listening in on them.

"Good job Sharp. You were doing pretty well for a while there." Tolah said.

"If you keep mollycoddling her she's going to make a mistake and a mistake out here gets someone killed. I'd rather her not learn the hard way." Sharp said.

"She's not going to change her mind."

"Know of any God that you think might side with

us?" Sharp said dryly.

"Apparently the Lord of Nature sometimes steps in if the environment is in danger."

"He must have a lot of arguments with the Lord of Fire then."

"No need to be flippant. Not saying I believe it happens but you asked."

"Let's just go to bed. Maybe ask if the Mayor can stop performing miracles long enough tomorrow to ask his advice. He'll know the area better than us." They dispersed except MJ who was only present in their last conversation in body, as he had been furiously redrawing part of his map.

"The landscape change since the last time you were here?" Sharp asked him.

"I guess... I'm just better at cartography now than I was." MJ said, not looking up. Sharp said nothing further and left to their room.

Chapter 13

Sterling didn't join them for breakfast. According to Tolah, she had already gone by the time they rose and as soon as Tolah herself had finished eating, she dashed off without waiting for her food to digest. The guys also dispersed as they left the inn, Sharp supposed there was nothing more to discuss. Not without Sterling anyway. Any discussion without her would seem like going behind her back, though any WITH her was probably just going to go around in circles. Sharp knew that the biggest teacher was failure but here? Failure came with too high a cost. Best scenario, only one of them died. Worst, they all died and subsequently, the rest of Mistmore if their quest really did hold the ramifications he suspected it did. He decided to find the Mayor. Shouldn't be too hard, he would just have to follow the light shining out of his arse. Turned out the beam of light he should have been on the lookout for was Sterling's smile. He saw them before they saw him and immediately darted back behind the wall he had come from. He recognised the Mayor instantly and on reflection realised no one had said his name as they were singing his praises yesterday. Oscar Pleiss. Blond hair, blue eyes, fantastic personality, modest, an expert fighter, amazing at any job he tried and minty breath. Great, now he was going to have to deal with that while they were here. It certainly explained the devotion to him. The man had more charisma in his little finger than most people had in their entire body. It had been six years since he'd last seen him and was hoping it would actually BE the last but now he was going to have to deal with him again. Not right this second though. Sterling could deal with him, they certainly were two of a kind. He walked in the opposite direction and avoided Quickly when he saw him to take a detour into the woods alongside the town. It was rare to find a village willing to build so close to an area where creatures could strike from so he decided it was probably safe and took a stroll. He took his swords but the place felt... peaceful. The leaves were a beautiful shade of orange both the few that were on the branches and the piles that had collected on the ground. He took a furtive look around and, seeing no one, jumped in the nearest pile, sending the leaves flying. Sharp continued to walk for a time and saw no hint of anything dangerous, a few squirrels and birds fled at his approach but that was it. He found himself walking into a glade. A bench had been set up here next to a small pool, a sliver of the sun that could be seen behind a cloud was reflected in its surface. He looked up and imagined that in the summer this place would be extremely pleasant to sit in if the air cleared. He was tempted to return later during the night to see why the town was Starglade and not Sunglade. He took a seat and allowed himself to become lost in thought. His brain felt as though it was filled with a swarm of... something. He had never imagined he would ever see Pleiss again. How had he come out here of all places? Sharp wasn't curious enough to ask, he just wanted to leave now but they were meant to be talking things over here and he knew that Sterling was going to like Pleiss. Would they leave if he explained himself? He lay back on the bench and closed his eyes. He probably should have put on an extra layer. Since he wasn't moving around, the numbness he felt creeping through his chest was probably from that. Sharp let himself drift off, he had nowhere he needed to be. Let the others sort out their problems, he'd just go along with it. Like he'd been able to influence what they did so far anyway, why bother trying?

He woke up when rain starting hitting him in the face. He rubbed the back of his head where it had been resting against the wood of the bench and yawned. Sharp was freezing so he started walking to get the blood pumping again. It had been nice to not do anything for a while but now he was going to have to go back into town. He looked around before emerging from the wood as if Pleiss was going to ambush him for some reason, but no one paid him any attention so he straightened his jacket and headed towards the shops. Time to stock up on warmer clothing. They probably should have done so earlier but with so few towns and other things on their minds, it had just been pushed onto the back burner.

The shopkeeper was overly enthusiastic, it seemed Pleiss really had turned this place into a great town to live in. Sounded like him. As he flicked through the winter gear ("That would look FABULOUS on you!") a noise behind him startled him out of his task.

"So I DID see you go in here! Where have you been all morning?" Sterling. Don't be with Pleiss, don't be with Pleiss, don't be with Pleiss.

"Hello, Sharp." Crap. Sharp turned round.

"Oh hey, Mayor Pleiss is it?" Hopefully Sterling and Pleiss hadn't already been talking about him.

"Oh, er, yes. Pleased to meet you." He caught on quickly. Of course, he did. Mr Perfect.

"Oscar was just telling me about the village, did you know he almost SINGLE HANDEDLY keeps the monsters away from Starglade?!" Great. first name basis.

"That's somewhat of an exaggeration. I have guards to work with me." Probably not an exaggeration.

"How does the wood stay safe?" Sharp asked.

"Oh, we have a fence! The wood isn't actually that big so it wasn't so difficult to surround it. All we needed was to" Pleiss trailed off into technical details that sounded like white noise in Sharp's ears.

"Isn't that AWESOME?!" Yup, Sterling was on team Pleiss.

"Yeah, fantastic." Sharp turned back to his task.

"Don't be rude Sharp!" Sterling said.

"You don't tell fish not to swim." Pleiss laughed a genuine laugh. As if he had any other. "He's just worried about your travelling attire. It has been getting colder and if you really do have as long to walk as you say you'll be needing warmer gear."

"Oh, of course!" Sterling shouldered Sharp out of the way to take a look herself.

"If you would allow me." Pleiss picked out a coat and handed it to Sterling. It looked fantastic on her.

"Oh, that's perfect! Thank you! Pick one out for Sharp as well please!" Pleiss picked another and handed it to Sharp. It was warm and the colour matched his eyes. It was perfect. Sharp shoved it back on the rack and grabbed another at random.

"Well, that one is good too! How about a mayoral discount?"

"Oh, how generous!" Sterling exclaimed. Sharp was already planning on how to get away. It wasn't difficult to do. Sterling's attention was entirely on Pleiss and Pleiss himself could see what Sharp was trying to do and didn't draw attention to him when he sidled off into the crowds. Sharp did some more shopping, preparing for the upcoming journey (if he was optimistic perhaps one they would be embarking on soon... oh who was he kidding they were here for ages). It was getting late but he was sure Pleiss and his fan club (probably numbering four now if he had met the rest of the team) were there so he ate elsewhere, then as the sun was setting he decided to try his stargazing in the glade idea. He swung his new coat over his shoulders to find it was slightly too big and itchy. He liked the fur lined hood but then he'd have to take off his hat... At least it was warmer as he waited on the bench for night time. It was strange having so much time to himself. It was all he'd craved since setting off but instead of feeling secure like he always had before, now he just felt... empty. He lent back on the bench and allowed himself to doze until the sun was fully set and the stars came out. There were no clouds tonight and the stars seemed closer than he had ever seen them before. He had the sudden feeling that this would be the last peace he would have in a long time. The feeling was both melancholic and relieving at the same time, like being in the eye of a storm.

Pleiss came to the inn each day after that. Sterling always met him with a wide smile but perhaps he had come to attempt to talk to Sharp? He certainly looked as if he had something to say, but what could be said? Sharp didn't let it happen anyway and as soon as he could, he slipped back to the glade or took walks through town, Sterling dragging Pleiss off somewhere and the other three going who knows where? They didn't seem to be trying to follow him at any rate. He had no idea how many days this went on. Could have been three days, could have been three weeks, he was tired of trying to steer the journey. Let it get colder, he didn't care.

One morning Pleiss didn't show up as early as he usually did. Sterling was there waiting for him like a dog waiting for its master's return but suddenly she turned and faced the group.

"While we're all here," she glared at Sharp. "I want to discuss something with you. I know you all want an army to take to Stillhaven and I want a smaller group but we could meet halfway. How about adding to our current number?"

"No." said Sharp.

"You didn't even know what I was going to say!"

"You want to invite Pleiss to join us."

"Well, why not? He's been saying he's been craving some adventure and he can always return to Starglade when we're done! I've been training with him and he really is an outstanding fighter. If he was a hunter he'd shoot up the ranks! Would certainly overtake me! He's probably the nicest person I've ever met. You all like him don't you?" This was aimed at the group.

"Yeah he's really nice." said Tolah. The other two nodded.

"I don't like him." Sharp said

"Oh, you don't like anyone." Sterling snapped.

"If he comes along, I'm not going with you." There was a stunned silence.

"You came when I invited everyone else."

"I draw the line here."

"I don't understand why! Why is THIS guy the line you won't cross? Maybe if you had more than a ten second conversation with him, in which he was VERY nice and you were just plain RUDE, you'd be okay with him!"

"You wouldn't understand."

"Of course not if you don't explain!" Sterling said. Sharp said nothing. "Fine, maybe I WILL invite him to come with us. You can do what you like."

"Sterling, wait a moment." Tolah said. MJ's mouth had fallen open and Quickly was looking torn. Sharp stood and walked out. "Sharp!" he heard Tolah call to him but he didn't stop. Let Sterling do what she liked. She claimed to want to help people but only if it suited her apparently. No one followed him so he went back to his favourite spot.

He was dozing on the bench as it got dark as

usual when the other three found him. He heard Quickly lumber through the bushes so he opened his eyes in time to see Tolah and MJ stumble behind in the larger man's wake. They stood for a moment awkwardly.

"You following me now?" Sharp wasn't annoyed, his emotions felt worn out. Just filling the silence.

"Oh no, Quickly found you. I think we should talk." Tolah said.

"Sterling inviting us all to the wedding?"

"She is going a bit over the top." Tolah sighed. "We need to leave. We needed to discuss our options here but, well, you and Sterling are usually the ones deciding things and as Sterling keeps blowing me off we decided to come and talk to you."

"Seems like our options have been settled to me. Sterling always overrides my opinion anyway."

"What is going on with you lately? You don't usually tell us a lot but something happened to you here and we need to know what it is!"

"Why?"

"We're WORRIED about you, you idiot! We like Pleiss, not going to lie, the man has something about him that's impossible not to like (except to you I guess) but I'm not willing to leave you behind if that's what it costs to take him! I don't think one extra person would make much of a change to our fortunes anyway." Sharp looked at her. She seemed really upset this time and he wondered when she went from hating him to genuinely caring how he felt. He certainly hadn't done anything different to change her attitude. Perhaps... he hadn't been fair. It had been so long since he'd had actual friends he forgot that if something impacted him it could impact them right back.

"I'll... think about it."

"I suppose that's the best I'm going to get. Just

remember that even if talking about it can't solve it, it might make you feel better. Is there anything we can do for you right now?"

"Just... stay with me for a while?" he was surprised how pathetic he sounded.

"Okay, sure." Sharp swung his feet off the bench and she and MJ took a seat.

"What have you been doing out here anyway?"

"Stargazing mostly." Tolah craned her neck back to look.

"Whoa, this is why they call the town Starglade?" She hadn't noticed the view until he had mentioned it, it seemed.

"I guess."

"Bit of a strain on the neck though."

"I usually lie back on the bench." Tolah jumped off the bench and lay down in the grass. Luckily for her it hadn't rained in a couple of days. MJ did the same so Sharp followed suit. Quickly moved the bench out of the way for space and they lay in a line for a time, just looking at the night sky.

"You want to tell us about the stars don't you?" Sharp asked.

"Soooooooo badly." Tolah said.

"Go ahead."

"Really?!" Tolah didn't wait for confirmation but launched into the constellations they could see. Sharp had no idea how she had knowledge about pretty much everything. He would probably know more if he actually bothered to listen now and then so he decided to make an effort this time at least. It was actually fairly interesting. He wasn't going to be changing career or anything but it passed the time better than when he had been here alone. He managed a couple of questions and MJ surprised everyone with a fair few of his own. Quickly said nothing as usual but seemed to be enjoying the ambiance. It was comforting to spend time with the party again, even if they were one short.

They got back late but Sterling had been waiting for them. She looked worried.

"Where were you guys?"

"Sharp wanted an astrology lesson." Tolah grinned.

"Er, is that code for something?" Sterling asked.

"Nope. We were actually stargazing." Sharp said.

"Without me?"

"You were on a date."

"I'm NOT dating Oscar!" Sterling looked ready to erupt again. Sharp probably shouldn't have been winding her up but he was too tired to dial it back.

"I'm going to bed." He would probably just annoy Sterling more if he said anything further.

Sharp made the effort to get up early enough to eat breakfast with his friends. Sterling was there but stood quickly when Pleiss came in. Pleiss started when he saw Sharp. Sharp just paid attention to his breakfast.

"Morning Lydia."

"Morning! Ready to go?"

"Ah, yeah, that's the thing. I actually have a lot of paperwork to do today, it's been a while since I really sat down to clear it. Perhaps we could do this tomorrow?"

"Oh, er, yeah, of course, no problem."

"I'm sorry but duty does call sometimes." He gave a beaming smile. What a jackass.

"So, what did you guys want to do today? Seems I'm free." said Sterling after he had left.

"Want to know why this town is called Starglade?" asked Tolah.

"Sure, why not?" Seems Sharp's personal

getaway was now completely public. He didn't know how to feel about that.

She was suitably impressed at least.

"It's better at night. You can really see the stars clearly here. Well, when it's not overcast." Sharp frowned at the clouds that had collected again. He sought for a topic of conversation but fell short. Sterling had one though.

"What do you think Oscar was doing before he came here?"

"Didn't you ask him?" asked Tolah.

"I did but he avoided the question."

"Maybe he was doing something shady and is trying to redeem himself!" said Tolah. Sterling chuckled.

"I bet he was a hunter but he didn't like the limelight so he left before he got famous!"

"Or he could have been fighting a DRAGON and that's why he got so beaten up!" MJ chimed in.

"He was a guard captain." said Sharp, leaning back on the bench and pulling his hat down over his eyes.

"You're meant to outdo the last person's suggestion Sharp." said Sterling.

"It would make sense though. He does know how to run a town and being a guard is an honourable thing to do. He would be protecting more people than if he were just a hunter." Tolah said.

"Okay, so maybe he was the guard captain of Golden! Protecting the biggest mass of people in the land!" Sterling bounced back.

"Nope. Tiny town in the back end of nowhere." Sharp said.

"Come on Sharp, I really don't think you get the game."

"Wait a second Sterling. How did he lose his job

Sharp?" Tolah motioned Sterling to be quiet.

"He made a mistake."

"What sort of mistake?" asked Sterling curiously.

"All his men were out on jobs so when two separate reports came in, he had to pick which one to attend to first. One was a domestic dispute and one was a bank robbery."

"Wait, so he went to the domestic dispute?" Sterling asked.

"No, he went to the bank robbery."

"Sounds like that wasn't a mistake. OW!" Tolah elbowed her in the ribs.

"The bank robbery was a pathetic man acting on his own in a desperate act who was easily taken down by the guards the bank itself had employed."

"And the domestic?" asked MJ.

"He went to that after. It was at a farm on the far outskirts of town. A young married couple had taken it on recently so the woman who reported the incident just thought they were having a lovers' spat. This, however, was a real robbery. By the time Pleiss got there the place had been turned over. Goodness knows what they thought they could take from a farm. He found the woman first..."

"And?!" MJ was on the edge of his metaphorical seat.

"She was dead. A violent death." Sharp took a breath before continuing, bending forwards and twisting his hands together. "The man had been bleeding a while and his attempt to crawl to the door hadn't made it better. However, Pleiss got him back to town in time to save his life." MJ sighed in relief.

"What happened next?" asked Sterling quietly.

"Pleiss waited until the man woke up so he could apologise. He didn't go back to work until he did."

"What did the man say?"

"Nothing nice. He blamed Pleiss for what had happened. Told him he should quit and a lot of unrepeatable things."

"Still don't think it was his fault. He took the option he thought would save lives. How could he know otherwise?" Sterling asked. "Is this the reason why Pleiss quit?"

"I don't know." said Sharp sitting up and pushing the hat off his face and staring right at her. "As soon as I could walk again I left town. The only thing I took, other than the clothes on my back, was an old sword I found sticking out of the ground. Maybe Pleiss quit out of guilt, maybe he was kicked out for avoiding work for that week or maybe his own extensive ego expanded to the point where he could no longer fit in town." Sterling was quiet for a time, the only sound was the rain which had just started to drizzle.

"And you're still angry. After all this time?"

"I needed someone to blame for Mary's death. It doesn't matter if he did the right thing or not. It was the only thing that kept me focused and got me out of bed every morning. Blaming him stopped me from blaming myself. That would have been something I could never come back from, so yes. Yes I still blame him and yet he still gets to live his life in this paradise he's managed to create. As if he was some god or something with all his perfect qualities and all his followers who do nothing but love him. Meanwhile I'm stuck with all my ugly qualities and a horrendous personality that repels people like a bad stench that I can't seem to shake." He had stood without realising and his voice had been getting louder but now he fell back onto the bench, his voice muffled and breaking. "I just... need you to decide what you're doing so I can just leave. I don't care what you choose, just choose." Sharp gripped his head in his hands. He felt as if he was falling apart.

"Okay." said Sterling. "Let's go back to the inn and get our things. I should say goodbye to Oscar so wait for me on the path leading out of town."

"Come on Sharp." said Quickly softly and Sharp allowed himself to be led back to the inn. They collected their things in silence, Sterling said goodbye to the surprised looking innkeeper and then disappeared as the rest of them made their way out. She wasn't long and they all marched out of Starglade. The rain had picked up so Sharp took his hat off and pulled the hood down low on his face, blocking out everything but his own feet keeping a steady pace as they walked down the road.

Chapter 14

Sharp said nothing for the next few days. The rain refused to let up and had a chill to it. The coats they had bought offered a certain amount of waterproofing but it couldn't keep out the puddles accidentally stepped in or the odd drops of water dripping down a collar. The wind didn't help and was whipping the raindrops so they fell almost horizontally at times. Quickly was suffering the most, there was no coat that fitted him so he had the biggest one he could find draped over his shoulders with the clothes he had set off in looking more than a little worse for wear underneath. The landscape offered them little protection itself and it was a miserable group that trudged along, no decisions had been made, old wounds had been reopened and people were grasping at whatever words they could to fix things that had been broken.

One evening they were all sitting around the fire, Quickly was shivering. MJ sighed and grabbed the coat off his back and started unpicking the seams.

"What are you doing MJ?" Sterling asked.

"Fixing his coat."

"You can do that?!"

"Yeah. My friends and I used to larp but we needed costumes so we all took turns making them." His fingers moved confidently and skilfully.

"What the heck is larping?" asked Tolah. Something Tolah didn't know was always entertaining to learn about. What could be less interesting than rocks?

"Oh, er, you kind of... dress up as if you're a fighter and... have mock fights..." MJ trailed off, it was hard to tell when a ralli was blushing because of all that fur but his nose was bright red. Less interesting perhaps and more just unimportant enough for Tolah not to have bothered with the topic.

"Take out the word mock and that's my actual job." said Sterling. Sharp could kind of see the appeal. All the excitement but with none of the danger. The way he was putting Quickly's coat together proved his devotion to the appearance, at least. Sharp wondered how satisfying that life could be. It definitely skipped the whole maybe being brutally murdered thing. He had a brief image of a bunch of rallis hitting each other in clumsy MJ-like ways, perhaps apologising when accidentally giving their opponent a stubbed toe or perhaps damaging their perfect outfits and immediately felt embarrassed he even granted MJ any suggestion of respect for his hobbies. He stayed silent, however, wouldn't want people to think he had another reason for thinking MJ was insane or anything. No one said anything further but watched MJ work. It was clear the attention was putting him off which was odd since attention was clearly what he was after all the time. He had to butcher some of their other clothes but it was out of season for them and Quickly needed not to have frostbite. Less for them to carry as well, Sharp reasoned with himself. When MJ was done he handed the coat back to Quickly. The yeti slipped it on gratefully, it fitted perfectly.

"Thank you." he said to MJ.

"Can you do mine?" Sharp asked. They all jerked at the first words he'd spoken since leaving Starglade.

"Er, sure. What's wrong with it?"

"Too big and itchy." MJ took the coat and worked on it for a while.

"You think I should have taken the other one." Sharp said.

"No." said Sterling. "Nothing could have fixed the problem with that one." MJ was stripping some of the fur from the inside of the coat which was quite mesmerising to watch. Sharp couldn't help wishing he would hurry it up, it was getting rather cold. When he was done Sharp slipped it back on. It fit like a glove and the itchiness was gone. He huddled gratefully into it, warmth spreading back through his body. Clearly, the fur had been the cause of the itchiness and had done nothing for heat.

"Another thing you're good at." Sterling said.

"Oh, thanks." MJ didn't seem as happy as Sharp thought he would be. He absent-mindedly turned his needle in his fingers and Sharp was reminded of Sterling and the seal. He hadn't seen that thing in a while.

"You okay MJ?" Sharp asked him. MJ gave him an almost convincing smile.

"Of course!" He replied in a fake happy tone. Sharp didn't bother asking anything else. If he didn't want to talk about it that was his prerogative.

The next day the map they were following showed another large field of crosses. Sharp turned to look at MJ.

"Zombies again? Or should we just find out when we get there?"

"Erm, find out when we get there I think." MJ said. Sharp sighed.

It wasn't another zombie field. They could clearly see what it was from the outskirts. Apparently, X meant death in MJ's map making world. It was an old battlefield, ancient even, judging by the state of the weapons sticking out of the ground. The years, the weather and the occasional creature had taken its toll on the place. They stood for a moment on the edge but there was no danger to be had here, the place was still and open, any dangers there would be seen from a mile away. It just seemed... depressing, Sharp supposed. He was the first to walk forward and the others followed shortly afterwards in silence. Perhaps it was the fact they were walking over a mass grave or perhaps it was a stark reminder of what they were soon going to be facing themselves. Sharp tried to guess when this battle had taken place, he didn't remember hearing about any war being fought out here for hundreds of years. His expertise on how a weapon or landscape degraded over time was non-existent so perhaps it was from as far back as the one he knew or perhaps people had simply never heard about it this far out from civilisation. He examined a few weapons as he passed them, they were all various sizes and various types. All kinds of species had fought here. The handles on some seemed odd, perhaps species he had never met or maybe even no longer existed. One axe stuck out, towering above his head and even Quickly seemed dwarfed by it. Sharp could only imagine a monster wielding such a thing, perhaps a giant? But who could ever tame a beast to fight a war for them? Other weapons were tiny, Sharp supposed they could have belonged to gnomes, a race he at least knew of but who were seldom seen and shunned other people. Why would they fight in a war beside another species? There were, of course, weapons he recognised. Human-sized was the standard size for most species after all and this battlefield wasn't about to try and change any stereotypes.

    They had been seeing fewer and fewer tracks from other travellers as they went but here they could see the traffic had picked up somewhat, a number of rallis had passed through from the shape of the tracks and a large amount of humanish species. The ones that worried him were the large footprints. The owners had been wearing no shoes and had left deep prints in the dirt. They must have weighed a great deal and coupled with them came what Sharp could only have described as fist marks as if the footprint owners had been also using their knuckles to walk. The footprint part of the set seemed rather familiar.

"Quickly?" Sharp called out, his sudden voice echoed over the expanse of nothingness and made everyone jerk out of their own personal daydreams.

"Yes, my friend?"

"I wonder if you could indulge me for a moment?" He pointed to the footprints. Quickly wore shoes (he had adopted them shortly after leaving his village) but you could immediately see his feet were smaller than the ones Sharp had found. He took his shoe off anyway as everyone crowded round to see what was going on. Quickly made a footprint inside the bigger one before sliding his shoe back on. It was almost a complete match (apart from the scale).

"So what does that mean?" asked Tolah.

"I don't suppose you know of any oversized versions of you walking around?" Sharp inquired. Quickly shook his head, looking worried.

"All the books I read about yeti told me they were different from what I actually met. I assumed the yeti had somehow evolved but what if they separated at some point and the others stayed the same? I suppose that sounds crazy." Tolah said.

"I think most of what you say sounds crazy but that does make sense. I've read a small bit about yeti myself and I saw the same that you did in the yeti village."

"You want to follow the footsteps to meet them don't you?" Sharp asked Tolah.

"Of course not! Are you crazy?! The books all said they were vicious creatures! Look at the size of their feet, and they walk using their knuckles! I think I'll stick to the cultured version, thank you very much." Tolah patted Quickly on the arm.

"Let's just hope they aren't going in the same direction as us." Sterling said.

"Not for now at least." added MJ, his head buried in his map.

"Then let's move on. I think we have enough to worry about as it is." reasoned Sharp. They all nodded and continued on their way.

It took a couple of hours to clear the battlefield. It must have been a humongous fight and to have been forgotten? Sharp wondered if the casualties were worth it. Perhaps the world would be different had the result gone the other way, maybe they would all be someone's slave or have to kill just for their next meal. Well, Sharp supposed he did that now but he made the CHOICE to.

Ah yes, rain. Something he knew all about. The temperature had dropped and they were now definitely into winter so the rain was threatening to become more like sleet. There was no cover so they rigged up a canopy over the firepit. They could have eaten dried food but Sharp was craving something hot in the cold and the others all quickly agreed. MJ spread out a map to study. He'd been doing that a lot lately. Sharp leant over and was surprised to see how much ground they had covered.

"How long do you think we'll be?" he asked.

"If we keep going at this speed? About two weeks."

"So we'll beat the weather."

"Unless it suddenly gets a lot worse and assuming this fight will be the end of our journey." That was the thing, wasn't it? They were all looking at Stillhaven as being the end of the road but all it was was the town name Sterling had given them when they set out and that Augury had also encouraged them to visit. It was simply supposed to be the start of the investigation. Luckily MJ seemed to be thinking ahead. Actually, it was lucky he had come along period, not that Sharp would have admitted it. He had mostly stopped the worship, nothing like seeing what your heroes were really like to start seeing them as real people and not just icons. He had also been talking to the other two as often as he spoke to the hunters. They were a team now. Sharp had seen it more since they had left Starglade. The ralli was still a pain in the ass but Sharp no longer wanted him as far away from him as he could throw him.

"Are there any towns between here and Stillhaven?"

"None."

"So the devastation hasn't reached any further out then? I was worried we were making too many stops but it would have hit Starglade had it hit anywhere and that town still looks like a unicorn vomited a rainbow over the place." They all stopped to think about it but everyone knew that they would only get answers when they got to Stillhaven.

"Game of cards anyone?" MJ took out a pack.

"Yeah sure, what we playing? Poker?" Sharp asked, taking the cards that were handed to him. "Why does this card have a dragon on it? And why does it have a health number and a magic number? How can you measure life? Like if I get stabbed in the head it's fine because I had," he squinted at the card "100 health? And how do you measure magic with a number?"

"Don't be critical Sharp! Let's just give it a go!" Sterling said. MJ was smirking.

"What's the joke?"

"Well... you think you have the same hit points as a DRAGON! That's hilarious! You have, like 20 hit points at most!" MJ said this as if it was the most obvious thing in the world.

"This is going to take all evening to explain isn't it?"

It didn't take all evening but it did take an hour. Sharp was fairly sure Quickly didn't get it but he didn't ask any questions. It was a more entertaining game than Sharp had foreseen (the dragon was in actual fact, an amazing card) but it turned out Quickly DID get it and ended up steamrolling over everyone including MJ who was half impressed and half annoyed that a newbie was beating him. It passed the time at least.

Sharp woke in the middle of the night. The rain didn't usually wake him but tonight it was really hammering down. He left the tent and saw that Sterling was already outside. As far as he could tell she was doing absolutely nothing but she seemed to be happy. He felt a bit mean disturbing her but he was bored and couldn't sleep so she was going to have to deal with it.

"Hey, what are you doing?"

"Oh, er, nothing really." He sat down beside her. She had managed to get her hands on some of Quickly's sweets so he helped himself. Sterling wrung her hands for a moment then said "I'm sorry about Starglade. I guess I got caught up in... stuff and lost track of the mission and of what you were going through."

"You aren't my babysitter. It's not usually a problem but I never expected HIM to be there. To be honest I'm surprised you took me rather than him. This was the only chance you were going to get to ditch me without me making a fuss you know." Sharp said, looking out over the gloomy landscape. Sterling looked shocked at the implication. Of course she did.

"Of course I wouldn't ditch you! You're part of

the team! You're... my friend. You ARE my friend, right?"

"Yeah. You stuck with me even after I acted like, well, myself. And I no longer want to be anywhere but here."

"That's enough for you to call someone a friend, huh?"

"You have no idea how rare that is." he said. Sterling laughed.

"I don't know how you can go through something like that. I don't know how any of you can go through what you've all been through. Quickly's got his anger problems, Tolah has troubles with her family, you have your wife and MJ has had to suffer a great deal of his family dying in various ways." Sharp agreed that MJ had issues but not the sort that Sterling was talking about. "You just all seem so strong. I don't think even an army stands a chance."

"I think you may be overestimating how good we actually are based purely on our ability to have life punch us repeatedly in the face. Anyway, why don't you count yourself in with us? You're the second strongest person in our profession and our profession is pretty brutal."

"You assume I'm not as strong as you because people know your name more than mine? Maybe the person who drags their bloodied kills through town is slightly more memorable than the person who's generally nice to the people she deals with and keeps her fights out of the public eye."

"Okay first, we need to duel for real at some point (Silver didn't count), second, I did that ONE TIME and suddenly that's what everyone knows you for (that and killing giant chipmunks), and third I did that for a REASON. That guy wasn't paying up and I had to make a statement. Can't have people refusing to pay the piper or that's what everyone is going to do."

"You WANT to be the guy who people are afraid is going to lead their children into the river if they don't pay for the rat extermination?"

"I want to not be treated like an idiot."

"People don't treat ME like an idiot."

"That you know of." he retorted. Sterling just glared back at him. "Okay so you think you're better than me but you don't think you can stand with us?" he moved the conversation away from one that would get him punched.

"It's not a physical strength thing. I'm confident in a battle but I've never been through anything like you."

"No one died? You get on with ALL your family?"

"No one, I even have all four of my grandparents. I have a brother and sister whom I have the odd spat with but we get on just fine most of the time. They both have families now whom I visit when I can. My parents have always been supportive of my decision to be a hunter although they are worried about me of course. They're proud of what I've done and where I've been and I'm happy more than most people can claim. I have no money problems and not many regrets. All in all, I've not been tested. I suppose... I'm afraid I wouldn't pass any such test that was handed to me."

"You shouldn't HOPE something horrible happens to you just so you can feel as if you can appreciate your admittedly pretty great life."

"You have any other family?" Sterling enquired.

"I have a father somewhere I think. Haven't seen him in a while but he's a good guy. No one else, but I never felt as if that was a bad thing."

"What happened to your mother?"

"Oh no no no, I think you have enough of my backstory. You always ask for other people to talk but never say anything about yourself."

"That's because I don't really have anything to say. I don't need comforting."

"And you think we do? We appreciate that you care but we can deal with our own issues sometimes, you know. You talk to people the way you think they need to be spoken to. When we first started out you talked to me constantly, I suppose you thought I was quiet and wanted the silence filled. You go quiet around Tolah because you know she likes talking, you try to make Quickly feel comfortable with who he is (even though we both know he needs to make some changes) and you're constantly comforting MJ whenever he tells you one of his macabre stories about a dead relative. You should just talk to us like you want to. You refused to abandon me even though you had a much better option standing right there that you clearly liked better than me, why would we do the same to you just for not changing to make us happy? We're fine with however you want to be."

"I didn't prefer Oscar over you and I wasn't trying to stop you rejecting me. I just wanted you to feel better about yourselves."

"You aren't our counsellor, we already feel fine with ourselves. Stop it."

"I guess... saying it out loud does kind of feel patronising." Sterling looked embarrassed.

"So tell me something about you then."

"Like what?"

"Well, how about what you were doing when I came out of my tent. You were just... sitting there."

"You're going to think it's stupid." Sterling flushed slightly.

"I think most of what you do is stupid. Indulge me."

"I was... listening to the rain." Sharp cocked his head. Sounded like regular sleep disturbing rain to him.

"You like the rain? Seems like a pain in our line of work."

"When I was younger my family used to go camping sometimes. We would go to the middle of nowhere and although my Mum would always pick the time she thought would be the sunniest it ALWAYS rained. I'm not sure I can remember a single holiday it didn't."

"Sounds about right."

"My Dad would rig up the canopy next to our tents just like this one and we would play card games and eat ALMOST completely cooked meat. It would get dark and the rain wouldn't let up. My parents would then always argue about the rain. My Mum hated the sound on the canopy roof and my Dad found it soothing. It was never a real argument, they always used this jokey tone of voice so no one ever believed they were actually arguing. But they did it every day it rained. Out of everything I remember as a kid, that always stood out the most for some reason. I loved it. After that, I always felt at peace when it rained, even when I became an adult. My nerves might be shot, my brain might be buzzing but as long as it's raining I can relax."

"So you agree with your Dad then?"

"I guess I do." Sterling smiled. "Don't tell Mum."

"I'll try to restrain myself." Sharp smiled. They sat in silence for a time, listening to the rain. He still preferred the rain when he was inside but it wasn't so bad out here. Eventually, he felt like sleep might beat the sound of the rain and rose to return to his tent.

"Sharp?"

"Yes?"

"Did you ever think it might be less painful to just... forget her?" Seems Mary had been on her mind.

"Sometimes. But then I think about what it would be like without her at all and that just seems so much worse."

"Right. Well, goodnight Jasper."

"Goodnight." He returned to his tent and finally managed to fall into a mostly restful sleep.

The rain kept up. Good for Sterling, Sharp thought. Not so good for the fletchins they met further on down the road two days later as they navigated their way around a ravine that ran parallel to their path. There were two of them. A woman with red skin and red eyes and a man with blue skin and blue eyes. They would have stood out like a rainbow against the gloomy landscape had they not obviously been walking in the wet for so long and instead looked water-drenched and ticked off. They saw the incoming party and stopped to wait until it caught up with them. They smirked at each other then went to stand in the party's way. Sterling went to step around and they moved to block her way. These were fletchins and so their rather large bulk blocked a great deal of the road. Sharp sighed. He was really not in the mood for this.

"Look if you're trying to stop us then just go ahead and say, so I know whether to draw my swords or not."

"It's a free country. We aren't stopping you!" Red thought she was hilarious apparently.

"Quickly, clear the road if you would." Sharp had used this one before. He liked to see how high he could make people jump. He had learnt not to do it while the victim was standing under a low hanging branch though.

They had at least managed to stop the bleeding before moving on.

Quickly walked in front of the two fletchins and ROARED. They didn't jump that high but to be fair they did weigh about double of most of those people Sharp had tried it on. The ground shook slightly as they landed again with suitably terrified looks on their faces.

"Okay, you can go now." Sharp made a dismissive motion. They backed away slowly down the road, keeping their eyes on Quickly.

"Was that necessary?" asked Sterling.

"Probably not. Fun though. Whoa, wait a second man!" Quickly had made a motion to follow so Sharp grabbed him by the arm to pull him back. "We don't actually want to chase them down you know!" Quickly turned to face him and Sharp recognised the dilated pupils that preceded a berserker rage. He backed off in shock, Quickly had never done this outside of actual battle before.

"What's wrong with him?" Sterling asked.

"Why are you asking me?" Sharp said.

"You like him the best out of us, right? So I'm counting him as your best friend."

"Not right now you can't." Quickly turned and saw Tolah. She must have looked much the same as the fletchins who had now fled in the pouring rain. He roared again, This one sounded different and, dropping to his knuckles, he charged. Suddenly Sharp had a flashback. It was all in the wrong order but he saw the charging yeti, the terrified look on Tolah's face, his heart pounding in his chest and he realised he was running. This time wouldn't be the same, he wouldn't leave Tolah again. But when he got there he realised it would end EXACTLY the same as Quickly's flailing fist swung out and hit him full in the chest, knocking the wind out of him as he felt his ribs crack all over again.

"Sh-"

He flew backward at a speed faster than before, not having the 'luxury' of trees to slow his flight. All he needed now was... ah yes, there it was: the ravine. Gravity decided to take hold of him juuuust as he reached the edge of the cliff and suddenly he was falling vertically. He closed his eyes and felt the back of his coat snag on something, yanking his shoulders back as he felt his head spin, hoping he didn't get whiplash.

"-it!" He looked down and decided actually, whiplash was fine. The ravine didn't have the decency to have water below but was instead lined with some kind of spiky rocks. Stalactites? Stalagmites? Whatever the pointy up ones were (weren't they only in caves?). He looked up and, half blinded by the rain, couldn't see any handholds on his side. An attempt to twist round gave no results anyway, his coat was too tightly caught. The other side was far too far away by a long shot. He heard a creak and suddenly he was contemplating religion, no reason really. It wasn't something he usually thought about, it was just so HARD to pick one. Of course, if they were all real he had a much better chance of picking just fine but most of them declared the others were all fake so he was just going to have to pick the right one. Crreeeeaaakk. Of course, a lot excluded him just for being him. There were the species only ones and the ones that only liked magic or people who owned a boat or some such nonsense (Sharp was shocked how many of those there were), so at least he could discount those. If they were real he wouldn't get into any kind of afterlife they offered anyway. He could always pray to all of them but again, most gods hated you for worshipping anyone else, so he may as well pick one that declared itself the only one and he'd still be covered

by the less exclusive religions.
CRRRREEEEAAAAKKKK. HE COULD ALWAYS EXCLUDE THE ONES WITH NO AFTERLIFE BECAUSE WHAT WAS THE POINT WITHOUT THE REWARD?

SNAP.

Well, that had passed the time. He fell straight down until an outcropping of rock loomed up and he hit it and flew away from the wall while spinning. He saw the sky, the wall, the spikes, the wall, the sky again, the wall, his lunch, the spikes, the griffin, wait, what? He hit the creature, who had been flying through the ravine, with a SQUAWK. He scrabbled to find purchase but slid off while grabbing at wet, slippery feathers that pulled out under his hands. The griffin reached for him and he found a giant talon gripped round one arm and up they flew, his arm feeling as if it was being pulled out of its socket. Sharp realised the griffin was carrying him away from the team and he could see they had run after him (all four were there or at least four tiny, roughly them shaped people). If he recalled correctly from the map, on the other side of the ravine there was a forest. Hopefully, MJ had been correct and it had softish trees. He was going to have to risk it. He reached back with his free hand and drew his sword, thrusting it deep into the side of the griffin where he knew its heart was. It let out a brief cry before it died and Sharp untangled himself from it and closed his eyes to brace himself for the trees. It didn't happen. He looked down and although the map HAD been correct, the other side of the ravine had not been flat and there was a steep drop before the treeline actually appeared. Of course. He free fell for a time and managed to hit the first tree which slapped him across the face and again he spun briefly, hitting the trees as if he was the ball in a game of tennis where the rackets were made purely of wood and the players thought the ball had insulted their mothers. The spinning stopped and he was miraculously the right way up. His descent was finally halted when he landed on a log, legs apart, right in the groin. He slid sideways off and onto his face into the mud. In the few seconds he had before his adrenaline faded and the pain hit at least he decided which god was definitely real. There was only one that had that sense of humour. A crashing above him revealed the griffin's body that landed on his back with a squelch.

"Praise Boffo." he squeaked before the most blissful unconsciousness finally caught up with him.

Chapter 15

Before he opened his eyes he lay there listening to the rain on what sounded like a tent. Sharp felt as though he had been run over by a cart. He must have broken several bones, he knew his face must be cut and bruised beyond recognition, who knew about internal injuries and certain private areas of himself were asking him why he hated himself. He opened his eyes and found he was indeed in a tent. Outside he could hear a muffled conversation, sounded like Sterling and Tolah. With a massive effort, he managed to stumble out of the tent, grabbing his coat neatly folded beside him. They had put together a rather crude canopy as well as the tent he had been in. A pathetic looking fire (with something nice smelling cooking over it) had Sterling, Tolah, and MJ looking miserable around it. Sterling had the seal in her hands. At his approach, Tolah leapt to her feet and wrapped her arms around him. He tensed up in pain.

"RIBS." he gasped.

"Oh, I'm sorry!" Tolah let go. The other two had watery smiles, he saw no sign of Quickly so he had to think that was the reason for the distress. He couldn't imagine it was his current state. He looked down at the logs they had pulled over for seating.

"Any chance of an ice pack?" he asked Tolah who rustled around and found a pouch of water which she froze and handed it back. He sat down with the assistance of the pack, Sterling passing him one of Quickly's healing herbs. "How long has he been gone?" The herb's effects numbed some of the pain immediately.

"About three hours. He stayed long enough to help dig you out from under the griffin then as we were putting you back together he slipped away. We didn't want to leave you so we stayed here."

"You didn't think to follow him and leave Tolah and MJ here?" Sharp was irritated. It was going to take ages to track him down now. The thought of just letting him go never even crossed his mind.

"I didn't want to split the party up even more than it already was." Sterling's expression shut Sharp down. She wasn't flipping the seal but turning it slowly, staring at it rather than at Sharp. She suddenly stopped spinning it and stared him in the face. "And I was worried about you." Her expression wasn't one of anger, she looked worn down.

"Yeah, I'm sorry. As soon as I can walk we'll go find him. I don't think he'll have gone far." Sterling nodded and put the seal back into her coat.

"Want a griffin leg?" asked Tolah. Sharp narrowed his eyes at the proffered meat. He took it and bit into it. It was actually pretty good. Eating his targets had never had much of an appeal for Sharp. Those sort of people always struck him as a bit... weird.

"How did you get down here?" asked Sharp.

"There's a bridge." MJ pointed it out for him on the map. It was depressingly close to where he had been thrown. "After that, we just followed where we saw the griffin drop you, the broken trees, the torn clothes, the patches of blood and we found your belt buckle!" He handed it over. The lady in a bikini now had a big scratch through her. Sterling raised an eyebrow.

"It was a gift." Yeah, from himself to himself. He returned it to his belt. He held up a sleeve in front of his face and realised it had been patched back together. It must have been almost destroyed when he fell (he had no idea how badly, it wasn't exactly on his mind earlier) but now you could barely tell. "You did a good job on this MJ, maybe you should take it up as a career."

"I guess." MJ looked grumpy.

"Or not. Just do what you want to do. You can either do what you love or what you're good at, there's no point in doing something that isn't going to make you happy. Unless what makes you happy is being a mass murderer or something."

"Even if what I want to do I'm terrible at?"

"Sure, as long as you don't get anyone else killed, then who cares if you're having fun?"

"I might ACTUALLY get you killed."

"We can take care of ourselves." Sharp looked at Sterling who nodded her agreement. To be honest, the ralli didn't need watching anymore. He might not be the best fighter Sharp had ever seen but he could definitely hold his own now.

They finished their meal in silence, each deep in their own thoughts. Sharp still felt as if he had been, well, punched off a cliff then attacked by a griffin, several trees and the ground but the longer they left Quickly, the further away he would get, so with a groan he managed to get to his feet.

"Are you okay to be walking?" Sterling gave him a concerned look.

"Not in the slightest. Let's go get Quickly so I can actually sleep some of this off and we can finish saving the damn world. I'm getting sick and tired of this quest."

Tolah and MJ were pretty useless at this point but the other two knew how to track a target and Quickly had made no attempt to hide where he had gone. Sharp figured he'd just picked a direction and left with no real plan. He hoped this would have slowed him down since the man had long strides and could be hard to catch up with if he put in an effort to get some distance and Sharp was in no state to travel fast. Annoyingly, Quickly seemed to have picked a direction away from their destination and they were going to have to stray from their path before finding it again. Sharp hated going back on himself before finishing a journey, nothing more annoying than re-walking the same path if you forgot something back at home. They followed the trail into the woods for several hours, Sharp needing to take breaks every so often slowed them slightly but they found Quickly shortly after nightfall. He hadn't bothered to even put up his tent but had laid back onto the muddy floor, letting the rain fall on his face. He must have been freezing cold even with the extra layer of fur and the newly fixed coat.

"Stay here." Sharp said to the other three. Sterling looked as if she wanted to say something but didn't and instead led the other two out of eyesight. Whether they were out of earshot as well, Sharp didn't know. Quickly sat up at Sharp's approach and Sharp had the sudden thought of looking at a wet animal left outside in the rain. He looked miserable. Sharp sat down beside him and neither said anything for a time.

"Are you..." Quickly began.

"Okay? Yeah, I've had worse and it's not as if I haven't been punched off a cliff by you before." More silence.

"Why... did you follow me?"

"Don't know why you have to ask that one. I may not be a social person but I'm not going to leave my friend behind when he's obviously hurting more than I am."

"I can't come with you if I'm going to hurt my own people."

"I don't know the solution to your problem but I do know what it is to be angry. When Mary died, I just wanted to kill something. I was lucky that the first thing I saw wasn't a person or I may have gone down a different road. I just killed one animal after another but it didn't help. After I found out I could get gold for doing what I was doing I started on bigger targets, which paid the bills but still wasn't enough. I ended up focusing on getting to the top but it was still only a distraction until eventually the wound of anger turned into a scar that hadn't healed right and I just became bitter towards everything. I don't know if talking about it would have helped or if that's even what you need but it can't be a bad thing to have someone to confide in."

"I just don't get why I'm not like everyone else in my village."

"Like your father?"

"Yes."

"No offence man but I didn't like your father." said Sharp. Quickly seemed taken aback.

"But he's a great man! He organises everything perfectly, the people are all happy and no one wants for anything!"

"Bet you they do. You have to hurt some people to make others happy. Not saying he's doing a bad job of course." He back-pedalled at Quickly's expression. "But I wouldn't want to travel with him. Out of that entire village, you were the most interesting thing in it."

"That why you tried to kill me?" Quickly asked. Sharp laughed.

"To be fair, at that point I hadn't actually met you. How about we work on your first impression and also on my reaction to someone's first impression?"

"Sounds fair." More silence.

"So you'll carry on with us? I don't want to have to share a room with only MJ."

"Okay. I wouldn't want to be responsible for MJ's death." Quickly had a small hint of a smile.

"So maybe help me out with some tents? I'm soaked to the bone here."

The others appeared as they were putting the tents up but no one said anything as they focused on the task of getting out of the rain. Sharp didn't know if they overheard the conversation or were just assuming he managed to say the right thing but they didn't bother asking either of them anything. When it was done, Sharp sat down with a slight wince, it had been a long walk in his current state. Tolah handed him another ice pack and Quickly held out a herb. He took both gratefully.

"Erm..." Quickly stuttered. They all turned to look at him. "Maybe... we could take a different road to Stillhaven?"

"Is there a reason we can't take that road?" asked Tolah.

"A lot of people have been walking it lately. A lot of fletchins and rallis mostly."

"How do you know that?" asked Sterling.

"I can smell them."

"Through the RAIN?"

"Yes."

"What do fletchins smell like?" asked Sharp. Tolah gave him a look. If Quickly's answer was less than complimentary Sharp was going to be the one to feel it and right now even a poke in the ribs would be agony. Quickly thought about it.

"Like light and silver and static."

"Describe colour to a blind man I suppose." Sharp said. "Okay, so assuming Duke's army is taking the main road we need to find another way around. MJ?" MJ was buried in the map. "What's this bit here?" Sharp pointed at a point on the other side of the road. Far, FAR from his favourite ravine. It was marked with several large Ms in a row.

"Er, not as bad as an X?"

"Yeah, really raising my hopes with that MJ. You

know what? I don't care, I don't want to be anywhere near the ravine and we can't take the main road so we don't have a lot of choices. Let's take our chances on the Ms."

"Okay, well, I can get us there tomorrow. It shouldn't add too much time on our journey."

"That okay with you guys?" Sharp realised he hadn't asked the others.

"Sure, sounds fine to me. I'm not eager to run into any more fletchins." Tolah said.

"You okay Tolah? You never said anything bad about your people before." enquired Sterling.

"Oh, you mean the people who decided to change their entire way of life because someone more powerful showed up and told them to do it? No, of course not." They all looked at each other. "Oh, unclench, I'm not going to do anything crazy. I may not have agreed with my family all the time but I never thought they would join a damn cult."

"They aren't the only ones who ever respected someone for being stronger than them. I'll bet everyone here has done that at least once, even if it didn't lead to making a life-changing decision." Sharp said. "We show them that Duke hasn't been sent from above and you can go back to your plan of teaching them to get out of their chairs for a reason other than domination of other people."

"Yes. Right. That's what we'll do." Tolah paused. "How exactly are we going to do that?"

"We can't fight an entire army. But cut off the head and the body dies." Sharp said.

"You think we should go for Duke." Sterling replied.

"Better than walking into a death trap."

"But where IS Duke?" Quickly asked.

"Think you could follow his scent? asked MJ.

"I don't know what an orc smells like. Also, I'd need a trail to follow. The most likely starting point would be in Stillhaven, if that's where his army is, but maybe he's staying back. It's the sensible thing to do."

"We told Augury we would meet him in Stillhaven." said Sterling.

"Can't possibly stand up the guy who wants to murder us horribly with an army or anything." Sharp said dryly.

"He might be willing to talk."

"Like he was last time?"

"I can't believe he'd be willing to hurt his sister."

"Just because you have a nice family doesn't mean everyone else does." He turned to Tolah. "You think your brother would start on you and your friends?"

"We never saw eye to eye but I don't think he would attack me. Even if he was inclined to, I think he would be too afraid of my father's ire. You guys, however..."

"Great, so one of us will probably be fine."

"You can always go-" Sterling said.

"I'm not going home." Sharp cut her off. "I think we should try to talk to the man, with no other option available to us. Our aim should be to get the location of the boss. We should then leave and let him have his victory. If a fight breaks out, we retreat. I'm alive now because I know to back out of a fight I know I'm not going to win and I don't have to even see our opponents to know we don't have a hope. I do, however, think we need to make this meeting, we need information to know where to go next."

"Maybe I should sit that one out. Talking isn't my forte." Quickly looked at his feet.

"You do whatever makes you comfortable." said

Sterling. "No one here wants you to do anything you don't want to, in the same way you don't want us to do anything WE don't want to."

"You don't want to have this meeting with Augury." Quickly replied.

"I don't know, I kind of do." Sharp drew one of his swords from his sheath and turned it over in his hands. At a glare from Sterling, he stopped turning it and instead pretended he was only oiling it.

"It's okay Quickly. We can handle it on our own and we aren't doing anything we haven't chosen to do. Sharp refuses to go home for instance, even though I keep giving him the option and that's clearly what he wants to do." Sterling said. Sharp shrugged.

"Let's just eat and then get an earlyish night. We have to contend with some Ms tomorrow." Sterling declared. There were no complaints.

Perhaps it was the earlier than usual night or the various injuries but Sharp found himself unable to sleep. He found there was something on his mind he couldn't quite pin down no matter how much he tried and he ended up only falling asleep when the sun had just started to rise.

There was a path leading back to the main road from where they had camped. It wasn't easy going. The rain had slacked off slightly but was still drizzling and Sharp's injuries and lack of sleep didn't make it any easier, but the others were willing to help him out at least. Quickly even carried him at one point. The yeti was chattier than he used to be but bearing in mind that he barely spoke, that wasn't difficult. When they got back to the main path they hovered slightly.

"We didn't meet anyone this far down last time but is there still heavy traffic here?" Sterling asked

Quickly. He nodded.

"Same amount as further on. Seems as if it isn't very often travelled but if we do meet someone, it will be along this road."

"Then let's make a beeline for the Ms." Sterling said. MJ found them a route and they were off.

"Calling for bets. What do we think M stands for?" Sharp asked.

"Monsters." Tolah and Sterling said in unison.

"Pessimism, a rare call from you two. I like it. Quickly? MJ?"

"MJ doesn't get a vote, he made the map." Tolah cut in.

"He clearly doesn't know what M means. He gets a vote."

"Mountains?" guessed Quickly. "Monsters might move so I doubt it's that."

"Mushrooms?" MJ guessed tentatively.

"Ah yes, we haven't had poisonous landscapes yet, that could be a winner."

"He didn't say they would be poisonous." Sterling said.

"Sterling, sometimes your common sense has to win out over your positivity."

"Not sure how expecting the worst is common sense but sure, we'll try to restrain the urge to eat everything we find on the floor."

"What do you think it is Sharp?" asked Quickly.

"Going with maelstrom."

"Don't they only form in the sea?"

"It's the worst thing I can think of - I'm not changing my guess."

It was a few hours to the Ms. MJ stopped and looked at the map. He lowered it then raised it a few times.

"This is it?" Sharp asked. They were standing in front of a canyon, the sides rose high on either side of them, the passage dark and gloomy in the distance. "Okay so... anyone think of a word meaning canyon that starts with M?" There was a collective murmur that no one knew. Quickly was leaning over the map so MJ passed it to him.

"Oh, it's the shape of an M." Quickly said. He traced out the shape with his finger.

"Well, I guess we're going into the scary gorge then." Sharp set off with a brisker stride than he felt. The passage was wide enough that they didn't need extra light walking down it but it still felt slightly claustrophobic. Quickly was slowing down until he stopped and Sharp walked into his back.

"Quickly?"

"Rallis have been through here."

"Ah, what are we concerned for then?" Sharp carried on walking.

"Wait, so we're concerned by a couple of fletchins and not by a horde of rallis?" MJ sounded insulted.

"Quickly, is it a horde?"

"No. Maybe about twenty or so?"

"What if they're armed?" asked MJ.

"You know a lot of vicious ralli fighters going around in groups? It's probably a workforce." Sharp said.

"You don't know that! Maybe Duke collected all the fighting rallis together! Maybe we should be careful!" MJ looked to Sterling and Tolah for some kind of backup but they just shuffled their feet awkwardly. Rallis weren't known for their fighting aptitude. They happened, of course, Slick was a good example, but it was a rare occurrence and if they were to team up, they would usually pick someone of larger stature. Perhaps they were willing to team up with others of their own kind, but if even one was a rarity then finding twenty with the same way of thinking was almost impossible. Stereotypes existed for a reason.

"Okay MJ. Quickly will tell us if we're about to come across anything but old tracks and we can prepare then." Sterling nudged Quickly forward so he was now at the front of the pack. He looked a little nervous at suddenly having to lead but at a thumbs up from Sharp he straightened up and strode forward. Probably a bad idea in hindsight. Letting the person with the largest stride set the pace was exhausting but they were making good time at least. Until he stopped of course. The party collided with each other. Sharp had been behind Sterling and in the pile that resulted, ended up with a shield in his complaining ribs and a sword hilt threatening to explore his nostril if he looked as though he was going to move a millimetre in its direction.

"Smell something then?" said the muffled voice of Tolah from somewhere at the bottom of the dogpile.

"Yes." said Quickly's voice from another direction. They all struggled apart and to their feet.

"How many?" asked Sterling, dusting herself off (well more mud than dust).

"About five."

"I'm fairly sure stopping dead in your tracks should be reserved for at least a hundred rallis. Unless they're armed with crossbows on fire or something. Can you... smell crossbows on fire?" Sharp was suddenly concerned, his luck hadn't been amazing lately.

"I can't actually smell what people are carrying you know."

"Well you know... there'd be like... smoke and..." he trailed off at the looks he was getting. He coughed. "Anyway let's go meet our horde of martial experts shall we?"

They weren't far. It was six in actual fact, not that that mattered. They were clearly not the great warriors MJ had been wanting. They were all a boring shade of brown, dull brown eyes and were carrying various tools that Sharp could only guess were made for building. It wasn't an area of expertise he was familiar with. Actually, they looked kind of similar to someone he knew...

"Twenty Seven?" said one of the rallis.

"Crap." said MJ.

"Friends of yours?" Sharp asked.

"More like siblings." said the ralli. "Decided to join us after all did you?

"Definitely not. I'm on an all-important mission to save the world." MJ replied. The rallis all cracked up laughing.

"And who are these people?" the ralli got out between laughter, "Victims you've saved along the way?" They lapsed back into hysterics again.

"I thought all your family was gone?" asked Sterling. She seemed genuinely surprised.

"Whaaa you still telling people that one?" said a different ralli. He turned to Sterling. "Nah lady, our family is pretty much complete. No grandparents but that's pretty common really. All thirty of the Jarzembowski siblings are fine though, as well as our parents."

"But... all those stories... so much detail... I comforted you. I..." Sterling trailed off. Sharp felt a pang of sympathy for her. She really was far too naive for her own good. Everyone else looked as if they were avoiding each other's gazes. Sharp understood. Popping Sterling's bubble could make you feel like a terrible person.

"So you invited MJ to join you on a job?" Sharp asked one of the rallis.

"Pfh MJ? Nice nickname."

"You called him by a nickname."

"I called him by his number. We all have the same name so calling each other by our numbers just makes sense."

"Wait you're ALL called Mac-something or other?"

"Macgillivray Jarzembowski. Yes. Our father was the first and didn't have much of an imagination. He named all of us, male or female, after himself."

"What was wrong with your mother's name?"

"Her name was Zona Krill. Can you imagine giving anyone else that name?" A round of laughter from the other MJs."

"And that's... a worse name?"

"Hah, you are one funny human, you know that?"

"Yeah sure. My humour is what I'm known for. You know that's not how numbers on names usually work, right? Like it's meant for long and distinguished lines?"

"For humans maybe. We have big families, we'd run out of names!"

"Riiiight. Well, what number are you then?"

"Nine." Number Nine seemed proud for some reason.

"And you were all the way out here? To do a job? Take it not in this canyon." Nine gave him a look as if sizing him up.

"We told Twenty Seven where we were going. He didn't tell you?" The four people NOT called Macgillivray Jarzembowski turned slowly to stare at MJ who appeared to be trying to sink into the ground.

"You KNEW what we were walking into?!"

Sterling towered over the cowering ralli.

"I did tell you I knew."

"But then you didn't tell us WHAT you knew! I assumed you didn't know much since you seemed surprised when we found out about Duke's plan. I thought you just wanted to make yourself seem as if you knew more than you did so we would take you with us but your family is WORKING out here! You were steering us into a DEATH trap!" Sterling stopped to take a breath. "I would have taken you even if you knew nothing." She finished quietly.

"I didn't know what the job was. Four told me we had a job and that the whole family was needed. It was a big project, a big opportunity for us but he didn't give me any particulars. But I don't want to be a builder or a blacksmith or whatever they wanted us to be."

"No, you want to be a world famous hunter like that Shark guy or that Starling woman. As if a ralli ever became famous! Stick to your strengths brother. No ralli ever became noticed for anything other than being part of a group that works hard and doesn't stop until the job is done. It's something to be proud of and any worker worth his salt knows not to go against the grain. Why try to be something you're not when you can be good at something that worthwhile?"

"So what IS this job you're doing?" Sharp got that everyone was emotionally charged right now but they could deal with that later. Right now he was looking for an edge over their enemy.

"It's a secret to those not involved. I assume you AREN'T involved since you aren't travelling the main road."

"YOU aren't travelling the main road." Sharp retorted.

"This road takes a day off travelling time if you

don't have to share it with too much traffic and you aren't bothered with small spaces and the dark. Some of our... allies can get a bit claustrophobic." Definitely talking about the fletchins, stuck up bunch of upstarts.

"Fine, so maybe we want to be involved. We can fight and one of us is a fletchin! We know you guys have a lot of them working as well." Tolah tried to stand taller than she was.

"Most of the fletchins didn't join." Nine looked critically at Tolah.

"Wait, they didn't? I thought they mostly all jumped on Duke's bandwagon!" Tolah said.

"He got the ones directly under the King and a fair lot of the higher ranking nobles. It seems not everyone believed what he's selling however. You look like an unbeliever."

"Are you a believer?" Sharp asked.

"I'm not paid to think about it." Nine said. "I was hired for a job with my family and many others like them and I will do the best job I can in as short a time as I can. If Duke has more jobs for me afterwards then I shall do those with the same amount of gusto or move onto another job with as many of my family as are needed."

"Well, how about you tell Twenty Seven about it?" MJ looked crestfallen at the numbering.

"He's not part of the project. Rallis understand that sometimes a whole family isn't needed and won't ask for information about a job if it is to remain a secret." Nine crossed his arms. From their postures the others seem to agree. Sharp supposed the lowest number got to be the spokesperson and the others just went with it. Rallis did love following authority figures.

"Maybe he's changed his mind. Fairly sure Ster- I er mean Lydia is going to fire him after this." Probably not a good idea to let the MJs know they were the hunters their brother idolised so much, they probably wouldn't believe he would leave them so easily and that was Sharp's plan. Sharp gave MJ a meaningful look which MJ couldn't possibly have seen through the layer of tears currently building in his eyes.

"But I don't want to go with them!"

"Yeah? What are you going to do on your own in the middle of nowhere?" Sharp could tell that trying to portray his plan through facial expressions was going to be too subtle for MJ. Sharp looked at Sterling to see if she could get where he was going. She looked MAD.

"I agree with Jasper. Twenty Seven should go with his family. His fighting certainly left a lot to be desired and this work sounds like something to be respected." Sterling growled. Sharp wasn't sure if she was going along with his plan or was simply that angry. She was using Sharp's first name which made him think the former, but using MJ's number suggested the latter. However, Sharp couldn't imagine Sterling could ever be that dismissive to one of her friends, even if that friend had been lying constantly since the day they met, but he supposed time would tell. He never did like MJ very much but thinking about ditching him for real made him feel kind of despondent. The rallis looked self-satisfied by the work-related compliment and unconcerned about MJ's feelings. Sharp could see why MJ had wanted nothing to do with the project, the whole situation seemed so impersonal.

"MJ, come here." Tolah said. The ralli walked towards her. She bent down to meet his eyes and Sharp could see her slip a note into his front pocket using his body to stop the other rallis seeing what she was doing. Sharp hoped he would have the foresight to read it in private, assuming he would have time to himself. Rallis rarely did anything not in a group and this lot looked as if it wasn't about to break any stereotypes today. MJ still looked as if he was the saddest man in the world but at least he seemed to get the general idea. "Sorry MJ. I'm sure this is for the best. We'll maybe see each other after this has blown over, okay?" Tolah said. MJ didn't say anything but wandered back to his siblings who welcomed him to them with metaphorical open arms.

"Okay, so we're kind of going in the same direction." Sharp said.

"You aren't travelling with us. You wouldn't be able to keep up anyway."

"We caught up to you before."

"We were conserving our energy. You won't see us again."

"We can only hope." muttered Sharp.

"What was that?"

"I said we can only lope. It's not the best way of getting about but you know us humans, not exactly sensible." He saw Tolah facepalm on the edge of his vision.

"Right, well we'll just be going then." Nine had his eye on Sharp as if he might be going a little insane and it could be catching. The group shuffled off. MJ kept a lingering eye on the party until they finally disappeared into the gloom at a pace which impressed Sharp. He was hoping they would actually be able to catch up with them after all or it really might be the last time they saw MJ. Sharp wasn't sure how to feel about that, an odd mixture of emotions battled their way in his brain. His group didn't move or speak for a few minutes. Finally, he turned to see what Sterling was looking like. She looked conflicted.

"You had to know he was lying."

"I trusted he wouldn't lie to me! We were meant

to be friends!"

"So you didn't get suspicious when he couldn't read the map he made? When he couldn't fight his way out of a wet paper bag? When he wouldn't give us any details about the plan that would, in fact, hurt a great many people (presumably) because he thought we would kick him out?"

"I thought he might not be telling us the whole truth, maybe exaggerated, but people can't memorise that much map. Maybe he managed to avoid encounters rather than fought them and maybe he really WAS worried we would ditch him! I was trying to get him to trust us enough to tell us what he knew on his own terms!"

"It's nice that you trust people but you can't reject common sense when you do so. People will lie if it protects themselves."

"I don't lie to people."

"We know and we all appreciate that." Tolah cut in. Sharp backed off, he knew he wasn't the right person for this conversation. "But not everyone feels the same way."

"I just wanted to help him." Sterling sounded lost. Sharp had never foreseen her as someone who needed anything from anyone. She could be gullible for sure, but could always deal with the consequences as long as it involved being solved via the edge of a sword. At least that's what he had heard.

"I know Lydia, but I don't think he meant anything bad by it. We should catch up to him and see if he managed to get any information for us and then we can talk about why he lied to us. He must have had a good reason and I don't believe he wanted to hurt us at all." There was a small, polite-sounding cough. They all turned to look at Quickly.

"Erm... I don't think he wanted to hurt anyone either." Quickly said quietly.

"You know something?" Sterling's voice suggested an accusation.

"Oh er, no. I just... think he wanted to be the lie."

"What do you mean?" asked Sharp.

"There are lots of times I don't want to be myself. I think maybe he told us he was who he wanted to be in the hope he would be able to live up to it when he needed to."

"I sincerely hope the dead family wasn't one of the things he wanted to make a reality." Sharp said. Tolah gave him a scathing look.

"He corrected the maps as he went, he was training on the way. I saw him do it on his own a lot while everyone else was sleeping and he was learning about the enemy alongside the rest of us. Perhaps he wanted to tell us the truth later but I think he was planning on becoming the person he had told us he was." His piece said, Quickly fell quiet again. Sharp wasn't sure if Sterling was won over or not but at least she wasn't grinding her teeth any more.

"What did you write in the note Tolah?" Sharp decided to change the subject.

"Oh, that we didn't mean what we said... we DIDN'T mean it right?" They all exchanged looks.

"Well he DID lie to us and I AM mad at him." Sterling said. "I don't think he should go with his family though. He should be allowed to be who he wants. Did you tell him we'd catch up with him?"

"Yes, in three days. Hopefully, he can get us some information in that amount of time. I also said that we were sorry." Tolah added.

"That'll give us time to decide whether to ditch him somewhere then, yeah?" Sharp asked. Sterling gave him a death stare.

"That was a joke yes?" she asked.

"Oh, erm yeah of course. Of course, we won't ditch the guy who lied to us and is actually no help to us whatsoever and talks with his mouth full I mean, COME ON, you can wait until you've swallowed to tell us about how sister number twelve died!!"

"We won't leave him. I just... I just need to talk to him."

"Talking doesn't solve everything you know."

"We need to talk to him to get any information he has anyway. We should just follow them for three days then decide on what to do then." Quickly cut in to stop yet another repeated conversation.

"Yes, Quickly is right, we should do that." Sterling said. "They took off at quite a rate. Do you think we can even keep up that pace for three days?"

"Not many exits to this trench. We can probably just power through without checking to make sure they didn't branch off. We should cut down on sleep as well until we catch up with them." Sharp suggested.

"Wha, wait, we're doing what now?" asked Tolah.

"Oh, hunters can pretty much keep going until we catch our prey. We can go without sleep for a while and only eat what is necessary to keep up our strength. It's a handy way of keeping up with speedy monsters."

"Yeah, well good for you but us normals need to eat and sleep to live. You going to leave us behind as well as MJ?" Tolah sounded frustrated.

"Ugh, you know I'm not going to leave you. Maybe cut me some slack, yes?"

"Yeah, fine, but we still can't keep pace like you two."

"I can probably lose some sleep and my strides are longer than yours." Quickly said.

"Let's just give it a go. The idea isn't to use speed but rely on stamina. We travel while they rest." Sterling said. "We can take turns carrying you if you don't mind." Tolah looked round at them.

"I'm a drag factor again."

"Only in the travelling aspect." Sharp said casually. "We'll be sure to call you when we need something incinerated to a point where we don't need to recognise it any more." He flashed Tolah a grin. She smiled back.

"Want to volunteer?"

"Ask me again after I've had to endure MJ's company for a while again."

"You're fine with him rejoining us then?" Sterling asked.

"You ask as if I have a choice. We all know you aren't going to leave him out here on his own because he'll not last a day and you also aren't going to make him stay with his family seeing as he looked absolutely miserable with them." Sharp replied.

"If we take down Duke then his family has no employer. They could just go back to their home town." Sterling said.

"And then MJ will have to go back to being the person his family wants him to be." Quickly interrupted.

"Helping someone isn't always killing the thing trying to kill them right?" Sterling said. "Okay let's just make tracks and make a decision when we find him. Thanks Quickly. You should talk more often."

Chapter 16

They started to trail the MJs. They paused every time there was an exit to the trench to make sure their targets hadn't left and took a short break to eat when needed, but other than that they just powered through until past sundown. The canyon seemed smaller at night, the lights from Tolah's flickering flames crept up the walls and made everyone's shadows jump around menacingly. As the time went on the light started to die and Sharp turned around to see Tolah almost asleep on her feet, the flame in her hand dying. Sharp stooped and picked up a sturdy looking stick.

"Quickly? Some oil?" Quickly tossed him a wad of oil which he applied to the stick then caught the last of Tolah's dying flame before she couldn't keep it up any more. Quickly caught Tolah as she fell. She didn't wake as she hit his arms and she was already snoring slightly as he swung her onto his back with the assistance of Sterling.

"You okay for a while Quickly?" Sharp asked.

"Hhmm for a bit I think. I was used to being awake at night but then I slept a lot during the day."

"We really haven't saved a great deal of time Sterling. I don't think the others are going to be able to keep up this pace. They're going to be exhausted tomorrow." Sharp said.

"No." Sterling didn't need details to know what he meant. Despite insisting on not leaving Quickly and Tolah behind earlier he had said it more for an easy life than believing it was the sensible thing to do.

"Wow, not even thinking about this one? At least in the past, you PRETENDED to take on what I had to say."

"Fairly sure I never pretended." Sharp cast his

mind back in time.

"Huh, I guess I just imagined having any respect from you, however slight." Sharp gestured to Quickly to take a seat, which he did so gratefully.

"We already split up with MJ. I don't want to break us up even more."

"I'm suggesting this FOR MJ. We don't help anyone if we can't even catch a bunch of short-legged... handymen!"

"Creeping into racism now are we?"

"Sterling, they admitted that they're performing handyman related jobs for him."

"Well, they might be doing other things for him as well!" There was a snore behind them. Quickly and Tolah were now BOTH asleep, leaning back against the uncomfortable looking craggy wall.

"I guess this is where we stop for tonight."

"I can carry Tolah tomorrow." Sterling said.

"Oh, I see where you're going. I'm not carrying Quickly." Sharp replied. Sterling smiled to herself.

"I'm not leaving anyone else behind. We'll just have to go at the pace the other two can keep. If we take turns carrying Tolah, Quickly can walk at his own pace and we can match it. At least he has speed if not the stamina."

"And hope we catch up to them before they leave the canyon?"

"If we miss them we can track them all the way to their destination." Sterling reasoned. Sharp thought about it. It would mean they wouldn't even need to rely on the word of a liar as to where Duke was hiding out (presumably the MJs would be going towards the boss). It would also mean no information on what Duke was actually doing but Sharp was getting really bored of this journey and was willing to just put a sword through the orc's face so he could go find somewhere with a lot of alcohol where he could set up camp for a few weeks.

"Fine." They set up the simplest camp they could, something to soften the floor and a canopy to stop the rain. They coaxed Quickly and Tolah into consciousness enough to make it to the camp and all four fell asleep. The one good thing about walking until you were ready to drop was the instant way you could fall asleep and Sharp was still having trouble with his injuries. He found himself in a dream where he was chasing one after another of his friends who kept running in different directions and he was unable to catch them all.

He woke up without recollection as to which of his dream friends he had chosen to follow and allowed his brain to forget and it faded from his memory.

After an early and quick breakfast, Sterling took the first turn carrying Tolah. She didn't complain and after a time managed to drift off. Quickly dragged his feet but kept up a steady pace. None of them spoke, all energy was directed to their complaining feet and Sharp found himself almost able to doze while walking. He usually liked to pay attention to his surroundings but he had three other people who could share that duty and the trench had shrunk slightly so that only two of them could walk side by side comfortably. He was almost hoping for the thing to end so that he could see wide open spaces again, as convenient as having a hallway to follow was.

This was how the next four days followed. They had missed their deadline but none of them spoke of it to each other. He could tell Sterling still wouldn't break the party, she was stubborn, but if he was honest, he was too tired to have made any more progress on his own anyway. The light was fading on the fourth day when they found the tracks coming from one of the exits to the canyon. Sharp let Tolah down and the two hunters took a moment to check them. They were clearly coming in from the outside rather than leaving and Sharp could recognise the tracks as belonging to more rallis. They joined the tracks of the team they had been following so that now they numbered a great many, Could have been fifteen, could have been fifty, the tracks were too scuffed up to count them accurately. What was evident, however, was that their quarry had slowed down significantly. Spurred on by the discovery, Tolah refused to be carried again and they made their way into the encroaching darkness.

They didn't have to walk far. The light was the first thing they saw. It was creeping from around a bend in the path, which was then followed by the noise of many people talking. Sharp took a quick look around the corner to the large circular area cut out of the trench before darting back.

"How many are we looking at?" Sterling asked him.

"Around twenty." Well, it could have been worse. Sterling pushed him out of the way so she could have a look. As if a second pair of eyes was going to reduce the mass of rallis in front of them.

"See any sign of MJ?" asked Tolah. Sharp took another look.

"Er, they kind of all look the same."

"Your bigotry is showing again." Sterling looked disapprovingly at him.

"Alright. Which one is he then?" Sharp retorted. Sterling took another look.

"Oh erm, obviously he's the one with the..." Sterling trailed off. Quickly took a look.

"I'm fairly certain he's the one crying in the back corner." The others all scrabbled over each other to confirm.

"Oh yeah, that's him. He has the same look that the world is ending that he had when we left him." Sharp conceded.

"We didn't leave him. We're here aren't we?" Sterling sounded insulted.

"Late though. He must think we ditched him."

"Then let's solve that right now!" Sterling struck a heroic looking pose.

"Right, well you take the ten on the left and I'll take the ten on the right." Sharp said dryly. Sterling didn't have anything to say to that one. The prospective fight was not an attractive one. They were all on the verge of collapse and when Sharp thought of the enemy, the word swarm came to mind, which was a word that Sharp had never heard in conjunction with anything good. The group took a moment to think things over but Quickly was looking back and forth between the other members. Finally, the yeti got to his feet and strode around the corner towards the group of MJs (Sharp could only assume they were all from the same family) before anyone could react. The other three leant to get a look, torn between the urge to help and the urge to see what would happen to Quickly without sharing in his demise.

Twenty pairs of eyes followed the giant suddenly in their midst and twenty mouths fell open as Quickly picked his way over to an equally stunned looking MJ.

"Sorry we're late." Quickly said, his head bowed slightly in apology. "Would you like to come back with us?" MJ's head turned to see the three heads poking out from behind the bend in the road. Tolah gave him a wave.

"Yes please." MJ said meekly. One of the rallis broke out of her stunned silence and stumbled to her feet.

"Twenty Seven, you'd leave the best opportunity our family has ever had? You could be part of something great! We could be building things that the world will be talking about for an eternity!" the ralli said.

"Sorry Ten, but I already am part of something great. We'll see how your work stands up to ours when we catch up to Duke." MJ walked away and back towards a relieved looking party. It seemed Sterling had momentarily forgotten she was angry.

"And his name is MJ." Quickly told Ten before following his friend.

"I thought you weren't coming for me." MJ said.

"Your family was too fast." Sterling said.

"I got a lot of information for you!"

"You going to actually tell us this time?" Sharp asked.

"Of course! I actually know stuff this time!" For some reason MJ seemed proud of not lying. Sterling suddenly remembered she was supposed to be pissed off and her expression changed in an instant. Sharp had assumed she had been trying to decide whether to let him back in the team or not but it seemed the decision had been made for her, not that Sharp thought the result would be anything different if she HAD had a choice. Sterling bent down so she was face to face with MJ. He started slightly at the sudden invasion of his personal space.

"You are going to tell us EVERYTHING about yourself and EVERYTHING about what you know."

"Oh, that might take a while? Like I know a lot about tabletop games and sewing and pretty much everything Tolah ever told me, but I suppose you already knew that..." MJ trailed off at her expression.

"You know what I mean. You LIED to us. We're supposed to be on the same side! Didn't you trust us?

And how can we trust YOU now?" It was difficult to see if Sterling was mad or sad.

"Let's not do this here." Sharp saw a couple of faces appear round the bend and pulled Sterling's arm. The group sombrely walked back until they couldn't see the lights from the MJ camp any more. The darkness had almost completely wrapped around them so they stopped to make camp. Proper camp this time. Sharp was happy to see the tents appear again, he was getting really tired of the freezing wind at night.

"Any chance we can talk about this after getting some proper sleep?" Sharp asked, knowing it was probably fruitless.

"No. We have to sort this out now. I can't have one of my team lying to me all the time! I don't even know why! You gained nothing from it and it could have put all of us in danger!"

"What? No, I never told you anything that would get any of us hurt!"

"So you came out here before did you?"

"Well, no."

"So we've been following a made up map then? We could have become lost in the wilderness!"

"Not made up! Whenever a traveller came by I would take maps they had made and combine them into one, then redraw it so it looked professional. The basic landmarks have all been correct, I've just been correcting any inaccuracies and missed features like the mansion we passed. I put an X where the man who gave me his map had written. He was the same person who had written M. I'd have drawn an actual canyon had I known what it was that he meant but he wasn't one to talk for long stretches so I was just focused on getting the base map." MJ held up his copy of the map (Sharp only just realised he had taken the maps with him when he left. In hindsight leaving him to his family could have been very bad as they could easily have missed getting to Stillhaven) the Ms had now been changed into a very clear illustration of the canyon which Sharp could easily use to trace its route. It looked as though they needed to leave it very soon. MJ turned and looked Sterling straight in the eye. "I would NEVER have lied if you could have been hurt from it." he repeated.

"You've never fought before."

"Only in my training area and I'd only been training for a couple of months before you arrived."

"What about the dead family thing? What was the purpose of that?"

"I guess I wanted you to feel sorry for me. There are plenty of other people who could give you maps and know the area far better than I do so I figured I'd play the sympathy angle a bit." He faltered a little at Sterling's unimpressed expression. "I'm not stupid. I know there's nothing special about me so I thought maybe a tragic backstory might at least make me slightly interesting. Yes, I know it was stupid but I was put on the spot a bit."

"And you really knew nothing about our enemy."

"Only what I learnt from my siblings when our family got the job. It was a big project and many families were invited to help out. We would get paid a lot and it was a job we could then use to obtain other work later. I refused to work on the project so my family didn't tell me anything further. It was an insult to refuse such important work."

"So why did you?" stepped in Sharp. This was the question he had been interested in. MJ paused for a moment.

"I didn't want this to be all I was. I'm fifteen now. If I'm lucky I get another fifteen and then that's it. No one remembers number twenty seven and the good, if slightly bog standard, work he did on some ruler's stable or whatever. I don't want to be a number. I want to be remembered as a great hero. Like you guys! Everyone knows you and the good works you've done!"

"Well, you picked up a lot in the few months we've known you I suppose."

"Rallis always pick up new skills quickly. It's why we always get hired for jobs we've never done before." MJ looked anxious. "Am I... fired?"

"Nah. Need your maps." Sharp said. MJ looked crestfallen.

"I think what Sharp means," Sterling narrowed her eyes at him. "Is that we need you in a fight. We can keep training you on the way and after this is done you're welcome to tag along with me as long as you like. Call it an apprenticeship if you want. I'll make you into a hero!" MJ looked as if he had just been told all his birthdays had come at once.

"You really going to let him follow you forever? Because that is what he's going to do." Sharp asked.

"It won't be forever. As soon as he can defend himself he can go off and become a hero in his own right. Or are you scared of the competition?" Sterling nudged him playfully. Sharp was not amused. As if MJ could ever be a threat to his position. However, even he couldn't bring himself to pop his bubble.

"I guess time will tell. I guess it's no skin off my nose if you want a sidekick. You sure do forgive easily though."

"I guess I get why he did it. Not that he's EVER GOING TO LIE TO ME AGAIN."

"Oh, of course not." MJ cowered.

"Speaking of which, I assume you managed to ask some questions about Duke in between your bouts of sobbing in the corner?" Sharp asked.

"I wasn't sobbing in the corner."

"Well sobbing against a wall then."

"ANYWAY." Sterling stopped it before it could go any further.

"Oh right. The job was mostly building armour and weapons. There was also a blueprint for what looked like a giant machine on wheels. It had weapons on it, covered like spines on a hedgehog. Some of the armour was... strange. As if it was built for an animal that walked on all fours, massive too, so the animal had to be strong. I'm thinking for those beasts Augury was talking about. The amount we were to build seems to indicate a large army, I'd say at least two hundred just of the beasts. Then we had a large amount of much lighter armour, perhaps for the mages and a lot of average armour. We had to build fewer weapons than armour. A few big and heavy but I suppose the beasts must come with their own weapons built in." He punched the air as if to accentuate his point. "Fletchins don't need weapons to make magic, right?" He looked at Tolah who shook her head. "So I guess we're outfitting the random extras Duke has managed to obtain."

"How far along are these plans?"

"About halfway done I'd say. Duke seems to have taken on more workers over time but I can't say it sped things up a great deal. Ralli families don't work well together. We don't like the idea that our work alone wasn't enough and that others were needed."

"And your siblings were happy to give you all this information even though you were clearly not happy to be there?"

"Rallis don't turn on each other. Especially not families. The idea that I would leave at all would have been completely shocking to everyone, let alone then give this information away."

"So you're okay with doing that?"

"Well... not completely, but we're doing the right thing! Those weapons aren't built for making people's lives better. They're built for ending them. All my family is seeing is the gold and the recognition, not the result of their work."

"Okay, so big army problem. What about that war machine? See any weaknesses in it? I'm just going to go ahead and assume we're going to have to take it down because that would just be typical." Sharp had learnt a while ago that assuming the worst was usually the best way to not get impaled.

"How would you like to have a look yourself?" MJ asked, leaning forward as if they were in some kind of conspiracy.

"Er, sure?" Sharp said. MJ took a roll of paper and spread it out in front of the group with a flourish. It was a set of blueprints. The man had only gone and stolen it from his family.

"Wha, you STOLE the BLUEPRINTS?!" asked Sterling.

"Ah, there were a few of them. They won't miss one copy." MJ said nonchalantly. They all bent over the design. Even in a sketch, it looked terrifying. Whatever was to pull it was seated inside so it was well protected but the WEIGHT of the thing would be insane as it appeared to be covered in metal. It had spikes and room for spears to be stuck out the side or crossbows, as well as a large plough on the front, more of a tool for destruction of buildings than of people. Sharp could see a place inside for a single occupant as well as whatever was planned for the pushing of the thing.

"I don't suppose it has any weaknesses?" Sharp asked when he'd had his fill of looking at the murder machine.

"Of course not. It was built by rallis." MJ said. He wasn't boasting, he stated it as if it was fact.

"Can you... take it apart?"

"On my OWN? I'd have to get inside it... but no, no I don't think I could do it solo."

"Fantastic." Sharp took a piece of paper and a pencil out of his pocket and started to write.

"What are you writing?" asked Sterling.

"Just a list of all the things that will probably kill me before I get paid."

"What's on it?"

"Death machine is definitely number one. Then we have scary orc prophet, an army that outnumbers us probably a hundred to one, MJ's cooking and Sterling's optimism."

"Great. Nice to know all our concerns are now in black and white." Sterling said. Sharp looked at the list again and considered adding Quickly's name. One look at the man and he changed his mind.

"I don't suppose you happen to have remembered to ask where we should head for our impending doom?"

"Oh yeah, that's... kind of an issue." MJ didn't sound optimistic. Sharp paused with his pencil poised. "He's in Moremist."

"What?! With the monsters?! And the mist?! How does he see anything?!" Tolah asked. She had been quiet for a while, Sharp guessed they had finally reached a topic she was interested in.

"I don't know why the monsters don't attack Duke's people but they don't. I think he uses magic to clear the mist. Again, I'm not too sure, my siblings didn't ask questions, they just did the work they were assigned." MJ didn't seem too bothered but Sharp carefully wrote the 'The bloody mist and its monsters.' on the list.

"Okay so straight into the mist to confront Duke head on, right? That would solve the whole army problem." Sharp asked.

"How would we find him in there? We don't have the luxury of whatever he's using to guide his people." Tolah reasoned.

"Maybe I could smell the path they use?" Quickly asked. "If there's been a lot of footfall I can probably follow the trail."

"We could go back to the rallis and tell them we all want in. We can tell them who Sterling and I are and we know they would take MJ back. Arborious wanted Tolah to join him so she'd be fine and who's going to turn down Quickly? Walk right into their camp and take out the boss. I can't imagine we'd be able to just walk out of there afterwards but we can always retreat into the mist and hope that without Duke the rest of his army can't find their way around. Hopefully Quickly can then lead us back to Stillhaven. We should make sure he gets a good sniff of the brickwork, yes? Not that we should even go there if Augury has his people hiding in the shadows. Not sure he'll be as convinced as the rallis as to our sudden change of heart." Sharp laid out his plan.

"That's a lot of hoping." Tolah said.

"Well, I'm positive that if we go to Stillhaven like we planned and face Arborious' army, we are going to get destroyed. I'll take a maybe over a certainty if it involves my death any day. We were only going there to get answers anyway and now we no longer need that. I can't imagine it can be any other puffed-up prophet with a giant army and mist controlling powers that has suddenly decided to destroy a bunch of towns for no reason."

"We aren't doing that." Sterling suddenly cut in.

"You have a better plan?" Sharp asked.

"We should go to Stillhaven like we planned. MJ isn't going back to his family," MJ looked relieved. "Tolah isn't going to have to lower herself to dealing with her brother and we are not going to lie about what we are and what we're about."

"You going to finally shove that seal in someone's face? Because I'm not sure how much that'll do against people who are serving a god. Slightly higher than a King. Might make the rallis sit up and take notice I suppose, since they're probably the only ones to have not been taken in by the whole messiah thing. They can't fight but it would cripple his defences." This was actually sounding like a better plan.

"We aren't using the seal."

"And your reasoning for that would be?" Sharp was starting to develop a headache.

"It's too underhanded and you think the rallis would be happy at that? We can't command someone to stop being what they are! They'd feel as if they had betrayed their employer, I can't do that to them."

"Sterling, you are LITERALLY killing me."

"We should go to Stillhaven. Talk to Arborious. I'm sure he can be reasoned with, he can't possibly want the destruction of the world."

"You can't be that stupid. Sometimes you need to use underhanded tactics to win a fight, especially if the other side has a butt load of magic, giant beasts and control of mist that contains goodness knows what?"

"If it comes to a fight, I trust in everyone's abilities. We can win any fight now when we work together!" Sterling proudly stated. Sharp looked around. The other three all looked nervously at each other. Sharp was glad they, at least, hadn't gone seemingly insane. Sharp had never been in a situation where he wasn't the boss. He knew that no matter what he said Sterling was going to stick to her guns about this. He was certain she was going to get everyone killed but for some reason, he couldn't bring himself to go home. Perhaps it was the money, perhaps it was the fact he didn't want his friends to die or perhaps he was also too stubborn to give up. Well, guess he was going to have to die then.

"I'm going to bed." Sharp declared. He was still hungry but he had had enough for the day. Maybe the world would be less crazy tomorrow. He turned to his tent and fell asleep before he hit the pillow.

When he woke it was still dark. It seemed as if his empty stomach had roused him so he crawled out of the tent and rummaged around in his bag that he had left outside.

"Sharp?" It was Tolah.

"Yeah?" He sat down. Guess he was going to have his ear talked off now. He craved a single meal where he didn't have to worry about having to think at the same time.

"Are we all going to die?"

"Don't know why you're asking ME that. You seem to have at least a few brain cells and I'm fairly sure that's all you need to see the impending death trap."

"What are we going to do?"

"Why are you asking me? Sterling's the boss."

"Well, you're kind of second in command."

"Great, let's depose her and go with my plan. Going face first into the fog." Sharp found a small slab of meat. He scraped together an impromptu fire and indicated to Tolah to light it. She did so.

"You know how insane that sounds right?"

"There you go then. Both leaders have crazy plans. Feel free to pick your poison."

"No, the deposing Sterling thing. The fog plan I

think might actually work."

"Then you're also mad. Not that I haven't taken crazy gambits before but I only ever had to think about myself. My plan will probably get at least one of us killed."

"Sterling's will get everyone killed."

"She's not going to change her mind. Better pray to whoever you believe in that the end is at least quick."

"Perhaps she'll be willing to retreat when she sees the odds?"

"This is an army. First thing they'll do to a small group they know they can defeat will be to surround it."

"Well then what are we going to do? At least I'm thinking of ways we might live!" Tolah was right. She had actually called him second in command. He realised that was the closest he was going to get to being in charge, so he should embrace that at least. He had the most experience and although, when he wanted the position, he would not have considered his teammates, he now cared about their well-being and was the most qualified to keep them all alive. He supposed it was a good thing he had no power when they first got together, not that he would admit it.

"Alright, let's go over the facts. Sterling is not going to back down from facing Arborious' army. We should assume we can't beat it and that Sterling will at least understand the situation when faced with said army. This is the only time we'll be able to leave, but I'm assuming us to be surrounded by this point."

"Can we cause a distraction?"

"For the whole army? No, we need to cause confusion. Use their numbers against them, find a gap in their line and get as far away as we can. We can then go with either my plan or another that we come up with that might actually let us leave with our lives." He got to his feet and went to Quickly's tent. Here's hoping the man slept in clothes when on his own. He stuck his head in the tent and poked the (mostly clothed) man awake. He beckoned to him to come outside which Quickly did. After a thought, he did the same for MJ's tent and after receiving nothing but snores to his repeated poking, he grabbed him by the ankle and dragged him outside. The fresh air woke him, luckily in silence. Sterling probably wouldn't be happy about meetings behind her back.

"Let me bring you up to speed." Sharp said, retaking his seat and splitting the now cooked meat between the four of them. Quickly listened expectantly. MJ listened grumpily, his fur sticking out in different directions. Sharp quickly summarized what had been said in between bites.

"So my question, Quickly, is, do you have anything that can make smoke, or maybe a flash bang?"

"Bet I can make a flash bang with magic." said Tolah, as Quickly rummaged in his bag.

"How would you do that?" asked MJ. Tolah closed her eyes and snapped her fingers. There was a brief flash of light and suddenly all Sharp could see was white, then different colours pulsing in his vision. There was a yelp from MJ and a grunt from Quickly. He couldn't hear Sterling wake up, but who could tell?

"Great, thanks." Sharp said.

"Just making a point! I can help!"

"Right, well before we went blind did you find anything that could help us Quickly?"

"Er yes, I have some pollen bombs. I assume you want the non-poison ones?"

"Yes, I would ideally not like to die by our own hand." Sharp's vision began to fade back in, bright spots still hanging around his eyes. He took the proffered bomb. It looked like the head of a flower (it probably was) and felt delicate enough to fall apart if he squeezed too hard. He decided not to test it. "How many of these do you have?"

"Four."

"Convenient."

"I foresaw our need."

"Feel free to offer your ideas earlier than the last minute man."

"Oh, okay. Sorry." Sharp stashed the bomb in his coat. Quickly handed out two more and kept the last for himself.

"Should we give one to Sterling?" asked Tolah tentatively.

"She wouldn't take one and she'd be bummed out that we didn't trust her 'plan'. She might even guilt trip certain people to not taking one." Sharp replied. MJ was the only one still holding his bomb. He held it out to Sharp.

"I'm not taking one."

"Feeling suicidal are we?"

"I can't lie to Sterling again."

"What about the rest of us?" Sharp took the bomb and placed it with his first.

"I won't say anything about the rest of you. Not taking one is to stop me screwing over a friend again. If I grass the rest of you up then that's doing the same to you guys."

"What is it with the people I hang out with and picking morals over their own lives?"

"I think he's doing the right thing." Tolah said. "But I do agree with you that dying for it isn't going to do anyone any good." Quickly said nothing but looked suitably regretful. There wasn't really anything else that needed saying so they ate their midnight meal in silence before returning to their own tents.

Chapter 17

Stillhaven was only two days away. By powering through the trench they had managed to save some time but they still took the first exit they could. Sharp was glad. He had started to have recurring dreams about walls closing in on him and he never liked areas where he couldn't fight freely if the situation called for it. MJ found them a path that went parallel to the main road and, with the exception of overgrown grass they had to wade through, had no trouble. The small pollen bomb felt heavy in his pocket although Sharp knew it weighed little. Indeed he was more concerned about crushing it and choking himself on the ensuing cloud. He didn't know why he or the others were as concerned as they obviously were, it may have been underhanded to a teammate but it WAS to secure five lives. A small lie that hurt no one and a lack of trust in the person you were following seemed small by comparison.

Stillhaven wasn't what he had been expecting. It was just a generic looking village with an overly romantic name but he had been expecting smouldering houses, bodies lying where they had fallen. Instead, he saw clear signs of recent building work, even a number of complete houses. The workers had done a good job of preparing the place for the winter. Any farmland that had been around was now looking more like wasteland but that could have easily been due to the weather, which had become almost freezing, rain was becoming like sleet, the wind chilling. The place didn't look crowded by any standards but those people that they could see were busy, men and women were working on the houses, children playing with animals in the streets and getting underfoot. It seemed like a mostly elven place but Sharp could see a few other species as well as the signs of half breeds in some of the elves (a mixed species with elf blood was always referred to as an elf). There were obvious signs of the battle that had taken place, broken buildings were still half standing and as the party made their way through the town people noticeably shied away from Quickly and Tolah and Sharp saw some of the children had even hidden from the hunters. As he looked around he could see a makeshift graveyard placed slightly out of town, the number of gravestones far exceeded the number of living bodies he could see around the place.

"I thought no one would be here." said Sterling. She sounded concerned. This was the meeting place of Augury's army. No way could a battle be held here. The fletchin could not have had any idea that the surviving villagers had returned to their home and started to rebuild or why would he have suggested it? Sharp had a feeling he knew the answer to that one but his brain refused to dwell on it. The village clearly had a lot of work put into it, work that would have taken a long time and wouldn't have been hidden.

"I guess people out here are hardier than closer to Golden. It's just a day's travel to the Mistline after all." Sharp couldn't help but be curious. If he lived through the next few days he would like to at least see it. The Mistline was supposedly a hanging wall of mist you could put your hand through. It would stir in the air like other mist but would settle back to being a wall after a small amount of time. Truly an anomaly that only a god or suitably powered being could understand. Sharp despised being a tourist, he only went somewhere to do a job, but this was a situation he would make an exception for. Perhaps he could excuse it as a professional excursion. There was no sign of anywhere to stay for the night but as they had expected a bunch of rubble this was already taken into consideration. There was also no sign of Augury's army. They paused in the town centre. Centre indeed, Sharp could see all the edges of town from where they stood. At the sound of a small commotion behind them they turned to see a group of four elves coming towards them looking, well, nervous was an understatement. The rest of Stillhaven were watching from safe vantage points.

"May I ask what you are visiting our fine town for today?" One of the elves asked. His body and ears were a lot shorter than a full blood elf. Must have had some dwarf in there, Sharp thought. Despite his short stature though, the other elves were clearly looking to him to do the talking.

"You'd be the mayor of Stillhaven?" Sharp ventured.

"Yes, that's me." The mayor answered.

"We were sent by King Torrell to investigate the attacks on the towns near Moremist." Sterling told him. "I don't suppose you have any information you can offer?" The mayor looked to Sterling's companions.

"These two as well?" He nodded to Quickly and Tolah.

"Well, technically I was the only one sent. I picked up my companions on the way."

"Perhaps you should be more wary of the people you associate yourself with." The mayor said bluntly. The group all looked at Sharp.

"Fairly sure he isn't referring to me."

"My companions are loyal and also none of your concern." A moment of irritation from Sterling. Sharp cleared his throat.

"Can you tell us anything about what attacked you?" he redirected the conversation. The mayor turned and pointed at Quickly.

"Quickly wasn't here." said Sterling.

"He means other yeti. Right?" Sharp asked the mayor.

"Yes. A great horde of them. Bigger than your friend here admittedly but no doubt the same species. They walked on their knuckles, ten feet tall, grey shaggy hair, giant teeth that ripped people apart!" The mayor's voice got louder and more dramatic as he went on, standing on his tiptoes to make himself look more imposing. Even doing so he didn't reach the height of his three retainers.

"Sounds like the pictures I've seen in the books I read." Sharp said. "The way the yeti used to be before they disappeared all that time ago."

"Oh, I think I saw something similar." Sterling said. "But that was ages ago. The yeti aren't like that now!" Sharp looked around.

"It would explain the destruction of the town and Duke apparently having beasts at his command. The fact that we heard the word beast and not the actual name of the species suggests that it was a creature no one knew of. I think it highly probable that the mayor is telling the truth. His people saw this first hand and they have no reason to lie."

"But..." Sterling faltered. She turned to Quickly. He was looking crestfallen.

"This isn't an issue. They aren't the same species any more. They clearly look and act differently. Let's call the beast ones... proto-yeti." Sharp added. He took his death list out and wrote 'proto-yeti' under Sterling's name. Quickly was looking unhappily at his fists. Sharp patted him sympathetically on the arm and he got a weak smile in response.

"We were expecting a fletchin here. He said he

would meet us." Sterling said to bring them back on track.

"The only fletchin we've seen in the last few months has been that one." The mayor pointed to Tolah.

"That doesn't make any sense." Sterling mused.

"Plan B then yes? Let's go into the mist." Sharp felt a weight lift off his shoulders.

"No. If they come to Stillhaven then the people might be in danger again."

"If they come to Stillhaven then the people will be in even more danger if we happen to also be here. Augury threatened to fight us, remember?"

"Duke's army destroyed this town before without us. At least if we ARE here we can help to protect everyone." There was just no arguing with Sterling. Sharp felt the pollen bomb in his pocket. It wouldn't do any good if a whole town needed evacuating and Sharp wasn't so cold-hearted as to abandon them all. That and Sterling would probably murder him of course. The mayor's head had been moving back and forth between the two hunters as they spoke.

"Is Stillhaven in trouble again?"

"No, don't worry. We'll handle it." said Sterling.

"You don't think they deserve a heads up? They can evacuate."

"Where to Sharp?" Sterling asked. She had a point. They were in the middle of nowhere with the next closest village a week away. When the first attack happened they probably had nowhere to go and so that was why they returned here. Building on the ruins of your previous town was at least slightly faster than building from scratch. Depressing though. Without a reply to give he said nothing. "Is there anything we can do to help you rebuild?" Sterling turned to the mayor.

"We'd really feel better if you just left." the

mayor replied.

"Oh right, okay." A dejected Sterling led their retreat, villagers emerging from the houses behind them as they went.

They watched the town for two days. Sterling didn't move from the spot she had chosen, eating what they handed her. Sharp was tempted to hand her something inedible to see what would happen but now was probably not the time. If she slept he didn't know about it, she was awake when he turned in and she was awake when he woke the next day. Conversation levels were low, which would have been good had it not been for the tension and the rain in the air (Tolah had rigged up an umbrella for Sterling). Sharp was getting restless and he spent his time pacing, grinding his feet in the dirt as he went, trying to drown out the noise of Sterling flipping the seal.

It was starting to get dark when they saw the flames. They appeared suddenly and shot straight up. Not a natural fire indeed. The five jumped to their feet and, abandoning their gear, they sprinted to Stillhaven. Arborious was there. There were other fletchins there as well but he managed to stand out, probably due to an extremely sparkly coat he had found from somewhere, the fire's light reflected in it. It was probably not a tactical choice but was distracting. He had more troops in town than there were inhabitants left still alive. A mixture of other fletchins, some humans, elves, dwarfs (a few of these Sharp knew to be hunters) and at least five proto-yeti. He could see why they had been referred to as beasts by everyone who had seen them. He wasn't sure how anyone could think Quickly had anything to do with them, the two breeds were clearly different. The proto-yeti were bent forward, they walked on their knuckles and their fur was dull grey/brown. They had large teeth and Sharp could see the canines were oversized, even more than a wolf's. Their eyes were dull but attentive, Sharp could see them looking to Arborious, presumably for commands. Sharp wasn't sure how intelligent they were, were they with him for their own reasons or were they acting like a dog to its master?

The town was on fire. Sharp could see the townspeople desperately trying to decide whether to put out the flames or defend themselves from the invaders. He could see the mayor gripped in the hand of one of the proto-yeti and was struggling for breath and for release but the proto-yeti wasn't having any trouble preventing both. There were a few bodies lying on the street in front of Augury's army. The survivors weren't stupid enough to try to retrieve them, they were doing their best to get out of the way but in such a small and half-built town they had limited options with the large occupying force in attendance.

"Thought that might get your attention." Arborious said smugly to the group when he saw them.

"What are you thinking of man! Don't you think you've hurt these people enough?!" Sterling was livid.

"Well, you'd think, but the people out here are like cockroaches. Hard to kill and if you don't wipe them out they'll just keep coming back."

"That's terrible! What could they possibly have done to you to deserve this?"

"Everything I do is for Duke. Stillhaven was just unlucky, like the other towns we've hit. A road test if you will, to see how effective Duke's army is in wiping out a town. I think you'll agree they're splendid at it!"

"What happened to you? I know you were never sympathetic to other people, especially those you considered lower than you, but to do this?" Tolah asked gesturing to the burning village.

"I'm guided by a higher force now, sister. Higher even than the King! The heavens have seen fit to send us a messenger! The gods themselves are my commanders and I will be rewarded as I'm due when my job is done!" Arborious swelled with pride.

"Yeah this is definitely a cult." Sharp said.

"What?" Arborious was thrown off for a moment. "It's not a cult! The gods themselves predicted this! We're just fulfilling the ancient religious texts' teachings!"

"Your gods didn't help you arrive before us though did they?"

"You're kidding, right? Of course you got here first! You left before I did and you walk as part of your job, I clearly do not!" Sharp couldn't argue with any of that.

"Yeah, well, you're still in a cult." he muttered.

"And you're about to die." Again, Sharp couldn't really disagree. Arborious turned to his troops. "Kill them. Townspeople as well, I don't want these bugs coming back this time, Duke needs to know we can actually get the job done with no loose ends before we take this show on the road."

"You're going to hit towns further in?!" Sterling cried. She seemed as if she didn't notice the beasts walking closer.

"Oh, I wouldn't worry. You won't be around to see it." Arborious's hands flickered with lightning and Sharp pulled Sterling back in time to stop her getting her brains fried. Arborious disappeared behind two hulking proto-yeti. A fist swinging down was deflected by Sterling's shield but Sharp could see a slight dent in the metal, and Sterling reeled from the hit. This wasn't going to go well. He turned in time to see another proto-yeti in his face and suddenly he had his own problems. He ducked under its heavy-handed swing and stabbed up and under its armpit. It roared in pain but he had no time to finish the job as a root snaked out towards him like an arrow. An arrow with sharp barbs on it. Sharp ducked and weaved past the other attackers who were coming for him and completely lost sight of the fletchin who had tried to spear him with the root as well as his own companions. It was a chaotic fight and he found their attackers had multiplied somewhat, no doubt they had formed the circle to cut off their retreat but had closed in when they hadn't attempted to flee (not as though they could). He found himself on the defence almost all the time as many attacks came towards him. He barely had enough time to judge how to respond as his vision was filled with magic, fists, teeth and swords. The army was clearly unused to fighting together and he was able to take a few down simply by kicking one into another or by moving out of the way in the nick of time. A scream hit his ears even over the battle and it brought his attention back to the field they were fighting in. He tried to weave his way towards the screamer but was blocked by a dwarf flailing a mace at him. He dodged as best he could but took a weakened version of the attack in the side of the face. The vision in one eye went black but with lights flashing different colours, disorientating him. He prayed that his eye hadn't been destroyed and pushed the next blow out of the way with a sword and plunged the other deep into the dwarf's neck. The dwarf fell with a choke but was instantly replaced by another attacker in the form of a proto-yeti, roaring and swinging its fists at him. He could see no intelligence in its eyes. Quickly had no reason to compare himself to these beasts, they had clearly let their minds fail. Sharp had to abandon any ideas of saving the screamer as he scrambled out of the way of the beast, only to be faced with two fletchins baring down on him. He had no time to breathe. They were never going to win this, he saw no end to the enemy. The fletchins' hands flashed colours Sharp had no time to associate with an element so he lowered his shoulder and bull-rushed them both, knocking the air out of one and kicking the other into the path of the charging proto-yeti still on his tail. He didn't look but heard a yelp from that direction. Did he hear the crunching of bones over the deafening noise of the fray? He slammed the fletchin he had a hold of to the ground, knocking the wind out of her. He raised a sword to finish the job but stopped to dodge a pair of humans charging him with their weapons (an axe and a sword). This was ridiculous. He couldn't even finish the people he knocked down and his muscles were aching already, he was bleeding from various wounds, most of which he couldn't remember getting, and the side of his face was throbbing in time with his heartbeat. He looked around in the hope he could spot even one of his friends, he had no clue if they were even still alive. He turned in time to block a swing from the axe aiming towards his neck and raised his left sword to strike the user in turn but a flare of pain indicated the sword wielder had taken a swing at him and hit her mark. Sharp's hand gushed with blood and he hoped his adrenaline would make the wound bearable for a time, He found his grip on the sword to be weaker but he didn't drop it. He slammed the butt of the sword into his second attacker's face and was rewarded with a shower of blood from her nose. He kicked the legs from under the axe wielder and while still holding off the axe itself with his right sword swung the left round to take off the man's head. A scream from the sword user alerted him she had taken the man's death badly but he put her out of her misery quickly with an easy parry and a sword through the neck. He picked a random direction and dodged and weaved, looking for any of his friends. He stumbled over the debris of the work that had been done, a half made brick wall and more than a few bodies. Sharp was ashamed to admit it but he was relieved to see he recognised no one. The only body he could be sure he recognised was that of the mayor, his bright coloured coat was now covered in his own blood, his body abandoned by the wayside as if it was nothing. A cloud of pollen suddenly shot out of the crowd and he made his way towards it. He took down a few assailants as he went, taking advantage of the easy kills. He had abandoned the shame of an unfair fight a long time past. The pollen bomb user was Tolah. Her clothes were covered in dirt and blood and her eyes were wild. Sharp could see tears but they could have been from pure frustration as he saw her set alight a proto-yeti that roared and flailed around, setting fire to a number of its allies as it went. The pollen had cleared already. Sharp had hoped it would stay longer but the wind from thrashing weapons and limbs had probably sped up the process. She turned in his direction and a bolt of lightning shot out. He braced for impact but it arced over his shoulder and took down a charging human, electrifying his metal armour. Sharp could smell burning flesh as the man screamed in agony.

"Thought you were going to zap me there!" Sharp yelled over the noise as he parried a blow that had come from his blind side, his instinct taking over.

"No way! I'd recognise that ugly coat anywhere!" Pleiss would have gotten him killed with his perfect fashion sense. This made him feel good at least.

The two friends fell silent as they focused on repelling the attacks coming their way, at least they could now cover each other's backs and though they were still not winning by a long shot, he had time to plan attacks slightly rather than rely on his skill alone.

"We need to find the others!" Sharp finally managed to get out as he ran through an elf Tolah had tripped with a root.

"How?!" Tolah said breathlessly. She didn't have the years of fighting experience that Sharp had and if HE was tired, she must have been holding together through sheer will.

"There are no rallis here other than ours! We make our move and look low for MJ!" He pulled her out of the way of a strike and they set off running, Tolah stumbling from exhaustion and probably the wound she had sustained all that time ago. No time for guilt right now though. He pulled her along as they went, scanning the ground for any short fighter and aiming towards collections of the enemy focused on a single opponent. Other than Stillhaven's residents, the five of them were the only targets. The pair dodged and deflected as they went, taking down a couple of dwarfs that confused their ralli search on the way. Eventually, they saw a combination of both short and hairy and saw MJ, clothes and fur matted with blood. Sharp could see he was missing an ear. He wasn't doing a great deal of damage but seemed to have hit his stride with a hit and run tactic and his opponents were having a hard time making contact. The ralli darted towards Sharp and he felt a stab of pride as he was only just able to block the strike. It was weak but he had aimed for his face. He was trying to blind his opponents, a tactic Sharp had been trying to teach him. MJ saw whom he had almost blinded and stumbled backward, Tolah saving him by shooting ice towards a proto-yeti who had tried to take advantage of the tiny blur slowing for a moment. MJ recovered quickly and now they were three. It was a miracle they had found each other but it was easier to keep alive even though he now had to watch out for three people, having them watch out for him gave him more confidence than he had felt on his own, even when he hadn't been in an all-out death match.

"Who next?" shouted Tolah. That was the question, wasn't it? Quickly looked FAR too similar to most of their opponents and Sterling looked even more so.

"Time for your party trick I think!" Sharp yelled in reply. She looked confused for a second but then realisation dawned on her face. She nodded. Light danced on her fingers and MJ and Sharp both shut their eyes, praying that this wouldn't get them killed. Death didn't come in the next three seconds so Sharp risked opening his good eye.

"Come on Sharp!" Tolah grabbed him by his arm. Sharp looked around. He sprinted towards the nearest proto-yeti and with an annoyed grunt and a wild swinging of its arms, Sharp managed to climb to its head. He scanned the area quickly and located a circle of proto-yeti surrounding a single smaller yeti roughly 50 metres away.

"That way!" He shouted, and keeping Quickly in sight, jumped to the next proto-yeti's head. The other two scrambled to keep up as he kept the high ground so he wouldn't lose sight of his friend. It didn't take long to lose the opponents that had been blinded and he found a giant hand reach out and grab his leg, hauling him down and face first into the paved path below. His head reeling, he saw MJ jump at an unseen enemy and Tolah used all her strength to pull him to his feet. Stumbling, he struggled to remember the direction he had been running in and imitated MJ's tactic by slashing and moving in an unpredictable pattern, making sure his two friends were following him. He must have got himself turned around at some point as Quickly wasn't at the point he had thought and the other two showed equally confused expressions in between dodging strikes. Both were flagging badly in the extended battle and Sharp had to confess to not being much better, a disturbing ringing had started in the ear on the side of his face that had been bashed earlier.

"QUICKLY!!!" He yelled in exasperation. He could barely hear himself over the crowd, a roaring in the distance could have been in reply or it could have been from any member of the species. Sharp hoped Quickly had kept himself together, he couldn't have him running amok here. Suddenly another cloud of pollen arose but instead of having to go to him, Sharp saw Quickly charging through the fog towards them. He dived out of the way to see the yeti collide with a fletchin who had decided to take his chances and got his chest crushed instead. Quickly turned to them and Sharp braced himself but Quickly's expression wasn't one of anger. He was distressed. Sharp gestured for them to follow him. He led them back into the section of the town which contained the newly built houses and managed to locate one with the door wide open, all the while fending off attacks. They all rushed inside and he slammed the door in the face of a proto-yeti that was trying to follow. The noise of the fight was muffled slightly through the wall but now four of five targets were in one place, Arborious's army had set its sights almost entirely on them. Quickly leaned against the door.

"Why did we come back into the inhabited part of town?!" Tolah asked.

"Because we needed to regroup and also there IS no inhabited part of town now." Sharp replied through gritted teeth. Tolah couldn't argue with that. They must all have seen the bodies of the villagers.

"We didn't do anything to save them, did we?"

"We can't even save ourselves. Every time we take one down it's replaced by like ten more!!" MJ was freaking out. Sharp looked at his friends, they were all on their last legs. Quickly looked as if he was out of fight, Tolah had been casting magic almost constantly for the entire battle and MJ was the least used to fighting. Sharp could see his bubble had been well and truly burst. As for himself, everything hurt. He had no idea how much of the blood on him was from him or from his enemies and his adrenaline rush was really starting to dip now.

"We need to leave. This was never a fight we were going to win and the fact we're all still alive right now is nothing short of a miracle." said Sharp.

"We can't leave! Sterling is still out there!!" Tolah was indignant. The sensible thing to do was to start running and not stop. Well, the sensible thing to do was to not come here in the first place but that was totally on Sterling. The other three were looking at him expectantly. Great, he got to be in charge at the worst possible time. He already knew what he had to do. He had to do what was best for the team but that meant leaving Sterling behind. There was no way the rest of them could fight any longer. He took out his pollen bomb that had somehow not got crushed in the fight. He handed it to Tolah.

"You're in charge Tolah. Take the other two out the back and run. Use the bomb to cover your tracks and if you have any energy left, don't forget to use your flash spell. Don't attempt to stop and fight but run back to the trench. DON'T GO INTO IT but go into the forest on the side. Keep walking until you can't walk any more."

"Okay, I really don't see us making it that far but

more importantly, what are you going to be doing." It should have been a question but Sharp didn't hear the question mark.

"I'm just going to go get Sterling. We'll catch up with you later."

"You want us to leave you." Quickly stated.

"I'm in charge. I'm telling you what to do. So do it." Sharp tried to sound more confident than he felt. There was an eerie silence as the proto-yeti had stopped banging on the door (people this close to the mist really knew how to reinforce their doors). A second later there was a loud smashing noise and the beast's fist punched right through the wall itself, inches away from Quickly's head (apparently they needed to work on reinforcing their walls). "Okay, no more questions! Go!" Sharp pushed his two smaller friends out of the room and as they started running Quickly took off after them with one last reluctant look towards Sharp. The arm that had appeared in the wall became a head and the upper half of a torso as the proto-yeti struggled to force itself into the room. Sharp couldn't pity the thing, it was clearly a monster despite its similar appearance to his best friend. He dispatched it easily with a blow to the head then sought another way out of the house. He picked up a chair and lobbed it through a window at the side of the house and hurdled the window frame, ending up in an alley. As one, he saw the eyes of all those surrounding him turn in his direction. He backed up and felt his back graze against something. It was a ladder. He scaled it as fast as he could, imagining his pursuers breathing down his neck. As he reached the roof he yanked the ladder up with him, shaking off a dwarf who had managed to reach the bottom rung as Sharp had reached the top. Below him he could see a sea of heads, all craning up to see him, shaking fists and various implements with the idea to disembowel him. He dodged a couple of magic spells lobbed in his general direction, stomping out a couple of fire spells that had found their purchase in the thatch.

At a second look, he saw not all attention was on him. He could see a clear circle had formed a fair distance away from himself, a space large enough for the two combatants in the middle of it. It seemed Arborious wanted the kill all to himself as his army was taking pokes at Sterling if she moved too close to the edge of the circle but nothing more. Tolah had trained herself mostly in the field but Arborious had clearly been trained at least partly at home, the duel seemed to be fairly equal from what Sharp could make out from this distance. Sterling appeared to be limping slightly, her shield was damaged to the point that it was at a severe enough angle that he could see it even from his vantage point. Arborious was steady but moving slowly. Sharp imagined a fight that had lasted the time that it had must have been taking its toll on the out of shape man. At that moment, the fletchins surrounding Sharp's safe house seemed to agree that fire was the way to go and he found himself shifting back from a hail of flames. The thatch reacted in the way he had expected. There was no point in trying to put out this amount of fire so instead he struck down with his sword and carved a chunk of the burning thatch loose, shoving it down into the crowd below. He heard a collective scream and without waiting to see if the way was clear, he jumped down, hoping he wouldn't sprain anything from the drop. He stumbled as he hit the ground but without waiting to feel any damage he took off and broke through the line, imitating MJ's technique again as he darted and wove as much as he dared while making his way towards Sterling's fight. The race seemed to take hours to him and his journey wasn't a graceful one as he fell, was jostled and scrambled under attacks thrown in his direction. He was there before he had realised, bursting through the fight circle into the wide open space. The spectators prodded spears into his back and he found himself propelled forwards. He looked up at the two battlers. They hadn't turned to face him, they were so intent on their fight. Both of them had muddy, bloody and torn clothing. As well as the bent shield, Sterling also had a chunk out of her sword and was leaving bloody prints from one foot. Arborious had a number of small slashes oozing red but nothing life-threatening it seemed (Sharp was sure if he felt in danger he would have released his army to help) and an angry bruise blossomed over his face. Sharp raised his swords to help but found himself being yanked backward as a proto-yeti grabbed his arms to stop him from joining in. Pain shot down his left arm and he dropped his sword with a yelp. The other sword was grabbed by another giant, hairy hand and he saw it thrown away from him.

"STERLING! FINISH HIM! WE'RE LEAVING!" he shouted as loud as he could. Whether Sterling COULD finish it was yet to be seen but a little faith couldn't hurt, right? She gave no sign she had heard him but she launched herself towards Arborious in a reckless manner. He flinched and apparently she had been fighting conservatively up until this point. In his panic, he formed an ice spell on his right hand and reached towards her as she reached him. From Sharp's vantage point, he had a clear view. He saw Sterling's sword run the man through, he had been cocky enough to have turned up with no armour apparently and the blade cut straight through his heart. At the same time, his hand touched Sterling's face and Sharp saw the spell EXPLODE, shards of ice sliced through skin and he heard Sterling screech in pain as blood went flying. Sterling lost her grip on her weapons and they crashed to the ground as she held her head in her hands, blood flowing through her fingers. There was a gasp from the audience and Sharp took the moment to slam his foot onto the foot of his captor who loosened his grip enough for Sharp to get free. He raced forwards and caught Sterling as she stumbled, blind and weak. The crowd broke free of their stupor and went to attack them. He cursed himself for giving away his pollen bomb - Tolah would have been fine with her flash spell! His brain kicked him and he remembered. He had MJ's bomb! He rummaged in his coat and found it. It could have been a precious gem and he wouldn't have felt happier to have it in his hand. He slammed it to the ground and immediately his vision was blocked out. Sharp hoisted Sterling over a shoulder and grabbed her discarded shield with his other hand. He whispered a prayer, picked a direction and ran. He tried his best to avoid or block but mostly he just charged and hoped for the best, every second expecting a strike that would cut him down. Instead, he found the density of the enemy reducing until finally there was no one in front of him. He didn't stop or look at which direction he was running in but instead focused on stopping his legs from giving up.

    A few splatters of rain hit him in the face before picking up and he felt a deluge of freezing rain drench him almost immediately. He stopped finally and turned. He couldn't see the town anymore. It could have been because it was out of sight due to distance or it could have been the sheet of rain but he could at least use it to mask his movements. He immediately started to walk to the side to throw off anyone who had been directly behind him while desperately trying to remember MJ's map and the landmarks on it. He let Sterling down. Somewhere along the way she had passed out but when that was he couldn't have said. He took off his coat and shivered as he wrapped it tightly around Sterling's head, making sure she could still breathe through it. He could still feel her breath but it was weak. He was going to need Quickly and even then she had lost a great deal of blood and Sharp had no idea if she would live. Tolah had survived after losing more blood than Sterling. He had to hope for the best. He dropped the shield so he could carry Sterling better, the thing was useless anyway. Sharp lifted her back up and skirted around the town as best as he could see. Luckily he hadn't run in the opposite direction as he started recognising landmarks they had passed on the way to Stillhaven. He pointed himself in the direction of the trench and started walking as fast as he could. A run would have been far too much at this point and he knew it would take at least a day to get to the trench. He should have picked a point they could have actually got to but there was nowhere they could have hidden that was closer and that they knew about. He also didn't think he would be carrying someone bleeding out at the time.

    He was walking against the rain (of course) and so found himself having to close his eyes as he went (well eye, one side of his face was still swollen) and so he didn't see the rock in his way. He tripped, somehow managing to turn as he did so so that Sterling wouldn't crash to the ground. He found himself with the rock under his back and annoyed, he went to pull it out so he could throw the thing as far as his aching arm could manage. It wasn't a rock. It was Quickly's bag! He cast his gaze about and saw he had stumbled into their camp. He rummaged around in the bag and found a herb. He had to mash it and combine it with water (most of it ended up as rainwater if he was honest) but he managed to get Sterling to drink it. He helped himself to one which eased the pain and allowed himself a moment to breathe. He examined his left hand which had been feeling worse as he went and realised he had lost the middle finger. Damn. That was his favourite finger! He used it all the time! At least he hadn't lost any more of them and judging by the cuts on those left it had been close. Hopefully, the finger was flipping someone off on the battlefield. Okay, time to make a move. He slung Quickly's bag over his shoulder, a blanket, a handful of food and with a wistful look at the rest of their gear, decided he wouldn't be able to take the weight. Sterling's breathing seemed more even but he didn't want to risk removing the coat which was a shame because he was now soaked to the bone and absolutely freezing. Time to work up a sweat or as close to one as he could get in this weather. He certainly didn't want to stay this close to Stillhaven. He picked Sterling back up and started the long trudge back to the trench.

    He didn't know how long or far he had walked when it grew darker. The rain hadn't let up and he was finding it hard to see his own feet, let alone keep his direction. A lone tree was his shelter for that night, a pathetic looking thing with no leaves that served to block out only a portion of the wind. Sharp ate part of his rations and after feeding Sterling another healing herb, he wrapped them both up in the blanket and allowed himself to fall less into sleep and more into unconsciousness.

Chapter 18

Well, they were both still alive the next day. Sharp had to consider that a win as it was the closest he'd had to one in a while. To his relief, he found he could see out of both eyes again. He had been worried he had lost the left one but now his concern was the ear on that same side. The ringing had stopped but now any sounds he could hear were muted and all he could do was hope it would clear up as he went.

He really didn't want to get up. It was as warm as he was going to get. He knew he would have to force himself to carry on walking and at this point he was willing to give up walking forever. The rain had stopped, so as soon as he was able to pick himself and Sterling up, he set off again. His vision clearer, he was able to correct his heading. There was nothing of note on the journey, just a slow trudge through a muddy landscape which Sterling slept through. Maybe he should make her carry HIM for two days straight after this. Nothing seemed to be pursuing them. Perhaps their enemy had been thrown into confusion by the death of their leader, perhaps by the rain but Sharp made it to the forest on the side of the trench without being challenged. He could see evidence of the other three in the way of broken foliage so he followed it to a makeshift camp which had been cobbled together out of whatever could be found nearby. All three were there and at their arrival, Tolah didn't move but simply broke down in tears. Quickly came forward and took Sterling gently from him. The yeti unwrapped the coat from her face but Sharp couldn't see the extent of the damage through the dried blood. Quickly and Tolah fussed over Sterling so Sharp turned his attention to MJ. He looked even smaller than usual, his fur was soaked through and the missing ear didn't look as if it was healing well. Sharp handed a healing herb to him which he took very eagerly and then tried to look nonchalant about it.

"You did a good job." Sharp told him. It was the first time Sharp had ever seen him look unconvinced by something Sharp had said to him.

"I don't think I killed anyone. And I lost an ear."

"You were facing an entire army or at least a fifth of one, and you didn't die. You fought in the way you were trained and didn't forget it all when you were actually in a fight. Keeping a cool head can be hard. Also, battle wounds add credence to your claims of being a badass."

"But we failed."

"I fail all the time. Best way to learn as long as it doesn't kill you and last I looked all of us are alive."

"For now." MJ looked towards Sterling.

"She's less damaged than Tolah was and this is what she does for a living." Sharp decided not to tell him about his fears about her eyesight.

"I just wish I could help somehow."

"Just... let me rest for a few hours. Then we can go hunting, yes? Looks as if we all only just got here. A meal will make it better."

Sharp was right and a few hours later they were sitting around a moderate fire (they were trying to stay undercover after all) eating a deer that had been foolish enough to wander into their sights. Quickly had managed to get the bloodstains out of Sharp's coat and he huddled back into it gratefully. The meal was eaten in silence and afterwards they all looked at him expectantly.

"How's Sterling doing?" he asked.

"She's still sleeping but she seems to be okay." Tolah replied.

"Well, we should all be doing that. Let's turn in as well. Tomorrow we're going to grab some supplies so we can settle here for a while. We need to regroup." He had no complaints from the others. They were all probably as exhausted as he was and to have someone willing to call the shots must have been a relief. They must have only just reached this area a few hours before he had.

The next day it was still raining. Sharp was glad for the cover if he was honest.

"Tolah I'm leaving you here to look after Sterling. Quickly and MJ, you're coming with me."

"What are you going to do?" Tolah asked.

"Taking a stroll. Probably be around four days." He replied. Tolah said nothing else. She knew exactly what lay two days away from there. He made sure to leave the rest of the deer for her and they started the long walk back to Stillhaven. He guided them towards their camp and, leaving Quickly to pack up their supplies, he took MJ to spy on Stillhaven. It was deserted. Not a single one of Arborious's troops had stayed, their job done and their leader dead, they had left. Sharp took a guess as to where Sterling's fight had taken place and made his way there while trying not to look at the bodies surrounding him as a depressingly small number of them belonged to the enemy army. Arborious's body was where they had left it. An honoured leader indeed, they hadn't even bothered to collect his corpse. He didn't know what he had been expecting but he felt an emptiness inside. MJ had been following him in silence. Time to do what he had come for.

"Find some new claws." he told him. MJ didn't look happy about having to search bodies but did as he was told. Sharp had been concerned that they hadn't killed enough to have left weapons they could use but swords were fairly standard fare so he found three quality looking ones without much trouble. Seems the rallis that Duke had hired were doing a good job, at least in the armaments department. He found a shield that would fit Sterling after a short while longer and although he found that MJ hadn't been able to find replacements for his rather unconventional weapons, the various tools and bits of metal he had collected indicated his plan to make some.

"Done?" Sharp asked. MJ nodded. "Then let's never come here again." Another nod. They returned to Quickly and, each taking a share of the load, they made their way back to their trench camp.

Sterling was awake when they returned. She didn't say anything to him or even turn to them as they constructed the tents and when hers was done she disappeared inside.

"Any trouble?" Sharp asked Tolah. She shook her head.

"What do we do now?" she asked quietly. Sharp wished everyone would speak up a little, his left ear had been completely deaf for a few days now and showed no signs of getting better.

"We go home." Sharp said. Tolah looked shocked. He saw the same expression on the faces of the other two.

"We can't do that! We need to kill Duke!"
"I suppose we'd better go into the mist then."
"I hate you."
"After all the stuff I've done and a JOKE is your limit?" He was rewarded with a small smile. The rest of the day passed without incident and the rain even stopped. When it grew dark the others quickly made their way to their tents, probably glad to have them. Instead of doing the same he paused outside Sterling's tent.

"Sterling?" he called out softly. For a moment he thought she was asleep but as he was leaving he heard her reply.

"You can come in." He did so. Well, she had both of her eyes at least. The rest of her face was a mess of scars however, each spreading away from where the spell had hit.

"How are you feeling?"

"Alive at least. Tolah told me I have you to thank for that. You also seem to have put everyone together afterwards."

"You would have done the same."

"You wouldn't have gotten us into the situation we were in. I hope at least some of the townspeople escaped. I... couldn't save any."

"None of us could. It was an impossible situation we found ourselves in. You killed Arborious at least. If he really was Duke's second in command then that could have dealt a blow to him."

"He was Tolah's brother."

"He made his choice. You spoke to him, he didn't deserve her."

"I just... really messed up this time. You were right. I tried to take the nice option and ended up almost killing us all for nothing." She reached into her pocket and brought out the seal. Instead of flipping it, she took a long look at her reflection in its surface and then held it out to him. "You should take over. If you still want me with you then I'll follow you."

"Even into the mist?"

"Yes." Her face was determined. Sharp reached out and took the seal from her. It was warm to the touch. He ran his finger over the raised surface. "It's been a while since the battle, right? No one followed us?"

"Just over a week. We're in a bizarre hiding spot,

the rain helped to cover our tracks and I'm starting to think they just didn't bother to come after us."

"You think they'll hit the towns further in next?"

"Maybe." Sharp absent-mindedly flipped the seal in his hand before he realised what he was doing and abruptly stopped. "They may have some success out here but Duke is really going to struggle in higher populated areas, even with his troops. Well, it won't matter if we can take him down. A cult will fall without its icon." He made a move to leave. "We leave as soon as everyone is at a hundred percent. Who knows what we'll find in the mist, or if we'll even survive long enough to find Duke at all. You should come to talk to us tomorrow. Tolah has been concerned."

"Goodnight Sharp."

"Goodnight." He left her tent and found the other three had emerged from their own. He saw their eyes go to the seal in his hand and almost as one, they turned and went back to bed although, he noted, all with accepting looks on their faces. It took him a while to sleep, the seal kept digging into his side no matter which way he lay.

Sterling did join them the next day. Sharp guessed it had been the comment about Tolah that had done it. Tolah was definitely overjoyed to see her and the atmosphere of the group was also improved. Sharp handed over the shield and one of the swords to her and she had enough tact not to ask where he'd got them from although it was rather obvious, he supposed. MJ was diligently working on his claws and Sharp was amazed the collection of metal scraps could be turned into a weapon but they were coming together nicely. Eager to see them in action, he took MJ hunting again. The man was starting to come into his own as a fighter now that he had decided to focus on a single fighting technique.

The local animals didn't stand a chance.

"We should leave tomorrow." Sharp said.

"You have a plan for when we get in there?" asked Sterling.

"Not really. I have no idea what we're going to find."

"Fine." There wasn't really anything else to discuss.

Once again he found himself alone at the dying campfire. He held the seal, now cold, between thumb and forefinger as he gazed into the dying embers. A noise indicated Sterling had joined him. Well, she was the one he needed to talk to. Without a word he held the seal out to her. She didn't take it.

"Why are you giving it to me?"

"I don't want it."

"Could've fooled me."

"I'm not fit to be the leader."

"You weren't the one who suggested taking on an entire army because you thought you could talk your way out of it. I thought this had been settled."

"I would have ditched you the moment you joined me." Sterling looked taken aback.

"But I was inviting you to help me as a favour!" she cried.

"And I would have taken that favour and left you in the dust."

"Charming."

"I would have then waved this around" he indicated the seal, "and would have pissed off a lot of people."

"Maybe that would have got us here faster."

"I wouldn't have taken Tolah with me."

"She wouldn't have had to be involved in her

brother's mess and ultimate death."

"I wouldn't have even spoken to MJ."

"He would have found his feet. Maybe someone would have taken him with them or maybe he'd have left on his own eventually."

"I'd... I'd have killed Quickly." Sharp couldn't stop his voice from cracking. Sterling had no reply to that one. "I'm not saying I can't get us there but the WAY we get there does matter. You got us this far, you should take us the rest of the way. You keep saying that you think we're all so strong but we aren't strong because we survive what's thrown at us, we're strong because we get back up afterwards and don't let it stop us." He held out the seal again. "Please." She reached out slowly and took it from his hand. A weight he didn't know he had been feeling was lifted from his shoulders. Sterling returned the seal to her pocket and they enjoyed a companionable silence for a time until Sharp felt a cold spot hit his skin. He looked up and saw the first snowflakes of winter begin to fall. Sterling held out a hand and smiled as the white dots hit them. They were going to struggle if it started up badly when they were in the mist but Sharp couldn't help but feel relaxed with Sterling's reaction to what was awful weather for both their profession and current situation. He supposed she just liked bad weather in general. They sat there until the chill in the air forced them back to their tents. For the first time in ages, he fell into a peaceful sleep, even as he stood on the precipice of the unknown.

Sterling picked a direction that would go nowhere near Stillhaven. Sharp could tell the rest of the team was happy to have her back in the saddle but also seemed to be careful about what they said about the whole thing. Tolah seemed overjoyed that Sterling seemed up to full speed again and barely left her side the whole way to the Mistline. Sharp had MJ doing the same to him, the man seemed to think he had earned some kind of sidekick status. Maybe Sharp needed to pull back on the encouragement but it felt like kicking a puppy. Quickly had fallen quiet again which Sharp was concerned about as he hadn't really had a chance to talk to him, but he was impressed the yeti had kept his head in Stillhaven. Well, none of this emotional rubbish was going to matter if they all got horribly murdered in the mist.

They reached the Mistline in roughly three days. Sterling announced they should wait for a new day to go inside although Sharp doubted it would make much of a difference since the other side looked as though they were going to be mostly blind. The line reached up higher than Sharp could see and it really did hold an almost solid wall. He put his hand through it and swirled it around. The surface moved around where his arm had gone through but as soon as he removed it, it settled back into the wall.

"Weird." he said and stuck his whole head in.

"Whoa, watch it!" he heard Sterling say from the other side. It wasn't as thick on the other side. He could actually see about a mile away if you didn't count the trees and other various features, although it all looked hazy and unclear. There were no signs of monsters or death traps or whatever was meant to be so dangerous in here. A sudden swirling of mist next to him revealed MJ's head and then one by one the others all appeared as well.

"Doesn't look as if we're going to die immediately." Sharp said.

"I can't smell much around here. There might be more further in." Quickly announced. Sharp closed his eyes and walked the rest of his body through the wall. A slight chill hit him as he entered. He opened his eyes and... still nothing. That was a bit anticlimactic. The others appeared next to him.

"Smell a direction we should take?" Sterling asked.

"Maybe this way?" Quickly guessed.

"Better than nothing! Let's go." Sharp said.

Quickly led them further in. The chill that had hit Sharp as he entered was intensifying, perhaps as the mist was soaking through his clothes. Sharp could hear 'things' in the mist now and he couldn't help but feel as if he was being stalked.

The first thing they encountered was in a clearing in the middle of a small forest Sharp had been unhappy to enter but it was the only logical way forward. Who knew how long skirting it would have taken? The mist pooled at their feet on top of the standard mist that was everywhere in Moremist. Out of the fog came a beautiful creature. A white horse, but Sharp could see a long horn on its head. A unicorn. He gasped and heard Sterling do the same. Unicorns had been extinct for hundreds of years.

"Whoa, it's beautiful!" Tolah exclaimed. She walked forwards, her hand outstretched.

"Wait, Tolah!" Sterling said but it was too late. The unicorn lowered its head and charged. Quickly darted forwards and grabbed Tolah out of the way as the unicorn zipped past them. Its eyes glowed bright white.

"Unicorns are dangerous! Have you ever met an untamed horse? Well, these are just as wild but with a sword attached!" Sharp yelled. The ground underneath the unicorn's hooves crackled with electricity, the mist swirling and darting with the discharge. "Oh, and they also might be magic. That one was meant to be a myth."

He rolled out of the way as the first bolt arced towards him and singed the ground where he'd been standing moments before. Quickly ran forwards and tackled the unicorn to the ground as it neighed indignantly, electricity dancing around its horn. Sharp ran forward and stuck his sword through its neck. It fell dead instantly.

"That's one of the most depressing things I've ever seen." Tolah said, gazing at the beautiful form lying in front of them.

"Yeah, I'm tearing up." said Sharp, carving away at its horn with his sword.

"What are you doing?!" Tolah cried.

"You think people are going to believe I killed a unicorn without proof?"

"How would you like it if someone carved up YOUR body after you died?"

"Why would I care? I'd be dead. Take what you want." Sharp shoved the horn in his belt.

"We should have at least tried to scare it away first. Or calm it down. Think of the things we could learn! What if we just killed the last unicorn in existence?!" Tolah's face was distraught.

A noise behind them alerted Sharp to turn around. A line of VERY annoyed looking unicorns were watching them.

"I think we may be safe on that front." Sharp said backing up slowly. The others all followed his gaze and then copied his motion. The unicorns charged. As one they all turned and sprinted into the forest, taking sharp corners to try to slow down the deadly charge.

"TREES!" Sterling shouted from somewhere to Sharp's left so he leapt at the first tree he could find and starting scaling it. He turned to see MJ had followed him so he grabbed the scrabbling ralli by the back of his coat and helped him up. He could see the other three in trees of their own. Quickly's was looking a little bendy but other than that they were all safe. The unicorns roamed around under them for a short amount of time then, with a snort of annoyance, they wandered off. The group didn't move for a few minutes.

"Still think they don't deserve killing?" Sharp asked.

"Of course not!"

"Well the next mythical creature we find in here, YOU can deal with in your way."

"I'll hold you to that you know."

"Counting on it." This should be good for a laugh. They cautiously let themselves down from the trees.

"Amazing though. The unicorns all came here! Who knows what else did?" Sterling proclaimed.

"I imagine creatures with poachability." Sharp said.

"What do you mean?" asked Tolah.

"Unicorns used to be hunted for their horns and some magic potions required their organs."

"That's horrendous!"

"We skin animals for their fur. Cut them up for their meat." Sharp reasoned.

"That's survival and we don't pick on just one species!"

"I'm not arguing with you in the middle of a forest filled with things that want to kill me and that I can't see coming." he said. Tolah shot him a look that said this wasn't over.

"Which way should we go now?" Sterling asked Quickly. He took a sniff at the air and started walking without replying. They all fell into line behind him, taking nervous looks around as they went. It wasn't long before they found another clearing. This one had no mist, a strange sort of oasis. The grass was all charred and the trees had burn marks up them. In the middle of the clearing was the most beautiful bird Sharp had ever seen. Its feathers were different shades of red, its nest made out of white branches. It was asleep. Tolah gasped and took a look at Sharp. He shrugged.

"Hey, this one is yours." He said. Sterling opened her mouth but he put his hand on her shoulder and she fell silent. Sterling really shouldn't be so trusting. Tolah was walking slowly towards the phoenix, for phoenix it was if he knew his random etchings he found randomly in some random book in some random library. She bent beside it and Sharp and Sterling shuffled forwards, hands on their sword hilts. The bird woke. It took a moment to take in its surroundings, which it decided it didn't like. It puffed up its chest indignantly and then it BURST into flames. Tolah fell backward, her fringe and eyebrows smoking slightly, her glasses fogged up instantly. Sharp hadn't realised how strong the flames would be but the end result was suitably amusing so it overrode any guilt well enough.

"You want to calm it down?" Sharp asked her.

"We shouldn't just... kill it. It's a peaceful creature!" Tolah wiped the fog off her glasses.

"Tolah, its nest is made of bones." She wiped her glasses and squinted.

"Oh, right."

The phoenix had had enough. It flew, skimming the ground, aiming right at Tolah but Sterling got in the way with her shield. The phoenix collided with the metal, scrabbling with its claws, trying to get a grip while flapping wildly around the edge, flames blazing towards Sterling. The others were forced backward by the heat and Sharp heard a cry from Sterling, her hand must have been melting on the shield.

"Tolah! Hit it with ice! Sterling's going to burn alive!" Sharp yelled to her. Ice formed on Tolah's fingers and the spell shot towards the phoenix, the ice melting immediately and drenching the bird who fell to the ground, flailing around. Sterling threw the shield away. Tolah formed more ice and gripped Sterling's arm. It didn't look as if it had burnt, the coat had taken the brunt of it. A good thing as she certainly didn't need any more scars. The phoenix was shaking its feathers and trying to relight. Steam rolled off its body. They didn't have long so Sharp stepped forward and, grabbing a handful of feathers, he ripped them out and followed with a stab to the chest. The bird fell to ash around his blade.

"You are rapidly becoming a poacher yourself Sharp." Sterling said crossly.

"Not this time." he replied. "But maybe we should be making a move." The ash of the phoenix was smouldering. The others quickly followed him out of the clearing as an egg shape began to appear. Who knew what was going to end up forming or how quickly the egg would hatch if that was indeed what was coming.

"So the rumours were true? The phoenix is immortal?"

"I guess so."

"Then how could it have been wiped out? Or driven out, if this one is anything to judge by."

"Perhaps there is a way it can be killed. What if something happened to the ash?" Tolah suggested.

"How about an immortal omelette?" Sharp suggested.

"You think people would eat it?!" Tolah asked.

"People eat everything. Especially if there's a chance of gaining eternal life from it."

"You don't think that would be true do you?"

asked MJ, casting an interested eye back towards the egg that had now fully formed and was smoking slightly.

"I'm fairly sure you can't catch life from something just as you can't catch death from a zombie. I do, however, think people would try."

"You two remember a lot of random stuff you read about extinct creatures." MJ sounded impressed.

"Well we'll be in trouble if we meet any BORING dead species, those don't stick in the mind as much as flaming birds who can't be killed." Sharp looked at the feathers in his hand. They seemed to be drying off without any damage to them. He stuck the largest into the brim of his hat and then handed the others a feather each. They all looked appreciative. Nothing like a gift to make people forget you almost got one of your friends set alight. At a word from Quickly they once again readjusted their direction.

Nothing else challenged them that day although Sharp still had that feeling of being watched and phantom noises could be heard from places just out of view. Sharp had an inkling that he could see the perpetrators if he just walked a few steps towards the side but he wasn't sure if he wanted to know.

They stopped walking when it began to grow dark. The mist was bad enough but if they waited then visibility would have been close to zero. They made their camp in a circle with no tents in case they needed to make a quick exit and they left a guard throughout the night. When it was Sharp's turn, Quickly came to wake him.

"Your turn to watch."

"Oh, okay." Sharp hated having to break up sleep, he would have rather not have gone to sleep in the first place. "Any movement?"

"No. Whatever is out there has been keeping its

distance. I don't think they know what we are."

"So as soon as they classify us as prey we're going to get a faceful of myth."

"Maybe. We can face it together." Quickly sounded as if he believed it. Sharp was impressed with how he had picked himself up after Stillhaven. Everyone had taken a blow from that fight and no one had really spoken about it or known how to even bring it up.

"Think there's a dragon out there?" Sharp wasn't sure what he wanted the answer to be. Taking down a dragon would be a better feather in his cap than the literal phoenix one currently there but whether it was doable was the bigger question.

"Could be anything." Quickly replied. "So many smells I don't recognise."

"Hey, I never got the chance to say, you did a good job in Stillhaven. I thought for sure you wouldn't be able to keep it together. That fight was crazy."

"I don't know. I just... didn't feel angry. I guess I felt," Quickly thought a moment. "sad, I suppose and I know I can be what I want to be with everyone here." he paused, then said "I don't think I can return to the village after this."

"Well, maybe we can stick together, for a while at least." Quickly's face stretched into a wide smile. Sharp decided to change the subject. "You escape fine after we parted ways?"

"They ignored us when you set fire to the roof."

"Oh er, yeah, that's what happened."

"You did a good job. I thought we would never see Sterling alive and then you made her leader again."

"You think I would have done a terrible job right?"

"No, I just think she would consider it a failure even if we do manage to defeat Duke unless it was by her own hand." They both fell silent so Sharp took his lookout spot and Quickly returned to his bed.

Chapter 19

There really was nothing going on so Sharp let his mind wander. Teaming up with Quickly could be fun. Sterling was welcome to MJ and Tolah would probably go off on her own to study absolutely everything unless she decided to go back home. Eternal Heights had probably fallen apart with half of its people leaving to worship a prophet, so she would have probably been welcome, no questions asked. Of course, nothing would happen if they all ended up dead in the mist or killed by Duke's magic. Who knew how many of his men he had kept near him, or even how they were going to get through that metal monstrosity he had built. Everyone was feeling pretty good now but Sharp had never focused on feelings when the solution lay at the end of a sword. Come to think of it, Sterling had struggled with Arborious. How would she fare against Duke, a far stronger mage? He could take a go he supposed. If they tried to fight him together, they might just end up stepping on each other's toes. Perhaps the rest of the team could take on the army, keep them back while Duke was fought though Stillhaven had shown him that that technique wasn't a good one. Come to think of it, the best way to approach this was probably a single person taking Duke by surprise. Maybe that person could even do it so quietly that they could creep away afterwards. Actually, that might work. He hadn't realised but he had gotten to his feet. He looked at his sleeping friends, this was the best chance he had to not have them die. He pointed himself in the direction Quickly had been leading them and started walking.

The mist and the darkness wrapped itself around him as he went but with every step he was assured he was doing the right thing. The creatures in the mist were keeping their distance, who knew why, but so far his luck was winning out. He would just have to do what he used to do before he teamed up with other people and rely on his instinct. It had served him well in the past and after joining Sterling he had lost a finger, half his hearing, a great deal of his money and suffered more mental damage than he had had in about six years. He walked with confidence, creating as much distance as he could so he would have a long lead by the time the next watch started in a couple of hours, not that they knew which direction he had gone in.

    Dawn breaking in the mist was less impressive than out but it was still beautiful to see the red leaking through the fog, eventually turning into light so that Sharp could see more than just in front of his nose. The feeling of being stalked had finally subsided. Perhaps they had been following the team simply because of the size of the group and a single man must have been easier to slip under the radar. The snow had started at some point during the night but he only realised it when he paused to take in some breakfast. He wondered how long it was going to take to get to Duke. He would have to keep up his speed if he wanted to get there before the others as well as the actual sneak plan. He supposed he could lay off the sleep mostly, leaving just enough to stay awake at the goal. With renewed vigour he set off once again. It had been so long since he felt such single-mindedness, the breeze felt nice on his face, the bird calls soothing to his ears. He managed to keep walking until sundown again, finding he needed little in the way of food which, again, saved on his time. He was sure the party must have been left far behind in his dust. They would be angry or concerned but they would soon change their minds when he brought back Duke's head on a platter. Well, perhaps that was a bit too violent.

How about taking that machine of his? He could work out how to power it when he got there, it had room for a proto-yeti so perhaps he could walk it himself but it would be far more dramatic to ride in the main seat. He supposed he was thinking too far ahead. He walked through the dark for a few hours before deciding to settle for the night.

    He woke when it was still dark. By his estimation, he had only slept for a couple of hours but he felt refreshed. To be honest he hadn't felt that tired when he had made his camp but logic dictated sleeping in the dark would be better than sleeping in the daylight, not that he had been finding it hard to walk in the blackness. Actually, that was strange. He hadn't even tripped over a stray branch or anything, despite not being able to see his hand if he held it out in front of his face. Well, he was relying on instinct, right? He'd found his way in the dark plenty of times before. He shook his head and carried on walking. He strained his ears and heard nothing in the way of followers as usual. Even in a regular wood, he should have been attacked or confronted at least once. It wasn't as though there was nothing out here, he could hear the sounds of owls hooting and small animals fled from his approach on occasion. Maybe he had just been lucky? No, that couldn't be right. Every time he tried to pull his mind to a question, he found it was a concentrated effort to stop it from drifting to the happy place it seemed determined to visit. He tried to focus on something, anything. The wind blowing past his ears wasn't chilled even though it was winter and he focused on that. Wait, ears? That wasn't right either. When had his hearing come back to him? And when had he eaten last? Yesterday evening? No, he hadn't eaten then. Sharp stopped walking. Something was really wrong and his brain didn't seem to be functioning at all, not that he had noticed before. He turned and started to walk back the way he came. Immediately a feeling of exhaustion overcame him and he felt as if he hadn't eaten in a week. The cold cut through his clothes and the feeling of being watched was palpable. The feeling wasn't surrounding him so at least he could just walk away, or he could do if he wasn't completely blind. He tripped over something on the floor and ended up falling on his face. The darkness and the mist were back in full force, maybe more so than previously, but how could he tell? He turned around and instantly everything turned back to how it was before. It wasn't as if the scenery had changed, just his... perception of it. What was going on? With an effort, he turned back to where he had come from again. It was a horrendous feeling but he could think better, not perfectly, but better. Think Sharp, think! What could cause this? There was one option he could think of.

"Craaaaaaaaaaaaaaaaaaaap!" He started walking the way he had come from. The harder it was, the more he was sure he was going in the right direction. It was terrifying how sure he had felt of his bearing beforehand without any kind of reasoning for it. His body felt heavy and weak, he stumbled constantly, his head was killing him, his hearing came and went in his deaf ear as the creature was unsure if restoring his hearing would make him turn back or not. It had to be a mind flayer. The only image he had seen was from an artist who clearly hadn't had a good idea of what they looked like, possibly because anyone who saw them had their brains sucked out. The sketch had been the equivalent of mumbling someone's name because you didn't exactly know what it was. The edges had been so loosely drawn it could have been fat or thin, tall or short. The only thing the artist had been clear on was the tentacles, as if the creature had a squid for a head, which would wrap around the victims head before the aforementioned brain eating. They got inside your head psychically and forced you towards them. In Sharp, that had been making him feel that abandoning his companions was the right thing to do and then walking him towards itself. It would explain why there weren't any other creatures near it as anything else had probably either been eaten or terrified. Sharp was practically on his hands and knees, a sharp pain ran through his body now and he was finding it hard to move at all. He was finding it difficult to remember details but he knew paralysing was one of the flayer's abilities. He hadn't even seen the creature but he knew he didn't want it to reach him, terror was now all he could feel and he curled into a ball to try and block it out. Whether he couldn't move because he had reached his limit or whether the mind flayer had paralysed him he couldn't tell, it probably didn't matter.

    He didn't know how long he was lying there, tired, hungry, in pain, freezing and scared, expecting any moment to see the creature looming over him. They weren't known to go to their prey but Sharp was in no state to come to it so surely it would come. A shadow fell over him but instead of slimy tentacles, he felt fur as he was lifted up and carried away, the terrible feelings blazing until he fell asleep from exhaustion.

    When he woke up he was in a camp and it was light. It was a small camp and he could see it contained only one other person. It was Quickly. He struggled to sit up and the yeti thrust a plate of food in front of him. Without looking at what it was he devoured it.

    "Where are we?" Sharp asked when he was done.

    "No idea. I just walked you back as far as I could towards Sterling. We can pick our bearing when we get back to them."

"Thank you."

"Why did you run off? We thought something had taken you before I picked up your scent. You were walking at quite a speed so I went after you on my own. Luckily there weren't any monsters along the way."

"Did you carry me back far? We should go further!" Sharp heard desperation in his voice.

"Whoa, calm down! What are we running from?"

"A mind flayer! It messed up my brain and made me walk towards it! I thought it was a good idea!" Sharp's heart beat faster and he started breathing in bursts.

"It's okay Sharp." Quickly put his hand on Sharp's shoulder. "We can walk back to the others and then we can finish what we came here to do. Nothing is near us right now." Sharp felt calmer slightly.

"You just follow the smell of strawberries, right?" Sharp gave a weak smile.

"Sterling doesn't smell of strawberries anymore."

"Oh." Neither said anything for a moment. "Shall we just go?"

"Sure." They packed up and started the walk back to the others. Sharp was still tired, still hungry and had the feeling that someone had been rummaging around in his brain without his permission. After a while, he started getting that being watched feeling again and was surprised at how comforting that was. It took another day to return, Sharp's condition not helping. He was concerned about the amount of supplies they had brought and if they ran out it would be because of him. When he saw their camp emerge out of the mist he felt as if he had returned home. He got a hug from Tolah and even Sterling rushed towards him before stopping herself. She looked as if she didn't know whether to hug him or hit him.

"This had better be good." She said with eyes narrowed.

"Mind flayer."

"What?! You saw one?!" All anger gone.

"What's a mind flayer?" Tolah asked. Sharp explained the best he could. Sterling had little to add, knowledge of them not being common.

"I didn't actually see it. I'd have been dead if I had."

"Why did it take you?" Tolah asked.

"I guess I was just awake at the right time."

"Or it picked the easiest mind to trick." Tolah grinned smugly but Sharp didn't laugh. Quite honestly that had been a concern.

"I'm sure it was the timing." said Quickly.

"Sorry for slowing us down." Sharp apologised.

"Forget it. We're just glad you weren't killed by something in the night. From now on, two sentries at a time." Sterling brushed it off. Forgiving him was an easy thing for her still. He felt glad she was her. He personally wouldn't have reacted the same way.

"It seems all the things we thought extinct are actually in the mist." Sharp decided to change the subject.

"Yes. It might be something worth revisiting at a later date." Sterling mused.

"But everything in here is a killer, right? Why were they all driven out of Mistmore?" asked MJ.

"It doesn't matter how large you are. If you're a big enough threat, people will rise against you to stop you from hurting others." Quickly said. "I suspect the mist is where Duke found my brethren."

"I'm sorry Quickly, I didn't mean to imply your people were killers."

"Actually they aren't his people anymore." Tolah

said. They all turned to her. "I'm just saying, the yeti experienced allopatric speciation and so can't really be considered the same species any...more..." she trailed off.

"Er, what?" Sharp asked.

"They evolved in different places so now they aren't the same species."

"Was that so hard?"

"I thought you read books."

"Only if they help me stab things better."

"Humans look a lot like elves but you don't associate yourself with them right?"

"You never thought the two yeti species were the same?" asked Sterling.

"Well, no. You did?"

"Yes." said Quickly.

"Your people are intelligent, they clearly aren't and there are obvious physical differences." Tolah explained to Quickly. "Actually, I'm surprised they follow Duke at all without self-awareness. I agree they probably came from the mist."

"Think he can control everything in here?" MJ asked. They exchanged worried looks.

"He would have attacked us with scarier stuff before, right?" Tolah eventually asked.

"He only found out about us when Arborious did, he couldn't have had time to actually TELL Duke before we got there unless he sent a bird and I see no bird willing to cross the Mistline."

"So we don't actually know if he's expecting us and if we turn up he could sic an army of mind flayers on us?" A chill ran down Sharp's spine.

"Seems about right."

"Should we just deal with this like we deal with everything?" MJ inquired.

"Make it up as we go along and hope we don't get

horribly murdered?" suggested Sharp.

"At this point, I don't see any other options." Sterling replied. "At any rate, we should continue on, we've lost a lot of time." No one said anything regarding it being Sharp's fault and he wasn't about to bring it up so he got to his feet first even though he could really do with more of a break. Maybe the exercise would clear some of the feeling of having someone taking up residence in his head for a while. Quickly led the way but with Sharp walking beside him it was probably obvious that the hunter needed prodding to keep him walking in a straight line or perhaps they were trying to protect his manly pride. To be honest he would rather they helped him but he managed to make it to the end of the day. He had no idea what he would have done if they had met anything monster-wise that day. Probably taken a dive so the others could deal with it. Unless it had a valuable body part which would be another matter.

The next day he was feeling better. Quickly had picked up a proper trail at last - a clear scent of proto-yeti. Sharp fancied he could see footprints himself in between patches of mist at their feet but he didn't bother looking too hard, Quickly was their tracker in here. Suddenly the yeti stopped. Sharp collided into his back, Sterling collided into his and Tolah into hers. MJ paused for a moment before deliberately colliding into Tolah. Maybe he felt left out.

"What's the hold-up?" asked Sterling after detangling herself from the pile. Quickly pointed up. Looming in the mist was a wall. Sharp must have really not been paying attention to have missed THAT.

"The scent trail doesn't turn?" asked Tolah. Quickly shook his head. They carried on forwards, the wall seemingly growing bigger as they drew closer and what little light they had faded. When they got to the wall it was solid. Sharp looked at the ground, there were definite signs of footfall, all different sizes but they were cut off abruptly at the wall. Sharp ran his hand over the surface but it looked the same as what he could see stretched far out on either side. He turned to face the others.

"Well, I don't know. Any ideas?" MJ stepped forwards and opened his mouth to talk but nothing came out. He looked stunned and slowly stepped backward. "What?" Tolah also said nothing but pointed behind him. Sharp decided he would rather not know and didn't bother looking but walked straight towards them. Suddenly he felt something heavy and blunt hit him in the back. He fell and felt the thing press him down so that he couldn't move. He turned his head with some effort and took a gasping breath as he felt his lungs crushed. Really hating the mist now. At least make this something he could kill. He suddenly felt the weight lifted and Tolah and MJ pulled him out, each taking an arm. He got to his feet and got out of the way to see Sterling and Quickly had shoved the GIANT FOOT away. They darted back to join the other three and together they saw the foot was attached to an animal leg which was attached to a giant torso which had a giant female human head on top. Sharp couldn't see anything past this monstrosity blocking out what little sun they had. He took in the whole creature and saw that the lower half was that of a lion, or at least that was the closest animal he could compare it to. The whole effect was terrifying. The creature bent down to see the team cower, baring her teeth (more lion like than human) and stretched out her claws.

"Erm, what is that?" Sharp was stumped this time.

"Sphinx." Sterling said. Sharp was irritated she

knew one he didn't.

"What does it do?" Sharp asked, emboldened by the fact Sterling wasn't backing off.

"It asks riddles. If we get them wrong we get eaten. If we get them right, we can pass. Correct?" This last question was aimed at the sphinx herself. The creature's laugh shook the earth slightly below them.

"You are correct! Three riddles I will ask. Three correct answers I must have. Only then will I grant thee passage!"

"Time, footprints, a shadow." Sharp said.

"What?" the sphinx said.

"Every riddle I've ever heard has had one of those three answers."

"You can't answer before even hearing the question!!" Tolah said. "You're going to get us killed, there is no way we can fight her if she chooses to attack us!" They turned to look at the sphinx. She was looking as edgy as a woman the size of a house with a lion's body COULD look.

"One of those was ACTUALLY the answer?" Sterling asked, a smile creeping on one side of her mouth.

"Erm... no."

"What was it then?" MJ asked.

"This really isn't how it's done."

"Okay then ask us the second question." Sharp asked.

"Well the thing about that is... er..."

"I just answered every single one of the riddles didn't I?"

"You don't have more than three?" asked Tolah.

"People barely ever get them right and those that do I never challenge again!"

"Like the beasts, fletchins and rallis that pass

through here?"

"Their leader correctly answered the riddles and so they may also pass through unhindered as extensions of their master."

"How many would you say pass through here? Also, I don't suppose you can list any of the other creatures he may or may not have, the number of teeth and claws they have and how ferocious they are on a scale of one to ten?" Sharp asked.

"You answer MY questions. I don't answer yours. Now be on your way!" The sphinx rose to her feet and, stepping to one side somewhere in the darkness, a path opened up before them. They realised it was only a wall and not the entrance to a canyon that the sphinx had set up her vigil in which made Sharp more relaxed. He didn't want another episode of the detour they had taken leading up to Stillhaven. The sphinx had placed herself just past the wall. She glared as they passed her and they didn't dare try to converse with her further. As they walked away she moved back into her previous space and settled down. Her tail was definitely that of a lion's. Sharp considered taking back a little souvenir tail hair but Sterling grabbed him by his collar and dragged him away. Ah, it was indistinguishable from ACTUAL lion hair anyway, no way anyone would have believed otherwise.

Chapter 20

A further few hours saw them to their destination. It was plain when they got there as the mist just... ended. They could see movement on the other side of the mist wall so they didn't cross it straight away but backed off to a safe distance with Quickly's guidance. After walking around they found that it wasn't an end to the mist but a small pocket of clear weather, like the one in the phoenix clearing only bigger, perhaps three miles in diameter. Quickly led them to a place that he said had no people so they stuck their heads through the mist to take a look. They were in what was clearly some sort of weapon storage, the mist serving as a wall. It appeared that the armaments were in displays but not in any kind of structure. The distance was perfectly clear and Sharp imagined it to be fairer than in Mistmore but put it down to the fact he had been in mist for the last few days until he realised that it wasn't cold here. No snow was settling and as he looked up he could see it swirling high above their heads but it stopped before getting very low, seemingly melting (it was hard to tell with the mist and the distance) so that the effect looked as if they were in a dome of a sort. There were trees and constructs in the dome which allowed their group to be there without being seen but also stunted their vision. Sharp could see people scurrying around, mainly rallis, with no fear it seemed. Sharp suddenly saw two fletchins walking towards them along the edge of the line of mist. He grabbed the two either side of him (MJ and Tolah) and yanked them back out into the mist. The last two followed quickly. Sharp held his breath as the two coloured blurs walked past. When it was clear they weren't paying attention to anything outside he breathed easier and tried to make out what they were doing. They were casting fire spells, that much he could see. As they passed he stuck his head back through and could see the line of mist become more solid. They were making sure the mist stayed where it was.

"Guess we'll have to watch out for patrols around the outside." Sterling said.

"Bet you anything we could walk around in there without being challenged." Sharp said. "Duke's bound to have more of his people here and who knows what else? We should blend in fine. Everyone, that works for you?"

"Maybe. I'm worried that Quickly doesn't look much like a proto-yeti and the humans, fletchins and rallis seem to be working separately. Rallis are the builders and the other two are the muscle. I can't imagine the fletchins would want anything to do with the other warriors."

"Think Duke is in the centre?" asked Tolah.

"Maybe. I suppose one of us could go in and report back to the others." Sterling thought it over.

"Shouldn't we try to cripple the machine?" MJ asked. Everyone turned to him. He had the blueprints for the hedgehog out and held them up.

"Well, we don't know where that is either." Sharp said.

"It's right there." MJ said, pointing. They all stuck their heads back through the mist. What Sharp had assumed to be a wall was, in fact, curved, had holes in the side and was covered in metal plating. It was the size of a small building, bigger than a shed, smaller than a house. It was a few metres away so after a furtive look around they made their way carefully across to it. Sharp ran his hand over the surface, it felt very solid. He drew his sword and gave a half-hearted swing at it. It bounced off with a clang.

"What are you doing?" came a voice from around the side of the machine. They turned to see a couple of rallis. The speaker was taller than the other, with black fur that looked more burnt than natural, her fur stuck out at weird angles giving the impression that a small explosion had happened in front of her face. Judging by her apparent career it may well have done. The smaller and younger looking ralli said nothing but was looking curious, his arms weighed down by various tools. Quickly backed off so he was blocked by the machine.

"Just checking out the war machine." Sharp said casually. "No rule against it." Crazy Fur sighed and rubbed the bridge of her nose.

"You know full well there IS a rule against it. Duke has said many times that the fighters need to leave the workers alone! Even ANTS know how to do that! This machine is the most important thing in here and yes I am including you and myself in that. I am tired of the sword swingers treating the builders as if they think they're superior! If we weren't here you wouldn't even have any equipment to fight with! Give me your sword." Without waiting for his reply she slid up to him and, stretching up, grabbed one of his swords. She sighed. "This is one of mine. You'd think you would have some respect for the person who built your own sword! What have you been doing to it?!"

"Er, sticking it into things that want to kill me?" Sharp couldn't see anything wrong with it, he had barely used it since picking it up and it looked flawless to him.

"Have you been using it to cut rock?!" Her eyes went to the unicorn horn still sticking out of his belt. She gave him a weary look then grabbed him by the lower half of his coat and dragged him towards the racks of swords. She pulled out two swords seemingly at random and handed them to him. He was no expert on swords, he paid other people to be, but he knew what a decent weapon felt like in his hands. The weight was perfect for him and a few experimental swings felt perfect also. He drew his other sword (a snort of disapproval at the fact it didn't match his other) and sheathed the two Crazy Fur had handed him.

"Hey, thanks!" She reached up and grabbed him by the collar, pulling him down to her height.

"Do not use them on anything other than something you want dead. Do you understand?" She spoke as one would speak to a child.

"Yes, ma'am." Sharp would promise anything to anyone who gave him quality weapons for free.

"You." She pointed at Sterling who had been enjoying the show but now had the expression of one who had been picked from the audience to come on stage. Crazy Fur held out her hands and Sterling handed her weapons over. She gave Sterling a critical look but said nothing. Sharp could still see the burn mark from the phoenix flames on the shield. The ralli rummaged around and found replacements for Sterling who had the same reaction Sharp had done. She looked like a kid on her birthday.

"And YOU." She pointed at MJ who looked taken aback. "Stop showing the fighters the equipment. They know nothing of what we do and will do nothing but mess up our work. You understand?" MJ nodded meekly. "Get back to work and return those claws to where you found them." Without looking to see if the order was obeyed, she walked off, her assistant scuttling after her to keep up.

"Heh, she just equipped the enemy." Sharp said.

"Actually she doesn't have an enemy. She may have even been told to equip anyone who asked so she may not have even been going against her employer's orders. Rallis are hired, they don't take sides." said MJ.

"Think we can take the machine apart?" Sterling asked the ralli.

"No. It's been completed. No weak points and I can't take something apart that a lot of other rallis have worked hard to make. Also, it's clearly being watched. We would call the whole place down on us."

"Okay, so we try to find the boss before he can get here." Sharp said.

"How exactly are we going to do that?" Tolah asked.

"Asking someone is probably our best bet."

"You want us to walk up to the people who want us dead and just ASK where their boss is?" Tolah was incredulous.

"We aren't part of the army here." Sterling said.

"Just act as if you're meant to be here. No one has bothered us and we're standing right next to the death machine." Sharp replied. They stopped and looked around. They had a few looks from the odd ralli that walked past but they hadn't been disturbed further. "Quickly, if you could walk on your knuckles it could help." Quickly didn't look delighted at the idea but did as he was requested. "Righto, let's try it out." Sharp picked a direction he thought was to the centre of the camp and started walking. The others followed him looking furtively around except MJ who was getting a bit too into it and was striding in an exaggerated fashion with his arms swinging wildly. They weren't challenged so the other three stood up straighter (except Quickly who was meant to be slouched) and stopped looking so obvious. As soon as they did so they got fewer looks and ended up just being part of the crowd. They realised the camp had been separated somewhat by species. The rallis they had already passed, in clearly the area where everything was made. They saw a group of fighters, humans mostly but with a healthy spattering of elves and dwarfs. They had some sort of training ground set up and were currently gathered around some sort of competition between an elf and a human who were sword fighting. Sharp couldn't see much but it looked as though they were both pretty good and he would rather not have to face any more of them. There was also a chance some had been at Stillhaven and he would prefer not be recognised. There was a section that looked more like a zoo than anything else, a wall had been erected around it and there was a door with bars on it. Inside, Sharp could see proto-yeti roaming around. He was unsure how trained these beasts were if they needed such containment, they certainly seemed to know what to attack when Sharp had faced them last. The group walked as close to the gate as they dared and were rewarded with a chorus of menacing growls. The last section looked a lot fancier, another wall was there but seemed less to keep the occupants in and more to keep everyone out. It was also a lot nicer looking. Sharp peeked around the side of the door and saw that the wall didn't go all the way around the outside. Clearly, they were more disturbed by the rest of their own team than by whatever was lurking in the mist. A large fancy table was set up with fancy chairs and the remains of fancy food. The fletchins surrounding the table weren't breaking any stereotypes weight-wise and clearly not attitude-wise either. Sharp could see they had also set up their camp here. It had been so long since he had even SEEN a bed. The rest of the army had set up tents in yet another section of the mist free dome. All these things they saw while walking in a circle and ended up where they had started. The only other thing of note was the impressive looking campfire in the centre of the whole place. A number of people had gathered around it, it seemed to be the hub for cooking. The people were grouped together by their species but there were a wide range of these.

"Not a lot of mingling I notice." Sharp said.

"Not sure how an army that doesn't get on would be able to take on anything." Tolah said.

"If you point them in the right direction with the promise of gold and tell them to kill, personal gripes aren't going to matter."

"Let's just do what we're here for and leave sorting the racial divide for someone more qualified." Sharp said.

"How? There has been no sign of Duke as of yet and we're starting to get some looks. I'd rather not attract the attention of anyone who might recognise us." Tolah asked.

"Let's go ask someone who knows!" Sharp strode off before they could say anything about it. He headed towards the fire. Nothing like a friendly meal to get information out of someone (well booze usually did a better job but he saw no sign of that). He picked a small group of a mix of races (two dwarfs, an elf and a human) and sat himself down without waiting for an invitation.

"What're we talking about?" Sharp asked. The others shared a look but then one of the two dwarfs shrugged and handed him a plate of mystery meat. It looked good and it would have been a complete waste to not eat it so he tucked in.

"So how long have you guys been here?" he managed through a mouthful of food.

"About two months. You new? Didn't think Duke was hiring anyone else." the elf said.

"Well, he WAS sent by The Lord of Lords. When we heard about his crusade we had to join up! We begged until he let us enrol in his army!" said Sterling. She was met with four blank stares.

"We heard he was paying well for an easy job." Sharp said. The group laughed.

"That was pretty funny." the human said to Sterling.

"Oh right, yes, thanks."

"What are you doing here?" The elf aimed this at Tolah.

"Oh erm, looking for food?"

"Your beast gets served at its cage. Get it out of here!"

"Hah, they both look underfed, maybe they're the runts so they have to rely on the leftovers!" the second dwarf was a comedian it seemed. She was rewarded with a roar of laughter anyway.

"Fletchins have their own beasts?" asked Sharp.

"Wow you ARE new." the elf said.

"As if I'm going to go talk to a fire flinger about pet care." Sharp replied. He was rewarded by a roar of laughter from the group they had approached and a few others who had sensed a show. Sharp couldn't see the expression on the faces of his friends which was probably for the best.

"Then let me explain." The first dwarf said. "The beasts aren't scared of anything but magic so they each get assigned a handler who can keep them in line. They do whatever that handler says for fear of getting set on fire and they get fed INSIDE THEIR CAGE. Fletchins get their meals taken to them. Apparently, they rank higher than us but they have to control the yeti so I suppose I'd rather be rank and file."

"How about the boss. How does Duke get his food?" Sharp asked as casually as he could. He imagined his friends leaning forward behind him.

"Oh, he has a couple of elves to tend to all his needs." said the human. "And I mean ALL his needs." He nudged the elf with his elbow. She didn't look amused.

"Where does he spend his time?" Sterling asked.

"You ask a lot of questions." the human said.

"We got hired by a lackey. I always like to meet the person I'm killing for." Sharp replied.

"Well, you're going to be disappointed this time. He lives in another pocket of the mist that we aren't allowed to enter. Just take the money like the rest of us. It's enough to not bother asking questions in my opinion."

"Fair enough." Sharp knew when to stop asking questions. Plus Tolah and Quickly were still hanging around and that was just going to draw too much attention. "Well, I guess I should try to get some training in, lots of good opponents here. Also, the company could be better." He looked towards Tolah and Quickly who looked put out. "Thanks for the..." he looked at his empty plate.

"Basilisk."

"Huh." Actually, it had been pretty good. He rose to his feet to leave.

"Wait a moment." the first dwarf said. "I DO know you." Sharp's team held their breath.

"Oh, erm really? Can't say I recognise you."

"You're Sharp! The famous hunter! I'm such a big fan!" Oh, it was that again. It had been so long since he'd had to dodge fans he had become complacent. Even MJ had changed from fan to friend. Facing death together can do that he supposed.

"Yeah, that's me. Thought I'd jump on the band-wagon while it was still paying." He made a motion to leave but suddenly he was surrounded and found himself being sat back down. He cast a look towards Sterling to ask for help but she mouthed the word 'sorry' and with a grin, disappeared with the other three. Son of a- she was using him as a distraction! He may have given up the leader role but he never agreed to be downgraded even further! Oh, if she didn't find Duke he was going to have words with her later. Funny how he felt more on edge here than fighting something that wanted to kill him, but he did. He sighed. May as well make the most of it. He accepted another plate of basilisk and started answering the many MANY questions they had. He heard plenty of stories from the onlookers as well. There were a lot of things in the mist that Sharp hadn't encountered, some of them sounded as though the group wouldn't have had a chance against. Duke had a way through the mist, presumably the fire, but it hadn't stopped a load of his people from being killed by the monsters there. About an hour later the human from the original bunch they had spoken to tapped him on the shoulder.

"Yeah?"

"Did you still want to meet the boss?" Sharp thought about it. The other four weren't there but it would be funny if he found Duke before they did. He could always come back and get them, he had learnt his lesson not to do anything on his own.

"Sure do."

"Then I think you have your way right there." the human pointed over to another place around the fire. Sharp saw two of the most attractive elves he had ever seen, they stood out in this bunch of grubby recruits like a beacon.

"Duke's attendants?"

"That's right! You going to follow them into the mist?" The crowd around him leaned in eagerly.

"Damn straight I am!" Sharp figured the elves

couldn't go far, what with their species being unable to cast magic. The crowd cheered and he shushed them. He cast a look towards the elves but they hadn't looked towards them, they had an air of being above the rest of those present. It appeared they were collecting food, presumably for Duke, so he weaved his way through the crowd, blending in nicely. They weren't difficult to follow. The elves led him to the edge of the mist and without pausing, strode into it. Sharp gave a few seconds to think about it then followed them, making sure to leave obvious footprints and dropping a few things he had in his pockets. He followed them to two tied up horses that were waiting patiently for them. Sharp could see no reason for why the horses hadn't been killed by the mist monsters until the elves had mounted and he saw two magnificent wings unfold on each of the creatures. They were pterripi. That explained a lot. His brain mentally tried to calculate the best course of action. If he followed them he was in danger from everything in the mist but if he didn't they would probably never find Duke, Quickly couldn't smell airborne creatures. For some reason, the elves pulled back on their reins even though they weren't moving. The pterripi beat their wings. He would have to choose! As they took off, his legs decided for him and he tore off after them at a sprint, craning his eyes to keep them in sight. He focused on the dark coloured one, its outline easier to pick out in the mist. He had no idea how long he ran, he had to keep up a full speed run just to keep them in sight and he always excelled in a marathon rather than a sprint. The pterripi got smaller and smaller and eventually disappeared, to his panic. He stopped to allow his legs a rest, trying to listen to what might be nearby and wanting a meal. He straightened up again and continued to walk in the direction he had previously been taking, the elves hadn't changed course while he was following, he had to hope they were close. He left as clear a line of footprints as he dared while trying to remain quiet. He was fortunate, it was only around a fifteen minute walk until he saw the tethered pterripi. His course had only been slightly off but any further and he could have become lost forever, or at least until something suitably large showed up and cut that forever short. He could see another clear area ahead. It was a lot smaller than the one for the army, at least Sharp's team would have less to fight here and it was a suitable distance away from Duke's main fighting force. Sharp hesitated. He couldn't go in without his friends, but which would serve him better? Hiding around here and hoping he didn't get his brains splattered by a monster or track his own trail back and hope he didn't get his brains splattered by a monster. At least here he imagined the creatures had learnt to stay away but man, he hadn't even brought anything to read, hoping his friends caught up to him was going to be dull.

He made the decision to stay put. He pulled his pack round and rummaged through it in the hope he would find something that would entertain him. His hands met a book. Surprised, he pulled it out but he didn't even have to read the title to know which book it was. 'Exotic Rocks And How To Distinguish Them From Other Similar Rocks Found In Non Exotic Places And Their Properties'. Tolah was making him haul her stupid book now! He flipped to the first page and saw she had written something there.

'Sharp. No one said anything because we all know you would either brush it off or make some flippant comment about it but we all appreciate what you did in Stillhaven. We also appreciate what you did for Sterling to give her back the seal, we know how much you wanted it, but to lose it would have been so much worse for her. I know how much you like this book and it's the only thing I can give so that's what I'm doing. Thanks, Tolah.'

Fantastic. Now he had to lug around the heaviest, most pointless book he had ever laid eyes on and if he gave it back he'd be the biggest jerk in the world, at least in the eyes of the others. He flipped through the pages and tried to decide whether reading this waste of space was more or less boring than doing absolutely nothing.

"Okay fine, you win this one, Smith." Sharp muttered, he was at least in an exotic place. He cast his eye about and found a deep blue rock with a red streak in it. Very exotic. Time to see if Smith knew his stuff. Apparently, he didn't (although of course the book was about exotic rocks in NON exotic places). Not this one or the one with the glowing spikes or the one with the constantly moving surface. Okay, he was starting to be slightly more interested in rocks. Oh, he knew that one! Sharp picked up a triangular shaped rock, it was a red colour and was shaking slightly. According to Smith, it was highly explosive. The rock started shaking more violently so Sharp lobbed it as far as he could and saw it explode as it spun through the air. There was a commotion from inside the clearing so he dived behind a nearby (and non exotic) rock. He didn't need to worry, they were checking on where he had thrown the bomb. One of the two elves appeared as well as two of the biggest proto-yeti Sharp had seen yet. They must have been ten feet tall, it was hard to see with them bent over though. They had jet black fur and their teeth overhung their lips to the degree that they must have got in the way whenever they tried to eat. Their eyes were red and seemed to glow, piercing through the mist. They were so different that Sharp suspected them of being yet another branch of the yeti species. And in the middle of the two had to be Duke. He was... tiny. Sharp had expected someone small but he was smaller than a ralli though it probably didn't help that he was standing next to two guards who were roughly three times his size. From this angle it was hard to see anything else but he had the slightly pointy ears that an orc did, his skin a ruddy dark brown. He was bald but was wearing some sort of fancy hat which looked more like some sort of ceremonial headpiece than anything. He had the gear that might suit an explorer (robes could kill. Sharp had seen it before) but it was all a white colour with what looked like gold picked out on the seams. Oh, and a cape. If there was a better way to bring an outfit together than a cape, Sharp didn't know about it.

Duke sent one of his guards further into the mist but it found nothing, there was probably just a pile of gravel after all. They turned to go back to safety and Sharp peeked around his rock as much as he dared to get a better look at Duke's face. He was definitely an orc. He had unusually blue eyes for his species but other than that he looked just like any other orc only on a smaller scale. His lower two canines rose over his upper lip slightly but Sharp couldn't make out much more at this distance. His actions were confident but Sharp couldn't have imagined he got that from his own people, taking his size into consideration, as orcs were notorious for disowning any that didn't win bare-knuckled brawls on a daily basis. If they weren't so single-minded on beating each other senseless, the rest of the world might have a problem.

Sharp watched the group disappear from his sight but at a hand on his shoulder, he almost jumped out of his skin. He grabbed the arm of his assailant and threw them to the floor. It was Sterling.

"Hi. Nervous much?" she asked.

"Only when people creep up on me in the middle of a mist-filled death land with a deadly prophet with an army of killers sitting a few meters away."

"That's oddly specific. That happened to you before?"

"The mist is new." Sterling didn't ask any further questions but got to her feet, brushing the dust off her.

"Charging off wildly again?" Tolah asked, one eyebrow raised.

"Got here before you didn't I?" Sharp retorted.

"Yes, we planned on having Quickly pick up a scent while you distracted what seemed like the entire camp, kudos on the fame, by the way, I thought *I* had a lot of fans."

"Yes, it's a curse to be this good."

"In the end we picked up your scent leaving the area at a rate of knots it appears. Thanks for the clear trail by the way, Quickly couldn't smell what you were following other than the scent of a couple of horses that then vanished."

"Yeah It's why I went off on my own again. Thanks for abandoning me in the camp by the way, you never would have found this place. I was following them." Sharp pointed towards the two pterripi. He heard an impressed gasp from the rest of the group.

"I suppose we should be grateful you didn't try to stab them. Also, if you don't want to be left behind don't call your friends fire flingers." Tolah said.

"You DO fling fire. I'm not sure how that's even an insult. And as for the pterripi, they didn't try to kill me. As far as I can tell they don't possess magic like the unicorns do, just a couple of flying horses which, by the way, I would LOVE to own. Here's to hoping I pick up a little bonus from this quest."

"First of all it was the way you said it and second I thought you weren't a fan of flying."

"I think I could get over it if I owned a FLYING HORSE."

"Fair enough."

"We have to win the war before dividing up the spoils." Sterling interjected. "What's the situation?" Sharp described what he had seen.

"You want to sneak in there?" Sharp asked. "We could get the jump on him."

"I want to ask him some questions." Sterling said. "Asking him why he's doing this could help us stop it happening again."

"And I want to know how he got such magic without being a fletchin." Tolah added.

"I want to know what he can tell me about the yeti." Quickly said. Sharp turned to MJ.

"What? I just want to finish this so we can tell everyone how awesome a job we did." MJ said.

"I guess I could ask him how he was planning on actually taking over the world. Just his army wouldn't be enough."

"Wait, so you're actually going along with trying to talk him down?" Sterling was shocked.

"You've already made up your mind to talk to him and I'm not going to waste my energy arguing with you. I'll just wait until you're done then put him out of my misery."

"Well then. We're all agreed, or at least not arguing. Let's go!" Sterling said. Sharp said nothing. He was just glad Sterling hadn't decided to give an inspirational speech. She strode into Duke's clearing, followed by the others.

Chapter 21

Luckily the place wasn't overpopulated. There was Duke, of course, sitting on what appeared to be a throne and he was flicking tiny lightning bolts at a line of ants on the ground. Someone had decorated the throne in gold, bolts of lightning and fireballs and a variety of generic religious looking imagery adorned the surface. On either side stood the two black proto-yetis. They were chained to the throne but it seemed more for decoration than anything since they looked as though they could crush the chains with a single hand. They weren't doing anything to deserve them anyway and Sharp could recognise a pet trained with fear when he saw one. Duke's two elves were off to one side playing a card game, looking bored. The only occupant Sharp hadn't seen before was an overlarge bird perched on the throne. It eyed them with an evil looking expression as they approached but seemed uninterested in attacking them. Sharp guessed this was Duke's method of sending and receiving messages. All eyes turned to the suddenly appearing group.

"And who are you supposed to be?" Duke asked.

"We're going to take you down for destroying Stillhaven and the other towns you hit!" Sterling declared.

"Wait." Duke looked them up and down. "Are you the guys who killed Augury?"

"That's right! We killed your highest general and now we've come to finish the job!" Tolah said. Duke laughed.

"Augury wasn't my highest general! I don't even have ranks in my army! That man just threw his weight around (and there was a lot to throw). He was some high ranking person in Eternal Heights but I don't care about that. Everyone answers to me, but if they want to answer to each other then that's their prerogative. Augury may have been strong but there are plenty more where he came from."

"THAT'S how you run your army? No wonder they were all over the place in Stillhaven!" Sharp was shocked.

"Eh, they aren't important. I'm just using them to test the mettle of Mistmore anyway. The outer towns are meant to be the toughest but my army couldn't even wipe them out the first time they tried. Or you apparently." Duke didn't seem bothered. It appeared that he didn't consider anything a threat. The fact that he was talking to them at all was evidence of that, his proto-yeti were watching them but were still and the elves had gone back to their card game.

"I assume you're testing people on the outside because you plan to come and take over?" Sharp asked. Duke lounged on his throne, swinging his legs over one armrest and leaning back against the other.

"That's pretty much it. Standard stuff I know but I come from a standard group of people. Be the strongest, own the most stuff, be on top, step on whoever you want to get there."

"I'm surprised no one heard about the bloody trail of orc corpses you left lying around."

"Oh, I left them alive. It'll be so much more satisfying for them to see me rise after everything they said. They'll follow me like they've always done to the strongest, then I'll cast them off. Anything else before my yetis tear you apart?"

"Yeah. I'm still unclear on the how. Your army isn't big enough to take over anything other than single towns and I'm guessing good cooperation isn't in your battle plan." Sharp asked. Duke swung his legs back over so he was sitting how the throne designer had envisioned. He leaned forward as if letting them in on a big secret.

"Well you've been rather resourceful I will admit. No one else has found where I live, let alone been bold enough to stroll right up to me! I guess I'm impressed by your courage at least." Duke clearly thought a lot of himself. Sharp suddenly had the impression of talking to a small child who thought they knew more than the adult they were conversing with. "Ever since I found I could do this," He made a tiny fireball and flipped it through his fingers like one would do a coin. "I realised I was meant for greater things than what I was told."

"You believe you were sent by a god?" Sterling asked.

"Of course not. My people have no gods, and why would we? We crave being the strongest thing around. The idea someone could be stronger than the orcs is ridiculous. It was just a way to convince the hues to join me. They may be stupid but their magic is strong." He looked into Tolah's eyes. "With the right guidance, anyone can be useful."

"Like a dog?" Tolah had been quiet but Sharp could see her hands bunched into fists.

"I suppose."

"So how would you take over if not by the grace of a god?" Sharp tried to pull the conversation back towards some answers before Tolah decked the guy. Not that it wouldn't have been fun to watch but he was still unsure what this tiny man had going for him.

"Oh right! You almost distracted me from the best part!" Duke leaned forwards even further, Sharp was really hoping he would pitch forward onto his face. It would probably piss him off but man, would that be funny. "What's the biggest creature you've ever seen?" Duke asked.

"Chipmunk."

"Well I... wait, what?"

"Long story, feel free to carry on."

"Oh, well how about a DRAGON?!"

"Yeah listen, I'm just going to move this conversation on a bit. You're going to set a dragon on Mistmore?"

"Well, not just a dragon." Duke seemed annoyed that he wasn't being humoured. He must have become used to the worship. "I'm going to rid Moremist of its namesake and set EVERYTHING in here on the rest of Mistmore. Let's see them ridicule me then! When I'm RIDING a DRAGON and BURNING their HOUSES down!"

"You're going to slaughter hundreds of thousands of innocent people because some people picked on you?!" Sterling was shocked.

"Heh, I bet his name isn't Duke. Orcs name their children after their abilities or appearance." Sharp knew how to piss people off and angry people tended to lose their ability to fight well.

"What?" Duke had been yanked off the path he was trying to walk down.

"I'm going to call him... Runt." Sharp said.

"My name is not RUNT!" said Runt.

"What're you going to do about it?" asked Sharp.

"Er, Sharp?" Sterling muttered.

"Okay I was GOING to ask you to join my army but instead I'm going to make you the FIRST to be crushed under my REAL force!" Runt had climbed onto the seat of his throne. It was probably to make himself look taller but it just made him look like a child having a tantrum. There was a low growl and suddenly Sharp realised the pattern on the top of the throne was moving. Claws shot out and dug into the back of the seat, the owner using the grip to pull itself up and over the back. A scaly dull red head topped with two horns appeared. One of the horns had grown into an ugly looking spiral, two evil black eyes stared down at them and two thin lines of smoke curled out of flared nostrils. Yup, that was definitely a dragon. It was larger than a horse but not much though, certainly not the behemoth Runt had built it up to be. Runt beckoned to it and it jumped down beside him. He put his hand on its side but it flinched away at his touch. Whatever he was doing to these creatures couldn't be right. Runt struggled a little but got onto its back. Okay, fair enough, that was intimidating but you could remove its rider and the dragon would have probably looked even more so solo. Sharp found himself backing off slowly, the other four doing the same. You didn't have to know much about creatures to know what a dragon could do.

"FIRE!" shouted Runt. The dragon obliged and a red hot jet of flame shot out and cut deep into the mist as they dived out of the way. It cut a path briefly through the mist before it closed back up again. With a big enough flame, Sharp could believe Runt really COULD get rid of the mist. With enough mages, enough dragons. Sharp looked towards the dragon but it wasn't the problem any more. Runt's fingers glowed with an element Sharp hadn't seen before, it was as if he was casting light itself. Unsure of how it was going to cast he strafed to one side and headed towards the relative cover of the mist behind them without turning his back on the duo. It was probably for the best as the light split as it left Runt's fingers and Sharp found himself dodging beams as they hit the ground and shot back at different angles. He couldn't keep his eye on his friends due to the light blinding him every time he looked too close to it but found himself practically tripping over MJ as he went. He grabbed the man by his remaining ear and yanked him out of the way of a beam. Sharp could smell burning fur. He let go of MJ's ear and pushed him back into the mist, following close behind. The light shot off through the mist as they entered it and Sharp had to admit it looked pretty impressive. He saw the other three enter the mist after him, looking to each other for any kind of plan. Sharp figured he'd just play it by ear again but he wasn't sure how they were going to get close enough to do any stabbing. He heard stomping and prepared himself for the dragon. However, it was one of the proto-yeti that tackled him full in the chest and slammed him to the ground. He felt his ribs bend under its weight and cried out in pain. He looked around for anything to get it off (his swords were pinned to his back) and saw Quickly taking a run up and tried to shoulderbash it off his friend. The proto-yeti barely moved and turned to bare its fangs at the lesser opponent. Sharp felt some ribs crack under its weight and found himself uttering an undignified whine. Suddenly a lightning bolt shot out and hit the proto-yeti in the shoulder. It roared and let him go. Sharp saw it get some distance from them, its eyes didn't leave Tolah who was, of course, the source of the electricity.

"Are you okay?" Sterling asked Sharp holding out her hand. He took it and with some pain, managed to get to his feet. He gave her the most sarcastic thumbs up he could manage. Tolah was keeping the proto-yeti at bay and Sharp could see the other one had caught up but was pacing in a circle, wary of their magic user also. "We need to get rid of Duke to stop him calling on his army."

"Oh please. Runt isn't going to call his troops. He

has no faith in them whatsoever and I'm fairly sure I've irritated him enough that he's going to want to take us out himself." Sharp replied, taking a healing herb from Quickly. He stashed it for now, he was sure more pain was incoming.

"Yeah, thanks for that." Tolah said.

"Well, would you rather have a crazy light wielding orc riding a dragon or a crazy light wielding orc riding a dragon and his army?"

"Point taken, but still not happy." Just then they heard a roar above them. Lucky too, as had the dragon not announced its presence they would have all been ash right now. They all scrabbled out of the way of the fireball, Tolah trying to keep her concentration on the proto-yeti.

"We need to stop him from flying around!" MJ said.

"Well, how are we going to get up there?" Sharp retorted.

"I know how TWO of us can get up there." Sterling said.

"If you don't pick me I'm not going to be happy."

"Can you three take care of these guys?" Sterling asked the others.

"Leave it to us!" Tolah said. "Quickly, can you hold them still? I need a clear shot. MJ you can distract the other one for me." She slipped into a leader role quickly and Sharp wondered what she had been like when they had parted at Stillhaven. Sterling seemed a little reluctant to leave them but she did and they took off in the direction of the pterripi, hoping that they were still there, hoping that they would accept the new riders, hoping that they weren't hit by the invisible dragon flying around, hoping the creature couldn't see them any more than they could see him. The mounts were still there. Presumably the elves had wanted to stay out of it. Sharp didn't blame them. The pterripi were wary of the newcomers but didn't fight as they mounted.

"Now what?" Sharp asked.

"Well, you saw them take off. What did they do?" Sharp tried to remember.

"Oh right." He pulled back on his mount's reins and she beat her wings and took to the sky. He found the air pushed from his lungs as he was forced down on the pterippus's back. When he dared open his eyes he saw nothing but mist around him. If he concentrated he could see the tiny circle of clear air which was Runt's throne 'room'. A beating of wings beside him alerted him to Sterling's presence. She was dealing with this a lot better than him it seemed, her expression was one of ecstasy. She yelled something to him but it was lost in the rushing air. Once he pulled himself together, he found he could control the pterippus fairly easily by using the reins or by leaning. Sterling beckoned to him so he urged his mount to follow. She rose ever up (he decided to avoid looking down) and finally they broke through the top of the mist and could see that it stretched as far as the eye could see in every direction from here. It was like having a cloth removed from his eyes, as even in the mist free areas he had still been surrounded by it but up here he felt free. Well, he did until the big dragon showed up and blocked his line of sight anyway. He had enough time to roll out of the way of the stream of flame that came towards him, hanging on for dear life to the saddle. Sterling wasn't hanging around but darted forwards to take a swing at Runt. Her blow was deflected by his fist which had turned to rock. Runt's dragon was unable to get its claws into so close an opponent so Runt was on his own here. Sharp took the opportunity to fly close to his other side but Runt easily held off Sterling as he shot a bolt of lightning towards him. Sharp was relieved to have a spell he knew of until the sane (and very tiny) part of his brain reminded him that lightning was bad. It hit him. He gripped onto his saddle to try and keep balanced and he felt his hair stand on end, light spots appeared in his eyes and he tasted metal in his mouth. Runt's deranged laugh reached his ear and shaking his head, Sharp cleared enough of his vision to see Runt dive down into the mist.

"Follow him!" Sterling yelled and dived after him. Sharp spurred his mount on and he felt the cool air of the mist enclose him again. The dragon was easy to follow, it moved predictably and didn't speed off (if indeed it could) while keeping distance enough from the blades behind him. Suddenly the dragon dived again and the two hunters followed it. Sharp found himself close to the ground which would have been a relief had he not been an extremely suspicious person, which he was. A variety of statues rose up around them, Sterling and he dodging erratically as the sculptures weren't in any discernible pattern he could see. He flew close to one and saw the grotesque expression on its face. An elf. He twisted in the saddle and saw others in similar states, hard to see at this speed. They were all correctly scaled as far as he could see. Oh crap. He sped up so he was level with Sterling and waved to get her attention. She turned to him.

"GORGON!" he yelled to her. She shook her head, they were going too fast to converse. He repeated it but got the same reaction. He pointed to the statues then held his arm over his eyes. Alarm showed on her face as she got the idea. Runt was trying to lead them to a gorgon's nest. If their eyes met hers they would join her victims below. Sharp had wanted a statue of himself but this wasn't what he had in mind. Reluctant to abandon the chase, they rose higher but still in range of the drake racing ahead. They caught up to him as he reached what looked like an abandoned chapel. The dragon perched on top of the entranceway as if it was part of the decoration. The building had vines and other plants growing up the sides but the creepy factor overrode the lonely one because of the various statues which had grown more numerous here and Sharp could see them peering into the doorway, some had their hands on the shoulders of previous statues as they tried to take a look inside and it gave a strange sort of layered effect. The pterripi landed, they were not happy to be here. Their hooves danced on the spot, their heads moved quickly, looking for danger. As they lived around here, it wasn't a good sign. Sharp slipped his coat off and draped it over his mount's face and saw Sterling do the same. He pulled his hat brim down low, not that it would help.

"If in doubt, close your eyes and fly straight up." Sterling said. "Keep your eyes focused on him and only him." Sharp nodded. They managed to urge their skittish mounts forward. Runt was leaning on the dragon's head with a sort of childish delight. Sharp bet he used to pull the legs off spiders when he was a kid. He heard the hissing at the same time as Sterling it seemed.

"Behind us!" Sterling yelled. He turned by instinct to fight the attacker before his brain kicked in. He managed to close his eyes in time. He didn't meet her sight but he managed to get an eyeful of snakes which seemed to be sprouting from her head in place of hair. The rest of her seemed to be human at first glance and first glance was all he allowed himself, cursing himself for turning in the first place. Sterling hadn't moved at all so Sharp did a double take to make sure she hadn't been turned to stone somehow but she just gave him a disapproving look. Suddenly the ground started to shake.

What was THIS now? He raised his head to see Runt, with hand outstretched, was causing the quake. The ground ripped open at their feet and they managed to ride out of the way.

"Time to split up again?" Sharp said. "Which do you want to take?"

"The orc." Sterling growled without missing a beat.

"Don't get killed."

"Same to you." Sterling took off towards Runt. There was no room to avoid his attacks and Sharp saw him shoot some sort of black goop towards her. She used her shield to block it but some hit the pterippus and it neighed in pain and bucked. It kept going forwards however and Sharp saw the two hit Runt and his dragon full in the face. He had his own problems now though. He closed his eyes, dismounted then turned and flailed wildly in the Gorgon's direction. He felt his blade strike something a glancing blow and heard her shriek. A hand grabbed his arm too tightly for him to break out of. She tightened her grip enough that he felt it bruise then she threw him roughly to the ground. At ground level, he opened his eyes to see her feet approach and rolled out of her way. He scrambled to his feet, seeking out the pterippus, hoping that perhaps height would help (dismounting had seemed a good idea at the time) but with a roar he saw the dragon swoop down and without even her sight to help her, the winged mare was forced to the ground, cruel talons ripping through her with ease. With a final pained noise, the dragon ripped her throat out, staring at Sharp with blood dripping down its chin. Sharp felt as if the dragon's gaze had done the same as the gorgon's for a moment. The kill was brutal and almost instant. The dragon bounded towards him and Sharp dived back to the floor, sliding through its legs as it bit down at the place he used to be. Before it could react, he managed to sheath his blades before grabbing it by the tail and started to climb up its back. The dragon took to the air as it bucked and rolled in an attempt to dislodge him but he'd had more than his fair share of practice hanging onto flying creatures lately and he managed to climb onto its back. He grabbed it by the horns as it took a nosedive back to the ground again and rolled but this time trying to crush him. Sharp pressed himself onto its back, its wings too big to succeed in breaking all the hunter's bones. As soon as it righted itself, Sharp yanked its head back, aiming it towards where he remembered the gorgon was before he had lost all sense of direction, hiding his own head behind the dragon's body. The beast immediately froze and Sharp could feel its skin become cold under him. He looked down and saw stone creeping along its whole body and he scrambled off its back in case anything it touched was also affected (those stone statues had stone clothes after all). The dragon flailed for a few seconds as it tried to fight the unfightable but then turned completely to rock. Its pose was one of distress, wings outstretched, claws curled, teeth bared. It was one magnificent statue. A crash indicated the gorgon had caught up with him and one wing turned to rubble under a punch, stronger than the wielder's size should have allowed. He turned and found himself in the same situation as before but flailing had done nothing so instead, he used the remains of his hearing to avoid her. He drew a sword then cast his eyes around for anything, ANYthing that might help. Among the sea of grey distressed figures, his eyes fell on a rock of a different colour. It was red. It was triangular. It was shaking slightly. He sprinted forward and grabbed it with his spare hand. He then turned and ran in the general direction of the gorgon, eyes cast down to the ground. As soon as he saw her feet he swung with his sword, his hand caught yet again by hers. He thrust his other hand towards what he guessed was her face fighting every instinct not to as his brain told him he was plunging his hand into a nest of snakes. His fist met what felt like a row of teeth, however, and as she opened her mouth in pain, he dropped in the now violently shaking rock. In hindsight, he really wished he had looked. It could have cost him his life but it must have been spectacular. Instead, he turned and ran, his hands over his head. The explosion was less of a boom and more of a splat and fleshy, unidentifiable things rained down around and on him. A hissing by his feet directed him to something he COULD identify. It was the remains of half a snake, still writhing for a few seconds before lying still. Slowly he turned but he didn't need to worry, the gorgon had no head any more, let alone eyes. Her torso lay still, snakes scattered around. Sharp took a moment to breathe and took in the scene for a moment. Oh yeah, one dragon and one gorgon totally killed by him on his own. He decided to hope people just believed him this time, he didn't feel as if any souvenir he could take would feel good being carried around. His eyes rested for a moment on the dead pterippus and the sight made him far sadder than it should have done. It was just a creature, but all it had done was help him and pay for it. He tore his eyes away and looked toward Sterling's fight. She had removed the blindfold from her pterippus's face and her mount had done the sensible thing and got his distance, leaving his rider to her fight solo. The black goop had left an angry looking burn and he was flipping his mane in irritation. Sharp cast an eye towards Sterling's fight. She wasn't doing fantastically well but she was still alive and, more importantly, not looking his way. He sidled up to the pterippus and, grabbing it by its reins, held the healing herb out to it. It looked at him a bit suspiciously but took it. Sharp could see the burn fade and the creature stopped showing signs of pain. He nudged Sharp in gratitude and the hunter wondered how intelligent the pterippus really was. He ran to the area below Sterling's roof fight. Runt had a few cuts and was bleeding from a chip out of his ear, Sterling seemed mostly unharmed but was breathing deeply and he could see a burn through a rip in her coat's shoulder.

"BRING HIM DOWN HERE!" Sharp yelled at her. She showed no sign she had heard him but after dodging a light attack she tackled Runt and they both fell off the roof. Sharp ran forward and managed to catch Sterling, his ribs groaning in agony.

"Thanks." She leapt to her feet and together they faced Runt who had struggled to his own, shaking dirt from his cape with as much dignity as he could for someone who had just hit the floor face first.

"You'll PAY for that!" he squeaked and yet another spell Sharp hadn't seen before formed on his fingers. He looked at Sterling who shrugged. Runt's fingers seemed to be distorting the air itself until suddenly spikes shot out. He aimed his hands towards the hunters and Sharp sidestepped behind Sterling as she raised her shield to protect them both. The spikes were too numerous to estimate their number and they less pinged off the shield than hit it like a sledgehammer. Sharp braced against Sterling's back as she was forced backwards. The onslaught stopped and Sharp stepped to one side to check the damage. Sterling's shield was now peppered with dents, not rendering it useless but it was worrying how much damage the spell had done. Sterling stumbled slightly and Sharp looked down to see her legs had taken a few glancing blows. She was still standing but he saw blood under the tears in her trousers.

"You okay?" Sharp asked.

"Fine." Her gaze didn't waver from Runt's. She was really taking this personally. Sharp didn't get her thing with trying to beat up powerful magic users but everyone had to have a grudge against something he supposed. He had so many grudges himself that he had lost count of them. The spell seemed to tire Runt out so Sharp prayed that one wasn't coming again and ran forward as a close fight was going to be their best bet. The ground shook again and Sharp strafed out of the way, drawing his other sword, swinging with both blades as he approached. He was blocked with the rock hands from earlier but Sterling came at Runt from the other side and shield bashed him in the head. He was knocked to the ground but rolled and got back up, blood running down his face but he didn't look stunned. Orcs were known for having tough skin and hard heads, even the small ones it seemed. The two hunters nodded at each other and this time rushed him together. Runt held out his hands and suddenly the floor was ice. Sharp lost his balance and pitched forwards, sliding towards Sterling, taking out her legs and the two spun towards Runt. His hands shone with light and, powerless to block it, they were both hit full on with the spell. For a moment Sharp felt light headed but then pain ripped through him. He felt as if he was being burnt up from the inside. He curled up like a wounded animal and whimpered until the pain became more bearable. He craned his head and saw Runt charging up the spike attack again, this time aimed right at Sterling. Her shield had spun out of her reach and she was in too much pain to move. Runt was too far from him to reach but Sterling wasn't. She was going to die and he could stop it but he was going to have to give himself to do it. A sudden thought ran through his head. She didn't deserve it, she didn't deserve any of it. She didn't deserve to die, she didn't deserve to have her spirit broken, she didn't deserve to fail, she didn't deserve to have to put up with him for months but she had and cheerfully for the most part. His legs were moving without him giving the command, the pain from the light spell throbbing with every footstep. He didn't stop and reached Sterling just as the spell was cast.

He felt as though he had been hit with every single spike but statistically some must have missed him. He fell backwards, his vision fading, Runt's smug face was going to be the last thing he ever saw. For a moment he felt nothing but the cold, disconnected from his own limbs. He found his head was moving but felt nothing and Sterling's face came into view, a better last thing to see than Runt he supposed. She was talking but his other ear had joined his first and all he could hear was ringing. He saw she was crying and with the last of his strength he whispered with a smile,

"Thank you." Then there was nothing.

Chapter 22

Sharp had passed out. His face was covered in blood, his clothes stained with the same. Sterling felt her own blood run cold as she cradled his head in her hands. He couldn't be gone! Nothing ever stopped him before! He had always seemed so stubborn, so resilient. Suddenly the cold turned to burning as anger flowed through her, never in her whole life had she felt so much rage as she had in this entire journey, at this one point in time even. She had constantly almost lost her friends, her view on people had been torn apart again and again and her face had been rearranged to a point that she didn't recognise herself in a mirror any more. She put Sharp's head down gently and then stood. He had thanked her. Perhaps he had changed, perhaps she had given him some kind of joy when he never seemed to show any, some kind of hope in other people. What was it all for when it ended in his death? She wiped the tears from her eyes, she had to finish this. For Sharp, for her friends, for anyone who was in Duke's, no, Runt's way. Runt watched her, a smile playing on his arrogant face, doing nothing as she bent to retrieve her shield and sword. As soon as she was ready, light played on his fingers again. She hated that spell, it was unfortunate the orc seemed to love it. She charged, trying to leave him no time to cast but she was too slow. She raised her shield to block the blast and felt some pain in her legs (she was really going to need a larger shield) but she remained standing, her legs already hurting from the previous spike attack. She swung under the shield and felt it connect and he yelped as the blade sliced through armour and skin. Without giving him room to react she treated him to a shield bash to the face which did no damage but staggered him slightly. She lowered the shield and this time sliced above it, aiming at his face. A lightning bolt came from behind the shield and hit the tip of the sword, rippling down it and along her arm. Her attack was halted as the electricity made its way through her body and she fell to one knee, her legs failing under the constant barrage of attacks they had suffered. He snickered above her and she saw his hands held out and she recognised an ice attack forming, she still saw that spell in her nightmares. She stabbed directly up and through his right hand and used her shield to push his left hand up and away from her head, the ice shooting off randomly as he reeled from the sudden pain. She yanked the sword back out violently and saw three fingers and half his hand spiral away. Panicking, he gripped his injured hand, blood spurting out like a fountain, shrieking. Sterling didn't back off but swung her shield over her head, protecting herself as the ice fell down, shattering on the metal. Blood spurted out from Runt's head, shoulders and an outstretched arm as the icicles hit their caster. Now in an immense amount of pain, the orc fell to his knees and as Sterling slowly approached him, the face that turned to look at her looked younger than it had previously seemed, his face stained with tears and scrunched up with agony.

"Please." he begged. "I just wanted to be noticed, to be someone! You must understand that or you wouldn't be here, doing this!" He fell forward, his strength gone, clutching his crippled hand as he curled into a ball. "They called me pathetic, They called me worthless. They called me nothing." Runt whispered quietly, Sterling had to strain her ears to hear. She was unsure if what he had been called were insults, they could quite as easily been actual names, judging by the orcs' naming techniques. She didn't bother to raise her sword to give the final blow and for the first time in her life she wanted to see someone die slowly. He was less than an insect in her eyes right now, too small to even bother stepping on. She didn't have to wait long. His blood was pooling rapidly under him from all his various wounds and soon he lay still. She checked for a pulse to make sure her unwillingness to strike the final blow wouldn't come back to hurt her and others in the future, but he was gone. She felt no glory, not even the feeling of a job finished. Her blood felt cold again, the mist suddenly seemed claustrophobic, wrapping itself around her and the statues. She heard a quiet snorting behind her and turned to see her pterippus leaning down over Sharp's body, pushing him with his nose. He hadn't run? That was odd, he should have fled as soon as he had the chance. She returned to him and with a hand on his neck, he allowed her to take him by the reins. She bent down and took Sharp's swords and slowly slid them back into their sheaths. In many cultures, a warrior returning without his weapons was a shameful thing. Sterling had no idea of his beliefs or his background, he spoke little on these things but she couldn't learn those things now. She bent and lifted his body onto the back of the pterippus who didn't complain. Sterling mounted herself and, holding his body still, started the sad return to the rest of her friends. Hopefully, she hadn't lost any more people she cared about today.

Chapter 23

There was no pain. It had been so long since that had been the case and he was taken slightly aback. Sharp looked around and found he was on his feet somehow. The area around him didn't seem solid but at least there was no mist. He looked before him and saw a large circus tent rise out of the ground. It was impossible to miss. It was red with decorations in too many colours to count and made him feel... welcome, he supposed. With a smile he walked forward and through the tent flaps, wide open to allow guests to enter, but he had been the only one outside. The same couldn't be said for the inside as crowds of people were there and the closest ones nodded their recognition at him but then faced forward again to watch the show unfolding in the centre of the room. It was spectacular. Too much was going on to stop his eyes from constantly moving but he didn't feel overwhelmed. Animals and monsters danced under the commands of the ringmaster, dressed in glorious red, as other people juggled, balanced on balls or spun through the air on trapezes and balanced on tightropes, a variety of species. Music was matching the action perfectly and he couldn't see where it was coming from but the orchestra must have been sizeable from the amount of instruments he could hear. The ringmaster turned to him and he saw his face was made up in clown makeup, the smile painted on was nothing compared to the natural one underneath. They made eye contact and the clown made the biggest bow Sharp had ever seen and gestured to a seemingly random seat in the stands before returning to his conducting without checking to see if Sharp had got the idea. Sharp turned his head and saw a familiar face in the crowd, a face he hadn't seen in six years. A cry was caught in his throat and the audience seemed to move out of his way almost unnaturally as he made his way towards her, their eyes not moving from the act in front of them. There was an empty seat next to her, the only one he could see in the whole tent in fact, so he sat down. Mary turned and smiled softly at him and for a moment he said nothing. He tried and failed a few times to find the words he wanted to say but nothing seemed right, nothing seemed to fit. Her smile widened and she reached out her hand and took his. It was warm despite the warmth already surrounding them and for the first time in a long while he felt... happy. He closed his eyes and savoured the moment. Somehow over the music, he could hear another sound. Flip, flip, flip. He opened his eyes and looked down. In her free hand, Mary was flipping a coin, as it turned he felt a ripple of annoyance travel up his spine. He realised the music was dimming and he turned to see the colours of the tent were fading, the crowd blurring together. Desperately he turned to Mary who was also fading. He desperately reached out to grab her other hand but he found he couldn't and that coin was ever flipping. He suddenly realised the sound was only reaching one of his ears.

"No!" he gasped. Mary smiled once more at him.

"Not yet. You have so much more to do." And with that, she was gone. He found himself standing again, his surroundings were dim and suddenly he was back in the mist and that flipping sound kept on, and on, driving him insane. He fell to his knees and clutched his head in his hands but the sound was inside his brain now.

Suddenly everything stopped. He was aware his eyes were shut but he could hear the flipping sound still, only it was faint. He concentrated and suddenly he could make out other sounds, the soft sound of pages turning, the general noise of people that one blocked out on a daily basis and he felt a soft breeze on his face. He finally gave in and opened his eyes. He was lying in a hospital bed, he felt as if he had been unconscious rather than asleep as nothing felt refreshed, he just felt drained. He turned his head to see Sterling was sitting at his bedside, reading with one hand and flipping that stupid seal with the other. As aching as he was, he reached out and grabbed the hand with the seal to shut that infernal noise off. Sterling jumped with shock at the sudden touch.

"Stop. Flipping. That. Seal." he croaked. It was less stern than he had intended, his throat felt dry and he coughed weakly after the attempt to talk. Sterling smiled widely and said nothing but tears fell down her cheeks. She let go of the seal and Sharp took it. It was blank. He turned in confusion towards Sterling.

"I gave it back. The quest was over after all." she managed in between sobs. "Should I have kept it?" Sharp swallowed, struggling to regain his voice.

"No." he finally wheezed. "You never needed it anyway." They sat in silence for a time, Sterling trying to stop the tears and Sharp trying to move his limbs to see if he still had them all while trying to block out the overwhelming feeling that he lost part of himself all over again. Was it real? Was it just a figment of his imagination as he lay dying? He decided not to dwell, that way led only to sadness, perhaps even blame to those who had brought him back to a world he didn't care for. "Is everyone else..." he trailed off.

"Everyone is fine. Tolah led them well, maybe she should have been in charge the whole time! They managed to win mostly using the beasts' fear to keep them at bay." Sterling said. "You can thank Quickly for your own survival. I was sure you were gone. As soon as I was told otherwise I took the pterippus and you and we found the nearest doctor."

"Tell me it wasn't in Starglade." Sharp looked around, without the strength to raise his head however the room looked the same as any other hospital room.

"Then I won't." Sterling replied.

"Tell me I'm not still there?"

"You aren't still there. When you were stable I took you to Silver. Doctor Rothkar was ecstatic to see you again."

"My wallet maybe."

"We paid, don't worry."

"I wasn't, but go on."

"You were there a long time, the others managed to catch up to us by the time you were well enough to leave. Their journey back had been a fairly uneventful one, a lot of the places they passed were willing to help them."

"They could have used the death machine."

"It would have had to be powered by something so we left it behind. The King demanded it be demolished so the rallis took it apart again. They were paid for it so they didn't seem bothered."

"Oh. That thing was a bit anticlimactic in the end." Sharp said, strangely feeling little disappointed. Sterling shrugged. "What about the rest of the army?"

"I wouldn't have even called it an army. A lot managed to sneak off before they were seen and the King didn't bother to punish anyone that had just signed up for a job that paid. I think he wanted to avoid the paperwork and save space in the jail."

"The fletchins?" Sterling paused.

"Some tried to fight the King's army when it arrived. A few other members of other species tried to fight also, the ones who were taken in by what Runt was preaching apparently. I had warned them enough of the magic that they were prepared and the number left in the army was now tiny so the King had no problem." Sterling paused for a moment. "Most were killed. A few of the fletchins begged for mercy when their prayers went unanswered and they were taken for prisoners. We may have some trouble with Eternal Heights over that one but at least they will have to actually TALK to other species now. Maybe we can get some sort of a mixing of people now, I don't know, not really my thing."

"... And Runt?" Sharp finally answered.

"Dead. You opened him up for me." Sharp wasn't sure how true that could be when all he did was get hit by a lot of spikes. "I..." Sterling fell silent then tried again. "Why did you save me? You must have known it would... kill you."

"I just thought you should be the one to finish him." Sharp turned his gaze to the ceiling. This sort of emotional stuff was something he would rather avoid but this was Sterling he was talking to.

"You were willing to die for me. That can't have been all it was!" Sterling had clearly been thinking about this for a long time. He must have been asleep for months. He supposed she deserved more.

"Look, I'm not good at this. I just didn't want to see my friend die, okay? And the world deserves more than me, you always gave so much more. I only gave the minimum amount and took all I could. I'm sure your death would have been mourned far more than mine anyway."

"You've had a fair amount of fans trying to fight their way in here you know. The King sent guards to watch the door since he was very grateful for all we did."

"I'm talking people who actually know me."

"Tolah was distraught. MJ has been hovering around, he hasn't even been bragging about what he did or anything!"

"And Quickly?"

"Hasn't said a word since you've been out. He's going to be overjoyed." Sterling smiled at him but he couldn't return it. Typical, even in sacrifice he managed to hurt other people.

"I assume I'm not dying now?"

"No. You have a new set of scars, not quite as stunning as mine but you tried your hardest." Sterling smiled. Sharp would probably never tell her but he preferred the way she looked now. She just looked less... perfect, he supposed. "You're also going feel some aches in the cold apparently but you're alive! Really, we were concerned about how long you were out. Every time Rothkar threatened to put you out of your misery, Quickly looked as if he was going to put him out of ours. We ended up relocating you again mainly because of that. It was about time I reported to the King anyway so we brought you to Golden."

"What happened to the pterippus?"

"The King took it. Said it was deserving of royalty and no one lower."

"Awww, I liked that guy!"

"I thought you might. He seemed very attached to you for some reason. Maybe you can go back one day and try to find another."

"Forget it. It wouldn't be the same." Sharp sulked. A thought occurred to him and he brightened up. "Tell me we got paid and then some."

"We got paid and then some. I divided the reward into equal fifths, I was sure you wouldn't mind. I've been keeping yours for you and if you felt like retiring, you could do it." Sharp was probably lucky Sterling hadn't donated the whole lot to needy orphans or something.

"Who said I wanted to retire? I'm guessing you're

now number one. Going to have to work hard to sort that one out." he said more childishly than he had planned. Sterling smiled.

"Not that I don't welcome the competition but here's the thing." Sterling looked as if she missed having the disc to flip. Sharp didn't give it back. "There's a bit of a giant problem up in The Rugged Mountains."

"Lot of space for them up there." Sharp was listening.

"A few have been coming into the local towns, it's going to be a problem soon."

"And you can't handle a few giants on your own?"

"Well, a friend or four to watch my back wouldn't be a bad thing."

"I suppose if you can't do it solo, it would be irresponsible of me to let you go alone."

"You're all heart."

"That's what they say about me." Sharp yawned.

"I'll let you sleep. You'll be woken up when the others come by anyway. If you ever need a sleeping aid by the way I recommend this." Sterling held up the book she had been reading. It was 'Exotic Rocks And How To Distinguish Them From Other Similar Rocks Found In Non Exotic Places And Their Properties'.

"Oh, don't you insult Smith!" Sharp said indignantly. "That man saved my life!" He took the book and held it protectively to his chest.

"Erm, okay then." Sterling searched his face for signs of sarcasm but found none. He was going to read that book back to front. "I'll just let you sleep then." Sterling backed slowly out of the room. Sharp slumped back on his bed, what little energy he had was gone. He closed his eyes, arms still wrapped around the book. Maybe he would find his way back to the circus tent in the sky, just for a moment, but he doubted it.

A month later he was able to leave and he stretched his muscles as he stood outside in the sun. It was now full into spring, the breeze felt delicious on his skin as he took in the sight of Golden, the people scurrying about to simply fulfil their day to day routines. Quickly put his hand on Sharp's shoulder and smiled down at him. The yeti had seemed far happier lately than Sharp had seen during the whole previous journey. MJ was sporting the tackiest outfit Sharp had ever seen. It was certainly getting him a lot of looks, he figured that was what he was going for but the phoenix feather he had woven into his buttonholes gave Sharp a pang of pride. Tolah was complaining about the amount of work she was leaving behind as she had found a group of scholars eager to speak with a fletchin, especially one with the amount of knowledge she had. Maybe her people wouldn't be ready for her teachings any time soon but she would never want for an audience if she looked elsewhere it seemed. Sharp had suggested she stay behind but she had looked as though he had suggested they go kick some puppies so he said no more after that and just let her complain. He supposed it was about time someone other than him did it.

"Ready to go?" Sterling asked brightly. She was sporting a brand new set of quality armour the King had had specially made. She had also provided a set for Sharp but made sure his was more low key and was made of the leather he preferred. Her shield was the centrepiece of the entire group, it held the royal crest and was so shiny you could see your face in it.

"Almost. Just need to do one more thing." Sharp said. He led them to the pier, the sea air felt fantastic. He looked down at the metal disc in his hands. He gave it one last flip, drew back his arm and threw it as far as he possibly could. It dropped far away in the water and sank out of view.

The End

About the author:

A. L. Brooke was born in Suffolk in 1985 and spent most of her young life lost in books and eventually films and games. After deciding that living at home at the age of 27 was getting a bit much, she moved to Cardiff in search of a change of pace. After the move revealed no epic quests or;; fantastic creatures she decided to write about them instead.

Printed in Great Britain
by Amazon